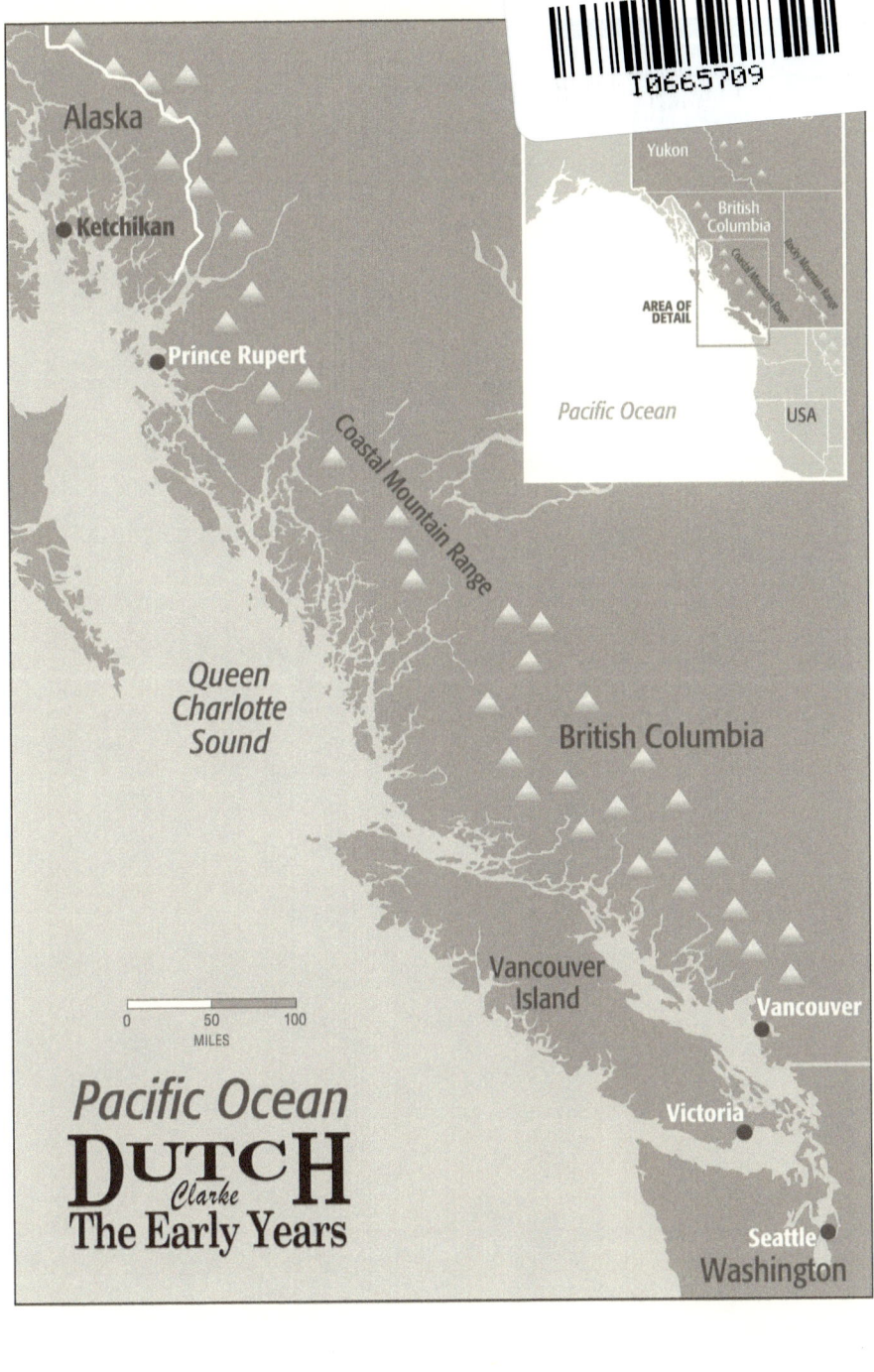

Alaska

Ketchikan

Prince Rupert

Coastal Mountain Range

Queen
Charlotte
Sound

British Columbia

Vancouver
Island

Vancouver

Victoria

Seattle
Washington

0   50   100
MILES

Pacific Ocean

DUTCH
Clarke
The Early Years

Yukon

British
Columbia

AREA OF
DETAIL

Pacific Ocean

USA

THE EARLY YEARS
Trail of Discovery

Brian D. Ratty

Sunset Lake
Publishing

Sunset Lake Publishing
89637 Lakeside Ct.
Warrenton, OR 97146
503.717.1125
#93-1015196

First Edition published in June 2006
Second Edition published in September 2009
Third Edition published in August 2014

ISBN-13: 978-0692254721
ISBN-10: 0692254722

Create Space Title ID: 4898943
Printed in the USA

For my Grandchildren: Alex, Emma, Maren, Seamus and Roan. I give you this story with all my love and affection. May your life be full of adventure, love, laughter and success.
God bless you all.

Authors Note

On May 31, 1942, my life began in a world that was full of turmoil and struggling for its very survival. World War II and related events would have a great impact on my life. There is no greater group of people who walked the face of this earth than the World War II generation. They saved the world from corruption and tyranny at a cost in human lives that counted into the millions.

During the war my family lived and worked in the small coastal town of Seaside, Oregon. Here, my father went to work with his father at nearby naval air stations in both Warrenton and Tongue Point. They both worked as civilian contractors for the United States Department of the Navy.

Soon after the war, my family moved back to Portland, Oregon, where my family lived for many years with my mother's sister. It was a simple time of simple needs and love. The phone, a party line, would ring twice for our family and three times for our neighbor. Our doors were never locked, and the people next door would always be there if you needed help, or just a friendly visit on the front porch. Our home was full of laughter, love and work.

As the boys came home from the war, so did images of the conflict. These pictures graced the covers and pages of such magazines as Life, Colliers and The Saturday Evening Post. They told a story about a country unprepared for war and about people pursuing normal lives until their way of life was threatened. Each story had its own hero, its own villain and its own destiny.

There was no escaping the aftermath of war in our community. We could see it in the faces of the people who were lucky enough to return. We heard about it on the radio and followed it in the newsreels at our local theaters. The war had taken and changed many lives.

In the early days of television, the nation was exposed to film documentaries such as "Victory At Sea" and "Industry on Parade." These stories and images depicted a sleeping nation coming to life to cope and conquer the dark clouds of a world at war. It was at this time that I became aware of the great photojournalists of my time, Robert Capra, Margaret Bourke White and W. Eugene Smith. Their stories and images riveted my imagination about our country's history and about how important it was to somehow capture and tell a great story.

For over thirty-five years I have been a professional photographer, inspired by these fine photojournalist. Today I write and photograph, not for profit or praise but pure pleasure. If others find my work interesting, entertaining and informative then I will have realized my rewards.

Everybody has a few good stories in them-maybe this is one of mine.

Brian D. Ratty

CONTENTS

CHAPTER ONE

The Trailhead

My gut had said no and my head and heart had agreed, so why was I on this miserable trail? Lost in the remote recesses of my mind I knew the answer: family.

Dirty gray clouds drifted across the landscape, changing shape as they traversed the blue-gray mountains and billowed across the tree tops. What lay underneath this dingy canopy was my fate.

Relieved that I had started, but upset that I had given in, I was blindly following this unforgiving path. At least the next year would bring closure to this foolish family notion.

A solitary eagle flew above me, its high-pitched shriek piercing the morning silence with needlelike shrillness that seemed to tell me to get off its trail, turn around and go back. The magnificent bald eagle reminded me that I was an intruder in its habitat, a visitor at best. As it flew over some trees in the distance, I became aware of all the sounds around me. The breeze moving through the trees as it tried to chase the clouds from the tops. The sounds of my animals as we moved down the narrow game trail, the rhythm of their hooves striking the solid ground, the breathing of my horse and the two pack mules that followed. The swishing and scraping of the dew-covered underbrush as it snapped across my chaps and then against the packs of the mules behind. Loud yet muted, these rich sounds reminded me of the lonely silence that was to come.

The morning was cool, damp and steel-gray, with diffused sunlight filtering through billowy clouds that hung low in the eastern sky. There was no rain yet, but it looked like it might start anytime. One thing I knew I could count on, over the next year, was rain, drizzle and more rain. This was no surprise, as it was springtime in Western British Columbia. Whatever Mother Nature had in store for me, I had made provisions for, or so I hoped.

Tugging on my watch chain, I reeled the cool, gold case into my hand. As I did so, my fingers brushed the engraved back, giving me solace. It opened with a solid click. The time was 8:11 a.m. I'd been on the trail just over two hours. With dawn brushing our shoulders, I had said goodbye to my Uncle Roy in front of the old hotel and café in Firvale. Roy had traveled along to see me off at that small, isolated logging village, serviced only by the Canadian Pacific Railroad.

As I turned to leave he simply remarked, "Dutch, life is full of tests and I guess the trail before you is one of yours. I wish you fair winds and following seas. May the wings of providence bring you home safely… see you this time next year."

Shaking his hand, I nodded my sad agreement and started the long ride towards my destiny. Somehow, it didn't seem possible that had happened only two hours before, and I had a foreboding sense that the year ahead of me could be longer than expected.

Swaying ferns some sixty yards ahead of me was Gus, also affectionately known as 'the dog.' He was mostly out of sight because of the tall underbrush, but every now and then he ran back down the trail, just close enough to see me and make sure I was still coming toward him. Without knowing a thing about it he seemed to relish this adventure, as he'd spent the first couple of hours barking out a staccato cadence to our steps. Now he was noisily breaking trail for my little pack train.

I had found Gus, and all my other animals, in New Mexico. He had been an uninvited ranch dog, half wild, with only the name of "dog." He was a beautiful animal. I guessed his breed as half German shepherd and half wolf. His ears, nose, chest and three legs were dark brown, while the rest of his body was light caramel. His eyes were bright and alert, his speed and agility brutally powerful. I named him "Gus" from one of the few Latin words I could remember after two years of high school Latin: "Augustus," which means "of stature."

I didn't consider him to be my dog, as Gus had little use for people and less use for any animal that crossed his path. He was one dangerous and tough creature. I placed his age at about four years, which I couldn't confirm as he wouldn't let me touch him, let alone check his teeth. The folks at the ranch told me that he had appeared there about three years earlier. They guessed that he'd been abused as a pup and then abandoned by his owner.

For some reason, Gus and I had formed a bond of sorts, back in New Mexico. The cowboys at the ranch had been surprised when "the dog" started following me around, and Gus had astonished all of us by jumping into the trailer as I loaded it with my other animals to leave. He was not part of my original plan, but I knew I wouldn't have to care for him, as he hunted for his own food and found his own water. I figured, why not? He would be better off with me than on that dusty, dry rangeland.

As I moved my little caravan up a steep slope, I became aware of steam coming from my horse's nose in the cool morning air. He, too, was a proud and magnificent animal. His name was Blaze. I'd been told that he was five years old and had been a saddle pony at the ranch for the last two years. He was a gelding, half quarter horse and half appaloosa, sixteen hands tall, of a gentle but determined nature. He had a white stripe on his face and two white stockings on his hocks. His mane and tail were dark while his body was a light chestnut with a few darker spots on his rump. The appaloosa in him made him sure-footed; the quarter horse gave him great stamina and strength.

Blaze was indeed a muscular and intelligent animal. But I hadn't picked him out of the herd, he picked me. One of the ranch hands was showing me an older sorrel, since the cowboys felt that an older horse would be more dependable, more sure-footed. Standing with my back to a group of horses, I was examining the mare when Blaze came up behind me and gave me a hard nudge in the middle of my back. Almost falling to the ground, I spun around to find him staring at me with a curious look on his face. I'm sure he'd smelled the carrots in my back pocket, but I like to think that it wasn't just the treats he was after. Perhaps both Blaze and Gus knew that I was preparing for an experience that was not to be missed. These two remarkable creatures would prove to be the most memorable animals of my life.

Twisting in the saddle I looked to the rear. If Blaze and Gus were unforgettable, I would soon forget the two mules, Harry and Harriet, or as I liked to call them, Dumb and Dumber. Their good points, and there were few, were that each carried four trail bags and a bag saddle, with a combined weight of over 250 pounds. They were strong animals, each gray to light gray in color, standing about fourteen hands tall. Their bad points, and there were many, were that they were stubborn, dumb, and smelled bad. Another thing: when a horse "whinnies," its sound has dignity; when a mule "whinnies," it sounds like an old woman cackling. And cackle they did, over miles and miles of trail. It about drove me crazy.

The path on which we traveled was a rough game trail that seemed to point in the general direction I wanted to go, north-northwest. The trail itself snaked through thick undergrowth but was pretty much out in the open, as the area had been logged off some years before. There were hundreds of large old-growth stumps scattered on the hillside. The old forest had not been replanted, but over the years it had started to grow again on its own. Here, new trees ranged from knee-high to over twenty feet, but the forest floor was mostly littered with tall, heavy underbrush.

A stiff morning breeze had come up, blowing the low-hanging, milky clouds higher in the brightening sky. Visibility improved and soon I could see my first objective: Thunder Mountain, some ten miles ahead. Its peak was over 6,500 feet and still had snow showing near its summit, which was in and out of view due to the moving clouds. Below the mountain's peak was a dense rain forest. That was to be my first obstacle.

After Thunder Mountain and a long trail northwest, I would turn south to cross another mountain. Comet was 6,300 feet high, and along the way I'd traverse three major rivers and many streams and creeks to get to my final destination, Nascall Valley. It would take all of six or seven days to travel those 90 miles. Had I been able to travel "as the crow flies," it would've been just a little over 50 miles.

It was May 15, 1941, the first day of what my grandfather called my "mission" and what I called, among other things, a stupid family legacy. I was to spend one year totally alone, in the wilderness of my choice, taking only what I could pack in. There were to be no boats, no planes, no modern conveniences, just what a horse and two pack mules could carry.

In this way, my family hoped that I would find my inner self, my destiny, or as Uncle Roy had said many times, "Maybe, just maybe, this adventure will clip that chip off your shoulder."

Sea Legs – 1937

Bang!

The green, foamy water thundered across the wheelhouse with such a force that I thought the windows would explode. Two gray-painted iron pipes ran across the ceiling of the little compartment and both my hands were wrapped around them, hanging on for dear life. All I could see through the smeared glass were mountains of white/green water, all rushing towards me. The boat was rolling in every direction, first up, then to the right, then down. Other than the dim light coming from outside, a single bare lamp burned above Captain Skip, who stood calmly at the helm. Next to him, on the other side, Jack was holding onto the pipe with one hand and drinking coffee with the other. Jack's casual posture reminded me of someone chatting at a church social. Both men were wearing yellow raincoats and hats. Outside, on the rear of the boat, Tony was checking to make sure the gear was lashed down securely.

I'd met all three of these guys just a few hours before, when we'd pulled out of the Ketchikan boat basin. It had been a wet, miserable day when we'd departed, and it had only gotten worse.

The boat rose in the air, twisted to the right, and crashed headlong back into the raging sea. Water again covered the wheelhouse with such a force that the door next to me flew open, spraying all of us with cold, salty seawater. Reaching over with one hand and using the weight of my body, I got the door closed again. My heart was in my mouth, and I was scared.

Captain Skip looked over at me. "Well, boy, how do you like fishin' so far?" Both he and Jack laughed out loud. Then Skip turned to Jack and asked, "How's that barometer doin'?"

"Still fallin', Skipper," Jack replied.

Another big wave broke across our bow, and this time the boat twisted almost 45 degrees. Turning to Captain Skip, I shouted, "Do you think we should get life jackets on?"

Both men laughed out loud again.

"Look, son, you can put one on if it makes you feel better, but the facts are that you wouldn't last two minutes, floating in the cold waters up here. Only way to stay alive in weather like this is not to fall in. Right, Jack?"

"You got that right, Skipper. Hell, there's more danger in having a little fun in the sporting houses of Ketchikan than in these waters."

Captain Skip spun the wheel to turn the boat into a large wave coming from the right side. Its green foam spread again across the wheelhouse. The sound of its crash was almost deafening, its force shook the whole boat. The little windshield wiper in front of the skipper's window stopped with the weight of the water and then began again.

Skip replied, "Come on, Jack, the boy just came aboard and you're already talking badly about our little fishing village. Why don't you go astern and see if Tony needs help?"

"Sure. Why not? There'll be plenty of time to show the boy how we live up here."

Jack slugged the last of his coffee, put the mug in a holder, and looked out the window for a few seconds, to time his exit with the waves.

Skip turned his head toward me for just a moment and said, "Look, Dutch, there's nothing to be afraid of. I've been in weather like this a hundred times, and the *Pacific Lady* is made of some of the finest timber man has found. She wouldn't let us down. You go below and get some rest. I put your gear in the forward cabin. Your bunk is the port side."

At first, I didn't know what to say. I wasn't sure I could let go of the pipes above me, and I certainly didn't know what "port" meant.

Skip looked over again. "You can make it. Just go slowly and hang on, you'll have your sea legs in no time. By the way, port is left, starboard is right. With this weather, it'll be hours before we start fishing. I'll call ya if and when we start fishing, or sinking."

A broad smile crossed his weather-beaten face. Forcing a smile back, I nodded my approval. Then, slowly, I turned and climbed down the rolling gangway ladder at the rear of the wheelhouse and lurched up a dimly lit passageway to the forward cabin. There I found my suitcase sliding back and forth on the floor next to a V berth.

Closing the cabin door, I looked around the small compartment. The only illumination inside the cramped quarters came from four small portholes above me. I was sure I wouldn't sleep, but I crawled into the left bunk anyway. Here, I could feel the front of the boat lift itself out of the water and then crash down again. Each time, I'd hang on to the sides of the bunk. Sometimes my whole body would become weightless as I was bounced into the air. Then I'd fall back into my bunk with a thud.

Damn! This was not how I'd envisioned fishing when Uncle Roy had told me about Captain Skip and working up here in Ketchikan, Alaska. Maybe, as much as I would have hated it, I should have stayed with Grandfather in Fairview for my sixteenth summer.

There was another wave, another loud crash. Then, for some unknown reason, I was asleep in a few minutes.

The next thing I heard was the muffled sounds of the boat's diesel engine as it pushed the *Pacific Lady* through calm waters. My eyes flew open and I saw sunlight coming from the small portholes above the cabin. Hopping out of my bunk, I stood on my toes to look out through one of the small, round windows.

The ocean was flat, the sun low in the sky, and seagulls were flying around the boat as it cut cleanly through the water. There was a rocky shoreline with tall trees growing between the rocks right down to the shore. The boat was slowly moving north, with none of the pitching and rolling of the day before.

Looking at my watch, I saw that it was 6 a.m.; I'd slept almost 10 hours! My legs were wobbly, but it was time to get moving. Swinging open the cabin door, I swayed down the passageway like a drunk. As I passed the gangway leading up to the wheelhouse, I saw Jack's legs behind the helm.

Just astern of the gangway, I entered into a small, smoke-filled salon with small windows above. This cabin served as a galley, with a diesel cooking stove on one side, which made the whole room smell of diesel, and a small eating booth on the other side. There, sitting behind the table, were Skip and Tony. They both greeted me with big smiles on their faces.

Tony said, "Hey, bait boy... good morning. I heard you wanted a life jacket yesterday. Here, you can have mine!"

He threw an orange life jacket across the cabin as he laughed.

Catching it in mid-air and turning to Captain Skip, I said, "Thought you were going to call me, sir. Sorry for all that sack time."

Skip looked up. "We didn't sink, and we're still a couple hours from where we'll start fishing. Thought a good night's sleep would help ya. When we get into the fishin' waters, there won't be sleep for any of us."

Sitting down on the corner of one of the benches of the booth, I was still a little bewildered.

"Help yourself to the coffee, and there's food on the stove. After you've eaten, I'll give you the first lesson on being a bait boy," Skip said.

The coffee was strong and black, and I poured a full mug. At the stove, I lifted the lid on a large, black, cast-iron skillet. Mixed in the grease from bacon and sausage were two cold, hard, fried eggs. The sight and smell of this mixture made my stomach turn, and I knew I was going to throw up. Turning, I staggered out of the cramped salon as fast as I could.

As I made my hasty departure, I heard Tony say, "Gee, Skipper, we won't need any bait on this trip. Looks like the bait boy will provide all we need."

Captain Skip soon joined me at the rail. "Don't worry about it, Dutch. It will take some time to get used to all the smells and rolling of a fishing boat. Let's get to work. It'll get your mind off it. Let me show you all about being a bait boy."

Even though I remained seasick for the next five days, that's exactly what he did. He showed me how to remove the barbs from the large hooks we were using and how to take a file to sharpen those hooks. He explained that if the barbs were left on, the fish would be hard to remove from the hooks.

As he helped me file my first few hooks, I really saw him for the first time. He was a tall, thin man in his late forties, with jet-black hair and graying temples. He was part Eskimo and part French, which gave him a love for nature and the temper to back it up. His face had strong features and his hands and arms were robust and thick. When he smiled, which he did a lot, he showed teeth that were white and straight. He was a man that fit his environment.

I took to him immediately. He was genuine with his instructtion and had a lot of patience for all my questions. Next, he showed me how to put the bait on the barbless hooks, how to handle the lines, where to throw the fish, and other tips for a landlubber turned bait boy.

My bond with Captain Skip came easily and I worked hard for him. It was important to me to do a good job and I never made the same mistake twice. On a working boat, you need to think ahead of the boat's needs and I took pride in being prepared to always fill those needs. There was no job I wouldn't do, no job I wouldn't try. My goal was to please him and the rest of the crew. I slept when they slept, worked when they worked, and joked when they joked. In time, I'd explored every nook and cranny of the boat. There was no part of that boat I didn't learn about and no piece of gear I couldn't operate. It was hard work, as hard as anything I had done in my life, but there was something I loved about it. It was the sea, the fishing, the rugged beauty of the Alaska wilderness and, most of all, my mates. By the end of this first trip, I had my sea legs and was never seasick again. I carried my weight and was by now a full-fledged member of the *Pacific Lady's* crew—and damn proud of it.

Between our five-to-seven-day fishing trips, we'd spend a day or two docked at the Ketchikan boat basin. Here, we'd sell our catch, refuel, re-supply, and re-rig for the next trip. Captain Skip allowed me to stay aboard the *Pacific Lady* while he, Jack, and Tony went home to their families. During these times, for the most part, I'd read, write letters, and write in my journal, which was never far from me. I loved to walk the streets of this unique, rough, and picturesque little fishing village. At the time, the only way in or out of Ketchikan was by boat or floatplane, so all the food and supplies were barged in, mostly from Seattle. Here, a nickel Coke cost a dime, a newspaper from the lower 48 that cost two cents was a nickel, and you could buy a hamburger and fries and pay almost two bits. The only thing that seemed to be cheap was the beer. Anyhow, it must have been, because there was a bar on every corner and a drunk on every sidewalk. Jack and Tony had asked me to go out on the town with them a few times, but I always found an excuse to say no. At sixteen, I might have a smoke every now and then, but going to those bars and what they called "sporting houses" just didn't appeal to me.

That first summer, I met Captain Skip's family only once, and that was when his wife had me to dinner, the night before I returned to the east. They lived in a modest house in the hills, overlooking the village and its harbor. His wife was a small, blonde-haired Norwegian lady named Louise, who cooked one of the best meals I'd ever eaten. The menu was simple—what she called seafood stew. While I can't remember exactly what kind of seafood she used, I remember telling myself it had been the best meal ever. At the dinner table that night were their two daughters. Laura, 17, was about to leave for college in Seattle, and Nancy, 20, was about to marry a sailor down in San Diego.

The next day, as Skip walked me to the ferry, he told me that while he'd miss "his gals," Ketchikan was no place to raise a family and that most young people got out as soon as possible. Later, as the ferryboat moved slowly past the city, I stood by the railing, looking out at the little fishing village. I felt sorry that Skip and Louise would be without their daughters, as I'd found this little hamlet so unique and picturesque, but then, I didn't have a family to raise here. With my pockets full of money and my head full of memories, I left Ketchikan for the first time. But I knew I would return.

As we moved through a small gully, I glanced up, watching the last of the blue-gray mist whisk away from the top of Thunder Mountain. Stopping my little caravan, I reached into my saddlebags for my binoculars. Through the glasses, I got my first really good look at that gigantic granite monolith.

What I saw frightened me, and for the first time in my life I tasted fear in my cotton-dry mouth. What loomed before me was a forbidding, unforgiving, massive wilderness that could swallow up my little party in one quick gulp. The trail ahead was pitted with dangers and I knew that I could count on no one but myself.

Replacing the binoculars in my saddlebag, I cussed myself for looking. Why didn't I have a spine? Why had I agreed to this adventure? Grandfather and I were utterly different, fire and ice. I never measured any man by his pocketbook. I never expected anything from others that I wasn't willing to give back and I never judged others, only myself. How had I turned out so completely my grandfather's opposite? Maybe, just maybe, I was more like my father, after all.

Missions

Life's a crap shoot when it comes to family, sometimes you win and sometimes lose. Families can have strange and funny traditions. In my case it was this "mission" stuff. This "back to the earth" notion was just so much bunk to me and from my earliest years, I let everyone know how I felt about it. This wasn't something that I intended to do or that I would even consider doing in the future.

That wasn't something Grandfather wanted to hear. For the most part, he wouldn't even listen to my loud protests. He simply ended our conversations with the same short, stale, stern statement: "You will return a man... a better man."

On the other hand, Uncle Roy would sit and listen to me point out all my reasons for not making such a journey. But in the end he would always tell me, "Look, Dutch, think of it as a colossal adventure. It would make your Grandfather so happy if you did this one little thing for him." A one-year ordeal in a wilderness didn't seem so little to me! But in the end and from his grave, Grandfather would, as always, get his way.

Grandfather loved to tell me about his mission, back when he was young buck. Dutch Eric Clarke was the first-born of a Mormon family near Denver Colorado in 1868. His father, Odo, from the Netherlands, was a dirt farmer. He owned a small farm a few miles outside the city. His mother, Grace, from Scotland, gave birth to seven children over the years. All were boys, but only two would survive. Uncle Roy had been born the last child, when Grandfather was already fourteen years old.

The Clarke family was hard-working, poor, and uneducated. When his father lost the farm in the 1886 drought and had to move into town, Dutch struck out on his own. Some months later, he had saved almost $20 from doing odd jobs around Denver. In those days, $20 was a good grubstake for starting a new life.

While working in town, he learned from some local silver miners about gold being found up in the panhandle of the new state of Idaho. He'd sworn never to be a dirt farmer, and the thought of free gold sounded awful good to young Dutch.

When he arrived north, he found that most of the gold claims had already been taken and that the mines were now being worked. Signing on with one of the local companies, he worked at learning the trade of mining. He would later tell me that working a mine was ten times harder than working any dirt farm.

While laboring in the gold fields, Grandfather befriended an old Indian who lived close to the shack he'd built near the company mine. The Indian told Dutch of a deep valley with a large river running through it, up in the northern mountains, close to the U.S. and Canadian border. He said that few white people had seen this land and that there just might be gold up there.

That's all it took; Dutch started his mission. With only two pack mules full of supplies and tools, he set off to find his fortune. After weeks of searching, he located the valley the old Indian spoke of. Nestled between navy blue and purple mountains, the valley was small, but did have a good-sized river running through it. Here he worked and survived on the banks of the river for a full year. It was hot, it was cold, it rained, and it snowed. He built a small cabin and hunted the forest for the food he ate. He did find gold, but never the mother lode or source of the gold in the river and streams. At year's end, he packed out over $10,000 of dust and nuggets on the backs of his two mules. This was a great deal of wealth in those days and these riches were to become the seeds of our family's fortune and future.

Dutch returned to Denver to find that his father had gone under and his mother dying of tuberculosis. Within the month, she, too, passed away, so Grandfather took his younger brother Roy and moved east. They settled in New Jersey, where Dutch worked for many years at a buggy company that was pioneering the manufacture of the new horseless carriages.

Just before the turn of the century, he quit this job to open a new venture, selling petroleum products from what were called "gas stations." With the growing number of automobiles on the road, he figured gas was a commodity that would be needed for years to come. He called his new venture Gold Gas Stations. Buying gas on the spot market from the few petroleum refiners on the east coast, he then had the fuel trucked to his stations. He was on the ground floor of a whole new industry. Dutch Eric Clarke was in the right place at the right time with the right idea.

Within a few years, Dutch had parlayed two outlets into thirty-five stations. After the turn of the century, Uncle Roy graduated from Harvard Business School (which Grandfather had paid for). Upon graduation, Roy started working for Grandfather. Some years later, they sold their gas stations to the Standard Oil Company of New Jersey for over $250,000 in cash and stock.

Taking some of this money, he and Roy bought one of the petroleum refineries that had once supplied them. Naming this second new venture Gold Coast Petroleum, they built a dynasty. By changing the way the oil was refined, they were soon producing not only gas, but also motor oil, diesel fuel, paint thinner, and kerosene.

Using Uncle Roy's expertise in business and accounting, Dutch acquired a dozen other refineries over the next thirty years. Because the company was without debt, when the Great

Depression came in the 1930s and the market for petroleum products started to dry up, he hired guards to oversee and protect closed refineries. He then reopened the plants as the markets improved.

Grandfather was a smug businessman, always working at work. The only thing he had time for was business: it was his life. Grandfather became a very rich man and he measured all other people by the size of their wallets. He was, in fact, quite arrogant, starchy and a skinflint when it came to his money. But of all his accomplishments, it was his "mission," his year in the wilderness, which he liked to talk about the most. Those stories were told and retold, always with reverence. It was he "who went into the mountains a boy and returned a man... a better man." The stories never seemed to change.

When the time came, my father had his own mission, although I didn't hear the stories from him. Instead, Grandfather loved to tell his tales to me. Dutch Clarke, Jr., was born into this austere and rigid family in 1892. His mother, my Grandmother Alice, was a generous and loving woman who could bring warmth to any home. For some untold reason, he would be her only child.

Grandmother made sure my father had a good education and a large family home in which to grow up, *Fairview Manor*. Dutch, Sr., built the house, at her insistence, on Long Island in 1901. Junior proved to be a very smart and talented son, and he went to the best schools Alice could find. At nineteen, he graduated from the University of Oklahoma with a degree in Geology. In September of 1911, he started his mission by traveling to the southwest territory of New Mexico, which was not yet a state. Here he would spend a year alone with a horse and two mules, doing a geologic survey of a large desert area.

He and my Grandfather had planned the trip well. Their objective was to find any oil deposits to which they might stake a claim after statehood. With the help of Uncle Roy, who knew one of the local rangers, my father had a base of operations for desert survival training and a point from which to start. Soon after his mission, New Mexico became the 47th state. In 1912, the Clarke's, Senior and Junior, staked mineral claims on twenty sections of government land. Of these sections, six proved to be "commercial" oil producers, which added to the mounting family fortune. Junior now joined the petroleum business with Uncle Roy and Grandfather.

In 1918, my father married his college sweetheart, Mary Wallace Person, in Oklahoma City. I was born in New Mexico on May 31, 1920, as Eric Dutch Clarke III. Over the years, I came to hate all those names... with the exception, for some reason, of "Dutch."

My mother and father were killed in an automobile accident in 1925. So it was then, at the age of five, I went to live at *Fairview Manor* with my grandparents. As I grew older, I deeply resented the fact that I'd lost both of my parents in a split second of squealing brakes and crashing metal. But, to tell the truth, I don't really remember either of them very well.

This was a time when there seemed to be a black cloud of death hanging over the Clarke family. Grandmother Alice died of pneumonia at age fifty-eight, just three years after I came to live with her and Grandfather. I have fond memories of that large, warm, and loving woman. Other than my mother, she was the only person I ever remember kissing or hugging me. In the few years we spent together, she tried her best to help me better understand and know about my parents, their lives and their tragic deaths.

Sad and shaken once again, I consoled myself that my beloved grandmother had joined my parents in heaven. From then on, I could only learn about my father and mother through the stories that Uncle Roy and Grandfather would occasionally tell. Most of all, Senior enjoyed recounting the details of my father's mission in the desert. He would take out old maps and point to the general areas of my father had traveled. Then he would rattle off stories about wild animals, Indians, survival, and finding just the right rock formations. He would always end the tale with his standard statement: "He went into the desert a boy and returned a man... a better man." As the years went by, it became an old sour story, told to deaf ears.

Green Sentinels

By mid-morning, I reached the forest line, where the logged landscape gave way to a rich and dense rain forest. The narrow game trail we'd ridden down eventually disappeared. From time to time, I'd find small creek beds that would lead my little party in the general direction I wanted to go. Other times, I'd dismount and use my hatchet and hunting knife to forge a trail. The forest was thick, and it made my work difficult and slow-going. The canopy of trees was so dense that at times I lost sight of the sun and seemed to be moving in a shroud of emerald-green twilight.

Most of the forest floor was littered with old trees and toppled snags, downed in many storms over the centuries. All trees—dead or growing—were covered with thick layers of green moss. The smell of damp and rotting vegetation permeated the forest floor. Growing through and around the downed trees was a crowd of green underbrush, and moving my horse and pack mules through these obstacles was taking much more time than I'd expected.

Every now and then, we'd come upon a small clearing where I could stop and fix my general position with compass and map. But these opportunities were few, as thick vegetation pushed through every nook and cranny in an attempt to reach an occasional ray of sun.

The animals and I strained through a patch of underbrush but soon broke through to a dry, rocky creek bed. The warm sun splashed my face. I looked up and over the large green sentinels and saw some patches of brilliant blue sky shining through. Many of these towering trees were hundreds, if not thousands, of years old, and at times made me feel like I was riding through a large cathedral, with the only light filtered by an immense green window from above.

Stopping every few hours, I'd give the mules and Blaze a rest and water. The mules each carried a heavy load of supplies. Blaze carried my 175-pound body, with an additional 100 pounds in my saddlebags, bedroll and backpack. Each time we stopped, I could see signs of the wildlife that inhabited the forest. There were tracks of deer, elk, raccoons, and cougar, but most of the tracks were from timber wolves, the most vocal citizens of this forest. Gus was having the time of his life, following all those smells.

At noon, I let my animals rest and drink while I ate a sandwich and an apple from my saddlebag. Having been in the saddle for almost six hours, I could tell by the feeling in my backside that it would be a long journey.

The weather had steadily improved throughout the day. Gus, who had been leading and exploring some few hundred yards ahead, now rejoined my little party and was soon asleep on some ferns in a sunlit area. He had been running, up and down, left and right, for almost six straight hours, and was exhausted. After eating, I stretched out under a large fir tree and dozed off.

Not long into my snooze, I was jolted awake by Gus's menacing bark and snarl. As I leapt to my feet, I saw the backside of a large mountain lion some fifty yards away, running fast through the forest with Gus in hot pursuit. Fumbling for my pistol, I called out for Gus to return, fearing that he would be no match for such a creature. I wanted to run after him, but I knew I couldn't leave Blaze and the mules unguarded in this environment.

For the next few minutes, I strained to hear the distant sound of a fight or a yelp, but my heart pounded in my ears so loudly that I heard nothing but that. Moments later, I saw the nearby brush quiver and then part. The hair was up on the back of my neck, and my pistol was cocked and ready. As I tightened my grip and dug my feet into the moss, Gus crashed through the underbrush and into our little clearing. His ears were up and he had what I swear was a broad grin on his face. I knew the lion had outdistanced him, but he was still very proud of his attempt. This was my first face-to-face contact with a wild animal, and thanks to Gus there had been no deadly confrontation. The encounter reminded me, however, that my animals were the keys to my survival. I would always have to be alert to protect them from the many wild predators of the forest.

Sobered, I packed up and we started our ascent of the trail again, with Gus at the point as always.

The *Pacific Lady*

As a young boy I don't recall that Uncle Roy had been responsible for this back-to-the-earth mission stuff, but also I don't recall his support for my loud protests. But then, I didn't hold that against him. He was Grandfather's brother and closest business associate, and he provided, after the loss of my parents and Grandmother, the only truly warm family relationship I had. Grandfather's and Roy's personalities were like night and day, ice and fire. Roy was relaxed and fun to be around while Senior was stiff, somber and always businesslike.

Uncle Roy told me that Grandfather's whole personality had changed after my father died. Then, after losing his beloved Alice, my grandmother, it only got worse. It was Roy who found time to come to my school ballgames. It was he who brought the presents that young boys wanted at Christmas time and birthdays. And it was always Uncle Roy who would sit down and take the time to talk with me. To Roy, I became the son he never had, and I had grown to love and respect him for that. Uncle Roy had always been there for me. Now I was here for him.

At age twelve, I was sent off to boarding school. Although this upset me a great deal, I soon came to realize that it was better than living with Grandfather in that musty, lonely house. I hated returning to *Fairview* at each summer break—except that it gave me a chance to see Uncle Roy and Hazel, our Negro housekeeper and cook.

The Christmas before my sixteenth birthday, Uncle Roy asked me if I would like to work in Alaska on a fishing boat that coming summer. It seemed that Roy had an old college friend, Skip Patterson, who owned a commercial fishing boat and needed some summer help from a strong and willing body. With Grandfather's approval, I jumped at the chance.

That was the first of four straight summers I spent with Captain Skip. He had a 55-foot wooden trawler named *Pacific Lady*, out of Ketchikan, Alaska. In the spring and summer, he and his crew fished for salmon. In the winter, it was halibut, shrimp and bottom fish. His crews were all expert seamen.

I fell in love with southwest Alaska the minute I stepped off the ferryboat from Seattle. Ketchikan was a small fishing, logging, and mining town with fewer than 5,000 people. With its wooden boardwalks, saloons, and sporting houses, the little community was as rustic and rowdy as any town in the old Wild West. Further, Captain Skip and his crews were just the opposite of the people I knew back East. For the most part, they were warm, honest, and hard-working, and they had no fear of man or sea.

In the first and second summers, I was what they called the "bait boy" and was paid for each day we were out fishing. My first few weeks on the *Pacific Lady* were a living hell, as the crew was suspicious of the "privileged" kid from back East. They loved to torment me and give me a bad time. But my biggest problem was seasickness. I hugged the rail and the head almost all the time. This meant nothing to my other shipmates. They required me, like themselves, to do all duties. And if we were fishing, I was needed topside, whether sick, wet, cold, tired, or hungry.

After I got my sea legs and gained the confidence of the crew, I started to connect with these men, the boat, and their way of life. Fishing the Inland Passage, with all its beauty, was truly something to experience. Here, for the first time, I saw bald eagles, bears, mountain lions, and fish of a size I could not have imagined. But mostly it was the captain and the other fishermen that I enjoyed. They seemed to know every rock, every inlet, and every bay. They knew where the fish were and how to catch them in any weather or water conditions. In and out of port, I spent hours listening to the crew and Skip spin stories about their travels up and down the Pacific Coast.

During my second summer, one of those stories stuck in my mind. Captain Skip told the tale of how he'd been trolling down the Queen Charlotte Sound for spring king salmon, the largest and most valuable catch in the salmon fishery, when a strong storm started to rage out of the southwest. With winds blowing at 60 to 80 knots, the barometer dropping, and gale force seas swelling to over 30 feet, Skip looked for relief. Soon he turned the *Pacific Lady* in at the protection of the Dean Channel alongside King Island in Western British Columbia. Using some old charts, he moved the boat through sheets of rain and white water some 40 miles up the channel before the weather improved enough to fish.

With the seas still running with six-to-eight-foot swells, he ordered the outriggers to be lowered. While Skip had never been in those waters before, and had no license to fish in Canadian waters, the fishing still looked promising. The crew soon had the outriggers lowered and the hooks baited as they moved further up the channel. Sure enough, they started catching a few very large kings.

Then, just past Edward Point, the northernmost point off King Island, the boat hit a rock or submerged log. The force of the blow caused the propeller shaft to bend, snapping off one blade and jamming the rudder. With the seas and winds still running high, the crew put the outriggers up and Captain Skip begin looking for a protective bay or cove where he might put in for repairs.

After a difficult search, they found Nascall Bay on the port side two miles further up the channel. Using the winds, the tide, and a small outboard motor from the dinghy, they limped into the bay and dropped anchor.

There they stayed for two days and nights, making repairs to the Pacific Lady. During this time, the weather improved, and on the last day they took the dinghy to shore to look around. They told me that above the bay they found a large freshwater lake, which on the chart was called Nascall Lake. A large, green valley of grassland spread at the base of this lake. There were two or three spring creeks running through the floor of the valley, with large groves of tall alder and oak trees on the perimeter. The rest of the area was surrounded with old-growth fir trees, which dominated most of the landscape. They saw many signs of wildlife—deer, elk, bear—and the clear water of the lake looked to be teaming with trout. Skip had called it, "The most beautiful and rich valley I have ever seen."

He went on to describe how the water from the lake flowed over large rocks, down some 200 feet to the bay and channel below. This waterfall and the rocks made for many large pools, some of which were fed by steaming hot water flowing out of the side of one tall cliff. He and his crew bathed and relaxed in one of the many hot springs. In another conversation, he talked about the bay being sandy and rocky, rich with shellfish, crabs, and fish. All agreed that this area was as beautiful as any they had seen in all of Alaska and Canada. Often, the crew would joke about returning to Nascall Bay and doing a little hunting in the valley they had discovered. These stories were repeated often, each time with the addition of yet another detail. Their tales and descriptions sparked vivid images for me.

At the end of each summer, with nearly $400 dollars in my pockets, I found it harder and harder to leave the *Pacific Lady* and my newfound friends. Each year, before I left, I'd ask Captain Skip if I was welcome back for the following summer, and each time he would tell me that I would always have a berth on any boat that he commanded. That made me feel good, like I'd found something I did well and friends who enjoyed me for who I was, not just for who my family was.

On the third summer of fishing, I was promoted to deck hand, which meant that I would share in the value of the fish we caught and sold. I left Ketchikan at the end of that summer with over $1,200 in my pocket. This was my money. I'd earned it myself and I would spend it myself. These summers gave me a feeling of freedom, fulfillment, and independence. For the first time in my life, I had my own money, my own friends and something I enjoyed doing. It was bloody hard work, but I was in love with Alaska, the sea and the men who fished for her bounty. These summers were the best of times.

Horsemanship

The way we were traveling turned better as my little caravan moved up a well-traveled game trail. It was now early afternoon, and, to my surprise, the weather was still improving. The bright sun felt warm on my body as I rode through the few forest clearings. Then, just starting up a small, windy hill, I turned to the rear to make sure the mules were in a correct path behind me. As I turned to the front again, a low, thick fir branch hit me squarely on the forehead.

The force of the blow rolled me off my horse and hard onto the ground. The crash knocked me out for a second, and I struggled to get my wits about me again. Slowly opening my eyes, I could see Gus clearly, some 50 feet up the trail. Blaze was standing in front of me with his head down, turning back looking at me, his reins hanging on the floor of the forest.

Both Gus and Blaze had puzzled looks on their faces. Blaze seemed to be saying, "You pointed the way, pal." As I got slowly to my feet, both the mules started to bray as if they were laughing at me. Embarrassed, I brushed myself off with hands and hat, dust rising into the still air. I had to remember that my head was taller in the saddle than Blaze's head on his neck. Basic horsemanship. As I mounted Blaze once again, I knew that, while my forehead would have a lump, the only real damage had been to my pride. This event only proved what I already knew: I was no cowboy.

Drifting

From old pictures, I could tell I'd grown up to look and be built much like my father. The difference was that he was taller and thinner than me, as I was 6'1" and weighed 175 pounds. He seemed to have had a strong, muscular body, the same as mine. Uncle Roy said that I had my mother's blue eyes, small ears, nose, and cleft chin. From her pictures, she was a very beautiful lady. I wished I had known them both; there were so many questions I would have asked.

When it came to brains, however, I didn't get my father's. Grandfather liked to say that I was academically challenged, and he was right. Every year, school was a struggle for me as I found only a few subjects interesting. I didn't blame my teachers for this because for the most part I was just not interested in a formal education. I did excel in science, geography, art, and athletics. But math, English, Latin, and history were another story. As it turned out, I had not become the scholar dear, old Grandfather had expected or the athlete that I wanted to be. Cynical with it all, I squeaked through senior year at boarding school as a C student and then attended a private college for almost two years, where I failed many courses. By then, I had a chip on my shoulder and knew it. I was just kind of drifting. Any wind could have blown me in any direction. In the early spring of 1940, I decided, over the strong objections of Grandfather and Uncle Roy, to drop out of school and return to the only thing I enjoyed: fishing in Alaska.

Sending a telegram to Captain Skip, I told him I was coming back and gave him my arrival date. I figured that if he didn't have a job for me, I'd find a berth on another fishing boat. Flying, for the first time, from New York to Denver and then Denver to Seattle, I made the journey in only 30 hours.

When I tried to purchase a plane ticket for Ketchikan, I was told that all the flights were full and that there was a five-day wait for a seat. When I inquired as to the reason, the lady at the ticket counter told me that it had been like that for the past six months, but that she had no idea why the delays were so long. Because of this, I decided to book passage on one of the ferryboats. While it would take three days of sailing, it was much better than waiting five-days for a seat on the airplane.

When I stepped off the boat, I found a much different Ketchikan than when I had left, nine months earlier. The streets were full of people, most of them wearing army uniforms. There were MPs (Military Police) on almost every street corner and hundreds of other "out of place" faces. Preoccupied with thoughts of the *Pacific Lady*, I hurried to the boat basin. My eyes quickly skimmed the docks to see if the boat was still in port.

Sure enough, there she was. Captain Skip had given her a new paint job, a white superstructure that contrasted nicely with the clean, bright green trim. She even had new rigging and gear on her afterdeck.

Captain Skip sat in the wheelhouse, cradling a steaming mug of coffee in his weathered hands. He greeted me warmly and, as he filled a chipped mug for me of the steaming brew, Skip brought me up to speed on the changes in Ketchikan. He told me that the Army was building a number of fortifications up and down the Alaskan coastline and that Ketchikan had almost doubled in size over the last six months.

From his descriptions, I didn't understand why the Army was in Alaska. I knew that some people were talking about a possible war in Europe, but why Alaska, such a long way from Europe? He went on to tell me that the locals hated having the military around and that there had been many fights in town, with the fishermen fighting the soldiers, the soldiers fighting the loggers, and the miners fighting everyone else. At this we both laughed. Clearly, the wild little fishing town of Ketchikan had gotten even wilder.

Captain Skip had waited for my arrival. One of his crew, Lucky, a good old guy with one hell of a temper, was in the hospital after being stabbed by a miner in a barroom brawl. One of his other crewmembers, a man whom I had not met, had returned to the lower forty-eight to join the Navy. We would be fishing short two crewmembers, a lot more work for all... but our shares in the profits would be more, too. The good news was that the price the packers were paying for fish had almost doubled over the past year. Stowing my gear in a forward compartment, I was eager to trade the port for the sea once again.

We fished almost non-stop from March on, with our average trip lasting anywhere from four days to a week. We'd then return to Ketchikan to sell our catch, purchase supplies, do maintenance on the boat, gas up, and return to the sea. Fishing had been excellent, and we were all making more money than we ever dreamed. While in port, we played hard, spending our money from café to saloon, saloon to café. But Captain Skip issued firm orders that the crew and I were to avoid any confrontations. Not that any of us were afraid of the townspeople. We felt that if we could master the sea, we damn sure could take care of ourselves in any port. We were rough, we were tough, we were fit... and that "chip" on my shoulder had never been so big. If it had not been for the respect I felt for Skip and his orders, I don't know what might have happened.

The *Pacific Lady* made the boat basin on July 12. We'd been out for just under a week, and our iced storage hulls were packed with pink salmon. At well over 15,000 pounds, this was about the maximum we could carry. As we tied up the boat at the packer's dock, a boy met us and said that there was a telegraph for me in the harbormaster's office.

Hurrying up the dock and the gangways, I reached the office and read Uncle Roy's simple message:

```
DATE: JULY 5, 1940
DUTCH CLARKE III
C/O PACIFIC LADY FISHING BOAT
KETCHIKAN, ALASKA


DUTCH SR.  DIED  JULY  4.  FUNERAL  ON  JULY  9.
COME  HOME  AT  ONCE.  FAMILY  BUSINESS  MUST  BE
RESOLVED.


    ROY
```

Only moments earlier, my life had been fulfilled and happy. Now, a simple yellow piece of paper made me feel uncertain and lost again. Grandfather had only been 72 and had seemed to be in good health; he should have lived forever. While I didn't shed a tear over Grandfather's passing, there was once again a hole in my life, a hole that would have to be filled.

Returning to the boat, I shared the news with Skip and the crew. I didn't want to leave the boat, for many reasons. Still, deep down, I knew I had to go, if for no other reason than to face Uncle Roy and that "Family Business" stuff.

Luckily, I got a seat on the next day's flight to Seattle, with connections to Denver and then to New York. Captain Skip, his wife Louise, and the rest of the crew saw me off at the airport. As I was shaking hands with Skip, he soberly said, "I'll save your berth, mate. You can ship with me any time. Just let me know if I can be of any help."

As the small plane flew out over the now-bustling hamlet, I wondered if I would ever see Ketchikan, the *Pacific Lady* and her crew again. With over $5,000 in my pockets and facing an unknown future, I vowed I would return. So help me God, I would return!

First Crossing

Late in the afternoon, my small caravan reached the banks of Thunder River, the first of three major water crossings. Having heard the loud roar of the river down trail for the last half-hour, I knew my first obstacle was at hand. At the point where I rode out of the dense forest alongside this river, I found a small ravine with large rocks on the opposite side, some sixty yards away. The water was deep and fast-flowing from the spring runoff. From its looks, I was betting it was bone-chillingly cold, too. The river was deep green, and boulders protruded from the fast-moving water, causing white rapids from shore to shore.

Reining Blaze to the north, I looked for a better crossing point. When I found none, I backtracked and traveled another quarter mile upriver from where I'd first come out of the forest. Finally, I found a place where there was a large logjam being held together by rocks on both sides of the river. This obstacle caused the fast-moving water to pool up and slow a hundred feet back from the logs. From what I could see, the water only looked to be about three or four feet deep at that point. The animals would have to traverse the river here, one at a time, and—because of the fast-moving current—it would have to be without their full, heavy loads. Each mule carried four waterproof trail bags; before crossing, I would unpack two of the bags from each of them. Looking at the river and the other side, I decided that I would cross first with Blaze, while stringing a safety rope from one side to the other. On a snag, I tied one end of my rope and coaxed Blaze towards the roaring river's crossing point.

With a great deal of caution, we entered the water. Huffing and snorting nervously, Blaze made one tenuous step at a time over the slippery riverbed rocks. By the middle of the stream, the cold water was up to my knees, and I could feel Blaze push his weight against the pressure of the moving undercurrent as we stumbled towards the other side. After reaching the other bank, I secured my safety rope to a large tree and took my saddlebags, bedroll, and saddle off Blaze before tying him to another snag. I also took off my backpack, coat, and gun belt, replacing my wet boots with canvas shoes to re-cross the river and retrieve the mules and supplies.

As I approached the riverbank again, I could see Gus in the middle of the stream, swimming towards me. With only his head out of the water, and his strong legs paddling with all their might, he was making good time in the water. It had taken no encouragement from me to get him to swim across, as he seemed to love the water.

After his safe arrival on the new shore, he greeted me with a big shake that flicked huge, cold droplets all over me. That was just a taste of more to come. Quickly, I ventured back into the river on foot. It was numbingly cold! I had to keep moving, as I knew the water could be dangerous. Holding on to the rope and moving hand over hand, I was soon on the other side again. It took me almost an hour and another six trips to get the mules and supplies all safely to the other side. All the while, Gus watched from the riverbank, moving back and forth, barking, almost as if he was shouting out commands to me.

After completing my last load, numb from the waist down, I couldn't believe how cold I was. Because of my fear of hypothermia, I quickly stripped my wet clothes off and dried myself in the late direct sunlight. Searching out some dry wood, I soon had a small fire made in a protected area of log snags. Damn! This was something I should have done on my first trip across. I had a lot to learn! There were dry clothes in my saddlebags, and I quickly changed into them. Wringing the worst of the water out of my wet clothes, I laid them out to dry by the fireside. Next, I searched through my saddlebags until I found the makings for a small pot of coffee, which I placed next to the fire. As the coffee started to brew, I made sure that the animals were fed and tied close to the camp and that all of the supplies were stacked and safe. Famished, I returned to the fireside, warmed a large can of beans, and ate some bread from my saddlebags. The area around my first campsite was breathtaking, from the dense rain forest on the other side of the river to the fast-moving white water and high rocky cliffs on my side. I was dwarfed by the sheer size and splendor of my surroundings.

Within a half an hour, the food and most of the coffee was

gone. Once my dinner fixings were cleaned up, I opened my bedroll on a sandy beach area close to the fire and lay back against a large log snag. By then, the light in the western sky was growing dim. Checking my pocket watch, I was surprised to find that it was almost 10 p.m. Because we were so far north, the days were much longer in the late spring and early summer.

Resting there in the faint evening light, with moths dancing around my fire, I reflected on my accomplishments. Not so bad for the first day... dead tired, a sore butt, a lump on my forehead, but it had gone pretty much as I had planned. Other than falling off my horse and getting lost a few times, the first day seemed to be a good omen.

My gaze soon came to rest on the stack of trail bags, full of my supplies.

For the thousandth or maybe even the millionth time, I worried about what I hadn't brought and what I might have overstocked. I remembered the detailed list that I'd drafted while trying so hard to anticipate all my future needs. What kind of weather would I encounter? What tools would be needed to build a cabin? Food: supplies... what to take and what to grow? Plans for the trip in and plans for the trip out, so many details. Despite having gone over and over my list of supplies for the better part of six months, I was still apprehensive. One thing I knew for sure: there would be no stores up in the Nascall Valley.

With the exception of my food, tools and animals, I'd purchased most of my trail supplies from Willis & Geiger, outfitters out of Wisconsin. The total cost to fund this journey was some $2,500, which had been paid for by Grandfather's estate. Therefore, I had made sure to purchase only the best outfit and supplies that money could buy.

My list of dry foods was quite long, since they would be my staples until my garden could be harvested. These staples, for the most part, were in moisture-proof containers that I could reuse for other foods. These supplies included such items as rock salt, vinegar, and sugar, which would be used in drying and pickling vegetables and game foods. Honey, dried fruits, and fruit juice were valuable for their sugar value and to help prevent scurvy. Most of my food items were packed on the mule Harry. On my mule Harriet, I carried my tools, building materials and farm implements. And the knapsack on my back held all my personal items.

In my saddle bags I'd packed food supplies for the trail: three loaves of hard bread, ten cans of beans and chili, one pound of coffee, a small coffee pot, can opener, six sandwiches, ten apples and ten candy bars. I'd brought the trail food so I could concentrate on traveling without having to do any hunting during my journey.

I also carried three firearms: a Smith & Wesson .32 caliber pistol, a lever-action Winchester Model 94 rifle, and a Winchester Model 12 pump action 20-gauge shotgun. Ammunition: eight boxes, 160 rounds of 20 gauge shotgun shells; two boxes, 100 rounds of .32 caliber rim fire pistol shells, with another 25 rounds on my gun belt; and four boxes, 200 rounds of 32/40 rifle shells, with another six shells in my rifle. Both my Winchester rifle and shotgun I had strapped in saddle boots on either side of Blaze. Other weapons were my 12" hunting knife and a small hatchet, both hanging on the gun belt, and a 6" switchblade knife in my pocket, all razor-sharp. In my bedroll, I'd stashed my sleeping bag, two wool blankets, a yellow rain slicker, a rubber poncho and two 4' by 6' waxed-canvas tarps.

This endless list of supplies kept rushing through my head like the river. Lying there, looking up at the countless stars, I thought, Details, details… whatever I've forgotten, I'll have to live without. Whatever I really need I will make, grow, or hunt.

When I tossed two more logs on the fire, it snapped and popped back at me, while the nearby river roared like a freight train. To this nighttime symphony, a single wolf added his contribution, crying out in the distance. His sounds reminded me that I would not really be alone on this trip, as these predators would always be with me. Slipping deep into my sleeping bag, I covered myself with a blanket and was soon in a cocoon-like slumber.

CHAPTER TWO

On the Trail

The early morning sun lit up the eastern sky with a regal, brilliant red glow rising behind the mountains. As I opened my eyes to the second day on the trail, it took me a minute to remember where I was and what I was doing. The morning was starting clear and crisp with heavy dew covering my supply bags and bedding. Rolling over, I faced the pool of river water I'd crossed the day before. There, on the other shore about three feet into the water was a young doe. She looked to be not much more than a yearling. Her hide was a beautiful light brown with white patches on her forelegs. Her mouth and nose were a shiny jet black. Backlit in the early morning light, she'd take a sip and stop. Sip and stop. Each time she paused, she'd raise her head with ears straight up and sniff the air for any scent of trouble, turning her head right and left. After a few more drinks of water, she turned and effortlessly jumped 10 or 15 feet back into the underbrush and out of sight. What a beautiful scene to start the day. Then I reminded myself that this was just the kind of animal that I would have to hunt and kill if I were to survive in the wilderness. Wondering silently if I could kill such a noble animal, I shook off the thought and began my second day.

Crawling out of my sleeping bag, I moved to the edge of the river to brush my teeth and wash. As I knelt down, I looked out to see two, then three, fish breaking water in the center of the pool. Fish for breakfast, not a bad idea! I'd save my washing for later so as not to scare the fish. From one of the trail bags I removed my fly pole, reel and a wet fly. In a few moments I was back at the dark green pool. Out of the corner of my eye I could see Gus, now awake, watching my every move. Maybe he was hungry too.

I was in luck, a strike on the second cast. I hooked a fat 14 or15 inch sea run cutthroat trout that knew how to fight. Reeling in the first fish, my long bamboo pole bent down with its tip almost in the water. It was a good fight. In the next few minutes, two more fish, each weighing about two pounds, joined the first, lying on the rocks of the riverbank. Now to put my knives to the test, stowing my fishing gear, I set to the task of cleaning the fish. As I threw some of the guts into the water, I noticed small crawfish coming out from under rocks and devouring the innards. Crawfish... I hadn't factored them in when I was planning my available food list. I wondered what other things haven't I thought of? Damn. I was still full of doubts, and things like this didn't put my mind at ease.

Overnight, the fire had burned down, so I stirred the coals, threw in bits of twigs and grass and the fire jumped to life. Warming my hands, I watched the white smoke rise into the air as the fire took hold. Nothing could be wasted on this trip, so I moved the tin pot of last night's coffee closer to the fire.

During my training in New Mexico, I learned a few outdoor cooking methods. "Indian style" seemed like a good way to cook these fat delicacies. Near the water, I found three sticks about 3 feet long, which I sharpened. With the sharpened end first, I stuck it into the fat end of the cleaned trout and slid them the length of the fish. Then I placed the other ends of the sticks into the sandy ground around my campfire. Securing the kabobs with rocks, the skewers now held the fish in the hot air over the flames. After a few minutes, I turned the fish. What a wonderful aroma, cooking fish, coffee and burning wood. Soon I began eating my first fish right off the stick. As I ate, I saw Gus move to within six or seven feet of the fire, laying across some small rocks and watching my every move. When I finished with the first fish, eating all but the tail and bones, I threw the carcass towards Gus... he didn't move an inch. The same thing happened with the second fish... he wouldn't move towards the remains on the rocks. About halfway through the third fish, I'd eaten enough. This time I threw the half-eaten fish directly at Gus's face and with one swipe of his powerful jaws, the fish tail, bones and meat were gone. A few minutes later both the remaining two tails and carcasses were also gone. This surprised me, for it was the first time that Gus had eaten in front of me or taken any food from me. A sign we were bonding? Maybe, but I couldn't count on it. Within a half hour I'd washed my dishes, cleaned up my camp and packed my bedroll, including the still damp clothing from yesterday. All these items were loaded on my animals and we broke camp to move up the next trail. By this evening's camp, I hoped to be on the other side of Thunder Mountain.

From The Grave

In Seattle I changed airlines and flew a new American DC4 to Denver and then on to New York. The plane was full again, not a spare seat to be found. As when I'd traveled from Ketchikan, about half the men on the flight were in military uniforms. This made me think about the war that was raging in Europe and how this event might affect my future. I'd wired Uncle Roy from Ketchikan, telling him the date I thought I'd arrive, and I planned on telephoning him from Denver with confirmation. These last two trips via air were new to me. During all my other trips to and from Alaska, I'd taken the train and the ferryboats, which had taken almost seven days of traveling time. From my departure at Ketchikan to my arrival in New York I'd figured it would take about 16 hours of airports and flight time, barring any delays. This was indeed an improvement in this new era of modern travel.

In Denver, I called Uncle Roy to tell him that my plane would arrive at the New York Airport at 11:30 p.m. He assured me that he would be there to pick me up. When I got to New York it was past midnight due to weather delays. As I got off the plane, I scanned the faces of the arrival crowd for Uncle Roy. Not seeing him, I headed towards baggage claim. I'd only taken a few steps when I heard a voice shouting,

"Master Clarke.... Master Clarke."

Looking around I found a Negro man, who I didn't know walking towards me.

"Master Clarke, I'm Mr. Roy's chauffeur, Henry, and he asked me to pick ya up and take you to *Fairview*."

"Oh, where is Uncle Roy? This afternoon on the telephone he told me that he would be here."

"He had to take the evening train to Pittsburgh, some kind of problem at one of the plants. He told me to tell ya that he would be back on the morning train. This way sir, I'll get your bags."

Things hadn't changed, only now it was Uncle Roy who was busy with business.

For the first time, I sat in the back of Uncle Roy's 1939 Cadillac Town Car. It was a luxurious automobile. I remember when he bought it that Grandfather had a fit about the way he was spending his money, not that it was any of Senior's concern. It was another two hours to Long Island and *Fairview*, so I made small talk with Henry for a few moments, then sat back in my seat and watched the city go by. It was a warm evening and I had one of the windows partly down as we drove towards the turnpike. The smells of the city drifted through the open window. It was a mixture of garbage, gas fumes and people. This smell symbolized why I had come to dislike New York City. It was too big, too crowded, too dirty, and the people who lived here seemed to have no faces and no personalities. Even as late as it was, I could see and smell that it had not changed. This city reminded me of how much I missed Ketchikan. My thoughts soon returned to that little fishing village and the way of life I had come to love.

We arrived at *Fairview* about 2 a.m. Henry hurried my bags up the grand staircase and placed them in my boyhood room as I looked around the old musty house.

The chauffeur returned and asked, "Master Clarke, should I wake the cook to get ya something to eat or drink?"

"No thanks, all I want to do is sleep. Tell Uncle Roy I'll see him in the morning. Good night, Henry, it's been nice meeting you." With this I climbed the stairs to my room.

The door swung shut on a creaking hinge behind me and I stared around my old room. It hadn't changed since the day I went off to boarding school. It was stale and drab, as was the whole house, yet clean and neat. The pictures and items of my youth still filled the space. Memorabilia, mostly of baseball and movie stars, brought back a wave of memories. Some were good, but mostly my thoughts of this house and room were of indifference. As I lay down on the bed and reached to turn off the light, I noticed the fading black-and-white picture on the nightstand. It was my parents' wedding picture--the only image I had of them together. My fingers reached over and stroked the frame. I'd held it in my hands and stared into their happy faces a thousand times before and always wondered how my life would have been different if only they had lived. Within a few moments, I was asleep, their picture clutched in my hands.

The next thing I knew, it was late morning. The bedside clock showed 10:20 a.m. I'd slept all night with my clothes and shoes on. I felt dirty, as I hadn't had a change of clothes, showered or shaved for almost three days. Thirty minutes later I emerged from the bathroom feeling like a new man. With hopes of finding Hazel and getting a bite to eat, I headed towards the kitchen. As I opened the door to the kitchen, I found a chubby older white woman working the stove. She looked up at me and said,

"You must be Master Clarke. I've heard all about you from your Uncle. I'm Bess, the cook. Would you like some coffee and breakfast or maybe lunch?"

"Only coffee... where is Hazel? I thought she would be here."

Bess took a cup from the shelf above the stove and poured the steaming coffee.

"She and her husband retired after Mr. Clarke passed away. They were so sorry you couldn't make it to the funeral. I know they wanted to see you before they left. I thought maybe Henry would have told you last night."

"No, he didn't say word. Well, I'm pleased to meet you, Bess. Just a little shocked with all the changes around here."

She handed me the coffee and I took a few sips; then I asked if Uncle Roy was here.

"Yes, sir, he's waiting for you in the study," she replied.

Thanking her, I told Bess that I'd return for some lunch in an hour or so. With that, I topped off my cup and headed to see Uncle Roy.

The large, inlaid doors of the study slid open easily. There in the dim, smoky window light, I found Uncle Roy seated behind Grandfather's enormous, hand-carved wooden desk, with papers stacked all over it. He rose with a large smile on his face and moved around to the front of the desk to greet me. We shook hands and embraced for a moment. It was good to see him again.

Roy was in his late fifties but looked to be in his forties. His fit body and brilliant "salt and pepper" hair made him look very distinguished. His handshake was firm and his demeanor commanding, as always. I could tell that Uncle Roy was now in charge, not only of the business but the family, as well, which also meant me.

We made small talk as I drank my coffee. He asked about Captain Skip and his family, wanted to know about my flight home and apologized for not meeting me the night before. I told him that we'd been at sea and that I didn't get his telegram about Grandfather's death and the funeral until it was too late. Next I inquired if Grandfather had suffered. With a softened voice he answered,

"No, thank God. The doctor said that he died painlessly in his sleep. Hazel found him the next morning lying peacefully in bed and called me for instructions."

I asked what had happened to Hazel and her husband, Buck. They had both worked at *Fairview* for as long as I could remember. Uncle Roy told me that Grandfather had made provisions in his will for $10,000 each, so they might retire in a little comfort. They moved to Illinois, where their children lived, the day after the funeral. He added that they were both disappointed at not being able to say goodbye to "Master Clarke." I then commented that it had been nice of Grandfather to take care of them.

At that Uncle Roy glared at me, his eyes staring at me over his wire-framed glasses riding low on his nose. He replied sternly,

"You know, Dutch, you just didn't give your grandfather much of a chance. You are surprised he would take care of those people... but why? There is a hell of a lot you would be surprised to know if you would've just given the old guy a chance."

"Now look, Uncle Roy, I didn't come all the way from Alaska to get into some kind of family feud with you," I answered angrily. "I know I must have been a disappointment to Grandfather, but in many ways he was a hell-a disappointment to me, too."

Uncle Roy moved behind Grandfather's desk again and sat down, still staring at me with those steel gray eyes, and said, "O.K., Dutch, let's not fight. I can see that chip is still on your shoulder... he's gone now and there's nothing we can do about that."

Roy reached down through a stack of papers and pulled out a blue bound document about 20 pages thick. He looked up at me and commented, "As you know, I was in life not only your grandfather's brother but also his closest associate, friend and confidant. In his death, I remain the same. I am the executor of his estate, and will to the best of my abilities follow his instructions to the letter."

His words were formal, unemotional and now riveting.

"Before I read you the part of his Last Will and Testament that relates to you, I want you to know that my brother bequeathed to me 75,000 shares of Gold Coast Petroleum stock, which added to the 25,000 shares I already own, makes me a 50% owner in the company. Now let me read the part relating to you. You may love it or hate it, but it's what your grandfather wanted."

Now to the son of my son, Eric Dutch Clarke, III, who has defied me with his attitude about education, the family business and life in general. In spite of this, I know in my

heart of hearts he is the blood of me and the soul of his father and shall truly become a man, in every sense of the word in the Clarke family. Therefore, I bequeath to him all the remaining assets of my estate, cash, securities, 100,000 shares of my business Gold Coast Petroleum, the home known as Fairview with all its furnishings and all other personal and private property contained within. This bequeath is made with only one reservation, which is that he, under the certification of my executor, will perform his family mission, if he has not already done so, starting within one year of my death. The mission will be defined as one year of survival, totally alone, in a wilderness area of his choice, packing in only what can be carried on animals, as both his father and I did. If my executor cannot certify, for any reason, at the end of the mission that the adventure has not been completed as to the terms and conditions set forth, then this bequeath will be given to the Mormon Church of Salt Lake City, Utah. If this mission has not been completed by the time of my death and until it can be completed under these terms and conditions, my executor will have complete control of this part of my estate. I say to my Grandson again, go into the wilderness and return a man... a better man.

Uncle Roy put down the papers and added, "The first part of the Will has to do with Hazel, Buck and myself. The last part has instructions on paying and transferring his assets through the probate courts. You can read the whole document if you wish."

He handed it to me. I sat there for a moment holding the blue bond papers, thinking about what my response would be. Placing the document back on the desk, I turned to Uncle Roy and said, "The Mormon Church? I knew that both Grandfather and you came from a Mormon family. But neither of you have ever practiced the Mormon faith that I can remember."

Uncle Roy reached for a cigar and began to prepare it for smoking. He cut the tip, looked up and replied, "You're right, there. I was as surprised as you are when I read his terms regarding your bequeath. Our mother was Mormon, but our father nothing as far as I know. After Mother died and Senior and I moved east, we never talked about the Mormon faith again."

Standing, I began walking around the room with nervous energy, holding my hands behind me. Stopping, I looked back at Roy, who was now lighting his cigar and said, "It doesn't matter. All this 'mission' stuff is just so much crap. I've always told you and Grandfather that I would never go on such an adventure. I don't want, or need, Grandfather's money, I have over $5,000 upstairs in my room. I made that money in just five months of fishing, so you can keep his damn bequeath. This is just so much shit!

Roy was surprised at my language and looked directly at me, blowing out some blue and white smoke as he replied, "I, I, I. There seems to be a lot of I's in your life. You certainly talk like a fisherman, but can you think like a man? Anyhow, we're talking about a lot more money than some lousy five grand. But Dutch, it's not about the money; it's what he wanted you to do for him, a way that he could be proud of you. You know, we all can't go through life just doing what we want to do. Sometimes we have to think about others and what they want."

Smugly, I cut him off, "Look, Uncle Roy, I know where you're coming from. I wish I could, but I can't and won't."

With fire in his eyes he raised his voice a little louder, "Dutch, if you won't do it for your grandfather, then how about thinking about me?"

"What do you mean by that?"

"Well, think this out. How might I feel about having the Mormon Church as my business partners? Do you think that thought pleases me? The last thing I need are some holier-than-thou folks running around our refineries. How about doing this for me?"

His statement caught me off guard and I shook my head as I sat back down. Panic welling up inside me.

"Uncle Roy, that's a low blow! You know how I feel about you. I would do almost anything for you. But what the hell do I know about surviving in a wilderness? I've never been on a horse, except for a pony ride in Central Park as a kid. Besides fishing up north, I've never killed an animal and I've never shot a gun. I don't know the first damn thing about living, let alone surviving in the backwoods."

Roy looked over at me with a slight grin, "It was the same with your father. Do you think he was born with all those outdoor skills here in the east? No way. Senior sent him out west for training. You remember us talking about the Lazy K Ranch in New Mexico? I still know Red Reed, who owns and operates the ranch that trained your dad. I'm sure he'd do for you what he did for your father. It was your dad who told Red there just might be oil on his property, and sure enough, he found oil right were your dad told him to look. He might be a little older now, but I am sure he and some of his cowboys can get you trained."

He was smiling a bit now, but he still looked determined and his eyes were burning my soul.

"All right... O.K." I replied, trying to find a new excuse. "Maybe I can be trained, but we are overlooking one little problem. From what I read in the newspapers, the government will soon be requiring all men from 17 to 35 years old to register for the draft. Seems there just might be a little war in Europe."

Roy turned serious again.

"Look, any war in Europe will be Mr. Roosevelt's war, not ours. Both your Grandfather and I have listened to Charles Lindbergh on this subject and he thinks the Germans and English will soon come to peace terms, making all this war talk just so much bunk. In any event, all men will have a maximum of one year before they have to sign up. *If* Congress, and that's a big *if*, passes the law before you leave, you can sign up. And if it's passed after you leave, you can sign up when you return. That is, if you feel you must sign up for Mr. Roosevelt's war."

I knew how both Grandfather and Uncle Roy felt about President Roosevelt and his administration and Uncle Roy wasn't going to let me use that as a way out.

Now I was in a bind. I didn't want to give in and was furious that even in death, Grandfather could still dictate my future. I didn't know what else to say or do. Standing up, I started walking around the room again, my mind racing. Who in their right mind would do such a mission? Was I to find more gold... more oil? No... no. If only life was so neat and simple. Uncle Roy had always been there for me, and like he said, maybe it was time I thought about someone other than myself. Just maybe there were too many "I's" in my excuse.

As I sat back down across the desk from Roy, my mind was still reeling. I started to talk, but he cut me off.

"I have something for you, Dutch." Reaching into a side desk drawer, Roy pulled out a gold pocket watch on a gold chain and slid it across to me. "When I was going through Senior's personal effects, I found this old watch. It's the one he gave to your father when he went on his mission."

Picking it up, I clicked the cover open. Inside I found a clear crystal protecting the face of a very old movement with Roman numerals. Above it, inside the cover, was an etched lighthouse, with the engraving of my dad's name and date of birth. Turning it over I found two more words etched on the back. The first word was Rimor and just below it, Votum. The words looked to be Latin.

Closing the cool golden cover, I looked up and across to Roy. "My Latin is a little rusty. Do you know what the words mean?"

Soberly he replied, "Rimor is 'explore,' or 'search'... something like that. And, if I remember right, Votum means 'vow' or 'prayer.' The words had great meaning to your grandfather, but the exact meaning is a little foggy to me, right now."

Slowly slipping the watch into my pocket, I forced a smile. "Well, I guess Grandfather will have my obedience after all. If this was once my father's, it's mine now. I'll use it with pride on my adventure. You better send Mr. Red Reed of New Mexico a telegram to see if he's ready to take on another tenderfoot."

Roy rose from behind the desk and extended his hand, which I took. Clasping my hand in both of his, he held onto me with a firm grip for a good long time. Looking right into my eyes, he finally said, "You know that Senior did this on purpose. He knew how I would feel about the Mormons and how you would feel about me. We both have been manipulated from his grave."

We both laughed. But it was a laugh of resignation, not joy.

All that night, I tossed and turned and reflected on my decision. Where would be a good area for my "mission?" How about some distant desolate island? How about somewhere up in Alaska? How about the same desert area where my father had roamed? How about that place in Canada the guys on the boat had talked about?

The next morning I sent a wire off to Captain Skip asking him to send me the charts and any maps or other information he might have on Nascall Bay in British Columbia.

Uncle Roy and I spent the next three months planning and outfitting my trip. I was to leave for New Mexico for "on the job" survival training in the middle of October 1940. I enjoyed this time with Uncle Roy, and I grew to know all the new faces around *Fairview*; they all turned out to be good folks.

Thunder Mountain

It was midday when I stopped at a large grassy ridge atop the last foothill before Thunder Mountain. Using my binoculars, I had a good view of the mountain some three or four miles ahead. The top of the monolith, 6,500 feet high, was hidden in a shroud of dirty white clouds. The place where I'd cross would be almost 4,500 feet up. I'd been told by an old trapper that there was a rough game trail that snaked up the east side of the mountain and down the west side. Unpacking the mules and taking the saddle off Blaze, I wanted all of us to have a little rest before our ascent.

With the animals safely hobbled, they began to graze on the thick grass. Pulling a bite to eat out of my pack, I began planning my climb up the mountain. From my perch on the ridge, I munched on a sandwich while looking north-northwest with the glasses, making mental notes of the terrain. The weather was looking threatening, with large black clouds moving down from the north. These dense clouds hid the top 1,000 feet of the mountain. Below the clouds I could see an outcropping of gray granite rocks. Here, I believed, I'd find the pass that would lead me to the other side.

Another 2000 feet below this outcropping was the timberline. In this rough and rugged region, there really was no distinct timberline, as some wind-blown trees had grown up to the top of the large mountains. But there was a place, about two or three thousand feet up, where the dense forest slowly blended with the much thinner trees that grew out of the granite face. Most of this high surface was blue-gray glacier-type rocks with patches of green. Through the binoculars, I could see areas were there might be a rocky trail leading up and over the pass. It looked like the last thousand feet above the dense timberline would be quite steep and that I'd have to walk and lead my animals up the trail. The path to the summit looked to be a narrow passage, some 1,500 feet below the top of the mountain. I took a bearing with my sighting compass and made a mental note of the general direction we'd have to take through the forest to emerge at the base of the rocks that would lead us up to the pass. As I packed the animals, it started to rain, light at first, then heavily within a few minutes. Pulling my poncho from the saddlebag, we began our wet ascent from the ridge.

The trail in the forest got steeper and steeper as we rode up the base of the mountain. I could hear the mules and even Blaze breathing heavily as we moved through the trees and underbrush. The temperature must have dropped 20 degrees since we'd left the ridge. It was still raining hard, but with the dense forest canopy we didn't seem to get as wet. A familiar pattern emerged—I'd lose the trail, then find it and lose it again. We settled into this kind of travel pattern for most of the afternoon. Late in the afternoon, we emerged at the thin timberline. From my recollection on the ridge, we were just below where the pass should be. As I looked up the last thousand feet, I couldn't actually see the pass, but knew pretty much where it should be. The trail up looked a lot steeper standing at its base than it did from the foothill. The route would wind up through outcroppings of rocks with some trees and brush growing out of the crevasses in the granite. Moving my little pack train to the foot of the trail, I started up slowly. This time Gus didn't take the point and instead wanted to follow Harriet, the last mule. Without the canopy of the trees to protect us from the rain, the way up was wet, muddy and slippery.

It was a cold, miserable trail. Still riding Blaze, I got no more than up the first section of the trail where it switched back to another direction. Just then, Harriet suddenly stopped, almost pulling me off, and over the back of Blaze. She started making that horrible noise, "*he haw... he haw.*" Gus began to bark at her and she kicked her hind legs at him. Letting go of the lead rope, I dismounted and moved Blaze and Harry up to a larger and safer spot. On the short trip back to Harriet, I was cold, wet and angry, calling her every name I could think of. As I approached her, I grabbed her rope and reins and gave them a hard jerk. She wouldn't stop her frantic and annoying braying and she continued to kick to the rear. With a misstep, I was afraid she would slide off the trail, dragging the gear and me down with her. The route was too narrow and steep for her to look back and I think this frightened her. Back in New Mexico, Red and the cowboys taught me that the first thing to do when working with mules was to get their attention. Taking off my leather gloves, with my open left hand, I hit her hard alongside the nose... once, then twice. Finally, she stopped her fussing and looked me straight in the eye, rainwater running down her face, her breath showing in the cool air. My slap seemed to calm her, as if letting her know I was in charge made her feel better.

Grabbing her lead rope, I slowly walked her up the path to the switchback area. By now I knew she'd be trouble all the way up the mountain, so I took two of the trail bags off and placed them on some rocks. Lightening her load would mean making two trips up the trail, but I thought it was the best option. Then I motioned for Gus to take the point, as I thought maybe he being behind her had added to the problem. Gus at first hesitated, and then moved forward up the steep track. Mounting Blaze, I soon had my party moving again up the narrow, rocky path. My horse proved to be strong and sure-footed as I rode him at the lead of the mules.

About an hour later we arrived at the pass. The trail here had widened with large rocky cliffs above us on one side and a steep ravine on the other side. Scattered about were some fallen trees lying across the rocks. Looking around, I searched for protection from the north wind, which was now howling though the pass.

Soon I found an outcropping of large rocks with a dead tree lying up against the granite. Hobbling both Harry and Harriet, I positioned my saddle rope, stringing it from a small growing tree to the dead tree so I could also tie them up. Next, I unpacked and unsaddled the mules, laying the trail bags behind some small rocks.

Then, I placed their packsaddles on top of the supplies for weight from the wind. Turning from the stack of provisions I told Gus, with both voice and hand signals, to stay with the mules. He wanted to come back down the trail with me but soon understood what I was trying to say and remained behind. Blaze and I moved down the trail again for another load. With rainwater pouring down the granite path, we walked and slipped all the way down to my remaining saddle packs. It was another hour and a half before we finally reached the summit again. By this time, in the cold harsh wind, the rain was changing to snow, then back to rain, then back to snow again. Gus had found a dry place, under a fallen log not far from the mules, I shouted to him to join me as I led Blaze back into the pass. But he was too smart... he was going to stay dry under the log.

By now it was starting to get dark. With no chance of moving on until morning, we would have to spend the night here. Unpacking Blaze, I hobbled and tied him to the rope. Surveying the camp site I spotted an opening that looked like a cave or perhaps some type of animal den. It was a large fissure deep in the crevasse of two boulders. Not wanting to find a sleeping bear or other wild animal inside, I removed a candle from one of the trail bags. Returning to the opening, I lit the candle by protecting the flame with my back to the wind. With my pistol in one hand and a candle in the other, I slowly crept inside the cave. It was eerie with the candlelight dancing off the inside rock walls. It took my eyes a few seconds to adjust to the dim light, but, as they did, the cave looked empty. It was small, about 25 feet deep and 15 feet wide, with a ceiling at the highest point of about 10 feet. There were some signs on the dirt floor that a bear and other animals had used the cave in the past, but they seemed to be long gone now.

Finding some dry wood and twigs at the rear of the cave I soon had a small fire going near the opening. Going back outside with Gus watching from his protected area, I carried all the trail bags, saddles, my bedroll, knapsack and saddlebags into the cave. My legs and arms were soaked to the bone. My boots had about an inch of mud all over, making them as heavy as iron bricks. But before I could rest and dry off, I would have to care for my animals. Soon I found the trail bag with the oats and feedbag.

Before leaving the cave again, I made some coffee, placing the pot close to the little fire to brew. Then, filling the bag half full of feed, I took it out and slipped it over Blaze's head. The rain and snow mixture had now changed to a heavy snow with big, wet, white flakes. The animals had no grass for grazing and no water to drink. Returning to the cave, I motioned and called for Gus to join me inside. He looked at me but still didn't make a move from his dry spot under the dead tree.

From the trail bags, I took out three thick pieces of beef jerky, two for me and one for Gus. Leaving the cave again, I retrieved the feedbag from Blaze and gave each mule a smaller, quarter full, helping of oats. On my final trip I threw the piece of jerky under the tree where Gus was. At first he just sniffed it, not knowing for sure what it was. After a few more sniffs he ate it with one gulp. Returning for the last time with the bag full of all the remaining water I had, I let the animals drink their share. As I stood there in the dark, waiting for each to drink, I could hear cries of wolves over the howling wind. Chills ran down my spine. The old trapper had told me how bold the wolves were up in these mountains. Finally, with the animals as secured as I could make them, I returned to the warmth of the cave and tried to dry out my clothes and clean my boots.

As I ate some warmed up beans from a can and drank hot coffee, the sounds of the wolves seemed to be getting closer. Beginning to worry about my animals I knew that I couldn't just sit there in the relative warmth and safety of the cave without watching out for trouble. It had been an exhausting day, but if I lost my animals, I would be much more than exhausted, I could be dead. Throwing more sticks and branches on the fire, I unrolled my sleeping bag at the cave's opening. Spreading out on my bag I had a view of the animals and could see some of the approaches to the trail. Putting on my wool coat and stocking cap, I wrapped a blanket around myself. With my back resting against a rock, I faced the night and my animals. My rifle was on top of the blanket, propped between my legs. The swirling wind was whistling through the pass and sometimes blew the snow on my face and coat. Straining my eyes to see the animals in the dark and blowing snow, I could still hear the cries of the wolves over the wind. Half of me was warm from the heat in the cave, the other half cold from the wind and snow. My nerves frazzled; I was dead tired, yet alert; hungry, yet fed; not alone, but lonely; cold, yet warm. It was going to be the longest and most miserable night of my life and I had to struggle to stay awake. Soon the snow turned to smaller flakes and I was sure we would have inches if not feet of snow on the ground the next morning. Drinking the last of the hot coffee, holding the warm tin cup in my cold hands, my mind began to wonder: Was this as cold and lonely as I had ever been? Maybe by weather conditions and place, but not as cold and lonely as I had felt growing up with Grandfather at *Fairview*.

Ghosts

Fairview Manor... I wonder why Grandmother gave that name to that house? From my earliest recollection, I couldn't remember any fair views. What I did remember was that house surrounded with other, more modern homes set on large parcels of land with tall trees framing long driveways. From what Uncle Roy had told me, it was Grandmother who had insisted that Senior build the house around the turn of the century. In its day, I'm sure that it was a fine, modern home. I understand that the original parcel of land was 35 acres, but that over the years, after Grandmother died, Senior sold all but five acres. The house was large, with three levels in the main house and an old wooden barn in the rear. The home was one of the first in the area to have electricity. It had four full bathrooms, or water closets, one on the top floor (the servant's quarters), two on the second floor, and one on the main floor. There was a large steam heating system in the basement that worked as hard as it could to keep the drafty house warm in the winter. The kitchen had state of the art appliances—as of 1905. For its day, this made *Fairview* very modern. But after it had been built, with the exception of a few coats of paint and basic maintenance, the house had never been changed or modernized.

It was at *Fairview* that Grandmother raised my father and, after his death, tried to raise me. I remember her as being a big, warm, loving lady who always wanted to do things for me. Between Grandmother and our cook and housekeeper, Hazel, the house was full of laughter, good smells, warmth and love. After the devastating death of my Grandmother, a black cloud seemed to hang over the old house. Years after her death, I was still playing a game where I would walk the halls of the second floor, opening doors to the bedrooms and pretending that there in the empty rooms were my mother and father having tea with Grandmother. They would always invite me in and talk to me.

"Oh, Dutch, what have you been doing today? Dutch, sit here and have some tea. How is school going? Dutch, we love you so much, please come back and see us again."

Then, more likely than not, a draft would fill the room and slam the bedroom door shut, which would startle me back to reality. They were all dead!

At first Grandfather tried to spend time with me, but it was hard for him because he was so busy. With schoolwork or a book in hand, I'd knock on the den door and ask for help on a project or even just a question about life. He would always give me the answer but never tell me *why* it was the right answer. If I pressed him, he'd lose his patience and say he was busy and would tell me more later, but later never came. During the holidays, Hazel and Uncle Roy tried to make them special. Although, I can't remember ever seeing Grandfather happy or laughing during these times. He would always escape into his den after spending as little time as possible with Roy and me. Roy always defended Grandfather by reminding me how much responsibility he had to the thousands of employees of Gold Coast Petroleum. But I'd always ask myself, What about me? Grandfather never had friends or business associates over for dinner, drinks, or any kind of get-together. *Fairview* had become just a place for him to eat, sleep and do business when he was away from the office.

For the first part of my education I went to public schools. It was here that I made a few friends and, most importantly, learned to play baseball. It was a game that I enjoyed, and the coaches told me I had some talent. Hitting the ball a mile, I could run and play all bases with ease. Getting better with each passing year of grade school, I kept learning and improving my skills for the game.

But my grades were only fair at best. This meant that if I wanted to play ball, I had to keep my marks to at least a passing level, so I worked as hard as I could.

It was the summer between the seventh and eighth grade that Grandfather called me into his den one evening. He told me that he had talked to several of my teachers and Uncle Roy about my future education. All had agreed that a school with stronger discipline and better academics would be better suited for me. Therefore, no matter what the cost and because he knew Grandmother would agree, he was going to send me off to a New England boarding school named Bradford Hall. He would hear no objections and didn't care what I thought, the subject was closed, and I was going.

Devastated once again, I would miss my last year in grade school with my few friends. Although I thought that not playing baseball for my team was the worst thing that could happen to me, Grandfather would hear none of my protests. I spent my eighth though twelfth grades at Bradford Hall. In boarding school, I did play baseball again, but it was just for a different team and never with the same joy. Growing apart from the few friends I had in public school, I had even fewer mates at Bradford. But as I look back on it now, it was better than living with Grandfather in that old musty house.

That old home was a ghost from my past, full of people, yet empty of love. It was a house big in size but small in caring. But my most vivid memory of those times was of me as that little boy, having tea from room to room in that damp, dusty, cold and dark home known as *Fairview Manor*.

CHAPTER THREE

River Crossings

Fighting off sleep most of the night, I must've dozed just before dawn. I began to dream that Gus was raising a terrible fuss and the mules were braying, kicking and pawing the dirt. Even Blaze was agitated, pulling on his ties and hobbles. The action in my dream became louder and more vivid, and I woke with a start. As I tried to shake the thick fog of sleep from my brain, I suddenly realized this was no dream.

It was dawn, just barely enough light to see. The snow had stopped, and the ground was covered with a thick, wet slush. Blaze and the mules were frantic. They continued to kick and pull on their ropes. Gus was at their side barking, looking down trail from where we'd come the day before.

Thankfully, my rifle was still in my lap. Jumping up, I quickly moved from the cave's opening. Peering over the rim of a large rock that had blocked my view, I saw what I'd feared all night: a pack of wolves! They were some fifty or sixty feet down trail, slithering on their bellies towards Blaze and the mules. Ten or fifteen feet behind them stood another wolf, howling at the forward attack wolves.

In that split second, I got a good look at the standing wolf, and his appearance sent chills down my spine. This wolf looked much different from the ones in front. He was bigger and fatter, but it was his ghostly blue eyes that caught my attention.

Shouldering my rifle, I squeezed the trigger. The sounds of three quick shots echoed off the stone ledges of the ravine and broke the morning calm. The mules and Blaze jumped and bucked with fear as the sounds reverberated off the mountainside. My aim was in front of two forward wolves. They stopped but did not retreat. After a moment, the blue-eyed wolf again started howling his commands to the forward wolves.

Their boldness frightened me, and I knew my animals were in jeopardy. Now I took solid aim at the front wolf. *Bam! Bam!* The two rounds hit him squarely in the chest. He bounced back and slammed to the ground, spattering the slush around him a bright red. His death howl echoed off the mountains.

Just then, the second wolf came into my sights. With a single shot, I stopped him dead in his tracks. Out of the corner of my eye, I saw the blue-eyed wolf turn and fly back down trail. As I spun to the other side of a large rock to get a better aim, he raced around a bend in the trail and was out of sight.

Bracing myself against the opening of the cave, my heart was pounding and my hands were shaking. I stood there for a minute, collecting my thoughts and running the incident over and over in my mind. I hadn't wanted to kill those wolves, just scare them off. But they wouldn't turn back and I'd had no alternative. The blue-eyed wolf was the most alarming. I'd never seen or read about such a beast.

After a minute or so, the animals started to calm down and Gus went to stand over the closest dead wolf, barking and sniffing the carcass.

Running towards him, I shooed him away. Then I bent low to get a closer look at the dead wolf. He was a skinny creature, with ribs showing through his matted, dirty fur. It must have been a long, cold and hungry winter for these wolves to be so bold. The remains had little value to me, so I didn't spend much time examining my first kill. With a hard kick I sent the body tumbling down a small embankment alongside the trail. He'd become dinner for some other predator.

The second wolf quickly joined the other over the embankment. As I stood there, looking down at the bodies sprawled across the rocks below, I was pleased that I'd saved my animals from this encounter, but I was still a bit dazed and full of sadness. Killing these mangy creatures was not something I'd enjoyed. But then, killing anything was still a hardship for me.

Shaking off those feelings, I walked over to my animals and put my face in theirs and rubbed each on the nose a few times, so they could see that things were right and safe again.

The morning was clearing, and the snow and slush on the ground was already turning to mud. Thanks to a slight breeze from the south that had blown away most of the clouds, I could now see the top of Thunder Mountain, still covered with a white canopy of snow. It was a cold and ominous sight. I had no idea what was ahead of me, but I wanted to get away from this hellhole and move on as quickly as possible. Breakfast would have to wait. Without food or coffee, I packed up my gear and placed it on the animals. We were off and down the north side of the mountain within fifteen minutes.

The trail down was much better and not as steep. The way was still muddy but not as dangerous as coming up the south side. In short order, we made it to the timberline.

After another mile or so, I found a grassy meadow with a small creek where the animals could feed and drink. We were all hungry, and the long night and adrenaline of the adventure back at the pass had sucked a lot of energy from all of us. Here I stopped for coffee and a breakfast of beef jerky and bread. Soon, Gus was off looking for his breakfast as well. As I ate, I wondered what Gus was hunting. I'd never actually seen him make a kill, but in New Mexico I saw him take after jackrabbits more times than I could count. I wasn't sure there were rabbits on this trail, but I hoped he'd get a good breakfast, this morning, as he deserved it.

We made good time on the downward side of the mountain with the weather getting brighter and warmer. Every now and then, when I could get a good look through the forest, I saw patches of blue sky behind the high white clouds. My plan was to camp for the night where the Dean River met the Dean Channel. From the map, I had considered crossing the Dean River upstream where it might be narrower, but every time the trail got close to the river, there was a sheer drop off down to the riverbed.

As we turned to the northwest to follow the river line, we crossed many creeks that flowed down the mountain to the Dean River. About midday, at one of the larger creeks about fifteen feet across, I pointed Blaze and the mules in the direction that I thought would be the safest to cross. Easing the animals into the water, I was confident that I could ride Blaze across and that the mules would follow.

The rocks were slippery and we began to cross slowly. When we reached the middle of the stream, Blaze suddenly stopped in his tracks. Kicking both my heels hard against his body, I told him to move. But Blaze held firm. Using my heels again, I spurred him hard and yelled out my commands. Instead of moving forward, he bolted to the left with such force that it hurled me into the air.

Splash! I landed hard on my rear end, sitting butt-deep in the cold water.

Sitting there for a few wet seconds, I tried to gather my thoughts. Finally, I turned to face Blaze, a few feet down the creek. His head hung low, and he looked sullen and angry. As if on cue, the mules again started braying. I swear to God, it was as if they were laughing at me.

Getting to my drenched feet, I picked my hat out of the water and walked through the flowing creek to the crossing point where I had been bucked off. Using one leg at a time, I explored what was under the fast-flowing water. All of a sudden, my right foot was suspended over a hole. With the heavy white-water current, it was hard to be certain, but with a little testing I guessed it to be deep, dropping off four or five feet.

Blaze had been right again. In the future, I'd have to learn to trust his instincts.

Moving the animals downstream about forty feet I tried again. This time, I walked the animals across. Leading Blaze, I tested each step to make sure I was on solid ground before I placed a firm foothold. There were no more drop-offs, and we made another safe crossing.

Shivering from the unexpected dunking, I stopped to build a fire and change into dry clothes. With my teeth chattering like castanets before the fire, I realized what I already knew: I was spending way too much time in the water and was running out of dry clothes. Once again, I wrung out my clothes and hung them on some tree branches to dry. Looking over to where Blaze was grazing I thought how lucky I was to have him with me on this trip. He was turning out to be one hero of a horse.

Tenderfoot

It was just like Uncle Roy had said. Red Reed of the Lazy K ranch was more than pleased to lend a hand in my training.

Arriving in Santa Fe via train on October 14, 1940, I met Mr. Reed and his wife, Norma, at the rail station. Red was in his late fifties or early sixties, about the same age as Uncle Roy. His face was dark from years of range riding, and his complexion looked tough as leather. He was a nice-looking man with salt and pepper hair, his body stout and well built. As we shook hands, I felt the rough, calluses of a working man. Norma was about the same age but didn't carry the years as well. She was a plain-looking woman, a little larger than most. There was no gray in her dark hair, but the wrinkles in her face gave away her true age. She was a woman who had worked hard all her life, and it showed in the creases on her brow. But there was still a sparkle in Norma's eyes that seemed to say, "This hard ranching life has been worth every minute."

They were both wearing western clothing, with cowboy boots and large leather belts with silver belt buckles. From the perspective of this tenderfoot, they were the real thing.

Red and Norma packed my gear into their Ford woody station wagon while explaining that it was another fifty miles to the ranch. I sat in the front seat with Red as we drove away from the station. It was still quite warm for that time of year, so the car windows were down, and the air smelled fresh and clean. As we drove, both Red and Norma talked about how my father had come to the Lazy K much the same way, so many years before. They talked with genuine affection about his time with them and their family, and how Red and the "boys" at the ranch showed him how to survive in the hot and dusty desert of Eastern New Mexico.

Red went on to explain that he and Uncle Roy had been boyhood friends, back in Denver, and that a few years after Roy had gone east with Grandfather, he and Norma went to New Mexico and homesteaded their ranch. They'd remained friends through all those years. Norma reminisced about how, just before my father left for his adventure, he'd told them that an area on the ranch had some good-looking geological signs of oil. At the time, both Red and Norma just humored him. He was so young; what could he know about finding oil?

It was five years later, after father and grandfather found oil out in the desert, that they began to believe what he had said. Sure enough, they found oil right where father said to look. Now, years later, about 20 percent of their 14,000-acre ranch was producing oil. He had helped them become rich, very rich, and I was as welcome as if I was my dad himself.

Listening to these hard-working Westerners, I knew I was in good hands.

We traveled on a paved road for about forty miles, and then Red turned off on a bumpy dirt road that would lead to the ranch. About hundred feet after the turnoff, we passed under an open gateway. The foundation of the gateway was made of rocks, which held two tall logs in place, one on either side. Above these logs was a third, running across the top. A large iron symbol of the Lazy K brand hung down from the timber. Curious about the name, I asked how it had come to be called the Lazy K. Red explained that there was a small creek that flowed through the ranch, a creek that the local Indians call "Kuawatch," which he understood to mean "lazy" in the Apache language. Thus the Lazy K Ranch was named.

As we bounced down the dirt road at a pretty good clip, I looked back to see a rooster tail of dust rising hundreds of feet into the air and trailing a half-mile behind the station wagon. Commenting on how dry the area looked, I asked how they found the ranch. Red told me that he and Norma had come to the valley after the turn of the century. It was all backcountry then, no roads, no phones, no electricity... nothing. They had packed in from Santa

Fe and made claim to the Territorial Government for two sections of land. They built a cabin, barn, corrals, and fences, and then stocked the ranch with the best cattle and horses they could afford.

"Some years, the land would be a dust bowl, others a mud bowl.... it was either too hot or too cold, cattle prices were up when our herd was small and down when the herd was big... it's been a hell of a lot of work, but we've enjoyed it all."

From the back seat, Norma nodded in vigorous agreement. She'd been beside Red every step of the way.

They had three children, all grown and gone now, but it was clear that this would always be their home, as well. These folks were so warm, friendly and down to earth that I could easily see why Uncle Roy called them his friends.

We arrived at the ranch by mid-afternoon. The complex had a large adobe main house, where Red and Norma lived, and a four-story wooden barn, which Red said was the largest in all of New Mexico. Near the barn was a large bunkhouse and kitchen for the hired hands, as well as a number of other outbuildings. The barn connected to a large corral, which in turn joined with barbed wire fencing as far as the eye could see. There were horses in one pasture and cattle in the other. The Lazy K was home to some 12,000 head of cattle, 1,000 head of horses and 22 working cowboys.

Red showed me around the barn and corral, introducing me to the ranch foreman, Axel, and some of the other cowboys who worked the ranch. Then he took me behind the main house to a modest-sized log cabin. The cabin was two stories high in the center, with single-story rooms on both sides. The little building was nestled between two large oak trees that provided shade from the hot desert sun. There was a small porch on the front center of the cabin. It was a charming-looking place, made of gray weather-beaten logs.

As we entered, Red explained that the center part, without the second story, was what he'd built in 1906. The room was long and narrow, with a large stone fireplace at the far end. He pointed out some general details about the construction and told me that his children had been born right there in the main room. After the first two children, he knew they needed more room. First, he went up, adding two bedrooms, then out with a new kitchen and dining room, and finally out the other way with two more bedrooms. The house didn't have running water or a toilet until 1919, and he ran electricity to the house the following year.

After they hit oil in 1927, he started to construct the new adobe house. When they had moved into it, he wanted to tear down the old cabin, but his kids and Norma would have none of it. Their kids now came out for vacations and stayed in the old cabin to show their children how they lived in the "old days" with Grandma and Grandpa.

Although this was no longer a wilderness cabin, Red told me that this was where I'd stay to get used to life in a cabin. He'd give me much more detailed instructions on building a cabin, fireplaces and furniture over the next few months. The use of this old cabin would help him illustrate some of his construction points. We walked through all the rooms and he made sure I was comfortable and had everything I'd need.

As he was leaving, he turned and said, "Your family is a little strange when it comes to this mission stuff. Roy told me how you feel about it, and that makes you just like your Dad. He thought it was so much crap, too. He was one hell of a good guy... so I look forward to helping you all I can. Norma will have dinner for us about six. See you then."

After he'd gone, the only thing I could think about was his last statement. So Dad thought this 'mission' stuff was so much crap, too. Now, that makes me feel a lot better!"

That evening, over a delicious meal of the thickest, freshest T-bone steaks I'd ever seen and steaming baked potatoes with all the trimmings, the Reeds talked about frontier life in the New Mexico wilderness. They told more stories about my Dad and Uncle Roy. I enjoyed hearing all their tales and respected them for the fascinate-ing life they'd lived.

Towards the end of the evening, Red told me that I should meet Axel in the barn at 6:30 a.m. for my first lesson in horsemanship. As we finished our last cup of coffee and a slice of fresh pecan pie, Red looked up and, with a grin on his face, said, "Look, Dutch, Axel and the boys love to get a hold of tenderfoots out here, so keep alert. And no matter what happens in the next few months, just choke it down with a good sense of humor. You're gonna need a positive attitude up north, and I know these fellers will help you out."

Assuring him that I would do just that, I excused myself from the table and after thanking Norma for the incredible meal, walked over to the cabin to turn in. Six-thirty in the morning would come around plenty early.

The next morning, I awoke fresh and ready to get started. Walking over to the large barn, I went in. There, grooming a beautiful horse was Axel. He greeted me with a firm handshake and a broad smile. We made small talk for a moment, and then Axel turned to me, with his hands on the horse, and said, "Dutch I'm going to show you how to ride and care for one of God's greatest creatures, the horse. They can be dangerous and wild unless their rider knows how to handle them under any and all conditions."

He went on to show me some of the basics: how to saddle and unsaddle the animal, how to insert the bit and fit the bridle, which side to mount the horse and basic riding commands. Finally he said, "Oh hell, Dutch, the best way to learn is just get up on the horse and do it."

"Okay, I'm ready."

I moved nervously towards my first horse ride since I was a kid in Central Park.

Like a traffic cop at a busy intersection, Axel stuck a large hand between the horse and me. "Whoa, Dutch. This is my horse. I have another saddled for you, over in a stall. His name is Rocket. Now, mind ya, he's a little frisky, a little wild, but he should be just the kind of horse you can master. Don't be afraid. I'll be right next to you."

As we walked over to the stall, I noticed an impish look on Axel's face. When we were in front of the stall, he reached down and swung open the wooden gate. There, standing on a thick, comfy bed of clean straw was an old, gray, sway-backed mare. Axel let the horse out of the stall and turned her so I could mount her. Her swayback must have been well over ten inches lower then her hips and shoulders. She looked worse than any horse I'd seen riding around Central Park.

Axel stared at me to see how I was taking it.

After looking her over, I turned to him with a broad grin and said, "Okay. She's a real beauty! I'll give her a go. Where would you like me to ride her?"

He held back laughter while I mounted and, through a barely stifled snicker, replied, "How about a couple turns around the corral?"

Turning Rocket with the reins, I headed for the open barn doors that led to the corral. As I entered into the sunlight of the corral, I could see about a dozen cowboys sitting or standing around the fence. They all began laughing, whistling and shouting to me.

"Hey, tenderfoot, don't let Rocket have her head."

"That's it, fellow. Watch out for her speed."

"Buddy, are you sure you can handle her?"

I knew what was going on. I'd been hazed and had jokes played on me many times at boarding school. Taking off my hat, I made grand sweeping and bowing motions with it as I smiled and rode around the corral. Out of the corner of my eye, I could see Red standing in the shadows by the barn, watching. He wanted to make sure that I'd kept my sense of humor, and I didn't let him down. I must've looked ridiculous, but I kept up the show and all had good fun. The story about my first real horse ride on Rocket was told and retold many times during my stay at the Lazy K.

We all worked hard for the next six months. Axel taught me how to select, ride and care for a horse. Some of the other hands showed me how to use ropes and the different types of knots used on the range. They taught me how to hobble and secure the animals when on the trail, and how to feed, groom and doctor a horse. They instilled in me the importance of caring and tending to all the needs of my mount. That was first and foremost: no matter how tired I should become, no matter what my ailments might be, the animals would have to come first.

There were no mules on the Lazy K, but there was one cowboy, Pete, who had been a muleskinner. He and Axel went to a neighboring ranch and selected Harry and Harriet as my pack mules. Pete showed me the basics of mule skinning: how to lead the animals, what to feed them, how to use the pack saddle, how to distribute the weight of my trail bags, and so on. But the most important lesson was how to get the attention of the mules. They were stubborn and pig-headed by nature, and knowing how to get their attention was essential.

Norma taught me about gardening in the wilderness and how to preserve the food I would grow. She gave me instructions on dressing out game, which part of each animal was the best to eat, which parts to use for stews, and which parts of the remaining carcass to use for lard, soaps and candle-making. There was almost no part of dead game that could not be put to use. She explained how to safeguard game food with salt, smoking and drying. We baked cowboy biscuits together and wrote out recipes for simple stews, soups and other meals that would be nutritious.

But of all the help I got from these wonderful folks, it was Red who worked the hardest on my behalf. He showed me how to select and fell the right kind of trees for a cabin; what wood was best for construction and what was best for a slow-burning hot fire; how to make joints for wall construction and how to build a roof that would be weather-tight; how to use river rocks to build a fireplace that would keep me warm in the winter; how to build not only a sturdy cabin, but also a smoker for preserving game and an oven from rocks for baking biscuits. He taught me which types of clay and mud made the best pottery. He showed me all the tools I'd need and how to use them safely. He seemed to enjoy teaching me as much as I enjoyed learning from him.

Red's other areas of expertise were tracking, hunting, shooting, and dressing wild game. Until this time, I'd never shot a rifle or shotgun. We would head up to the local foothills early in the morning. Here he'd have me search for signs of game and then track the signs. Most of the time, it was a mountain lion, bobcat, or wolf. Then, depending on how well I'd tracked, I'd shoot the game and Red would dress it out, showing me different techniques. We'd take the pelts back to the ranch, where he'd instruct me on how to dry and tan the hides.

While we saw some signs of deer, we never got one. He told me that it was so late in the season and that most of the white-tail deer had moved down the valley into the desert for the winter. We shot a lot of quail, which is a small, fast-moving game bird. Norma would then cook the little birds, which I found very tasty. We didn't see any signs of bear, either. Red guessed that what few were around had already returned to the caves up in the mountains to hibernate.

One day, while talking about bears, Red said, "Look, Dutch, the bear we have around here are a hell of a lot smaller than the bear you're going to find up north. But keep this in mind: never corner a bear, never mess with a mother bear or her cubs, and if you have to run from a bear, never run uphill or up a tree, always run downhill."

I thought for a minute. I understood not cornering a bear and that fooling with a mother and her cubs could be trouble, but I didn't understand the downhill stuff.

Red saw the puzzled look on my face and said, "It's simple. A bear has longer hind legs than front, so he can climb trees and run uphill faster than you can. If you get him running downhill, you will have a chance—but only a chance."

Red was full of tips like this for every aspect of surviving in the wilderness. I prayed I could remember them all.

When we returned to the ranch, he'd take me out behind the cabin, and we'd practice shooting the rifle, shotgun and pistol for hours. He even had a hand-held skeet thrower, and I'd shoot the shotgun at clay pigeons as long as his arm and the ammunition held out. In the end, I became a fairly good shot with both the rifle and the pistol. But the shotgun was my favorite. I was accurate and enjoyed going after clay birds on the fly.

Every now and then, some of the "boys" would invite me into Santa Fe for a Saturday night fling. I soon came to like these guys as they were much like my fishing mates up in Ketchikan. They were all hard-working buckaroos who enjoyed life and played as hard as they worked. We'd go from bar to bar, gambling and talking to the ladies. They'd share past stories of barroom fights and of the women they'd loved and lost.

But, since they were mostly very young guys, just like me, I'm sure the stories were just that—stories. The guys were curious about why I was at the Lazy K, trying to learn the life of a cowboy, but they didn't ask me many direct questions, and I didn't volunteer any information. Like most western folks, they never got too snoopy. Red and Norma respected me, and that seemed to be good enough for them. Why I didn't want to give them specifics, I don't really know. In retrospect, I guess I just wanted the guys to think of me as one of them. But, the boys loved hearing me talk about Alaska, the ocean (which some of them had never seen), and fishing. I related stories about Captain Skip and the crew of the Pacific Lady and described how we'd be out to sea for weeks on end, fishing in waters so rough that waves would crash over the wheel house of our boat. I told them about 100-pound king salmon and 200-pound halibuts that we'd caught. For the most part, my stories were true... but, of course, there was a little embellishment here and there, just for good measure.

They'd roll their eyes, laugh and say, "Sure, Dutch. That's just like your horse, Rocket. Come on, let's have another beer."

My best memory of the Lazy K was how I met Gus. It happened on one of my first days on the ranch. Axel and I had gone out to ride a fence line early one morning. We were riding single file, with me in the lead. I'd just shifted my weight in the saddle when a jackrabbit jumped out from some underbrush by the fence and crossed our trail, some ten feet ahead of me. He was hopping as fast as he could. Then, not twenty feet behind the little critter, came this muscular animal in hot pursuit. At first I thought it was a wolf, but they were both moving so fast I couldn't get a good look. Within a matter of seconds, they disappeared into the tall prairie grass. Turning to Axel, I asked, "Did you see that? Was that a wolf after that rabbit?"

"Nah, that was just the barn dog after his breakfast. That rabbit's toast by now."

"Barn dog? What the hell is a barn dog?"

Axel rode up beside me and stopped. He stood up in his stirrups and arched his long body to get a better look over the grass and brush for any signs of the dog.

"He's a mutt that hangs around the barn. Been here for a couple of years. Don't get close to him, Dutch. He doesn't like folks, he just likes other animals… like that rabbit."

"Who does he belong to?"

"He belongs to no one. We put up with him because he keeps the predators away from the cattle and horses. He fends for himself. He's a wild, tough dog." he said, and we rode on.

I didn't see the barn dog again for a few days, but I did ask Red about him. Red thought that the dog had been abused when he was a pup and then abandoned up on the highway. Somehow, he'd made his way to the ranch. Red said that, at first, they were going to destroy him for fear that he would start attacking the horses or cattle. But instead of going after them, he became a kind of protector. He only went after the predators and vermin—whatever he could find, hunt, chase, and eat—so they let him have the run of the Lazy K. But, like Axel, Red gave me strong and somber warning, "Stay away from that dog. He has no use for people."

The next time I saw the dog, it was early one evening. Sitting on the front porch of the cabin, I was reading a book and drinking in a desert sunset. It looked like God's colors had been tossed in a bowl and spilled out in an exotic concoction of lavender, red, and yellow. Looking away from the sunset, I found the dog lying on his belly, not twenty feet away.

He was staring at me with bright, glowing eyes, and his ears were straight up. It was the first time I'd really gotten a good look at him. He was one proud animal, with beautiful brownish coloring and bold features. He looked to be of mixed breeds, but in the darkening light I couldn't tell which kinds. Shepherd, Husky, or wolf, I suspected, but couldn't be sure. Slowly, I eased myself out of the chair and tiptoed into the cabin to see what scraps I could offer as a token of friendship. Returning, I threw a large, meaty bone to him. The motion of my arm made him jump to his feet and give me a loud growl, his teeth looking as mean as a wolf's, his face deadly serious. The bone fell three feet from where he was standing. For a few seconds, he just stood there, looking at me, still showing me his teeth and growling. He finally moved over to the bone, made a few sniffs at it, always with his eyes on me, and then turned and walked away into the dark.

My offering being rejected made me more curious about this proud, unpredictable and dangerous dog.

A couple of evenings later, I was in the barn, brushing down my mount, when I saw the dog come through the open barn door. He walked slowly over to some hay behind me and laid down.

Turning to him, I started talking. "Hi, fellow. Have a hard day hunting those rabbits? Hey, how about those Yankees? Think they'll take the World Series again?"

I just kept talking to him as I worked on my horse. At one point, he seemed to be listening, cocking his head as if to hear better. But when I bent down to pull a bucket of fresh oats closer to my horse and straightened up again, the dog was gone.

Soon, contacts with the 'dog' happened more and more often. Every now and then, in the evenings, he'd come for a visit… sometimes at the cabin or the barn, or just following me around as I walked. But, like a phantom, he'd soon disappear again.

Then he started to show up more often, when I was out riding, working a horse in the corral, or even behind the cabin practicing with the firearms. All the boys began to notice and talked about my shadow. They'd kid me that the dog was just sizing me up as a good meal. After I'd selected Blaze to be my horse—or, better said, Blaze had selected me—I noticed that the dog started hanging around him when he was out in the pasture, grazing. The dog would lie or stand a few feet away from Blaze, then start running around, barking at him, as if telling him that he was the boss. Blaze paid him little notice, but it was some kind of game the dog liked to play.

One day, as I watched him snap and nip within a few feet of Blaze's legs and heels, the Latin word Augustus came to my mind. I tried to remember the meaning; it had something to do with pride. That's when I started calling the barn dog "Gus."

Then the most surprising thing happened one morning when Red and I were out hunting. We'd seen signs of quail, and we walked our horses towards a large thicket from where we thought we could flush a large covey. We were already tasting Norma's spit-roasted quail with butter sauce and red potatoes.

While we were still about sixty feet from the thicket, three birds flushed. They flew straight up and out, like they'd been shot from a cannon. Swinging my shotgun up to match their flight pattern, I squeezed the trigger and pumped three quick shots at the fast-moving birds. Two went down, right in the center of the big patch of brush and brambles.

Out of nowhere, Gus came running from behind me and jumped into the thicket. Red started laughing. "Say 'so long' to those birds! You just shot that dog's breakfast for him. Damn, Norma will be mad when she hears this story."

We squinted, looking for any activity in the thicket. The brush moved, twitched, shook… and finally parted. In the next second, out popped Gus, with one bird hanging from his mouth. He walked over to me, staying about ten feet away, and dropped it. He then turned and ran back into the bramble.

Red looked amazed. "Ain't that the funniest thing I ever seen? A wild barn dog retrieving game birds for a tenderfoot. Don't that beat all!"

A few seconds later, Gus popped out again with the second bird and dropped it in front of me. Kneeling down, I tried to praise him, but he bolted and backed off. I still couldn't get within ten feet of him. Although I knew we were bonding, he still didn't trust me. But at least Norma would be serving quail that night.

Dean Channel

The trail made a sharp turn to the left, and I came out of the forest into a small clearing. The end of this trail was at hand.

It was here that the Dean River met the Dean Channel. We moved down a small bank to the edge of the river. We had dropped almost four thousand feet since this morning, and there was still plenty of light, as it was only 5 p.m. The mouth of the blue-gray river was wide and deep, over hundred and fifty feet across, with steel-gray driftwood littering expansive beaches on both sides. The weather was much improved, with hazy sunlight showing through thin, high clouds. To the west, across the channel, the top of the still-snow-covered Comet Mountain loomed.

I hadn't seen Gus for a couple of hours, and found him lying in the sun atop a large fallen log next to the river's edge. He watched me as I dismounted and unpacked the loads from the animals. Soon, I had a small fire going, fueled from some of the plentiful driftwood. Sitting on the beach, I watched the current of the channel as it flowed into the river. My plan was to cross the river with all my supplies high and dry. Looking at the shoreline, I could tell that the river was affected by the rise and fall of the channel tides. For all I knew, incoming tidal water could run for miles up the river itself.

At this time, the current was running heavy with a flood tide, which made it impossible to cross. The water was olive green, deep and cold looking. I knew the only way across would be to swim, but definitely not at high tide. Deciding to wait for the high ebb and slack water, I'd mark its time. Then, twelve hours later, we'd have another slack tide at the low ebb. This would give me about an hour or so to swim the animals across without their packs, then return and float a raft across with my supplies. I only hoped that the weather would hold through tomorrow, as I didn't want to cross that river in a pouring rainstorm.

Hobbling Blaze and the mules, I let them graze on the grassy knoll above the riverbank. Then, pounding some sticks into the shoreline as a gauge of the changing water level, I set about executing my plan. There were plenty of drift logs lying on the beach. Removing my axe and saw from the trail bags, I went to work.

Within a couple of hours I'd made a crude log raft, using some of my log spikes and rope to secure the logs together. It was about eight feet long and six feet wide. Building the raft close to the shore, I soon had it floating in the rising tide. As the water current began to slack, I tied it off with my rope, leaving about fifteen feet of extra line, knowing the raft would float lower as the tide dropped.

About 8:30 p.m., the tide had ebbed and began moving out again. That meant at 8:30 tomorrow morning we'd swim across the river... or at least I hoped so.

I don't remember ever having been so tired. Not sleeping most of the night before, combined with all of the days of outdoor activity, had left me drained. It was all I could do to heat a can of beans, which I practically inhaled. Then, still hungry, I ate the remains of the second loaf of bread. The thought of fishing crossed my mind, but I was just too tired.

After dinner, I brought the animals close to the fire and spread my bedroll on the sand by some driftwood. Gus had returned from his evening hunt and found a place under some logs to sleep. Sitting with my back against the driftwood, I watched the raft float lower and lower as the tide moved out. A few times, I got up and pushed the raft into the shallow, receding waters of the river, but by nightfall I decided not to worry about it. If I had to, I'd use the animals to get the raft back into the water the next morning.

Adding more driftwood to the crackling fire, I lay back on my bedroll. With my back propped on my saddle, I gazed out over the channel at Comet Mountain. The evening sunlight, now low in the western sky, bathed the world in a rich, warm light. The contrast made objects seem to stand out in relief. The blue sky, snow-capped peaks and green trees over the now-coral waters of the channel were incredibly vivid. It seemed that I could almost reach out and touch them. Few people, I thought, had ever seen such a rugged and picturesque sight. But it also looked ominous and dangerous.

Wow. What the hell was I doing out here! I had never expected much out of life, and now, because of my fate, I was facing this new challenge. But then, life often rears up and bites you on the butt. Soon, I was in a deep sleep, dreaming of Comet Mountain and the challenges of tomorrow.

I needed the nine hours of deep and restful sleep that I got that night. It was 7 a.m. when I finally opened my eyes to the bright morning sun. I had been lucky and hadn't overslept and missed the low tide. Washing my face with a cold, wet towel, I took note of the river's current. It was still moving outward into the channel. Next, I looked down the shore to the raft; it was out of the water by about five feet. I'd need to take care of that soon.

Gus was nowhere in sight and I guessed he'd already started his morning hunt. After starting my fire again, I led the animals up the bank to graze on the grass. When the campfire took hold, I started the coffee under clear skies. Looking skyward, I hoped that the cool dry weather would warm up as the day progressed. While the coffee was brewing, I checked out the raft. Using a long, thin log, I pried and pushed the craft back into the water.

After a quick breakfast, I stripped down to my long underwear and canvas shoes and packed all my clothes and gear onto the raft. Next, I secured the trail bags, backpack, bedroll and rifles on the raft. By this time, the current was slowing; I knew it was time to cross, so I whistled and called out for Gus.

Moving the animals down to the shoreline, I saddled Blaze. I'd never seen him swim before, and I was worried about what his reaction to it might be. Tying the mules close to the campsite, I secured one end of my saddle rope to some driftwood and then mounted Blaze and moved towards the river.

As we made our way, I let out more rope as my safety line. When I looked behind me, I saw that Gus had reappeared and was watching me from atop some logs. The river was now about sixty feet across and ebbing. Nudging Blaze ever further into the cold water, I could feel a cold breeze coming off the channel.

When the water reached midway up his body, Blaze stopped.

Reaching down to his neck, I patted him and applied some pressure with my knees. "Come on, boy. Let's go. Come on!"

He hesitated a moment, then jumped forward in a big splash. Instantly he began swimming with all his strength, with me holding onto the horn of the saddle. What a sight we must have been... me in my red long johns, with only a gun belt, hat and shoes on, bobbing across the river, hanging on for dear life. Damn, the water was freezing cold!

Finally, Blaze stumbled up the other muddy shore, both of us drenched to the bone and dripping river water. Once again, he'd done a great job.

Tying my saddle rope to a log snag close to the shoreline, I walked Blaze up the shore a bit and removed his soaking saddle and tied him to a large piece of driftwood. Once I had put both the saddle and saddle blanket on some log snags, I started a fire with the two matches I'd carried across in my mouth. Then, after the fire had taken hold, I dropped my hat and gun belt and returned to the river. Once in the cold water again, I used the rope, going hand over hand, to cross the river.

Gus had now moved down to the shore and was barking as I returned for the mules. For my second trip, I led Harry down and into the water. Both he and Harriet were saddled but without their canvas bags. Back in the water, I slowly began pulling Harry by the reins, but he resisted my commands.

Gus seemed to understand what I was trying to do and came up behind Harry, barking loudly. Finally, Harry moved into the deep water and started to swim. Continuing to pull him with one hand while keeping my second hand moving on my safety rope, we slowly moved across the river.

Harry soon started making his awful sounds, which only made me more determined to get him across quickly. Upon arriving on the other side, I praised Harry and tied him close to Blaze, taking his packsaddle off. In another few minutes, I'd returned to the other side for Harriet.

It was easier getting her into the water than Harry. She didn't hesitate and started to swim without much of a struggle. As we splashed across, I was thinking how simple things were going. But when we were about halfway across, she suddenly seemed to realize what was happening. She stopped swimming and started to thrash her body in the water.

I jerked her reins as hard as I could, but she pulled back so hard that I lost my grip on the safety rope and her reins. For a split second, I dropped beneath the surface of the water and sucked in a mouthful of the river. When I popped back to the surface, I was sputtering and coughing. Harriet started to sink, but her natural instincts finally took hold. She started swimming again—but up-river.

Gus was still on the south shore, running up and down, barking at her.

When I made a quick dive for Harriet's reins, which were floating on the water, I missed on the first try. On the second try, I snagged them. She was going to drown us both if she kept heading upstream.

I pulled hard again on her reins but it did no good. Now I was swimming alongside her, and in a desperate attempt to save us both, I grabbed one of the wooden braces of her packsaddle. With one powerful leap, I pulled myself up onto her back. She struggled for a few seconds with my weight on her, but I used her reins and nudged my heels hard against her body until she changed directions and started for the north shore. All the while, she was braying frantically.

As she stumbled ashore, I jumped off, water dripping from me from head to toe. I was cold and mad as hell. Tying her close to the fire, I removed her packsaddle, all the while telling her what I thought. But, as tired and cold as I was, I had no time to waste dwelling on what had just happened. For the last time, I entered the river and crossed the safety rope, hand over hand, to the other side. There, I untied the rope, took its end down to the raft and secured it. Looking up, I now found Gus standing a few feet from me. Patting the top of the saddlebags on the raft, I yelled, "Gus, you want a boat ride across?"

The dog made no move. With great effort, I polled the heavy, loaded raft a few more feet into the water. While holding onto the rope, I swam back to the north shore. From there, I pulled the rope with all my strength. Slowly, ever so slowly, the raft started to move across the river.

As the raft made its way across, Gus jumped into the water and followed it. All I could see was his head, bobbing above the water. Luckily, he was a powerful swimmer, and soon we were all safely across.

Securing the raft, I stripped my wet clothes off and dried myself by the fire. As I changed clothes yet again, I began to wonder if I'd brought enough.

After placing my long johns close to the fire, I got another pot of coffee going. Then I emptied the raft and pulled it to high ground, with the help of Harry. There it would remain for my return trip.

Sitting next to the fire, drinking coffee, I was still uneasy. I'd almost lost Harriet, which would've been disastrous. There was so much work ahead of me and, no matter what I thought about the mules, I needed them. My biggest fear though, was the fact that we had one more river to forge.

Salmon Wars

I could smell it before I could see it. We'd found a good trail leading north, away from the Dean River and up the Dean Channel. We were no more than a couple of miles from the river when the trail turned a corner around a large boulder. There, lying in front of me was what had stunk for the last half-mile.

I'd been told about it but could never have visualized it. Looming out of this wilderness was the eerie, abandoned skeleton of a fish cannery. It had been constructed on a high wooden platform above the waters of the channel. There were five weather-beaten gray buildings with tin roofs on top of a platform of rough-cut timbers. The whole complex was covered with seagull droppings that filled the morning air with a strong smell of ammonia. The trail led right up to the ramp that connected the old cannery to the shoreline.

It called to be explored. Tying the animals to some trees, I walked up the rickety ramp to the deck complex. The largest building was leaning nearly twenty degrees on its leeward side. All of its windows were without glass, and two large wooden doors in the front had blown into the building itself. Inside the semi-darkened room, there were old wooden tables lying on their sides and a large number of seagulls sitting around. Once in a while, they'd take a meaningless flight from one perch to another.

The birds seemed to have no fear and roosting there must have become merely a habit for them, as any fish remnants had been scavenged long ago. The large room smelled so strongly that I had to back off. Turning away and moving towards the smaller buildings, I was careful where I stepped, as many of the planks were rotten and exposed to the churning water and rocks below.

One small building, protected by two other buildings on the windward side, still had its roof and most of its glass was still in the windows. As I pushed open the door to the building, three barn owls flew straight out, missing me by inches. They startled me so much that I jumped back on the deck and lost my footing, hitting the planks hard.

When I got up, I noticed my clothes were now dirty and stinky with bird droppings. Brushing myself off as best I could, I decided I'd seen enough. Walking to the ramp, I looked back at the complex, thinking of it as a skeleton of the past. Here, man had killed millions of salmon. Now, the symbol of his greed was dying its own slow death. To me, these buildings were a monument to man's gluttony and to the power and beauty of the wild salmon. The salmon had, in fact, won the war.

As I rode down the trail, I remembered hearing Captain Skip tell stories about these kinds of canneries. And I had seen other signs of this madness at the Dean River. Less than a mile upstream was half-dozen pilings that had been driven into the riverbed, and I was sure I'd find the same kinds of pilings on the Kimsquit River, where I was hoping to camp tonight. The people who ran these canneries were not fisherman. They were mass killers of the fish in this area. Their technique of "fishing" was using "fish traps" at the mouths of major rivers. They'd spread their nets across the river from shore to shore. The salmon, returning to their natural spawning grounds by swimming up the rivers, would be caught by these nets. Most of the returning fish were killed using this method. During those salmon runs, the cannery people placed new sets of nets across the river while floating the filled nets down to the cannery where the fish would be processed. Because of this kind of harvesting, the market would be flooded with cheap salmon, which in turn drove down the price that real fishermen like Captain Skip could get for their catch.

Regular fisherman hated the people and companies that ran these fish trapping operations. There had even been salmon wars in the Alaskan waters in the late 1920s. Many fisherman and cannery workers had been wounded and killed during those wars. The combination of fish traps and canneries had been used up and down the West Coast for years. It wasn't until the early 1930s that the Canadian government concluded that this type of fishing was decimating entire species of salmon. By 1935, fish trapping had been outlawed in all Canadian waters. It was still allowed in Alaska, but only in a few, specific areas. The sight of this rotting shrine, with nothing but the skeletons of greed remaining, pleased me.

By late afternoon, I arrived at the mouth of the Kimsquit River, some seven or eight miles up from the abandoned cannery.

The condition of the trail from the crossing at the Dean River to the Kimsquit River was excellent. There were many signs that others had traveled this trail many times. I was sure it had been the workers from the cannery who had beaten down the trail during the years of fish trapping.

The weather had also held; it was still mild, with only a thin layer of overcast in the sky. The Kimsquit River was really the headwaters of the Dean Channel. At the point where this river entered the channel, it looked to be over a hundred feet across. Deciding to make my way upstream, I would look for a narrower crossing point.

Just as I'd guessed, I passed many pilings protruding from the tidal water. These pilings stopped at a spot were the tidal waters gave way to the fresh river waters. Here, the river narrowed to about forty feet. Riding a little further, I found a shallow, narrow gorge, some thirty feet across, with faster-moving fresh water below.

A half-mile above the tidal water, at a bend of the river, a large, dead tree had blown down across the gorge. This log was about thirty inches thick and fifty or sixty feet long. Using my hatchet, I removed some of the smaller branches and explored the log as a possible crossing point.

Soon, I had worked my way to the other side of the river. The log bridge was too narrow for my animals to cross, but wide and firms enough for me to carry my supplies across. As I returned to my animals on the other side, I paused on the log to look down into the clear waters of the river. Through the glare, I could see two or three large salmon making their way upstream to spawn. Smiling, I thought, Dinner on the fin. I'd return for a little fishing after getting my animals and gear safely across the river.

Once again, I removed the trail packs from the mules. One at a time, I carried them across the log bridge and down the other shoreline to a tidal water beach. With hand signals, I persuaded Gus to stay with Blaze and the mules, as they'd be out of my sight while I carried my heavy loads. If any trouble broke out, Gus would alert me with his barking.

After taking the second load to shore, I built a small fire close to the trail bags. As I brought each load over, I added more fuel to the fire.

It took me about two hours to get all my gear safely on the other side. Before returning for my animals, I opened my bedroll, took out my still-damp pair of long johns, and changed into them again. Standing by the fire, I tried to warm up wearing the cold, damp clothes, but that was hopeless, so I decided it was best to just get it over with.

Returning for my animals, I led them down the stream to a point directly across from my fire. The tide was still moving but was close to ebbing. The river looked to be about sixty feet wide, but I wasn't sure how deep. Having gained more experience in these river crossings, I decided that I would take all three animals across at the same time. This seemed to be the best strategy, given Harriet's fear.

Sandwiching her between Blaze and Harry, I prepared to get wet again. Gus had crossed the river on the log bridge and was now standing directly across the water from me. As I slowly moved the animals into the water, Blaze bolted out ahead of the mules and I couldn't rein him in. So much for the "Harriet sandwich" idea! Gripping the mules lead ropes, I pulled hard and shouted instructions; Blaze soon found his footing on the rocks under the water. By the time we were halfway across, he was still walking, while the water was above my knees. A few steps more and it was almost waist high. Looking back, I found the shorter mules now swimming. Harry seemed to be all right, but the look on Harriet's face was not encouraging. Afraid she'd be trouble again, I tried to hurry Blaze to the other side of the river.

With another splash, Blaze found shallow water, and within a few more steps the mules were also walking on the rocks of the riverbed. Harriet's attitude improved immediately. Seconds later we were across without any problems. Pleased and relieved by this success, I wondered if we were all just getting use to the cold waters.

After changing clothes again, I hobbled the animals and let them graze on some nearby grass. My fire was large and threw off lots of heat, as most of the wood that I'd used to fuel it had come from a dry oak snag. This crackling, sparking fire would be perfect for a salmon roast. After hanging out my wet clothes, I warmed myself by the fire for a few moments. Then, retrieving my fishing pole from one of the trail bags, I headed for my fishing hole.

The salmon wouldn't be feeding now, as they were in the fresh water, swimming upstream to spawn, so I selected a bright yellow and red lure. The only hope of catching one at this point in their life cycle was to get them mad enough to strike my brightly colored plug.

The log that crossed the river would serve as a great fishing perch. Flipping out a short cast, I pulled out about thirty or forty feet of line. The bright lure darted and dashed in the turbulent but clear pool. A few moments later, a solid strike. The pole jerked with such force that I almost lost my balance and had to grip it tightly with both hands.

The bamboo bent but didn't break. From the fighting action, I could tell that I'd hooked a large king salmon. As I played it out, it broke water a half dozen times, and I could see it was a magnificent fish. Walking off the log, I moved over to the shore-line.

Within a few minutes, I'd landed the fish onto some rocks. It was a big one, about twenty pounds, its color was still bright, but I could see signs of its nose turning dark and starting to curl. These were normal signs of a fish getting ready to spawn. Feeling starved, I quickly set about cleaning what turned out to be a buck salmon. I cut him into two large fillets, each about six pounds, more than enough food for many meals over the next few days.

At camp, I cut up one fillet and placed the meat into some empty bean cans I'd saved. The other slab of meat I cut into two pieces. That would be tonight's dinner and tomorrow's breakfast— even enough food to share with Gus, if he'd take any. As I cooked the fish and brewed some coffee, I spread out my bedroll and placed one of my canvas tarps over some high snags to protect me from any rain that might fall during the night.

All in all, it had been a good day. I'd crossed two major rivers and been able to divert disaster and calm my animals. I'd seen a skeleton edifice of man's greed and had sampled the bounty of this rich and beautiful land. My wet and clammy clothes were drying by a wonderful fire. And, when the time came, the dog even gobbled a piece of salmon that I tossed his way.

All was well.

CHAPTER FOUR

The End of the Trail

In the cold light of dawn, it looked still dark. There was a gloom in the air that was enhanced by the thick overcast and rain. Slowly waking, I flicked a dragonfly off my chest before stirring. By luck, I had some dry driftwood underneath the sleeping tarp from the previous night. So, in spite of the heavy drizzle, I was able to get a reasonable fire going. Snacking on cold salmon, I warmed up the remains of last evening's coffee. It was a day for rain gear and I dug out my most waterproof clothes and poncho. In this rain, I didn't think much would keep me dry, but it was worth a try. With drops of rain streaking down my face, I was glad we'd crossed the river the day before, when the weather had been clear.

Packing up, I broke camp about 7 a.m. With Gus in the lead, we started looking for a trail that would lead us west, up the side of Comet Mountain. As we rode along the river's shore towards the channel, I kept my eyes open, but the few game trails that we encountered always followed the river and never led up and west. With the forest line at the river's edge so dense, I hoped I wouldn't have to hack my way up. Finally, I came to a small creek from the west that flowed into the mouth of the river near the channel. As I turned Blaze and the mules up into the rocky, wet creek bed, their hooves made a dull, muffled clomping sound in the wet morning air. The creek seemed to meander uphill for miles.

The footing was not good, so I felt it best not to hurry. At times, it felt like I was riding at the bottom of an emerald Grand

88

Canyon, with tall, green trees towering over me on both sides of the narrow stream. Eventually, however, the creek seemed to turn north. Checking my position with my compass, I slid off Blaze and moved my caravan out of the creek bed and into the forest, heading due west.

As always, Gus would run ahead of us as though he was showing me the way. Sometimes he'd be out of sight for hours, but if I made a course correction, he always reappeared, not at the rear or sides, but once again in front of us.

It was slow going through the forest, which was littered with fallen trees and heavy underbrush. This was truly a rain forest. Every tree was covered with long, hairy strands of green moss. The forest floor had thousands of white wildflowers, which looked like some sort of lily, and there were large groups of toadstools growing everywhere. As we moved up the mountain, I looked for a game trail that wouldn't be too steep for the animals. Many times, with the cool damp air smelling like dead and rotting vegetation, I picked and hacked our way through the tall brush only to find that our way was blocked with downed snags some ten to fifteen feet high lying on the forest floor. Each time this happened, I had to turn around and look for a different route.

The old trapper back in Firvale had told me to go directly up the side of the mountain until I reached its rough timberline and then turn due south. It was still raining when we reached that line about 2:00 p.m. and turned that direction. A heavy overcast blocked the view of the mountain peak above me, and low clouds blocked my view below. It was like moving through a gray and eerie tunnel. I could see a little to the front and rear, but everything else was obscured. Due to the altitude, the forest had thinned out dramatically, which made traveling along the timberline much easier. With map and compass as my steady companions, I guessed we were about 4,000 feet above the channel, making good time as we traveled the wet south slope of Comet Mountain.

Late in the afternoon, a southerly wind blew up, driving the rain directly into my face. An hour or so later, I felt the rain rolling down my back under my yellow rain slicker. I'd had enough for one day and started to search for a place to camp.

About 6 o'clock, I found a grassy knoll where the animals could graze and where I could build a makeshift shelter from the weather. Here we'd camp for the night. There was a dead tree that had fallen alongside a big boulder at about a 45-degree angle. Taking my hatchet, I chopped away some of the branches and attached one of my canvas tarps over the log to make a lean-to tent. On one side of the shelter, the boulder provided protection; on the other side, I stacked my trail bags. A second canvas tarp would serve as my floor on this wet night, and I spread it on the ground inside the tent. It was my hope that this would keep the soggy ground from soaking through to my bedroll.

The opening of the tent faced west, up the side of the mountain where my animals were grazing. Being cold, I began to search for dry wood to make a fire but found little. Protected by some boulders, I scraped together a few dry twigs and sticks, which I laid out. After about three tries, I got a small flicker started, but between the rain and wind it was soon out. The rest of the night was spent in a cold camp.

I'd been in the saddle for almost 11 hours, and my body ached all the way to the bone. Although my little makeshift tent kept most of the rain out, I had no hot coffee, my clothes were still wet, and I was freezing. Hoping this night wouldn't turn out like the one in the cave on Thunder Mountain, I was determined to make the best of it. Gus, who had just returned from his evening hunt, found a mostly dry area at the base of the big boulder. As I ate more of the cold salmon, I threw some pieces his way, but he paid them no attention; he must have had a successful hunt.

Just before going to sleep, I moved the animals down closer to the tent and still well within my view. Then, back in the shelter, with great effort, I pulled off my wet and muddy boots and moved them and my slicker to the back of the tent. There was little hope that things would be dry in the morning, but I still laid them out as best I could and crawled into my sleeping bag. With my rifle leaning close to me and my pistol and gun belt on top of my bedroll, I tried to relax.

By now, the heavy rain was falling sideways, with the wind whistling through my little shelter. Every now and then, I'd hear thunder and see lighting flashes in the distance. Outside, the rainwater running down the hill turned my footprints into mud puddles. My animals, standing in the downpour with their heads down, water flowing off their bodies, looked like three drowned rats. As I closed my eyes in the waning gloom, I thought, Why am I here? Please, Lord, no wolves tonight...and may tomorrow be a better day.

Green Thumbs

Spring, with its warm sun and cool evening breezes, has always been my favorite season. It's a time of new life and renewal, even for those of us who lived at Fairview. Each year, with care and determination, Grandmother would plant a large vegetable garden out back, alongside the barn. She'd work the soil with the help of Buck. He was married to Hazel, our cook and housekeeper. Buck also worked for Grandfather as our gardener, driver, and general maintenance man. He was a tall, good-looking Negro with graying hair, a chiseled face and powerful black hands. As a very young boy, I remember watching Grandmother till the ground with Buck in harness, pulling an old, rusty plow made for horses long since sold. Grandmother would work the plow end, using all her strength to keep it in the soil as Buck struggled to pull it. They seemed happy as they worked together talking, disagreeing and planning the garden. Both had strong opinions about where to plant what seed and how deep it should go. Then they'd quarrel about how much water, sun and fertilizer each plant would need. Part of the joy of their friendship was in their verbal jousting, although Grandmother seemed always to win the battle of gardening ideas, as her plans were more or less adopted. By seasons end, their gardens were always beautiful and plentiful.

The first spring after Grandmother passed away, Buck took me into the garden for the first time and taught me his way of planting and harvesting a vegetable garden. As we worked, he'd tell me stories of his grandfather and grandmother, who had been slaves on one of the biggest farms in Kentucky. He told of how they would work the ground from sunrise to sunset, planting every kind of crop man knew.

"Corn for as far as ye can see… vegetables larger than you, boy… cotton whiter and softer than those clouds… tobacco taller than them there trees."

Each story was full of God in all His glory and of Mother Nature, who would always provide for those who worked her land. Along with the stories, he showed me how to work the soil, how to lay out the rows, which seeds should be planted deep and which shallow, and how to mound the dirt and dig the ditches so the rainwater would run off. He always claimed, in his good-natured way, that his methods were the best, as his kin had been planting vegetables for hundreds of years.

When I grew a little older, Buck made gardening tools that fit my small size: a hoe, shovel, and rake only three feet high, small clippers to fit my small hands. After the plowing and planting was over, it was my job to maintain the garden. I'd spend hours working with my little tools in the warm spring sun, keeping the plants watered and weeded, with loose dirt around the seedlings. Each day, old Buck would come by to watch me and give me pointers and encouragement as I worked from row to row. One of my most vivid memories is of looking up at this tall, black, handsome man, backlit from the afternoon sun. In his booming voice, he'd say, "Master Dutch… your hands are almost as brown as mine, but when you're a gardenin' man, ye gotta have green thumbs, so ye keep workin' till those little thumbs turn green!"

And green my thumbs and garden would turn each warm and wonderful spring.

Missed Opportunity

By mid-morning, I found the lake that the old trapper had described. It was just visible through the rocks and trees below my trail, so well hidden that, had I not been looking for it, I would've ridden right past it. The morning had been cloudy but with no more rain. Last night had passed without incident, other than camping out in a major rain and windstorm. When I had woken, I'd been relieved to find the rains gone and the sky brighter.

From this position on the trail, I guessed we'd traveled three or four miles from where we'd camped the night before. The lake was 500 feet below the timberline and looked to be a half-mile long and a few hundred yards wide. The old trapper had told me to drop down to its level and then follow the land's natural contour, which would begin to lead me down the mountainside. His words rang in my ears:

"Along the way, the game trail will cross three major streams. At the third one, you should be overlooking a large lake, Nascall Lake, with its valley beyond."

Moving down closer to the small lake, I could see what looked like birds on the water. Using my binoculars, I saw about twenty ducks on the far side. I hadn't expected to see ducks this early in the season; these were either new arrivals, or, for some reason, they had wintered this far north. Riding to within a few hundred feet of the lake's shore, I dismounted Blaze and tied up my animals. After the cold meals of salmon and beef jerky, a lunch of warm cooked duck would help fill my empty belly.

Once I'd pulled my shotgun from Blaze's saddle, Gus and I moved to some rocks along the shoreline. As quietly as I could, I slid the three shells into the gun's chamber, pumping the breach. I remembered how good a shot I'd been with those clay pigeons back at the ranch; now, I'd find out if I could be as accurate with live, moving ducks. Silently, I moved behind a large rock and found just the right position with the ducks in view. Moments later, when I jumped up from behind this rock, my feet slid on some loose gravel, and I lost my balance for a split second. As I reached out to the boulder to regain my stability, the shotgun went off, pointing straight up at the sky.

Boom!

Its loud roar reverberated off the mountainside and the surface of the water. In a great flap of wings the once mirror-like surface of the lake came to life with the spooked ducks flying off. The blast had startled and stunned me for a moment. By the time I recovered, all I could do was pump off two rapid shots at the distant birds, which were now well into the sky and flying away.

Boom...boom!

By this time, however, they were well out of range, and I missed with both shots. Watching them disappear over the treetops, I silently berated my clumsy self. Then, as I turned to walk back to the animals I saw Gus standing behind me. He, too, seemed disappointed. Turning to him, I said, "Okay... a duck hunter I am not... the beef jerky and cold salmon will do just fine."

As I returned to my animals, I knew that I'd have to become a much better hunter if I were going to survive the coming year. But as I moved my caravan on down the trail one bright spot lay ahead, lifting my spirits. Tonight, with any luck, we'd be at our new home.

Gus

Uncle Roy came out to the Lazy K on the first of May 1941. He'd made the arrangements to get my animals, my gear, and me to Canada. He planned to enjoy a few days with the Reeds before we had to leave. Roy and Red spent hours sitting around the dinner table, talking about the 'good old days.' They told stories about a time in the West when the land was open to anyone who wanted it and would work it. They talked about guys they knew who had made fortunes and other drifters that had ended up dirt-poor. They reminisced about the gun fighters, frontier sheriffs, and old Western towns. They talked so long that both Norma and I would excuse ourselves and go to bed, leaving these old friends to reminisce until the wee hours of the morning. I don't think I'd ever seen Uncle Roy happier.

On May 5th, we loaded the animals and gear into a large truck to be taken to the rail station in Santa Fe. Having just put the last trail bag in the rear of the truck, I was reaching to raise the ramp when I noticed Gus watching from behind some bales of hay.

Red had also seen him and walked over to where I was standing, "Dutch, are you going to take your dog?"

"My dog? Don't think that animal is anyone's mutt, but he can come with me if he wants to."

Turning to Gus, I gave him a hand signal and yelled, "Well, boy, do you want to waste a year with me up in the great Northwest? Come on... get in if you do."

While we might have bonded a little, I really didn't think he'd come, as he still didn't trust me or any other human being. He just stood there, not moving a bone, watching Red and me. Turning to Red, I said, "Looks like he's staying with you."

Reaching down, I started again to pull up the truck's ramp and had it about three feet from the ground when Gus leapt to his feet and running full speed, jumped over the ramp and into the back of the truck. Once inside, he looked back at me, with his tongue hanging and a strange expression on his face. Gus had made his decision. There'd be five in my little party.

Uncle Roy's arrangements for getting us to the trailhead in British Columbia included renting a utility rail car from the Santa Fe railroad. After we loaded it, the railroad would pick it up, joining it to a freight train to Billings, Montana. At Billings, the Northern Pacific Railroad would take us and the car to Vancouver, B.C. We'd leave Vancouver on May 12th via the Canadian Pacific Railroad, arriving in Firvale, B.C., on May 13th.

After Roy had told us about these plans, Red and Norma decided to go with us as far as Vancouver for a little vacation. The utility car was half living quarters and half freight car. The rail crews used cars like these when they were working on the right-of-ways in remote areas. The front of the car had four small sleeping compartments, with a small kitchen and eating space at the end. The other half was just a large freight car. Here we loaded the animals, a dozen bales of hay, three bags of oats, 50 gallons of water, and my gear. The trip north would take us a total of six days, so, before we departed, we all went into town and stocked our little kitchen with food and supplies. The last thing Red brought aboard was a case of whiskey. "For those long dinner chats with Roy," he said with a grin.

The journey was slow, but the scenery was magnificent. We all marveled at the spectacular lands, from the barren desert to the snow-capped mountains of the Rockies. For some unexplained reason, the railroads always seemed to have their tracks in just the right places for views that were overwhelming. Along the way, the tracks led us through one of our most spectacular national parks, Yellowstone. Here we enjoyed not only the scenery but also the sight of all kinds of wild animals. Traveling through this park with family and friends was a sharp contrast to the solitude that lay ahead.

We parted ways with the Reeds at the rail yard in Vancouver. It was hard saying goodbye. We'd enjoyed their company and Norma's meals on the trip. And they'd enjoyed the adventure of living, for a short time, in the primitive surroundings of a working rail car. As Red and his wife were leaving, he turned to me and remarked, "Dutch, no matter what happens to you up north, always keep three things in mind. Never kill more then you need, never risk more than you can afford to lose, and never look back."

Shaking his hand in agreement and hugging Norma, I thanked them both for all the time and effort they had given me. I couldn't have asked for better people to help teach me how to live and survive in the wilderness. I prayed I would be able to do justice to the knowledge they'd given me.

We arrived in Firvale, British Columbia, early morning on May 13th. Trains stopped at Firvale twice a day: the morning train from the south and the evening train from the north. Firvale was a logging town, nestled between two mountains. It had a large lumber mill that rough-cut the timber coming mostly from the north and then shipped that milled lumber down south to Vancouver. The mill, with its large buildings, ponds, and storage areas, was close to the rail station. The town itself was small, about 300 people. One dirt main road ran from the station for a quarter-mile to the only hotel in town, the Firvale Hotel, Café, and Bar. Along the way were a dozen other businesses, including a dry goods store, a blacksmith's shop, a market, stable and feed store, a church that also doubled as a school house/movie theater, and so on. Behind the dirty, muddy main street were the small homes and cabins of the townspeople. There were few automobiles but many large log trucks that were used in the nearby forest. It was a typical mill town, caught up in a time warp of the early 1900s.

The stationmaster helped Uncle Roy and I move my animals and supplies down to the stable. We made sure that the animals were rubbed down and well fed. We also warned the stable keeper to keep his distance from Gus and to pay him no attention. After giving instructions to the blacksmith to re-shoe all three animals and provide me with an extra set of shoes for Blaze, we checked into the hotel.

The hotel was a two-story wooden building with a half dozen rooms, boasting a bath on the top floor and the cafe and bar on the lower floor. A large French-Canadian named Frenchie and his wife, Margaret, were the proprietors. Roy had sent them a telegram, telling them of our needs and the dates we would be there. After we checked in, Margaret led us up a dark stairway to a pair of small rooms that overlooked the main street. The rooms had the stale smell of years of use and mildew from the Pacific Northwest dampness, but they were clean and simple. She showed us the bathroom and, beaming with pride, pointed out that the hotel had a bathtub with both hot and cold running water and an indoor toilet. Frenchie had installed these new additions just a year earlier.

Being strangers, we could tell that everyone was curious about what these Yanks were doing in their little town. Most had asked leading questions, like "How long you folks going to stay?" or "Up here to do a little fishing?"

But when we gave vague answers, their questions stopped.

In the afternoon, we went back over to the rail station and cleaned the utility car, then made arrangements for the evening train to take it back to Vancouver. Roy bought a ticket for the late train on the 14th and sent a handful of business telegrams back to the States.

With that taken care of, we returned for a few beers and dinner back at the hotel. The bar and cafe made up one large room on the street-side of the building. A wall with a pair of swinging wooden doors divided the eating area from the bar room.

Roy and I went into the bar and sat at a round wood table with hard wooden chairs near the front windows. Looking around, I noticed that five stuffed heads of local game were mounted above the bar: bobcat, mountain lion, elk, deer and, in the center, with a rack of antlers nearly eight feet wide, a large moose head. Below the animals was a narrow mirror, running the full length of a 30-foot mahogany bar. In front of the mirror were glasses and bottles of beer, wine and liquor. During the day, the entire smoky room was lit only by the sunlight coming in the windows on the street side. There was an old man seated at the end of the bar and three other guys sitting at another table.

Frenchie came out from behind the bar as we sat down. After placing some peanuts in a wooden bowl on the table, he took our drink order. Then I asked him if I could order a half-dozen ham sandwiches, apples, candy bars and three loaves of baked hard bread 'to go' for early the next morning. He wrote down the order on a small pad he took from his apron, asking what time in the morning I would need the food. I told him 6 a.m. He assured me it would be ready.

Roy and I made small talk through our first beer. Soon Frenchie came over with a second round we had not ordered.

"What's this?" I asked.

"It's on the house. Sounds like someone's going traveling and I thought another beer wouldn't do any harm. So, where you going, kid?"

I turned to Roy, who was grinning, then back to Frenchie and replied, "Nascall Valley. You know where that is?"

"Nope... but old Sam the trapper man would." He turned and shouted across the room to the old man sitting at the end of the bar. "Hey, Sam, the kid here is going to someplace called the Nascall Valley. You ever hear of it?"

Sam got up from his barstool and shuffled to our table, carrying his beer. Looking at Frenchie, I asked, "Does Sam have a last name?"

"Nope, not that I know. But then, I never asked. Everyone just calls Old Sam 'old Sam.'"

Sam sat down, facing the window light. He looked much older than Roy, with a weather-beaten face and a long, gray, unkempt beard. On the right side of his forehead, he had a fading, ruby scar about six inches long. He was wearing a faded pair of blue overalls with a dirty wool shirt underneath. As he held his beer, I noticed his hands were rough, with large brown aging spots.

"I've been there... some years back. Why you going there, boy? Lookin' for gold? If you are, you won't find any, 'cuz I looked up and down that valley while I was trappin' and didn't find any gold."

Assuring him I was not looking for gold, that I was only going there to explore the valley and the lake and to do a little fishing, I soon gained his confidence. Over the next two hours and three more beers, he told us how he'd trapped and prospected the whole Dean Channel area in the 1920s. As we talked, I went up and got the map from my room and showed him the way I planned to travel. He gave me pointers about landmarks and made trail suggestions, which I noted on my map. In the end, Old Sam had been a good find. This interesting character was a fountain of information about the wilderness that I was about to travel in. But his last statement stuck in my mind like flypaper:

"Get out of the valley no later than the middle of September. Don't get trapped by the winter. If the weather don't get ya, the wolves will. They are bold, with no fear. They'll kill you, boy!"

Destination

There were many small streams flowing down the side of the mountain, but I'd been told to look for the three largest ones. As I came to the first large creek, I remembered what the old trapper had told me: the three main streams would all have waterfalls where the water flowed down the mountain through steep and narrow outcroppings of rocks and that the trail would get narrower as I approached the third and final stream.

About a mile after the first major stream, I came the second. Its waterfall rushed down the rocks some 100 feet above me. It formed a small pool before flowing on again, down the mountain. After crossing the shallow pool, I dismounted and climbed a large rock to peer down the mountainside with my binoculars. With the weather now much improved, I could see clearly down to the Dean Channel, some 1,000 feet below. The sheer drop-off of the rocks caused the water to flow down well over 500 feet before the next pool. From the angle of my perch, I couldn't see anything that looked like the Nascall Bay or King Island, which was what I'd been told to look for. Remounting Blaze, I continued down the trail. In another few minutes, the trail narrowed to no more than a few feet wide and turned west.

Within a mile, I came to the third and final major stream. Here, the creek came rushing from a few hundred feet up and formed small, shallow pools of cold water. The landscape now was almost all rock, with only an occasional tree trying to grow from the cracks of the blue granite. There was plenty of fallen wood, though, as it had been blown down from above and now lay by the sides of the pools.

Crossing the stream, I found a patch of grass and scrub brush. Stretching a rope between two small spindly, scrub trees, I secured the animals. With my binoculars in hand, I walked out onto a rocky point alongside the stream. From there, in the clear, late-afternoon light, I could see parts of King Island to the south and parts of Dean Channel running west. The view was so breathtaking that I sat down on the rock to survey my surroundings and soak in the incredible panorama.

About 600 feet below me was Nascall Bay. It was a crude U-shape, with a rocky shoreline in the center and two sandy beaches on each side. At its widest point, where it opened into the channel, the bay looked to be about a half-mile wide. Some 200 feet up from the rocky shoreline was the eastern end of Nascall Lake. From the lake, a large flow of water ran down a series of waterfalls and pools into the bay. Beyond the lake, to the west, were two large, tree-covered mountains. According to my map, these were Nascall Mountain, in the foreground, and the larger Eucott Mountain in the background. There were also other, smaller tree-covered mountains directly across from my view that weren't named on my map.

Set between two of these smaller mountains was a large, green valley of mostly grassland that ran from the lake's shore, up a mile or so, to the base of these smaller mountains. This was the Nascall Valley, where I'd spend the next year. The sun was now low in the western sky, its golden light causing mountain shadows to fall across the lake and the valley below. The color contrast caused by the late afternoon sun was brilliant: the deep blue of the lake and channel set against the rich green of the trees and grass, highlighted by the white of the snow on the distant mountain peaks. I sat there for at least a half-hour, gazing at the valley's beauty and making mental notes of the area.

Eventually, reluctantly, I returned to the knoll where the animals were munching contentedly on the scrub. It was too late in the day for us to try to go down into the valley, so I unpacked and set up camp. On this last night on the trail, I wouldn't be feasting on fresh, hot duck; instead, I'd eat the last of my salmon and a can of beans.

After tending to my animals' needs, I made my coffee and dinner. As I ate, I perched myself on the rocks, eager to see the view again. With the light now growing dim and a cool breeze in my face, I ate my last spoonful of beans. At one point, I looked up to find Gus standing next to me, no more than a few feet away, looking out over the same view. The last six days on the trail had been long and hard, wet and cold, empty but yet fulfilling. We'd traversed three major rivers and dozens of smaller creeks and streams. We'd climbed up the face and then down the backside of two tall mountains. And we had made it here, to our destination. I felt pride in this little accomplishment. Reaching into my pocket, I pulled out my father's watch and examined it again, reading the Latin words. Turning to Gus, I said,

"We have searched out this valley, and tomorrow we'll explore it. And I pray we make it through the coming year."

Gus turned his cocked head towards me with an inquisitive look as if he understood.

CHAPTER FIVE

The Nascall Valley

At first light, I made another small fire and heated last evening's coffee, then ate the last apple and candy bar from my saddlebags. The day dawned clear, and I could even see some late evening stars in the distant western sky.

After breakfast, I broke camp and began planning our move down to the lake and valley below. Before packing up, I decided to walk down a short distance to see the condition of the rough game trail that led to the lake. The path was steep and narrow, switching back and forth erratically. On the way down, I stumbled and slipped on the loose rocks. Walking some five hundred feet down to the lake, I found the entire length of the path to be treacherous. As I walked back to the animals, I knew I couldn't ride, nor could I hope to lead all three animals down at once. Deciding to take Harry first, I quickly loaded him with his trail bags. Then I led him by the reins to the narrow trailhead.

Before we started down, I coaxed Gus to stay with the other two animals. He soon lay down in some tall grass, close by Blaze and Harriet. Cautiously, I moved Harry one very careful step at a time down the path. He hesitated a number of times, unsure of his footing. He'd slip and slide a few steps, and I'd steady him. After each slip he'd stop, lock his front legs and tremble. Only when I put my face right in front of him and yelled could I persuade him to come along.

In the swirling wind, I smelled sulfur in the cool morning air. A few steps more and I noticed steam erupting from small streams of water that flowed out of some cracks in the rocks. Soon, all these small hot springs joined together to make a larger flow of water, rushing down the mountainside. As Harry and I reached the lake level, I saw that the hot water springs had formed small waterfalls that fell down into pools in the rocks just above the bay. These pools of steaming hot water then mixed with the cold water of the lake's falls, also flowing down to the bay. These were the hot springs that Captain Skip had told me about. From the rim of the lake I could look down another two hundred feet and see all this water mix together and then rush further out and into the seawater of the bay. These hot springs were truly miracles of nature.

It was too dangerous to leave Harry on the small, rocky rim, so I searched for a way to cross the lake's flowing water to the valley beyond. At the point where the lake water began its run down to the bay, the current was strong, and it appeared deep. Some fifty yards up the lake, the water was still and clear. The crossing looked to be about 100 feet. Through the clear water, I could see a rocky bottom not more than two or three feet below the surface. Pulling off my boots, I draped them over one of Harry's packs. It was a simple crossing, shallow and relatively safe. Harry and I crossed without incident.

It had taken me 45 minutes to get Harry down. Tying him to a sturdy tree that I knew would be well within my view on the climb back up, I set off for Harriet, Blaze, and Gus. Within a couple of hours, I had my little party safely on the valley side of the lake.

The crisp morning was bright, with a warming sun. The steam rising from the hot springs below the lake looked inviting, as I had not shaved or bathed since leaving Firvale. I felt dirty and gritty from head to toe, and a few times on the trail I got a whiff of myself and it wasn't pleasant. Thank God, the animals couldn't complain.

Although I wanted to take a bath, I hesitated to leave my animals tied up by the lake, as they'd be out of my sight. On foot, I explored the rocks below the lake, looking for a way to get the animals down to the bay. A few hundred feet east of the flowing water, I found a well-traveled game trail leading down to a sandy beach below. No doubt this was a bear path that was traveled frequently to fish the waters of the bay and channel. This concerned me some, but the notion of a warm bath was getting the best of me. After some hesitation I decided to try the trail.

It proved to be an easy path down, and I was soon walking my animals on the floor of the bay. The channel shoreline was littered with steel-gray log snags. Tying Blaze and the mules to one of these snags, I explored the area.

The small, sandy beach looked like a war zone, with the snags, all the way up to the high-tide line. As I moved into the bay and got closer to the lake's waterfall the ground was covered with rubble, rocks, and boulders that formed the actual pools of hot water. Quickly, I unpacked my shaving kit, bar of soap, towel, and all my dirty clothes used on the trail. By trial and error, I discovered that the pools closest to the bay were only warm, while the pools closest to the lake's waterfalls were much hotter. Within a few minutes, I'd selected a pool forty feet from the shore. With my boots and gun belt lying on a nearby rock, I climbed in, clothes and all.

I can't remember a time when warm water felt so good. As I undressed in the pool, I washed each piece of clothing, and then hung them all to dry in the sunshine on the warm rocks nearby. After all the clothes had been washed, I lathered my face and, using my straight razor and small mirror, removed six days of beard. After my travels, this experience felt decadent, and I spent an hour soaking in as many different pools as I could, climbing from one to another. If someone had been watching, they'd have thought I was crazed: a naked man sitting in a pool for a while, then gingerly crossing a series of rocks to plop down into another pool. Like a kid in a candy store, I wanted to try them all.

From my vantage point, I could see across the channel and a little south down to towards King Island. It was an outstanding view. At the south-western horizon, just over the valley ridge, the channel turned towards the Pacific Ocean. There, I could see a large gray fog bank, rising miles up into the dark blue morning sky. Retrieving my binoculars, I looked for any signs of boats that might be fishing in the area, but saw none.

Nascall Bay had two small, sandy beaches and a rocky baseline. I reflected that the rocky baseline could be a good resource for shellfish like clams and maybe even mussels. I knew that the channel would have fish, and I hoped it might also have some crabs and other seafood. The whole area looked just as rich and bountiful as Captain Skip had described.

Soon, Gus was exploring the hot springs. He moved easily across the rocks and, with tail erect, sniffed every crevice and stuck his nose in every pool. During the trip, he'd proven to have no fear of the water and had, in fact, seemed to like swimming and wading. I watched as he explored the lake's waterfalls by walking in and out of the flowing cold water. Then he went behind the sheets of the cascading water and was out of sight for a few moments. All of a sudden, he poked his head through the falls. He looked over at me and, to get my attention, he barked. Now he put on a show as he tried to stop the water with the powerful snapping of his jaws. It was quite a site: a dog's head floating in a sea of foaming white water! My minds-eye image of Gus's head sticking through that waterfall is as vivid to me now as it was then.

By noon, I'd packed up my animals and moved up the trail to the lake above. A few hundred feet up from where the lake dropped off into the waterfalls was the beginning of the large valley. A narrow band of trees followed the lake's shoreline. These trees were mostly alder and hemlock, with a few large fir trees a little further up the shore. The valley was at its largest at the lake shoreline, about a mile wide. Our party moved from the lake towards the open grassland, and we followed the valley's contours until we were about halfway to its widest point. Now I could clearly see up the valley, which was nestled between two small mountains. These mountains rose above the valley a couple miles up the basin, then gradually sloped back to the lake. There were three small spring creeks that ran from the far mountains through the valley floor and into the lake. These creeks were just a few feet deep, no more than a few feet across, and had rocky bottoms.

There were also a few small groves of oak and alder trees scattered about the valley. The grass in the meadow was green and young, no more than a foot tall. Along the shores of the spring creeks, the grass was thinner, longer and paler. The colors of the valley ran from the pale yellow of the spring creeks' grasses to the light green of the valley and on to the darker green of the trees around its perimeter. These green colors and all their hues seemed to blend together like a museum watercolor. The ground cover was beaten down in several places with small game trails and animal bedding areas. Most of these signs of wildlife led to the lakeshore. From my vantage point atop Blaze, I surveyed the valley with all of its magnificence and looked for a suitable campsite.

Near the center spring creek, I found a large grove of oak trees a few hundred yards up from the lake. Here the terrain seemed the flattest, and I decided to make this my camp while I explored the rest of the valley.

In short order, I unpacked the animals and hobbled them so they could graze on the rich, young grass nearby. Pacing off the area, I was excited to make plans for my camp. The first priority was my tent. I tugged it out of a trail bag and set about making the needed wooden poles and stakes from oak tree branches. The weather had been with me all day, but I knew it couldn't last, and I was determined to stay warm and dry for a change. Within a few hours, I'd completed setting up my canvas tent, which was firmly secured to the land with poles and stakes.

Fire was next. Collecting rocks from the creek, I built a small fire pit. Dry wood was abundant in the nearby grove, and I soon collected an ample supply of firewood. Next, I stowed my bedroll, knapsack, and trail bags in the tent for safe and dry keeping.

With the basic necessities in place, I was ready to explore. I didn't want to take the mules with me, but I was afraid to leave them, so I moved them to an area where they'd always be in sight during my ride. It was late in the afternoon when Blaze, Gus, and I set out. Giving Blaze his head we galloped up the basin.

It was wonderful to have the wind and sun on my face, my eyes full of Mother Nature, and to be riding such a proud and beautiful animal in God's country. We rode as far as the tree line at the base of the two mountains. Here, the center creek flowed into the valley from the mountains above. I didn't know if these mountains had names or not, but I decided to give them names; the smaller one was Harriet and the larger one, to the south, Blaze. On the other side of Blaze was another, smaller peak that I named Harry.

The forest growing up the face of these mountains was dense, dark, and deep. There were signs of wildlife everywhere: deer, elk, wolf and mountain lion droppings. I even saw a few old droppings of what I thought to be bear, reminding me of the dangers that lurked in this rugged wilderness. Gus, too, had found most of these signs as he darted from one area to another, his nose working all the time. Then, all of a sudden, he'd furiously bark at a pile of droppings and drop to his shoulder and roll. Blaze and I would race up to him and shoo him away as fast as we could. The last thing I needed around camp was a dog that smelled of game dung.

Before dusk, I returned to camp, feeling like the area I'd chosen for my first site was as good and level as any I'd seen. The trees gave me shade, a little windbreak, and firewood, and there was even a creek for water. As the shadows of the mountains grew long across the valley floor, I walked to the lake and easily caught two trout for dinner.

Sitting in front of my tent drinking my evening's coffee, I felt relieved to have found this lush and beautiful area. Captain Skip had been right when he described this valley as the marrow of North America. This little slice of land was full of surprises, richness, and opportunities.

Later, I climbed into my sleeping bag and gazed out of my tent at my glowing campfire, with small sparks floating into the dark, evening sky. To the serenade of a distant, crying wolf, I reflected further on my day. For some reason, I felt disappointed that I hadn't seen any fishing boats out on the channel this morning; it reminded me just how desolate this location was. But what had I expected? Did I think I'd look down the channel and see the Pacific Lady making her way towards me, her outriggers out, her crew working the lines, with Captain Skip waving from the wheel house?

No. I was alone. Totally alone.

Things to Do

The sleeping bag was toasty warm, and I lazily looked out over the landscape down to the lake. Then I noticed the heavy layer of dew that had fallen over my camp. The morning was gray with a threat of rain. Reluctantly, I pulled myself out of my cocoon, tugged on my boots and light coat, and lit my fire with some of the dry wood I'd placed in the tent the night before. I'd been warned that the climate here was so wet that, even on dry days, it would take hours for the dew to dry off the wood. On the trail, the secret had been to find dry wood under the damp wood, under the trees and rims of rocks. Here I'd have to do the same.

Last evening's coffee warmed up quickly and I cut three slices of bacon from a slab I carried in one of the trail bags. Once the thick strips started to sizzle in the pan, I added a large cup of water-soaked beans. Cooking the meal in the hot grease didn't look very appetizing, but I was hungry.

Gus was nowhere to be seen. Apparently, he'd already set out for his morning hunt. The other animals seemed to be enjoying the early cool air as they grazed nearby. My breakfast table and chair were a couple of dead logs that I'd rolled into camp. Plopping down on one of the logs, I savored my beans, bacon and coffee.

With Comet Mountain in the background, my mind began to race with the thoughts of a thousand things that needed to be done. It was then I decided that I needed a good game plan to determine what tasks should be done first and how I would manage my time doing them. The garden would be first, then a barn for the animals. What about an outhouse? A root cellar? I'd have to hunt and fish and, of course, build a cabin for the winter... a thousand things to do.

Stooping creek side, I cleaned my pans and utensils in the cold water and then set out to carefully survey the area of my camp.

The stream to the south was a hundred yards away, the one to the north just twenty yards away. This creek would be my water supply and cleaning creek. Between the two creeks, I hoped to find soil under the grass that would make for a good garden. The sun this valley got would shine the longest in this area. I'd need to dig with a shovel and pick to examine what was below the grass line.

All the heavy tools I'd packed in were without handles, so my first project was to make wooden handles for my shovel blade and hoe/pick. Working with my hatchet, knife, and a small wood saw, I soon had two oak handles that fit snugly into the tools. As I worked, I scheduled my daily routine for the coming months. The mornings would be for gardening, the afternoons for building the barn and a fence around the garden, the early evenings for hunting and fishing, the late evenings for everything else. I would need a cool, secure root cellar for my supplies and game, a table with a chair, a bed to be above the damp ground. All this would take time and work, lots of work.

With a thud, I swung the narrow blade of the pick into the soil. The ground split under the blow. Next, I loosened the ground with the heavy hoe-type blade and peeled back the grass turf. With the shovel, I turned the dirt and examined the soil with my hands and nose. The soil close to the creeks was mostly clay, while the ground under the turf, out in the open, was rocky but rich. From the nearby oak grove, I cut some branches and laid out an area about forty by sixty yards. This would be my garden, which would have to be cleared of all the grass and rocks, then plowed, and plowed again. I figured it would take a couple of weeks to get the soil ready for planting, and another two weeks to build the fence around it. In the meantime, I'd empty four of my trail bags of supplies and fill them partially with soil. Here I'd plant some seeds to see if I could get plants to start, and then transplant the seedlings in a few weeks into the main garden. The idea would be to keep these bags inside the tent at night, out of any bad weather, and outside whenever it was warmer and sunny.

By noon, I had the four partially dirt-filled bags in the tent and began planting some of my seeds. It began to rain lightly, and, by the time all the bags were planted, it was raining hard. It looked like I'd be spending the rest of the afternoon in the tent, but there was still plenty to do.

With my knife, hatchet, and saw, I crafted crude oak handles for the rest of my tools. At one point, the rain was coming down so hard that even Gus warily moved just inside the open flap of the tent to keep dry. Looking out of the tent, I saw the areas that I had checked for soil quality were now nothing more than large mud puddles. It was still early in the season up here, and I hoped the weather would soon improve. The mud puddles reminded me of the problems I'd have growing anything in this kind of environment, so I was more determined than ever to get seedlings going in the trail bags to avoid having my precious seeds washed away in a sudden downpour.

By late afternoon, the rain had stopped, and there was even a little blue in the northern skies. It was now time for more exploration and, checking out the fishing further down at the lake. With food supplies and trail bags safely inside the tent, I secured the flap. This trip I'd have to take the mules, as I wanted to venture to areas where they'd be out of my sight. We'd be safer if we stayed together. I'd be back before nightfall, so the only other items I took were my fishing poles and weapons.

Gus sensed what we were about to do and ran in tight circles as we started off. We rode down to the lakeshore and turned west for about a half-mile. At the point where the valley ended and the forest began, a little creek dropped down from Blaze Mountain. We crossed the creek and continued along the shoreline. There was a strip of open land that ran against the shoreline, fifty or sixty feet wide. Here the trees were sparse; beyond that, the forest was dense as it climbed up the mountainside. We came to a small peninsula that protruded into the lake. The peninsula was a beautiful grassy meadow that I noted would be a good grazing spot. Past the peninsula, we came to a large creek, flowing from a plateau above us. Turning the animals, we headed up the rocky creek bed towards the plateau. Along the way, I saw many signs of deer, elk, and other wild game. At one point, I heard noises not far ahead of me. In one smooth motion, I slid my rifle from its sheath and slipped a bullet into the breach. The sound of me cocking the rifle echoed off the rocks of the small canyon.

We climbed a steep grade of loose rocks and soon came to the headwaters of the creek. As I rode up and around the last large boulder, I could see a small lake through the trees. It looked to be no more than a few acres big, with tall grass and reeds growing out of the muddy bottom all around its shoreline. The pond also had dead trees lying in and out of the water but it was clear and open in the center. Here a dozen ducks were swimming and fishing the lake's bottom.

It was time to see what kind of hunter I could be this time. As quietly as I could, I dismounted and tied the animals out of sight of the lake. Stowing my rifle, I pulled out the shotgun. As I walked towards the lake, Gus moved ahead of me, quietly walking into the grass where he, too, could see the birds. Crouching low, I crept the last few yards until I was alongside a dead tree that I could use as a blind. Stealthily, I pumped my shotgun breach and placed a 20 gauge round in it. On the ground, I found a small piece of driftwood. Standing quickly, I threw the driftwood into the center of the lake, scaring the birds.

In a split second, all the birds were flying into the sky, moving as fast as they could. Raising my shotgun to my shoulder and taking aim at the lead duck, I pulled the trigger. Boom! The bird fell to the lake. I pumped and panned for a second duck. Boom! Another bird was in the water. I got a third shot off at a fast-moving, more distant duck. *Boom!* Not surprisingly, I missed the last bird... but was happy with my first two shots. Duck for dinner sounded great.

Gus was in the water before I got the second shot off. He swam directly to where the first bird had hit the water. Within seconds, he'd brought the bird back to me, dropped it on the shore, and left for the second one. Moments later, as he walked from the lake, carrying the second bird, he shook his body, giving me a shower of cold lake water.

Holding my arms up to protect my body from the flying water, I laughed and shouted at him to stop. He finally did and stood there for a minute, looking at me with his bright eyes glowing and his tail wagging, the colorful Mallard duck hanging from his mouth. He dropped the bird on the shore, turned to the lake and started barking, as if to tell the other birds how dangerous he was.

In a matter of seconds I had fresh game, thanks to his efforts. It was still amazing that this half-wolf, half-Shepherd dog seemed to understand retrieving and hunting as well as any fancy retriever or pointer. He was quite an animal.

On my way back to camp, I stopped at the little meadow by the big lake. The animals grazed while I took my fishing pole to the waters' edge. The lake was crystal clear, and I soon found a deep drop-off not twenty feet from the shore. Using a small, bright lure, I cast out beyond the hole and let the lure sink as I slowly reeled in my line. On the second cast, I got a strike. With the line moving out towards the deep water, I set the hook with a jerk and started fighting the fish.

My pole bent as I began reeling in my catch. The fish broke water once, then twice, rolling downward each time. He was big, as big as some salmon we'd taken on the Pacific Lady. Releasing the drag on the reel, I let him run out again, as I was only using an eight-pound test line and was sure the fighting trout was twice that weight. Soon, he began to tire, breaking water once again but just rolling on the surface. Slowly, I reeled him towards the shore. With my trout net, I reached down and trapped him inside.

He was brilliant in color—bright silver with blue and red stripes running down his sides. As I reached down and picked him out of the net; I was sure he weighed 15 or more pounds. He was as beautiful a lake trout as I had ever seen. Gus and I would get many meals from this single catch.

When I returned to our camp, I found that some type of small vermin, most likely a raccoon, beaver, or fox, had made its way through the holes in the tent flap and had started to claw at the canvas of one of the food bags. Our return must have scared it away. The heavy grass turf around the tent kept me from seeing clear signs or tracks, and I couldn't identify what kind of animal it had been. While it hadn't gotten all the way through the canvas, the incident reminded me that I would have to build a secured cellar for my foodstuffs in the near future.

Cleaning the fish and ducks at creek side, I removed all the scales and feathers, then I cut the game into sections. Building a good-sized campfire I fried one whole duck and a slab of trout in my large skillet.

Soon, the smell of the cooking game and burning oak hung heavy over my little camp in the still evening air. Gus was lying close by the campfire, his nose twitching. Cutting a large piece of duck and a chunk of fish, I took a full tin plate over to him. When I bent down to place it in front of him, he jumped back a few feet, watching my every move, but he didn't growl or snarl at me. This was progress. As I moved back to the fire, he put his face into the plate and, with a few quick slurps of his tongue, lapped up all the cooked game. Then, as I sat down with my plate in hand, he looked back across the campsite as if to say "thank you."

With the sun now deep in the western sky, I leaned against the log and ate the most delicious meal I could have imagined. This little valley was indeed a paradise in vision and bounty.

Bonded

For the next week, I worked only on my gardening project. In the mornings, I removed the heavy grass turf and plow the exposed dirt. In the afternoons, I would fell small oak trees in a nearby grove and use the wood to build a fence around the garden area. The fence would only protect the garden from larger animals, including my own. For protection from the smaller animals and birds, I'd build a scarecrow after planting.

With the help of Harry and Harriet, the dirt was plowed with little effort, but I had to remove hundreds of rocks as we went. Then I used these rocks to brace the fence posts that ran around the perimeter of the garden.

For the most part, the weather was predictable: light rain in the mornings with clearing and some sun in the afternoons. The temperature seemed to warm a little more with each passing day. With such a short growing season, I wanted to seed the garden as quickly as possible. At the end of the first week, the seedlings I'd started in the trail bags had begun to show color. My plans were to seed the new garden first, and transplant the seedlings in another week or two. Planning my garden, I laid out the rows-carrots here, and onions over there, potatoes down here, and so on. Finally, the ground and fence were ready; tomorrow, I would begin planting. Soon, I'd find out if I had what old Buck had called "those green thumbs."

It took two full days to seed the garden. On the second day, which was bright and clear, I had only a few last rows of corn to plant. To keep my rows as straight as possible, I laid out my rope. There on my hands and knees, I placed each corn seed along the edge of the line.

It was then that I heard the first blood-curdling cry. It was an agonizing howl of pain, and the hair stood up on the back of my neck when I realized it was Gus. He was somewhere beyond the forest line close to the meadow. Jumping to my feet, I ran to the fence and vaulted it in one large leap. My gun belt was hanging on a fence post, and I grabbed it as I ran past.

Blaze was grazing nearby. He, too, had heard the cry, and stood taught and tense, listening with ears back and eyes wide. Another loud, angry cry echoed through the valley. This time, I also heard sounds of wolves as they began barking and howling. Quickly, I untied Blaze's hobbles. Grabbing his tack, I placed the bit in his mouth and strapped the bridle on. There was no time to saddle him up properly so, holding onto some hair of his mane, I threw myself onto his bare back.

A few more cries came, from the same general direction. Blaze automatically began moving that way. I dug my knees deep into his sides, and we were off at a full gallop in a matter of seconds.

We crossed the grassy meadow to a grove of trees, then through the trees to a creek on the other side. I could still hear the growling and barking of Gus and at least a couple of wolves. Blaze turned onto the rocky creek bed and we raced upstream with water flying.

The creek made a sharp turn to the left some fifty feet from where we'd entered. As I turned the corner, I spotted Gus ahead of me, one front leg deep in a pool of water and the other legs on the shore, pulling backwards hard, as if he were stuck. Behind him, only five or six feet away, was a large, dirty, gray wolf, snarling and about to spring on him again. Behind the front wolf were two more wolves, howling encouragement to the front one. Behind them was another, even larger wolf... and by God, if he wasn't blue-eyed!

As I slid off of Blaze, I removed my pistol from the holster. Landing solidly in cold, ankle-deep water, I squeezed off two shots at the front wolf.

Bang-bang…

The loud sounds bounced off the rocks. He let out a whimper and fell over dead.

Twisting my body, I took aim at the three others. Hands trembling, I realized how frightened I was. Furiously, I squeezed off three more shots, but they all missed their marks as the wolves raced back into the heavy underbrush.

Still shaking, I clumsily splashed through the shallow water to where Gus was standing. There was blood dripping down one of his shoulders, where the lead wolf had attacked him. I could also see blood running down the top of the leg stuck in the water.

Kneeling in the water in front of him, I began talking to him. "It's OK, boy... It's OK now. Calm down."

He stopped moving, frozen in place, his eyes looking right at me as I got closer and closer.

"Damn... don't you bite me, dog."

Never taking my eyes off of his, I slowly slipped my hands under the water and searched for what held him. Soon, I felt a rusty game trap that had closed on his left front paw. I tried to force it open with my hands, but I couldn't get a good grip on it. All the while, Gus snarled and growled at me. My mind flashed back to old Sam, and I cursed him for leaving behind one of his traps. As hard as I tried, I couldn't open it.

Feeling around for what was holding the trap to the streambed I finally found a rusty length of chain. With a sharp tug, I snapped it, freeing the trap from the creek bottom.

As I lifted both the trap and Gus's leg from the water, he looked as though he was about to attack me. Looking him straight in the eye, I shook my head and shouted, "No, Gus. NO! Don't give up on me now!"

He seemed to calm down a little, but between his wildness and his pain, he was as unpredictable as the weather. Soon, I found the lever on the rusty trap and pulled on it as hard as I could. Grudgingly, the trap's jaws finally opened... and Gus was free.

Holding one leg in the air, he backed off a few feet and let out a soft whimper as he fell to the ground. The fight just seemed to slip out of him, and his eyes rolled back into his head, his body shaking from fear and shock.

I'd gone this far with him and hadn't been bitten, so I couldn't let him down now. Bending low, I picked him up in my arms. He was heavy, ninety or more pounds. Stumbling through the water, I hurried back to Blaze. Draping Gus across Blaze's bare back, I stepped on a large rock to mount myself behind the big dog. Then with the reins in one hand, I guided Blaze back in the direction of camp.

We moved downstream as fast as we could, through the grove of trees and out into the valley. Within a few minutes, we were in front of the tent.

Slipping off Blaze, I gently hoisted Gus off of his back. Carrying him just inside the tent, I placed him on top of my yellow raincoat. His breathing was labored, and he whimpered every so often. He was in shock and semi-conscious.

Opening my medical kit, I removed the supplies I'd need. First, I filled a small syringe with Novocain to ease his pain. Then I stopped the bleeding from the wound on his shoulder with two hemostats. With the scissors, I cut back the fur around his leg wounds. The bottom wounds were where the trap had cut open his lower leg. The top wound, I realized, was where he'd started to gnaw off his own leg in an attempt to free himself.

I cleaned and examined all three areas. The cuts were deep, but the leg didn't seem to be broken. I sewed up the lower cut with a couple of stitches; the upper cut took a couple more.

By then, the bleeding from the largest wound had stopped. Removing the two hemostats, I sutured six stitches in the cut made by the attacking wolf. Before bandaging the wounds, I placed an antibiotic ointment on each. This must have stung, as it was the only time that Gus lifted his head to give me a growl. Finally, I filled the small syringe with tetanus vaccine and gave him a shot in the rump.

When I'd finished, I was exhausted. Kneeling there, I looked down at him for a long moment. He was lying across my bloody yellow coat, breathing heavily, his body not moving. Shaking my head, I thought, I've done all I can, but will it be enough?

Then my mind raced back to the blue-eyed wolf. Could this be the same animal we'd encountered on Thunder Mountain? It couldn't be. He would've had to travel all those miles... and for what? To get back at us? No, this had to be a special breed of wolf only found up here in the North Country.

But if that was so, why hadn't old trapper Sam told me about them? For now, I'd call this type of wolf the "blue-eyed devil," and I hoped to find the answers to my many questions when I returned to Firvale a year from now.

After cleaning up from my first aid work, I built a fire and put some coffee on. Later, as I sat on my log drinking the coffee, I watched Gus through the open tent flap. I had grown to love this dog. He'd become a valued member of this adventure. From Day One, he'd been not only my companion but my alarm to any danger. Now, if he made it, I'd be his alarm until he recovered.

Like a nervous parent, I watched him for hours. A few times, I took him water and dropped small amounts around his mouth. He'd move a little, drink a little, and then drop off again. In the future, I would have to be much more careful with my animals. These wolves were bold and had little or no fear of us... and just maybe the blue-eyed devil had some kind of score to settle. There and then, I decided to hold off hunting any large game until I could complete a barn that would protect Blaze and the mules. Soon, I'd also need a secure root cellar to store any game meat, as the scent of any dead animal would be an open invitation for these bold wolves.

In the afternoon, I finished planting the corn, but I was never out of sight of the tent where Gus lay just inside. That evening, there was little change. Placing more wood on the fire, I rolled out my sleeping bag next to Gus and tried to sleep. I tossed and turned for hours and in the distance, I could hear sounds of the wolves' haunting cries over their dead comrade. It made it impossible to sleep. Each time Gus's breathing changed or he moved, I looked over to him. Keeping the fire going all night, I finally fell asleep just before dawn.

When I opened my eyes, it was bright inside the tent, and it took me a few seconds to collect my thoughts. Once I realized where I was, I looked over at Gus but found only the bloody yellow coat empty. Jumping to my feet, I went outside to the burned-out fire. Quickly, I turned towards Blaze and the mules. They were all right, but there was no sign of Gus.

Turning the other way, I spotted a tail above the grass at the creek. Walking toward it, I found Gus drinking from the stream. As he turned and walked out of the grass, limping on three legs, he looked directly at me, then sat down, keeping the injured leg off the ground.

Inching my way in front of him, I knelt down and looked at his bandaged leg. He didn't back off or let out a sound as I put my hands on the leg. In a low and calm voice, I said, "Hey, boy, you look a lot better. Let me take a look. Good dog, don't move."

There were no signs of new bleeding; my sutures were holding. He sat there with patience as I examined the three bandages. After I was done, I slowly moved my hand up the side of his face and stroked the top of his head and ears. His eyes were bloodshot, but there was a little brightness in them.

"You're gonna be okay, Gus. Just give it some time. You hungry, boy?"

Sighing with relief, I knew he was going to make it. Thank God!

Within a couple of weeks, Gus was back to his old self, off early and late for his hunts. He seemed to have no fear that the creeks might still hold other forgotten traps or of the wolves. But his attitude towards me had changed a lot. One morning, while I was down at the creek washing my face and brushing my teeth, something poked my raised rear end from behind. The force of the poke caused me to lose my balance and fall into the cold creek with a splash, face-down. The cold water dunking had me fully awake in an instant. Jumping to my feet, I twisted for my pistol on the rocks.

When I turned, I saw Gus standing behind me with a big grin across his face. Head and chest down on his front paws and his rump raised in the air with a wagging tail, he wanted to play and had found the sight of my butt in the air too much to resist.

Water dripping from my head to toe, I took off after him in a playful manner. He'd run through the grass and then come to an abrupt stop and turn and chase me. He even let me wrestle him to ground, all the while barking and playfully pawing at me. It was such a joy to see this proud animal playing and enjoying the company of a human being. It seemed hard to believe that, just a few months ago, he would not have trusted nor cared a dime about anyone. There is something about a man and a dog, like a mother and child, or the moon and the stars… inseparable. We'd bonded at last, and we would continue to deepen that bond in the weeks and months to come.

Working with the mules, I cut down and pulled about sixty logs to the site I'd selected for the barn. The layout of the structure would be twelve feet long and ten feet wide, with a six-foot overhanging roof at one end. Under the open overhang, I'd store wood and dry grass for the winter. The logs I used were all alder from the groves around the edge of the valley. Selecting straight trees that were eight to ten inches thick, I cut them two feet longer than the barn's inside dimensions to leave room for the notches.

A fourteen-foot alder log that is ten inches thick is very heavy and I could hardly lift one end at a time, let alone raise it up to the next course of logs. So, using split logs as a slide, along with ropes and both mules, I rolled each log up to the next layer of the barn, notching each end to fit snug and tight to the matching cross log. In the morning hours, I cut down the trees and moved them to the site. In the afternoons, I cut the logs to the proper length, slide them into place, and chop out the notches. During all this building and cutting one of Red Reed's old sayings kept racing though my mind: Measure twice, cut once. My plan was to saw out two doors, one on the side, the other in the end, after building the entire shell of the barn. Positioning the barn close to the garden, I'd use the fenced-in area as a corral after harvesting my vegetables.

The garden was slowly becoming green, with little sprouts coming up in most of my rows. Some weeks before, I'd transplanted the starter plants from the trail bags, which had grown well from being moved in and out of the tent as the weather allowed. These plants were now two or three inches above the dirt. The birds soon found my little garden, so I'd taken my plow and buried its handle in the dirt and made the blade the skeleton for my scarecrow. With sticks, some winter clothes, my baseball cap and stuffed grass, I built a reasonable semblance of a man. Empty tin cans, lids, and fishing lures were the hanging decorations, moving in the slightest breeze and making a jangling sound that I hoped would keep most of the birds out of the garden. In the end, though, Gus, who loved to chase the birds, scared most of them away.

In the evenings, I started digging two large holes. One was on the other side of the little grove of trees behind my camp and would serve as an outhouse. It was close enough for convenience but far enough away so that any smells would not offend. The other hole I dug was close to my tent, and would become my root cellar. I planned a log-lined room, eight by six feet, and some nine feet deep. I'd cover the last two feet with a layer of logs, and rocks, with dirt on top. At one side, I dug out an opening, at 45 degrees, which would lead down to the dark little room. This opening would be covered with a large, secured wooden door made out of split logs. When it was completed, I'd move all my food, vegetables, and any fresh game into the cellar for preservation and safekeeping.

The work had been hard and long, the days full of sweat. I had not returned to the hot springs or even "Duck Lake," as I'd named it, because of my concerns for Gus and the well-being of Blaze and the mules. My meals were mostly fish from the lake and the beans and rice that I had packed in. In addition, once or twice a week I would bake some biscuits in my makeshift oven of flat rocks buried under my fire. While my menu was limited and monotonous, it would just have to do until my animals could be secured.

July Fourth

With the barn nearly completed, I planned to make the 4th of July special. By boarding up the unfinished barn, I could keep the mules relatively safe while I explored more of the countryside. Gus was now back in top form, with patches of short hair beginning to cover the scars of his wounds. The garden was growing nicely, as both Gus and the scarecrow were good at keeping the birds and other small animals away. Having finished a secured root cellar, I could now store food and any game away from all the vermin. And the outhouse was almost done. Later, I'd have to build a small house around the log frame commode to protect me from the winter weather. For the time being, however, it was truly an outdoor outhouse.

I'd even built a chair and small table from the alder scraps. It was nice to sit and eat at a table again. Such a little thing, but then, it was the little things that I found myself missing the most. It had been over six weeks since I left Firvale, and I'd accomplished a lot, although it had been damned hard work. My labors had lasted from sunup to after sundown, and I'd promised myself that July 4th was going to be a day for a "hot" bath in the springs, not the cold ones I had been taking in the lake. It would also be a day for relaxation and exploration.

The day started with low clouds hanging over the lake, but, just behind Comet Mountain, I could see patches of blue sky. With the weather looking promising, I let the mules graze for a couple of hours before I moved them inside the barn. Since the barn doors weren't finished, I nailed split logs across the two openings. Then, taking extra clothes and some food in my saddlebags, I saddled Blaze and we rode off towards the mountains behind the camp.

It was about a half-mile up to the end of the valley so I let Blaze have his head again. Not to be outdone, Gus was staying with us stride for stride as we galloped across the grassy valley floor. Blaze ran with such grace and speed that we made the distance in no time. Finally, we slowed up as we came to the base where Harriet Mountain and Blaze Mountain joined. Here, between the two mountains, flowed one of the small creeks that split the valley. Turning Blaze into the creek, I headed up the rocky path.

I had often wondered where the headwaters of this creek came from. The forests on both sides of the creek were dense with thick underbrush that grew below the tall fir trees. We climbed a few hundred feet up the rocky creek bed until we reached a small waterfall. Dismounting Blaze and taking him by the reins, I walked up and around the falls. The going was steep but not as bad as when we came down the side of Comet Mountain. On the topside of the waterfall, I found a well-used game trail that seemed to run right down between the two mountains. Remounting Blaze, I climbed further uphill.

A half-mile up the trail, we came to a lake about the same size as Duck Lake. But by contrast, this was a deep lake and had no grass growing around its perimeter. On each side of the lake were tall, rocky cliffs with hundreds of small springs flowing from the granite. Over the years, the natural trickles of water had discolored the cliff walls, making it appear as if there were white lines drawn on the granite face. At the front end of the lake were large boulders and rocks that helped retain the water inside the lake.

The far end of the lake looked to be higher, with trees growing up a gentle slope. We made our way around the lake by keeping on the narrow trail that zigzagged under cliffs on one side. When I finally reached the other end, I stopped and looked back over the lake, with the Nascall Valley in the background. In the distance, just over the tops of the trees, I could see my barn and garden and the big lake. The view was breathtaking, with the two giant granite cliffs framing the vista on each side and the deep blue of the lake in the foreground. There and then, I decided to call this lake "July."

As I paused, I thought about turning around and going back down the path to the hot springs at the bay, but decided to explore the trail for another hour or so. It felt so good to be away from camp and learning more about the area that I was living in. Turning Blaze, I rode farther up the trail.

As we moved through the dark forest, I smelled seawater. In another half-mile, the trees started to thin out and the way became much brighter. Gus, as always, was ahead of me, but he soon turned and ran back down the trail, coming alongside me. In a few moments, I rode over a small knoll and emerged from the forest.

There before me was a spectacular view of the Dean Channel, with King Island and beyond. The day was bright and sunny, with the mid-morning sun still low in the sky. From this vantage point, I could see south down the channel all the way to where it turned west to the Pacific Ocean. With my binoculars, I searched the view for any boats or other signs of life but found none. It was a lonely thought that I was the only human seeing this most beautiful site.

Shrugging off the loneliness, I moved on.

The game trail turned and moved downhill through a few scrub trees, rocks, and grass. It was a gentle slope with good footing, and Blaze strolled along easily. The old map that Captain Skip had given me showed a small cove, named Eucott Bay, a few miles south of Nascall Bay. This trail looked as if it would lead to it.

Sure enough, within the hour I'd dropped four or five hundred feet to a bay that ran from the channel north for about a half-mile. It was a narrow bay, only a few hundred yards wide. A number of small creeks dropped out of the mountains, surrounding the bay and then flowing into the channel. The tide was out, and the floor of the inlet was covered mostly with rocks and mud. Scattered around the higher shoreline was tons of driftwood, bleached white from years of exposure to sunlight.

Further down the trail, I turned Blaze through some driftwood and out onto the mud flats of the bay. There was a strong smell of sulfur, which meant some of the creeks flowing from the mountains were hot springs.

Next to some of the rocks in the inky black mud, I could see something moving under the muck. Hopping off Blaze, I walked over to one of the moving mounds and reached down to expose the object. Burying my arm deep in the muddy goo, I came up with a large, hard-shelled clam. Washing the clam off in a nearby tide pool, I examined it. The shell was half round and dark blue, thick, and about the size of a softball. The clam had a neck, also blue, sticking out of the shell four or five inches long.

My fishing mates had told me about clams like these. They were called Geoducks, and they'd make a real delicacy for the evening's meal. Quickly, I gathered more, washing them as I went, and placing them in an empty trail bag.

After about a half-hour of clamming, I remounted Blaze and rode towards the narrow end of the bay, where the creeks merged. We moved slowly through the mud onto a rocky shoreline. At the very end of the bay, I found a large number of streams dropping down the rocky face of the mountains above. Some had steam rising in the air, as the water flowed from the mountainsides into small pools below. Tying Blaze to some driftwood, I tested each pool for its temperature to find just the right one. Clothes stripped off, I eased myself down into the steamy, wet heat of the pool and took a long-overdue bath. Spending over an hour in the hot water, I bathed, shaved, and relaxed in the warmth and sunshine.

I would've stayed longer had it not been for the turning tide. Being concerned that it might flood the narrow area we'd traveled, I feared the tide might trap us inside the bay. After drying myself and getting dressed, I mounted Blaze and rode back across the flooding mud flats without incident.

As we crossed through some driftwood on the upper shoreline, I noticed a green glass ball lying in some debris. It was a Japanese fishing ball that had floated all the way across the Pacific Ocean. The size of a basketball, it had a dirty white net around it. The bright sun shining on the sphere showed off the crude and uneven texture of the deep green, hand-blown glass. Reaching down, I picked it up, hanging its loose net over my saddle horn. I wasn't sure how I could use it, but I decided to take it back to camp anyway. If nothing else, it was colorful and interesting.

With that, we left the beach, turned back up the game trail, and headed home.

It had been a splendid day. We returned in the late afternoon, galloping at full speed down the length of the valley. The weather had gone from warm to hot, so I gave Blaze a bath with cold water from the creek and then a good rubdown. In the early evening, I moved the animals across the stream, letting them graze in some fresh grass.

Cleaning the clams down by the lake, I watched the crawfish take some of the remains. I would only eat selected parts of the clams, as I remembered that the darker parts of their bodies could be poisonous. Over a hot fire, I fried the necks and tails in leftover bacon drippings. The fried clams, about three pounds worth, made a delicious meal. Even Gus begged for more after I threw him a small sample. In the end, I think he ate as much as I did.

The evening was warm as I sat at my small table rolling a cigarette and watched the sun slowly fade in the west. The rapidly changing light sparked a vibrant show of color, across the lake, on the side of Comet Mountain. The long shadows made strange patterns on its face as the sun dropped further in the western sky.

Soon bright brilliant stars appeared overhead. It was such a warm, beautiful evening that I decided to sleep in the open, under these stars. Unrolling my bedroll on the thick grass alongside my tent, I lay down and fixed my gaze on the clear sky above.

Gus soon came over and joined me. There was a crescent moon rising in the east, and the stars were so bright that I thought I could hear their twinkle. Every now and then, a shooting star streaked across the sky, leaving a faint trail of yellow light behind.

It was just like watching fireworks without the noise. But the sounds of Mother Nature more than made up for the silence of these fireworks: the gurgle and bubble of the spring creeks as the water danced over rocks, the melody of crickets in the grass and frogs down by the lake, the soft rhythm of a woodpecker, the crackle of wood burning in my campfire, an owl calling out from the oak grove, even a wolf howling in the distance. It was the Lord's symphony of sights and sounds. I was in harmony with God and my surroundings. It was indeed a 4th of July I would never forget.

CHAPTER SIX

Fool's Errand

It was cold and wet. It poked me, not once but twice.

When I opened my eyes, I saw Gus standing over me, staring down at me, his nose in my face. Wiping the sleep out of my eyes, I sat up in my sleeping bag. It was early, very early, just light enough to see.

Gus nudged me again before he turned and ran across the camp and stopped at the grass line, looking back at me with his tail wagging. He turned his head towards the lake, then back at me again. I knew there was something he wanted me to see. Crawling out of the dew-covered bag, I crept over to Gus in a low crouch. Dropping to my knees, I slowly raised my body to look over the grass.

There, halfway between the lake and my camp, were three elk grazing. Gus must have heard or smelled them and alerted me.

In a low run, I went back to camp and slipped on my boots. Grabbing my rifle and binoculars, I strapped on my gun belt. I was still in my red flannel long-johns, but there was no time to change. Slipping into the gully of the creek bed alongside camp, I gave hand motions for Gus to follow as we made our way towards the lake. Quietly, I moved a few hundred feet downstream, stopping at a point where the taller grass gave way to the shorter grass. There was some patchy cover here, so I sprawled out on the creek's bank, which gave me a clear view of the elk. They were no more than a few hundred feet in front of me and with a light breeze in my face, I was sure they wouldn't pick up my scent from this position.

Through the binoculars, I watched over the brow of the bank as they grazed. There was one big bull with a rack of antlers almost five feet across. He stood six feet tall and was almost kneeling down to reach the grass. His chest and neck was almost jet black, while his body was dark brown with a tan rump. I guessed his weight at well over 800 pounds. Not far behind him was a cow about half his size. She'd eat some grass, raise her head and smell the breeze, then return to grazing. Next to her was a yearling with only small spikes as antlers. I guessed his weight at about 250 pounds. He and the older bull seemed to pay no attention to any possibility of danger; that must've been the cow's duty. All three were grayish-brown in color, with dark brown chests and legs, and each had a white patch on its rump. The bull was majestic in size and appearance, dwarfing the cow and yearling. They all were as beautiful as any animals I'd ever seen.

Gus joined me on the creek's bank. He lay a few feet from me, looking out at the three elk. Reluctantly, I knew the time had come to kill one of these extraordinary animals. Quietly, I cocked my Winchester Rifle, and pointed it in the direction of the elk.

At just that moment, I could hear Red Reed's voice in my head: Don't kill the big bulls—their meat is tough and there'll be too much of it. And don't kill the cows, unless you have to. Kill the young bucks.

Panning the rifle barrel from the big bull to the yearling, I aimed. It would be an easy shot, as he was no more than 200 feet from me. Slowly moving my finger to the trigger, I watch a drop of my cold sweat fall on the rifle breech. Just before I squeezed off the shot, the yearling stopped eating and looked up in my direction, the morning light forming a halo around his head. In that split second, his face was etched in my mind forever and I was unnerved. Finally, with sweat pouring off my brow, I pulled the trigger.

The shot broke the morning calm, and it startled even me. The yearling went down, with the older bull and cow on the run towards the lake.

Gus leaped to his feet and was off in their direction, barking. Jumping up from the bank, I ran toward the downed elk, all the while calling for Gus to return. He soon turned from his chase and joined me at the side of the dead elk. Or was the animal dead? As I walked to the front of the elk, I noticed he was still alive, looking at me with his big, brown eyes. I'd aimed for his heart for a quick kill, and instead, my bullet went through his shoulder and into his lungs. He wheezed as he tried to breathe, and a whimpering sound came from his mouth.

I was sick that I had only wounded him. The yearling was suffering because of my botched shot. All of a sudden, his hind legs started to move as he struggled to get up.

Feeling sorry for him, I rushed over and placed my rifle barrel directly above his skull. His young face was clear in my vision, with his velvety black nose and mouth twitching like he was trying to say something to me. I swear there was a tear running down his cheek as he stared back up at me.

Cocking the lever, I pulled the trigger, cocked and pulled again, cocked and pulled again. The sound of my three shots cut through the still morning air like a knife. My hands were shaking and my knees buckled. Dropping down in front of the dead elk, blood running from the three holes in his skull, I shouted, "Damn! Why do I feel this way? He's just an animal!"

I hadn't felt this when I shot the wolves, nor the ducks, nor the thousands of fish I'd caught, so why now? Maybe I'd never really looked at their faces before. Maybe I hadn't thought of these animals as living beings before. Maybe their beauty and pride, and their role in nature, had never crossed my mind before. And maybe I'd better get a grip on myself if I'm going to survive out here! I told myself sternly.

I knelt there in front of the dead elk for almost a half-hour with these thoughts and feelings rushing through my mind like a whirlpool. Gus must've sensed something was wrong, as he soon was sitting close to me, intently watching my every move.

Finally, I composed myself and returned to camp, where I dressed and saddled Blaze. With ropes, we dragged the dead elk to the lakeshore. There we found a sturdy fir near the shore. Tossing the rope over a tall tree limb, I strung the young bull up by its front legs. Still numb and only going through the motions, I forced myself to remember what Red had shown me about dressing out animals, using some of his cattle as an example.

With my hunting knife, I split opened the elk's belly from tail to neck. Reaching up inside the chest cavity, I worked on cutting out his insides, my arms and hands soon slimy with blood and entrails. He was still warm and, with more cutting, his steamy guts began dropping to the ground. I'd read how the Indians would use or eat almost 100 percent of an animal they killed, but I wouldn't. The only thing I kept from inside the elk was its liver. With my boot, I pushed the rest of the guts into the lake. Then I worked on skinning him and cutting off the two meaty hindquarters. Each quarter seemed to weigh at least 60 pounds, more than enough meat for my needs.

Carrying each of the slabs of meat back to my camp, I stored them in the root cellar. Still trying hard to choke down my feelings, I washed up and started working around my camp. It was late morning by now, and, surprisingly, I even felt a little hungry. Building a fire, I set out the coffee pot and began slicing the elk's liver, frying about two pounds of it in some bacon grease. It tasted sweet and rich. It was good and I knew it was good for me, but in the end Gus ate most of it; I was still having a hard time getting the elk's face out of my mind.

After my meal, I returned to the lake with Harry and cut down the remaining elk carcass. Draping him over the back of a mildly protesting Harry, I walked deep into the forest to discard carcass. The remains would no doubt draw wolves, so we traveled at least two miles from camp, where I was sure it would attract no danger to us. Here, other scavengers would finish the deed I'd started.

As I walked back to camp, I made a promised to myself; I would eat as much duck, fish and seafood as I could find, and I'd only kill other game animal if there was no other food for my needs or if I were in danger. I'd also make sure that the shot would be straight, to kill the animal with the first bullet.

The morning's events had been a revelation to me and proved what I had guessed for a long while: the mountain man deep inside of me was as soft as a three-minute egg.

The hundred twenty pounds of meat stored in the cellar were more than Gus and I could eat before it went bad. I knew I'd have to try to preserve half of it. That afternoon, I rode down to the bay and began boiling seawater in my largest cooking pot. It took almost six hours to boil down enough seawater to make two gallons of a salty slurry. With the slurry stowed in the feedbag, I returned to camp. Removing one hindquarter from the cellar, I sliced the meat thin and soaked it overnight in the salt solution. The idea was that the salt would remove most of the meat's natural moisture, which would then allow for drying the meat in the sun.

Early the next morning, I started to build two large drying racks. These I made from some oak branches that crisscrossed each other and were fastened with vines. Each rack was about 5 feet square. By midday, the warm sun was out, and I placed the strips of meat on the racks. Each rack was placed about five feet off the ground and positioned in direct sunlight, close to camp. One of the books I had packed in said it would take two or three days to totally dry the meat, so I feared two problems: weather and big birds (seagulls, hawks, and eagles). I'd have to remain close and alert, taking the racks inside the tent if the weather changed or if animals approached them. But luck was with me and I had no problems in the next three days.

During the time it took to dry the meat, I tanned the elk hide. The process had been taught to me by Red and detailed in one of my books and turned out to be extremely time-consuming. In the end, however, the hide was soft and clean, and it didn't smell sour or gamey.

During this time, I also worked in my rapidly maturing garden. In fact, as I thinned the rows, I ate some of the young vegetables. There was even enough that a couple of handfuls of carrots were shared with Blaze and I used some young potatoes and onions to make elk stew. After three days, I had about 30 pounds of elk jerky. It had little flavor and was tough to chew, but it seemed to be well preserved. When I had more time, I'd build a smoker and see if that would be a better way of preserving my game.

The Cabin

While waiting for the meat to dry, I began planning the construction of my cabin. The overall size would be 20 feet long and 12 feet wide. The length included a six-foot covered porch for dry storage of firewood, so the living area of the cabin would only be 14 x 12 feet. The sidewalls would be five feet high, with the end walls and the roof hip nine feet high. At the porch end would be a single door to the cabin, and at the other end, a large rock fireplace. The floor would also be rock, built over the natural soil. I wanted a window, as I feared how dark and drab the cabin would be without one, but I hadn't packed in any glass, so I resigned myself to doing without.

From the nearby and now depleted alder grove, I'd built the stable. The only other large alder grove was a half-mile up the valley. That would be too far to pull the logs, so I decided to build the cabin out of hemlock, which was plentiful around the perimeter of the valley. Most of the hemlock trees were tall and straight, with few branches growing close to the ground. The trees' diameter changed very little from the ground up to twenty feet or higher. There was a good selection of trees with the girth and length that I needed and with the help of Harry and Harriet, I could handle logs of this size.

My first task was to lay out two puncheons (flat sides of halved logs), each 22 feet long. These puncheons would act as the foundation for the cabin.

Splitting a log of this size was not easy. First, I would fell the selected log using my axe, then remove any branches, and cut the log to its rough length. Next, working with ropes and both mules, I dragged it to my building site. At the site, I squared the log to the correct size, cutting it with my large crosscut ripsaw. Studying the growth rings at each end of the log, I looked for just the right place to split it lengthwise. Using iron wedges and a sledgehammer, I would start a straight split. After hammering and prying for hours, I finally got two equal halves that I could then move into place. The first half was placed just outside the opening to the root cellar, where I'd use my shovel and hoe to level it to the ground. The second half was squared and leveled to the first at 12 feet across.

With this layout, I would have a small cellar opening inside the future living area.

This whole process of building the foundation took one long day. Not much to show for all that work and sweat, just two half logs lying on the ground.

With the puncheons in place, I used a drawknife and broadax to hew a few inches off the top round of the split logs. Using my common axe, I made notches at the back ends and two more notches 14 feet up the puncheons. Into these notches I rolled two 14-foot logs, also notched and hewn. I repeated this procedure on two more logs and rolled the 16-foot logs onto the others to form the sidewalls. The trick was to get the notches just deep enough to receive the notch of the next layer. I wanted no more than an inch or two gap between the courses of logs. Where the notches came together, I drove a single large spike into the notch to hold the corners firmly together. My goal was to make each layer of logs fit together as snugly as possible. Later, I'd chink any gaps between the logs with mud and moss to add protection against the weather. I had learned these building techniques from Red Reed and a few chapters in my frontier books.

Determined that my cabin would be weather-tight, I worked hard at the construction process. But this process was a slow one. I decided not to cut the openings for the door or fireplace until all my walls were about five feet high, and then I would use my whipsaw to make square cuts for both openings. Into these openings I'd nail thick timbers that had been whipsawed from ten-foot-long logs. These timbers would hold the cut log-ends securely. On the front porch, under the overhang, I also made floor planks out of timbers that had been sawed to my needs. To accomplish this, I made a jig that held 12-foot logs straight up in the air so I could rip them lengthwise with my saw. Standing on wooden platforms, I could cut a log with a 20-inch girth into four three-inch-thick planks. It was difficult to keep my planks uniform in thickness as I sawed the full twelve feet of the log but, learning by trial and error—lots of error—I soon perfected my sawing proficiency.

Every few days, I'd load a couple of empty trail bags onto each of the mules and ride down to the bay with Blaze and Gus. After taking a warm bath and fishing or clamming, I'd search for rocks. On one mule, I'd load a trail bag with round rocks that ranged from eight to twelve inches in size, to use in the fireplace. On the other mule, I loaded a bag with large flat rocks no more then a couple of inches thick, for the cabin's floor. In both of the other bags, I'd place clean beach sand. With the mules' heavy loads, we'd walk up the rough game trail and return to camp.

If the rocks and sand were to be used in building the fireplace, they'd have to be washed first in fresh stream water. Fresh water would remove any salt residue so that the gravel would form a better bond when mixed with the cement that I'd packed in. As it was, I only had enough cement to build the base and the firebox for the fireplace. For the upper chimney, I'd use a mix of mud, grass, and sticks. After I'd completed the roof and had the cabin dry and weather-tight, I'd lay the flat stones for the floor and grout the cracks with sand.

It was a slow process, one log layer at a time. Days turned to weeks, and weeks turned into a month. But in this time the cabin had taken shape, with its walls now all in place. Using the strength of the mules, and aided by log ramps tacked to the walls and by the block and tackle, I was able to skid even the heaviest logs into place. The biggest was the 22-foot ridgepole, which formed the hip of the roof and would support the roof rafters. To lift it into its nine-foot position, I built temporary platforms inside the cabin and raised one end of the 400 pound pole at a time. Without the help of the mules, I could have never built a cabin of this design. Emotionally, I didn't have much use for them as compared to Blaze, but they did carry their weight and then some. This would make my future decision regarding their fate even harder than I had expected.

During this construction period, I maintained a planned schedule. Ever since leaving Firvale, I'd used my tide books to keep track of the days, weeks, and months of my mission. Each morning, I'd note the moon's position, as printed in the book, and make a mark on the day's tides. Without this, it would be easy to lose track of time. When the tides were high, I hunted for rabbits, worked in the woods and built the cabin. When the tides were low, I'd bathe, wash clothes, fish in the channel, clam, and search for rocks. There was always more than enough to do.

I worked long days, as the sun would rise around 6 a.m. and not set until close to 9 p.m. Without these long days in the north, plants would not grow and mature in the shortened summer season. There was always something to build, repair, or sharpen, and there was the garden and the animals to tend to. My energy level was high and with all this activity, I had a huge appetite. Each morning, along with whatever meat I'd fry, I'd open a few biscuits and pour some honey over them. The sugar in the honey was about the only sweet energy source I had. So when I found a patch of wild strawberries, I was delighted. While the birds had already taken most of the ripe berries, there were almost enough partly ripe and green berries to fill a gallon tin. These I took back to camp, where I laid them out in the sun to ripen. Over a period of a few days, I ate them. What a treat, Strawberries for breakfast and dinner. There were also acres of blackberry bushes. When the berries ripened in the late summer sun, I knew I'd be racing the birds to reap the harvest.

While fishing down by the lake one day, I spotted a large beehive, high in a tall fir tree. While I didn't like bees, I knew the hive could be a great source of renewal for my rapidly dwindling honey supply. Soon, I told myself that I had put off "the great beehive caper" long enough. From some straight hemlock limbs, I built a 20-foot ladder. Next, dressing myself in woolen winter clothing, I tied my pant legs around my boots, doing the same with my shirtsleeves around my leather gloves. To protect my head and face, I used an empty flour sack, cutting two small slits for my eyes.

During all these preparations, Gus watched me with great interest. In fact, when I tested the fit of the flour sack over my head, he started barking and growling at me. After chasing him around camp, I'd then remove the sack from my head, and he'd smile and wiggle his tail. He soon knew it was some kind of game, and nothing to be frightened about.

The time had come. Picking up the tools I'd need for this honey-gathering adventure, I stubbornly walked towards the tree with the hive. I tried to instruct Gus to stay in camp, but he would have none of my orders and came along anyway; he was determined to see why I was dressed in this funny-looking outfit on a bright, sunny August day.

The tree was just up from the lake, about a half-mile from camp. Before approaching the hive, I gave Gus hand motions again to return to camp. He just sat in the grass looking up at me. Finally I said, "Okay, boy. But when these mad bees take out after you, don't forget I warned you!"

At the base of the tree, I wedged the ladder into position. From my pocket, I removed the bag for my head and put it on, tucking the open end into my coat collar and zipping up the coat. Next, I put my baseball cap over the bag on my head. From my other pocket, I removed a second sack and a tin plate that I'd use as a scoop. It was difficult to see through the two small holes for my eyes, so I slowly felt my way up the ladder.

The hive was just inside a large knothole in the tree, some eighteen feet up. Just below the hole was a branch, where I rested my ladder. As I climbed up and approached the hive, I could see a few bees flying in and out.

Soon I was nearly at the top of the ladder, directly in front of the hole, chest-high. Spreading my feet wide on the rungs, I bent my knees slightly to get a firm hold. With the scoop gripped in my gloved left hand, I slowly moved it into the hole. I could feel the honeycombs through my gloves as I made a pass with the scoop.

Instantly, the hive came to life. When I removed my hand and arm from inside the hive, it was black, covered with swarming bees. Emptying the first scoop into the second bag, I returned for more. Bees were buzzing everywhere, on my arms, chest, and head. Then a few found their way under my protective head bag, and I could see more flying in through the eye slits. It was the noise that began to get to me, the loud sound of thousands of bees swarming and buzzing around my head.

After a second big scoop, I returned for more. Ouch! Ouch! I was being stung on my face and neck from bees inside my head sack. And more bees seemed to be coming in every second. The noise was driving me crazy, and the stinging was hurting like hell.

After placing a fourth scoop into the bag, I'd had enough. Tying off the bag, I dropped it and the scoop to the ground, and scrambled fast down the ladder—too fast. Halfway down, I lost my footing and hit the hard ground with a distinct *thud*.

The bees were still all over me, and some were still trapped in my head sack. Jumping up, I ran for the lake, a black cloud of bees matching me, stride for stride. At the lakeshore, I ran straight into the water, throwing my entire body under the cold water.

When I came up, the bees were still there. Sucking in a deep breath, I went under a second time, and waited over thirty seconds before lifting my head out of the water again.

They were gone. Thank God, they were gone. Easing myself cautiously out of the water, I began to walk to the shore, ripping off the flour sack from my head. A couple dozen dead bees fell into the water. Stumbling to the shoreline in my dripping wet wool clothes, I plopped down on some rocks. The welts were already swelling on my face and neck from at least a dozen stings.

Just then, I noticed Gus lying in the grass, a few feet away. He must've seen the whole episode, from the time I fell out of the tree to when I jumped into the lake. He was looking at me, his head cocked. Yes, he must've thought this was some kind of funny game.

The bee stings on my face and neck would heal over the next few weeks. But, in the end, all my efforts and pain only yielded a quart and a half of fresh, new honey. Quite a price to pay and I decided it was a game not to be played again.

Month of Pain

August turned out to be a month of pain. Not more than a week after getting all those bee stings, I had a serious accident up in the woods. I was working in a grove of hemlock trees, cutting down smaller-diameter logs for my roof rafters. The grove was about a half mile from camp, and I rode Blaze there early in the morning. My plan was to return with the mules in the afternoon, to drag back what I had felled.

While I worked, it was my custom to hobble Blaze to let him graze just outside of the grove. By now, I felt I was an expert lumberjack, as my cabin was nearing completion. Gus, as usual, was with me but out of sight while looking for prey.

I had chopped down three trees and was just starting on a fourth one. The forest floor was littered with branches, logs, underbrush, and wood chips. Moments before, I'd taken some time to sharpen my axe with the stone and oil I carried in my coat pocket.

Normally, when starting on a tree, I'd look carefully at its trunk to make sure there were few if any knots in my chopping area. This time, I didn't look carefully enough; on the second swing of the axe, I hit a large knot under the bark. I had put all my strength into the chop, so when the axe head hit the knot, the force was instantly reversed, causing the handle to break, which sent the axe head flying up into the air. It could come down anywhere, and it happened so fast I had no time to react.

The next thing I knew, I was on the ground, with the axe head buried deep in my right thigh. Looking down at my leg, with pain flowing through my body, I almost passed out. But with all my might, I shook it off. I couldn't pass out; there was nobody here to help me. Leaving the axe head in my thigh, I dragged myself over to the log snag where I'd left my coat. Propping myself up, I held my leg with both hands. There was some blood running down it, and I knew that when I pulled the axe blade out there would be much more. Removing my shirt, I took off my T-shirt to use as a compress. Then, reaching down to the axe head, I pulled it out with one fast jerk. The wound was deep and long, about four inches across and an inch into the skin. Blood came flowing out. Tying the T-shirt around the leg, I compressed the wound, but the fabric was soon saturated with blood. Knowing that I couldn't make it back to camp without first closing the wound, I searched for an answer. What I needed was my first aid kit, but I had become cocky and left it back at camp.

I had to stop the bleeding... somehow, I had to suture the cut. But how?

Then I remembered that, in the morning, I'd sewn a new button on my coat, and the needle and thread were still in one of my pockets. Soon I had found the needle, with about nine inches of black thread hanging from it, enough for a dozen or so stitches. Reaching down, I removed the T-shirt. With my right hand, I pulled the gash together, holding it firmly, with my left, I began to sew.

Each stitch felt like someone was kicking me in my thigh. Trying to shake off the pain, I knew that I would have to stay conscious and finish all the stitches... or else bleed to death. Finally, I reached the last stitch and tied it off. I could still see lots of blood, but it seemed to be old blood. With the T-shirt, I cleaned the blood away from the gash and it seemed as if the stitches had stopped the worst of the bleeding.

My head dropped back against the log, and I passed out.

When I came to, Blaze was looking down at me. He was still hobbled, so how or why he managed to come into the forest to find me, I had no idea. For a hobbled horse to walk through the obstacles that surrounded me seemed near impossible, but he had done it, and I thanked God that he had.

Soon, I was also aware that Gus, too, was standing by, watching me. Still feeling faint, with my head spinning and my body on fire, I shook off the feeling of sickness and the temptation to throw up. Leaning over, I slowly removed the hobbles on Blaze's legs. Then, carefully, I moved my butt to the top of the snag I'd been resting against. From there, I cinched down the saddle and pulled myself up, draping my body across his back.

He didn't wait for me to give him any commands. In an instant, he began walking through the forest and out into the valley, towards camp.

Every step that Blaze took sent shooting pains through my body, and I almost passed out again. The next thing I remember, I was sliding off the saddle and dragging myself into the tent. Once on my sleeping bag, I searched for the medical kit. Removing a syringe, I filled it with a small amount of Novocain. Giving myself a shot, close to the wound, I then laid back, waiting for the pain to subside.

Within a few moments, the pain became more bearable, and I felt somewhat relieved. Pulling off my blood-soaked pants, I cleaned the gash with antiseptic. The stitches were holding, and I could see no new bleeding. Finally, I placed a large bandage over the wound and took two aspirin from one of the bottles. After taking the pills, I lay back on top of my sleeping bag and went to sleep.

The breeze in my face woke me and I opened my eyes to find early evening. Gus was lying just outside of the tent flap, with Blaze standing over him. Struggling to my feet, I hobbled outside the tent. With more effort than I'd expected, I stooped to pick up a branch to use as a crutch. Using the stick, I picked up Blaze's dangling reins and walked him over to the stable, where I removed his saddle and bridle, and gave him the last of the oats we'd packed in. Putting my face to his, I thanked him out loud for being there when I needed him. Damn, he was a great animal.

It took me a good week to get back on my feet without the use of a crutch. During that time, I stayed close to camp and did small chores that I could accomplish on one leg. A few weeks before the accident, I'd felled a cedar tree that I'd cut into 30-inch lengths to dry. My plan was to use this wood for the shingles on my roof. Now, I had the time and could, while sitting split these short logs into shingles. Also, I found other things to do. Early on, I'd built a small rock oven for baking biscuits. When I built the fireplace in the cabin, I'd also made a much larger rock oven, one that I could now use as a pottery oven. After crafting a crude pottery wheel that I could spin with my good leg, I mixed clay and straw to shape some pots for food storage. After letting my pots dry in the sun, I'd fire them, one at a time, inside the oven. Using some roots and pitch, I even tried to make some pottery glazes, although it never did seem to work as well as I'd expected. But my pots turned out to be sturdy, and, although they weren't the prettiest things, they would serve my purpose.

Another project was to make a bed frame, something I'd thought about since arriving in the valley. Taking some of my "error" timbers that were not quite thick enough for porch planks, I made a frame 6'6" by 3'6". With hand tools, I attached four legs, each three feet high. Using my brace and bits, I drilled holes in the sides of the wood frame, six inches from each other. Through these holes, I wove lengths of rope, securing each end with square knots on the outside of the frame. The woven rope made for good support with just a little give. On top of the woven rope mattress, I laid the elk pelt and my sleeping bag. It was heaven, sleeping off the ground on a somewhat soft bed again. Each day, as my leg improved and my spirits were more optimistic, I continued to work on more creature comforts.

During this time of recovery, I became more observant of my environment and my animals, and spent more time grooming Blaze. The mules also had this time off, and I had to tend to them, as well. But it was watching Gus that I enjoyed the most. He was a curious dog, always on the move, with his nose in the air for any scent that might come his way. He could hear, see, and smell rings around me. Gus loved the garden area, and I'd watch him play and hunt in it almost every day. This green patch of dirt was his trap for any bird or varmint that dared to enter. He'd sneak quietly into the now-tall rows of plants and wait for some unsuspecting animal to intrude. Sometimes I'd look over to the garden and see just his tail pointing in the air above the rows. It was a funny and comforting site. But one day, while watching him patrol the rows, I was shocked to see him jump straight up into the air, well over the tops of the vegetables, and let out a cry that was more of shock than hurt. In an instant, he turned from the garden and raced to the creek, where he jumped into the water and started to roll.

With my rifle firmly in hand, I hobbled towards the garden. Was there a bobcat? A porcupine? What?

I smelled it first, then saw it. Turning the corner between the row of carrots and corn was a skunk! He was small and quick as he raced out of the garden and into the underbrush. His scent filled the air and drove me from the patch. Good God, I had never smelled such an odor in my life. Moving as fast as I could, I retreated to the creek, where I found Gus now rolling in the tall grass. He smelled bad, very bad. That skunk must have sprayed him good with its foul perfume.

I didn't know how good a job my soap would do on Gus, but I had to try. He got a good scrub-down in the cold creek, and all the while I held my breath. But the bath didn't seem to help one bit. Next, I gave Gus a haircut, but that didn't seem to help either. It would be almost a week before Gus and I would again enjoy the fresh and natural odor of the great outdoors. I hoped this was the last time either of us would run into a skunk.

As my leg healed, I got bolder with my activities. Soon, the mules had pulled all the logs from the grove down to the cabin site. Once I had the logs all laid out, I cut them to size, hewed, and notched them. There were nine rafters on each side of the roof. Once again, it was the mules and the block and tackle that made this work possible. Each rafter had to be fitted to the walls and the ridgepole. The fitting process required moving the rafters in and out of position as I chopped and fitted each joint. I had run out of log spikes a while back, so I finished the frame of the roof by drilling and placing wood pegs in all the major joints. The last thing I wanted was for the roof to blow off in some winter tempest. Lengthwise across the rafters, I nailed small, split branches to which I would nail my shingles.

Completing the roof was the end of the heavy work. To finish the cabin, I only had to chink all the walls with mud and moss, lay the stone floor, and build the front door. Then I could move in, an event I looked forward to.

While gazing into my campfire late one evening, mulling over the clams I'd eaten, it dawned on me how I could catch crabs in the bay. I knew they were there, as sometimes their spent shells were strewn on the beach. My problem was how to catch them.

My idea was simple enough: I'd make a trap out of small sticks fastened together with vine and nails. This trap would have two compartments. In the lower one, I'd place rocks, so it would be heavy enough to sink. In the upper one, I'd secure fish heads to lure the crabs in. To finish it off, I would craft a swinging gate on the top compartment that would only open inward, trapping the crabs inside. The Japanese float I'd found would be my bobber, and a rope would also be tied to the float so that I could pull the trap in from the water. When I sketched it out in my journal, it looked like it just might work, so I went to work on its construction. Soon my simple trap was completed and I waited for just the right low tide so that I could position it far out into channel. Then, when the flood tide came in, the trap would be deep on the channel's floor.

A few days later, when the time and tides were just right, I took my contraption to the bay. At the channel's edge, I placed rocks in the lower compartment and fastened three fish heads into the top. Lobbing like a softball pitcher, I hurled both the trap and float out as far as I could. Within seconds, the trap was sinking to the bottom with the green float bobbing above it.

Tying the other end of the rope to some driftwood, I looked for clams as I waited for the tide to change. Nascall Bay had none of the larger blue clams that I'd found at Eucott Bay. Here, the clams were the smaller, rock type, about the size of a silver dollar. My normal method was to scratch around in the sand in front of beach rocks to find them. They were tasty but, because of their size, it took a lot of effort to collect a meal's worth.

Within an hour, the tide had changed and was beginning to flood. By that time, I'd found three or four pounds of the rock clams, and I gave up the search because of the tide. The green float had been tugged a few hundred feet down-channel by the force of the flooding water, so the float and trap were farther out, in deeper channel waters. I was eager to see if my contraption yielded any results, so I untied my end of the rope and went to edge of the water. Arm over arm, I began pulling and pulling. I made little headway, as the force of the tide and the weight of the trap were just too strong for me.

Retrieving Blaze, I twisted my rope around his saddle horn. With his strength, we easily pulled the trap to shore. It was covered with strands of long, silky seaweed that kept me from seeing inside the trap for a moment. Stripping the seaweed away, I saw that inside the top chamber were three large crabs, each more than two pounds! For the next two days, I feasted on clams and crabs. My little idea for the trap had worked, and I was proud of both my contraption and myself. Again, I had proven that surviving here in the wildness could be done, with planning and self-reliance.

Death's Shack

Part of this self-reliance involved making hard decisions, and now I had to make an extremely difficult one. With the cabin almost completed and all the heavy work done, I no longer had the luxury of keeping the mules. They required too much of my labor to feed and maintain them. Also, I'd need the space they occupied In the stable for the storage of dry grass for the winter. Having pondered these points for weeks, I knew it was time for my decision. At first, I'd thought about taking them far from camp and killing them, leaving their carcasses for the wolves. But I wasn't sure, now, that I could do that. While I didn't respect them for their brains, I did respect their brawn. They had worked hard in both the journey to the valley and helping me build the stable and cabin. Therefore, I'd come to a different conclusion. If nothing else, I'd give them a chance at survival. My decision was to find a large, grassy meadow, far from camp, where I could release them into the wild. I knew their chances of living out the fall and winter were slim, but maybe, just maybe, they'd make it. In any event, it was better than me killing them. The problem I now faced was finding a grassy meadow far from my camp. With only Blaze and Gus, I needed to explore the western reaches of Nascall Lake for a suitable location for the mules' release.

We prepared to leave, with Blaze packed with enough supplies for us to spend a couple of nights on the trail. Making sure the mules had enough feed and water, I secured the openings to both the stable and the cabin.

We were off, early on the morning of August 26th. For the most part, the weather during late July and August had been bright and warm. We had low clouds most every morning, and sometimes a rain shower or two, but usually by late morning the sun would start dancing out from between the clouds. By the afternoon, the clouds were gone and the rest of the day warm and bright. Most of the day's temperatures were in the mid '70s, and at night they dropped to the mid '40s.

Towards the shoreline of the lake, and beyond the creek bed that led up to Duck Lake, was another large landmass that narrowed out into Nascall Lake.

The ride along the lake line was easy going. Numerous creeks and streams flowed off Nascall Mountain and into the lake, but we had little trouble crossing them. By late morning, I'd made it to the dense forest that was growing on the peninsula. Here, I rode through the forest to the point closest to the other side of the lake. Looking east, I could see my valley and even my camp, some two miles down the lake towards the channel.

Directly across from me, on the other side of the lake, were the high, rocky cliffs of Comet Mountain. These steep cliffs rose up over a thousand feet from the lake's surface. At its narrowest point, the gap between the tall trees and these rocky cliffs was no more then a few hundred yards. So I decided to name this point the "Narrows." To the west, I could see that the high cliffs of Comet Mountain ran the entire length of the lake's north side, while the south side had trees and a distinct shoreline. The lake itself seemed to be four or five miles long, on the western side of the Narrows. We continued our journey, heading west along the water's edge. Around every turn, I anticipated finding a valley or large meadow for the release of the mules. But I found none.

By late afternoon, we'd traveled almost the full length of the lake. Here, the terrain didn't seem as steep, so I began thinking about turning inland in search of a suitable place for the mules. Stopping at one of the larger waterfalls that flowed into the lake, I began exploring the area. The water was coming from a horseshoe-shaped bluff about 50 feet above me. The falls were beautiful, and I watched the water as it flowed into a short creek and then into the lake.

That's when I saw it. At first, it didn't register in my head and I started to move on. But after crossing the creek bed I stopped as it finally clicked in my head. Dismounting, I walked back to where the water entered the lake. Sure enough, there, sunk in about ten feet of crystal-clear water, was a log raft, joined together with rusty steel cables. Scratching my head I said aloud, "What the hell are you doing out here?"

The raft looked big, although some of the logs had broken away and it was difficult to see its true overall size. *A large, man-made object in the middle of this wilderness?* I thought.

Deciding to do a little more investigating, I scouted the area. Searching the lower portion of the waterfalls for about a half hour, I found nothing. But when I had just about given up, I saw a game trail that seemed to move up towards the bluff that formed the waterfalls.

We followed the trail up and through the underbrush, climbing over large rocks and downed trees. Soon, we were on top of the bluff. Here was a large clearing that looked to be a few hundred feet wide and about a quarter-mile long that narrowed into the side of Nascall Mountain. The cliffs of the mountain were tall and rocky, probably five hundred feet or more in height. Running off these crags and onto the floor of the bluff were small streams of water that came together to form the water of Horseshoe Falls. There were a few trees on the bluff, although it was covered for the most part with heavy underbrush. We moved across the clearing towards the creeks in the center... and that's when I made my second discovery: a large, rusty object that was nearly covered by a green blanket of underbrush.

Crossing the shallow creek to get a better look, I pulled back the blanket of weeds and found a large, old steam engine. The main smokestack had rusted away and fallen to the ground years before. What was left was a large boiler with rusty valves, gears, and wheels. Alongside the machine, I found another, smaller machine. It looked like some kind of rock crusher, but I wasn't sure. People had been here a long time ago, working the area for something.

Turning around, I took a careful look at the cliffs behind me. Just above the dense brush was an opening in the side of one of the cliffs. Tethering Blaze to one of the old engines, I walked to the opening and pulled back some of the underbrush. Within a few minutes, I'd cleared out the mouth of a mineshaft about seven feet high and three feet wide.

Peering inside the dark, cool opening, I tried to adjust my eyes to the dim light. After a few moments, I saw large wooden beams bracing the walls and ceiling of the shaft. They were placed every few yards down the dark mine.

Gus, who had joined me, walked into the cavern. I knew he could see a lot better than I could, so I followed him inside, feeling my way along the beams. The shaft was damp and smelled musty. This could be a good animal den; with that thought in mind, I cocked my rifle. The last thing I wanted was to be surprised by a drowsy bear.

The sound of my rifle cocking rolled through the mine and bounced back at me with a loud echo. Just then, I heard Gus bark, down deep in the dark shaft. Then, out of the darkness came hundreds of what looked like birds, flying directly at me while making a loud, high-pitched, screaming noise.

Falling to the ground in a cloud of dust, they passed over me. These creatures flew so close to my prone body that I could feel the breeze from their wings as they flew out of the mouth of the shaft. Then came Gus, in hot pursuit, leaping over my body and heading for the opening of the abandoned mine.

It all happened so fast that it took me a second or two to realize that what we had disturbed were bats, lots and lots of bats. They had scared me, but by now my eyes had adjusted to the faint light, and I could see more clearly. Moving only twenty or thirty feet further inside the shaft, I came to a point where it split, with one tunnel going in one direction and another in a different direction. There I found old rusty shovels, picks, and large hammers piled on the floor of the mine. Also lying on the ground were two rusty steel hats with kerosene lamps on top. Shaking both to see if there was any kerosene in them, I found none.

The mine was a spooky place, and I didn't like being in it.

As I turned to leave, I saw some wooden boxes against one beam. Moving over to the boxes, I used my hand to dust the dirt off the top box and lit a match. Peering down, I could just make out a faded word… "Dynamite!"

Quickly jumping back, I threw the match to the ground. I certainly didn't want to fool around with old explosives.

Next to the wooden boxes were two large wooden kegs, about five gallons each. These wooden kegs would be great for food storage, but I wasn't sure what was in them. Carefully, I slipped off their round wooden tops and found that each contained nails. One was about a quarter full of ten-inch rusty nails, the other about a third full of 16-inch rusty spikes. Satisfied, I hoisted a keg under each arm and turned to leave.

When I stumbled out into the brilliant sunshine, it took a few seconds for my eyes to adjust again. The sky had never looked so good as I took deep breaths of cool fresh air. Putting the kegs down near the old engines, I loosened Blaze's saddle, realizing that if miners had worked this mine, they must have lived here, too. There just might be a cabin up here, or maybe they had lived on the old sunken raft. I wasn't sure.

Looking around the bluff again, I spotted a large outcropping of rocks, about hundred yards up from the mouth of the mine.

Behind those rocks, protected from the wind blowing off the lake—*that would make a good site for a cabin*, I thought. Enjoying my detective work, I made my way through the underbrush, and around to the other side of the rocks.

Sure enough, there was a small shack. It was built out of corrugated metal sheets that, over the years, had turned to rust. Bushes and vines grew halfway up the walls. The whole structure was leaning backwards about eight degrees towards the rocky cliffs behind it. On the front of the cabin were two small windows, one on each side of a wooden door. There didn't seem to be any other openings in the shack.

At the front of the cabin, I pushed back blackberry bushes with my rifle butt. Trying to peer in through the windows, I found that both were boarded over from the inside. The door was made out of thick wood planks, supported with rusty iron plates running across the top and bottom. The face of the door bore faded scratch marks almost to its top. It was obvious that animals had tried to get in.

Shaking the rusty latch and pushing on the door, I found that both were stuck. Taking my rifle butt, I began pounding on the rusty latch, and it finally moved up to an open position. Trying the door again, I pushed hard, then harder, and it finally moved an inch or so. Now I could see that the door had been nailed shut from the inside. With my shoulder against the door, I threw my body against it, and the door finally popped open.

Inside, the room was dank and dark, but there was a small hole in the roof in one corner of the shack. From the streak of light pouring through the hole, I could see a rusted potbelly stove, broken in half and lying on the ground. Turning to the windows I found the boards covering them were actually shutters which had been nailed shut. With some effort, I pried them open, letting more sunlight filter its way into the shack through the filthy window glass.

The floor was dirt, and the metal walls and roof had been built onto a wooden frame attached to puncheons that made up the foundation. It was a single-room shack, roughly 12 feet by 12 feet. There was no furniture; only the old stove and what looked to be two corroded metal bed frames on the other side. As I moved over to the bed frames, I noticed old pots, pans, lamps, and plates scattered about. One bed frame seemed to have a dusty, old bear pelt on it. I could use that, I thought. Reaching down, I pulled a corner of the pelt up to look at the fur side.

Underneath a skeleton face with no eyes stared up at me. And, perhaps startled by the light, worms began to crawl out of the empty sockets.

After jumping back and catching my breath, I pulled the pelt all the way off, sending dust flying into the still air. I had never seen a human skeleton before. My hands were shaky, my knees a little weak. This was a complete skeleton of what looked to be a man lying on the rusty bed frame that had collapsed to the dirt floor. There was a layer or two of rotted wool blankets on top of him and underneath were shreds of his rotted clothes.

He rested on a mattress that had long ago decomposed. I could see some of his bones protruding from patches of denim. There was no flesh, just bones that were quite white. I looked at his face and at the dark holes where his eyes once were. His jaw was closed with no expression on his face. There were still a few strands of hair on top of his skull.

Then I saw the small round hole in the side of the skull.

As I bent over for a closer look, I noticed a rusty, old revolver lying directly under the bed frame. Picking it up, I struggled for a moment to open the tarnished breach. Finally it opened, and I found six spent 32-caliber shells in the six-round chamber. It looked to me like he had taken the last shot to his own head.

One thing was for sure: he'd been here a very long time. Needing to get some air I went to the open door and took three deep breaths.

Having just disturbed a dead man's tomb, now what should I do? Who was he and why was he here? He must have nailed the door shut from the inside, but why? And why was there no furniture? Did he kill himself? Questions with no answers. My mind was racing. I'd just made a sad and grisly discovery, and yet this little cabin had some things I could use. Would this be wrong? Should I leave him as I'd found him, or would it be all right to take a few things that would help me survive the winter? I could use the front door, with its metal hinges and working latch. Then there were the two windows, each about two by two feet, with nine panes of glass. These I could use—the shutters as well. While some of the panes of glass in each of the windows were broken, I could repair them into one window for my cabin. But if I took all these materials, I would leave the dead man's skeleton vulnerable to the wolves and other animals. That I couldn't do.

After wrestling with the moral implications of all this, I gathered my composure and decided I could use the items from his cabin. But first he deserved to have a decent burial. So I made up my mind to bury him in the old bear pelt that had been his shroud for all these years.

The ground was hard and rocky, but I managed to dig a shallow grave close to the cabin, using one of the rusty shovels from the mineshaft. Then I rolled him off the bed frame onto the pelt, which I dragged to the gravesite. Before rolling him into the hole, I went back inside the cabin. I wanted to find something, anything that might tell me more about this man. Some type of marker would have to be made, and I wanted to say something about him over his grave.

Under his bed frame was a pile of rotting clothes. Taking my rifle barrel I peeled back a few layers. There, under his clothes, I discovered a small metal box. It was about three inches thick by ten inches long and ten inches wide. I carried it outside into the sun to see what treasures this old miner might have left.

Sitting down on a nearby rock, I pried off the box's rusty tin cover. Inside, I found an old, dog-eared Bible; a gray journal; an ink pen with a bottle of dried up ink; some old, faded pictures; and a long, cowhide pouch. The poke was full of what looked to be gold dust and nuggets. For a moment, the sight of what I thought to be gold brought back memories of grandfather's mission and its outcome. That thought sent chills down my spine. History would not repeat itself!

Thumbing through the Bible, I found an inscription: To my loving husband, Lars. May God always keep you safe, Love, Nelly, June 12, 1923.

Fanning the pages of the Bible, I looked for any other notes but found none. Next, I turned my attention to the journal, where I found three letters stuck between the pages. All were postmarked from Seattle, with dates from April and May of 1929. They were addressed, in fine, delicate handwriting, to Lars Larson, c/o Northern Mining Supply, Vancouver, B.C.

The journal itself was about half complete and looked to be some kind of diary. Before each notation there were dates, starting in April of 1929, with the last date of entry February 14, 1930. The handwriting was difficult to read, and on some pages the ink had smeared, making it even more laborious to understand.

Gently, I returned all of the items to the tin, then snapped the lid back into place. Now, at least, I knew his name and the rough date of his death.

Late that afternoon, I finished burying Lars and said a few words on his behalf. That evening, I camped close to the shack and carved a rough wooden marker with my pocketknife. It simply read: Lars Larson, loving husband to Nelly. Died February 1930. The next morning, I nailed it to a stake and placed it at the head of his grave. Reinforcing the stake with a pile of small rocks, I said goodbye to the old miner.

Finding the mine and the skeleton of Lars had given me the creeps, and I wanted to return to my camp as quickly as possible. With my hatchet and some old rusty tools I'd found, I soon had the door and its hardware, as well as the windows and shutters off the old shack. Making several trips, I carried these materials and the two kegs of nails down to the lakeshore. Then, returning to the bluff, I made one last search for any other items that I might salvage. There was a rifle, but, like the revolver, it was rusty and beyond repair, and I couldn't find any shells for it. There were two more kerosene lamps in the shack, both empty of fuel. But I did find a white porcelain bedpan under a pile of Lars's rotting clothes, which I added to my backpack. All the other items in and around his cabin were in rusty or rotten condition. There seemed to be nothing else useful to me on the bluff. Saddling Blaze and placing Lars's metal tin in my saddlebag, I moved to the trail that led down to the lake. As I twisted in my saddle, I looked back for the last time at this mysterious bluff of gold and death, and realized that I was glad to be free of it.

Down on the shoreline, I cut some alder limbs and made an Indian skid for Blaze. On the skid, I placed the old door, the windows, the shutters, and the two wooden kegs. After lashing these items down with my rope, I attached the skid to Blaze.

Pulling the sled made for slow going on our return trip. It wasn't until late on the third day that we finally arrived back at our encampment. While I hadn't found a suitable place to release the mules, I'd found treasures to make my stay better. Quickly I went to work on finishing my cabin. First, I installed the rock floor, which turned out a little bumpy and cold but which was, for the most part, secure and sound. Next, I moved my belongings in from the tent. It was a pleasure to be sleeping inside a house again.

The door that I'd dragged from the shack was a few inches smaller than my opening. To fix that problem, I shimmed planks inside the opening and then hung the door by driving spikes through the hinges and planks into the wall's logs. It was a heavy, sturdy door that could latch closed tightly. Next to it, I cut a hole for a window. This, too, I shimmed with planks cut to the correct size.

The windows from the old shack had loose panes of glass, since the putty holding them in place was old and brittle. Selecting one window frame to use, I removed all its glass. Then I cleaned away all the old putty from the fame. Next, I removed only the unbroken glass from the second window. Taking some of the old putty, I warmed it near my fire to make it soft and pliable. To this, I added tree pitch, and then worked the mix with my hands. Using this new mixture, I set and secured nine unbroken panes of glass into the first window frame. Letting it set up overnight, I then installed the window into my opening the following day. Knowing the shutters would come in handy, I hung one on the outside and one on the inside of the cabin.

With the door, window, and shutters in place, my little home was now totally protected from the elements. During the day, the little window let just enough light inside the cabin for me to see, while at night, the light from my fireplace and candles provided the needed illumination. Next to the fireplace and close to the root cellar door, I'd placed my table for food preparation. On the other side of the fireplace was half a cord of firewood. At the other end of the room was my wooden bed frame and, across from it, under the window, my second table, which I used for eating. My single chair was placed in front of the fireplace, and I planned to make a larger, more comfortable chair in the near future. The firebox in my fireplace was almost five feet wide and five feet high. There was a stone oven at the base of one side of the firebox, upon which I could burn logs for needed heat. On the other side of the box was my grill, which was held up off the base with rocks. Here I'd build small cooking fires for frying, grilling, and making coffee. Above this surface, I'd placed two large log spikes into each side of the firebox, one two feet up, the other three feet up. These could hold my cooking pots—the ones I'd use for making soups and stews and for warming water—away from the fire itself.

All in all, I was pleased with myself for the way I had planned and built all the essentials of my cabin. It was by no means luxurious, but it was cozy. Here I would live out the long, dark winter.

Mule Valley

A week after moving into the cabin, I found an area where I thought the mules would have a chance to survive. It was a large meadow just below Eucott Lake, on the other side of Nascall Mountain. I'd seen it through my binoculars after Blaze, Gus, and I explored the timberline above Duck Lake. It looked to be a good day's journey, over the mountainside and then down to a lake and meadow. The afternoon before we left, I washed and curried the mules, even pulling out a few carrots from the garden for them to eat. There was not much more I could do for them. Although I was feeling a little guilty, I knew my decision was the right one.

Early the next morning, we were off. I was sure the mules couldn't understand why their backs were bare and they carried nothing, not even their wooden trail bag frames. By early evening, we'd reached Eucott Lake. Here I camped and fished, hobbling Blaze and the mules so they could graze on the rich grass of the meadow. That night, before turning in, I removed the hobbles from the mules' legs and took the bits from their mouths. Giving them a few extra pats on the nose, I spoke to each of them softly. We'd had our difficult moments but, all in all, they'd performed nobly and I thanked them. With a little slap on the rump I told them they were free now. Then I turned in, hoping that, when I awoke the next day, they'd be long gone.

No such luck. The next morning, the mules were still standing where I had released them, the night before. You'd think they were nailed in place. They were indeed as dumb as dirt. After breaking camp, I saddled Blaze and herded the two mules further down the mountain, stopping them in the center of the meadow, close to a spring creek. Dismounting, I went over to them, placing my face against theirs as I'd done so many times, and said, "Look, it's up to you now. If you survive the first winter, you'll be okay. Please try to use the brains God gave you. Stay away from the other animals, especially the wolves. Don't be so stupid."

Walking away, I had tears in my eyes and a knot in my throat. As I walked back to Blaze, I turned again and said, "Thanks, Harry. Thanks, Harriet. Without you two, I never would've made it this far. You'll be in my thoughts this winter. Good luck!"

Then I mounted Blaze and rode out of the meadow and up the mountain. A few hours later, just before leaving the sight of the distant clearing, I looked back with my binoculars, and there stood the two mules, still grazing next to the little spring creek, right where I'd left them. Shaking my head, I thought, *who am I trying to kid? Those two will be lucky if they live out the week.* And I rode on.

As we made our way down to Duck Lake, I rode through a small clearing. There, growing on small bushes was a field of wild huckleberries. It was early September and many of the blackberry bushes were about to ripen, but this was the first field of ripe huckleberries I'd seen. From the saddle, I reached down to taste a few. They were dark purple, almost black, and they were succulent and juicy. They were a real treat, and I decided to stop and pick some for my larder.

Swinging off Blaze, I removed his feedbag from the saddlebags. While I picked, I ate my fill of the little wild berries, even throwing a few handfuls to Gus, which he seemed to enjoy. It was a treat to be eating fresh fruit again. Within a half hour, the feedbag was full, and we rode on.

It was dusk as we approached our encampment. Gus had run off, looking for his dinner, so it was just Blaze and me slowly riding towards the stable. There was a breeze in my face and I could smell the saltwater from the channel... and then I noticed it, over in the garden. The young deer was so busy eating my plants that it hadn't heard or seen me.

I'd been true to the deal I'd made with myself, and hadn't killed a large animal since the elk. But now, with autumn coming on and fresh vegetables from the garden to make stews, it was time to break my deal. From atop Blaze, I slipped the rifle from my saddle and silently cocking it, took careful aim.

The deer never knew what hit him—it was a clean kill. He was a buck, about two or three years old, and he'd dress out to about half the weight of the elk. This time, I didn't have the same emotional reaction as I'd had with the elk; this was now part of my survival. It was now time for me to start thinking with my head—not my heart. As before, I gutted the animal, taking only what I knew I would eat, and then skinned him for his pelt. The remains were taken far from camp.

September was full of final activities in preparation for winter. Cutting about three acres of grass for Blaze, I laid it out in the sun to dry. Every day, I'd roll it over in the sun, to ensure it would dry thoroughly. After drying, I rolled it into bundles and tied them with rawhide. These bales I moved into the stable, stacking them to the ceiling. I had no idea how much grass there was but, other than Blaze's stall, the entire room was full.

Wood was my next concern. I would need lots of firewood over the next eight months. So I cut two cords of wood that I stored in my old tent, another cord that I placed under the dry front porch, and still another that I placed under the overhang of the stable. I figured that I would burn about a cord a month, but I had run out of dry storage, so I'd have to continue chopping wood throughout the winter.

My garden was harvested throughout September. Even though I'd built a fence and a scarecrow, and Gus had been on vigil all summer, we still lost about a third of the garden to wild game. Some of my crops had done well; the potatoes, onions, radishes, tomatoes, and cucumbers were large and firm. The carrots and beans, while small, were plentiful and sweet. The corn, however, was not so lucky. The cobs, for the most part, were tiny, about half the size I had expected. And the peppers and cabbage suffered the most. All were small and in limited quantity. In October, I'd harvest the rutabagas that seemed to be doing well. By the end of my harvest, I knew that if preserved correctly and consumed with diligence, my food supply would be ample.

After harvesting the garden, there were still plenty of chores to do, and I cleaned and repaired the wooden kegs. To protect them from moisture, I placed tree pitch in all of their wooden joints and made sure, with wax and more pitch, that the lids fit snug. I placed some of my vegetables in these kegs for winter storage. One large keg was full of potatoes, the other full of onions. The four smaller kegs, which I had packed in, contained carrots, tomatoes, dried corn, and cucumber pickles. I was also able to fill four empty trail bags with carrots, potatoes, and rutabagas.

For the most part, Blaze and I ate the cabbage as it was harvested. Added to my larder were a dozen pottery jars of blackberry and huckleberry jam and two gallons of berry wine. I also had an assortment of smoked, dried, and salted fish, deer, elk, and duck meat. The remaining supplies I had packed in were noted in my journal entry dated September 30th: 18 pounds of flour (to which I would grind in dried corn to stretch my supply), 4 pounds of sugar, 5 pounds of beans, 10 pounds of rice, 1 pound of baking soda, 1 cake of yeast, 10 pounds of coffee beans, half a gallon of honey, and one 64-ounce can of lemon juice. (I had used the lemon juice in my drinking water during the summer months as my only nutrition from fruit.) During the past four months I had eaten all the other packed-in food supplies. By the end of September, the root cellar was full, and I was confident that we would not starve during the coming winter.

With the first few heavy rainstorms, I knew the rivers would rise, alerting the fall silver salmon out in the Pacific that it was time to spawn. They would swim from Queen Charlotte Sound up the channels, heading for their fresh-water spawning grounds in the many rivers and streams of the area. This would mean that fishing down in the bay could be very productive.

After the second big tempest, I packed up Blaze and, with Gus tagging along, made my way down the old game trail to the bay. Having consulted my tide books, I timed my fishing for an afternoon flood tide. Tying Blaze to some driftwood, I rigged my pole with a large, colorful salmon lure and walked out onto a sandy spit to cast my line into the channel.

While coming down the trail, I had noticed fresh bear droppings, and I found more out on the spit. I had seen these signs before, but to date had not seen a live bear.

Strike. Fish on! Sure enough, within an hour, I had two large silver salmon cleaned and in my saddlebags. That was enough food for now, since I wanted to return to camp before dark. Looking around for Gus, I found him doing one of his favorite things down at the bay—chasing seagulls. Whistling for him, I began walking Blaze up the game trail.

About thirty yards up, the trail made a turn around a large boulder. Just as I approached the turn, a black bear appeared, coming from the opposite direction. At first, we both stopped, startled by each other. Then he started down towards me, slowly raising his body in the air.

He looked to be over six feet tall, and he was looking at me as if I was one of the salmon down in the channel. Moving back while still facing the bear, I backed into Blaze, giving him a hard nudge. But my nudge was too hard, and he turned and ran back down to the bottom of the trail. The bear was only thirty feet from me, still walking towards me and I needed my rifle, but it was in its sheath on my saddle, now at the bottom of the trail.

The bear let out a deafening roar. He was so close to me that I could smell his breath, and it was awful! Then the bear started a charge.

Stepping back as fast as I could, I drew my pistol.

He lunged at me.

Now I was running backwards as fast as I could. With a shaky aim, I fired three rounds at him, but he didn't break stride. There were small pools of blood coming from his chest, but I knew there was little damage, as his fur and fat were just too thick for pistol shots. If anything, I'd only made him madder, and he was still coming at me, picking up speed.

All of a sudden, Red's voice rang in my ears. Remember, Dutch, man can run faster downhill than bears, because a bear's front legs are smaller than its larger hindquarters.

Praying Red was right; I turned and ran down the trail. Racing towards Blaze at the bottom of the trail, I grabbed for the butt of my rifle from the saddle boot, barely snagging it out of the sheath as a petrified Blaze turned to run away again. I spun around to face the bear, and moved, cocked, and fired all in a matter of seconds.

Bam! Bam!

The bear stood straight up, stopped... and then dropped, his large front claws missing my legs by inches as he crashed to the ground. With my whole body shaking, I raised the rifle again. *Bam!* One final shot to his head, just to make sure.

By now, Gus had joined me, and was barking with all his might. Ordering Gus to stay away I took a long piece of driftwood and poked the bear several times to make sure he was dead. He was.

I'd been caught off guard and had never been so frightened. A few more inches and it would have been me lying there, dead on the trail.

After I regained my composure, Blaze and I dragged the dead bear back up the trail to the cabin. This journey took us hours, as the dead bear must've weighed well over 500 pounds. It was almost dark as we made our camp. Again with the help of Blaze, I hoisted the carcass high in a tree behind the cabin, where I'd dress him out the next day. All that night I tossed and turned in bed, replaying the bear attack over and over again in my head. Brushes with death are chilly reminders of the value of life. What could have happened, what should have happened, what did happen? All questions with no answers...I had been very lucky.

The next day, taking only what I thought we could eat or use, I skinned and dressed-out the bear. Later, I found the meat to be stringy, tough, and greasy, so I discarded all but the choicest cuts. While it made for a few meals and I used most of the bear's fat for lard, only the pelt was of any real value. For now, I decided, the bears could eat their fill of the salmon down at the bay. I wouldn't return to the channel until they were in hibernation.

Many evenings, I'd take my coffee and move my single chair to the porch of the cabin. Here, looking out over the lake, with Comet Mountain beyond, I'd roll a cigarette and watch the seasons transform. By the end of September, the colors changed and changed fast. Parts of my view turned yellow and crimson; the grass that was once a rich green turned almost amber. The weather also changed fast, from everyday showers to everyday rain. The once-blue sky had given way to large, gray clouds that shrouded the mountain peaks and treetops. Wind began roaring off the lake, making the trees and bushes bend with a rushing, rustling noise. There was a cool nip of fall in the air. The valley that was once bountiful and full of life now seemed drab and lifeless. What was amazing to me was that all this change occurred over a period of just a few weeks. This shifting of seasons soon turned my attitude sour, as I knew only lonely months lay ahead.

It seemed so strange that only a few short weeks ago, the dog days of summer had been vigorous and fulfilling. Now I could only look forward to months of loneliness and idleness. Soon the days would get shorter and darker, the wind colder and more powerful, and the rain heavier and more constant. My general attitude frightened me. This was only the middle of October and already I feared my future. How could I endure this isolation and the many days of wind, snow and rain before I hiked out to Firvale?

As the days shortened and the rains increased, I found myself held captive more and more in the little room of my cabin. I began making things: shelves for the walls, and a bigger, more comfortable chair that I placed in front of the fireplace. I also made a larger eating table, but soon my list of needs dwindled. Of course, I tended to Blaze each day, but that took only an hour or so, and I'd chop and replace the wood I had burned the day before, but that also only took an hour or less. Having been active all sum-mer, I now gave way to inactivity, napping, restlessness, boredom and the blues. I tried talking to Blaze and Gus, telling them my thoughts, but they could only listen; they could not comprehend my cabin fever. Many nights, I'd sit by the fire and think of Grandfather and Uncle Roy, and curse them both for throwing me into this lonely position. This adventure was indeed a fool's errand, with no rhyme or reason.

CHAPTER SEVEN

Ridge Of Gold and Death

Pacing around the little cabin, I had a long talk with myself. No one else could help me through this despair of stormy weather; I was on my own and I needed to quit feeling sorry for myself. Convinced that activity was the tonic I needed, I decided to stay outside during all the daylight hours, no matter what the conditions. So Blaze, Gus and I rode all over the valley and into the forest to hunt game, fish, and just explore. But with snow now showing on all the surrounding mountain peaks, we kept mostly to the lower elevations. By late October, I was confident that the bears were in hibernation and we even returned to fish and bathe in the bay. But the clamming, crabbing, and fishing in the channel had turned sour. For the most part, I also found the hunting in the valley to be poor. It was now rare to see any game at all, even at long distances. They seemed to have moved on for the winter. Only the lake fishing remained reasonably good. I didn't much mind, though. My cellar was full, and the few fresh fish that I caught from the lake were more than enough for our needs.

During this time, the weather was mostly wet, with showers and rain almost every day. As long as I wore my rain gear, however, it wasn't much of a problem. By early November, though, the big storms started. Lighting would streak across the sky, brighter than flashbulbs, with thunder rolling off the mountains like bowling balls. Then came heavy rains blowing sideways, with winds that raged across the lake. The trees bent low from the force of the gales and made rustling sounds throughout the valley. Sometimes you could hear a loud snap as limbs broke and fell to the ground. The lake itself was covered with waves and white foam as far as I could see. Storms, one right after another, each gaining in strength, finally drove me back into my cabin, even during daylight hours.

My attitude again soured, the isolation was proving unbearable, and I had to erase it with activity. I'd built another new chair, and put the bearskin on the floor in front of the hearth, so I had a warm place to sit and think. In my mind, I'd replay pictures of my childhood, with Grandmother and Hazel baking cookies in that large, warm and loving kitchen back in *Fairview*. But there were also images of my childhood with Grandfather, in that same dingy and cold house. These thoughts I came to dread as dwelling on them, I feared, would only worsen my disposition. That's when I remembered a line from an old movie: *"The best thing to do with bad memories is ride away from them."* This I would try to do.

Gus, too, had come to accept the reality of being house-bound and liked to curl up on the bear hide in front of the fire. Many times, warming myself by the fireside, I'd listen to the rain pounding on the roof, the wind whistling through the trees, and think how lucky I was just being inside. There, in the glow of the fire, I wished I'd brought more books... food for my mind. The two I'd packed in were now used as toilet paper, for they'd been read many times during the summer.

That's when I remembered Lars's tin box and the two books inside. Removing the container from my knapsack, I opened it for a second time. First, there was the Bible, which I'd never read. As I thumbed through it, I recalled how Grandmother used to read to me from the Bible when I was young. That thought recalled good times when the Bible stories would keep my attention for hours. It was as if I could hear her soft, loving voice again. Taking the book in hand, I decided to tackle a few pages each day until I'd finished it. Then there was his journal, with its letters and faded pictures. If I could decipher his handwriting, I might learn more about what had happened up at the mine. If I succeeded, I'd translate a summary of the entries into my journal. It would be a big project, and it would help keep my mind engaged during the long winter.

Reaching into the tin box, I gently fingered the faded pictures. I wondered if the couple holding the little baby was Lars and Nelly. There were two other pictures, both of the same young lady. Surely this must be Nelly. She was an attractive woman in her middle twenties, wearing a plain but smart-looking dress. I was curious about her and the baby, and what happened to them after Lars' death? Did she even know he was dead and how he died? What had brought Lars up here, and why had his body been left in this wilderness for over a decade? That's how it all started.

April 12, 1929

Hank and I arrived here in Vancouver this afternoon. I already miss Nelly, who saw us off in Seattle only a few short hours ago. She is so sweet and dear to me. How lucky I am to have her as my wife. The people from the Northern Mining and Supply Company met us at the station and assured us that our needs could be filled within a few weeks. They referred us to a local boat builder who will build our raft in such a way that it can handle our supplies and equipment and still be transported by rail to our launching point up north.

April 14, 1929

Today we approved the final plans, and work started on our steam engine and rock crusher. The final design is just a scaled-down version of the company's standard models but will be half their standard weight. They will have all work completed by May 10. Today we also began buying the building materials and dry goods we'll need for our trip. For both speed and convenience, we'll build our cabin out of metal sheets. This plan will free us from the time needed to harvest and build a log cabin. Everything we are planning is targeted around our desire to mine as much gold as possible in our short stay up north.

Last year, when Hank and I prospected the Nascall River and Lake, we traveled mostly by canoe. From that experience, we realized that good weather will only last until the middle of September, so we want to spend as much time as possible mining. In that summer of 28, we'd searched for gold in nearly every stream and creek downriver, taking us 2 months to travel the fifty-five miles from Mills Logging Camp to the Nascall Lake. By July, we'd become disgruntled, as we'd found little gold and no promising sites. Then we stumbled on the little creek from a horseshoe falls, where we panned half a dozen nuggets. Up at the top of the falls, we found a large rocky bluff and more gold. Hank and I spent the next month digging ore samples from the surrounding area to determine the position of our first mineshaft. In the last 2 months of our stay, we were able to dig out a small fortune of gold, more than enough money for us to grubstake this year's trip. As the weather soured, we abandoned our efforts and back-tracked our journey by walking up the river to Mills Camp. We didn't arrive there until the middle of October. We'd started back way too late in the season, as we had knee-deep snow and hard going all the way upriver. This year, we've made arrangements to be picked up by boat at Nascall Bay on September 15th. This should give us well over four months of mining time. With all the equipment and supplies we'll need being floated in by riverboat, we should have a productive summer. Our goal is to come out with over $25,000 in gold by late fall of this year… Ain't sure we can do it, but we'll give it a try, cuz our families really need the money!

April 20, 1929

Today we made the final arrangements with the Canadian Pacific Railroad. They will transport our equipment, supplies, the raft, and us to Mills Camp, leaving here on May 12th. The boat builder has come up with an ingenious design for our raft. It will be made out of treated logs, strapped together with steel pins and cables. The whole raft will be assembled here in Vancouver and thoroughly tested, then disassembled for shipment and reassembled by us on the banks of the Nascall River. The boat will be 30 feet long but only 10 feet wide, so we can navigate through the narrow gorges of the upper river. At the rear of the raft are two rudder points where we'll use oak oars to steer and propel the craft. We know from last years' experience that it will be a dangerous trip down river, with all the rapids and rocks.

While both Hank and I are apprehensive, we are also eager to go. The engineers at the boat works have ensured us that the raft will hold up to both the river's fury and the weight of our equipment. I hope they are right! It could be another long wet walk out if anything goes wrong.

Received my first letter from Nelly this morning... what a pleasure to hear from her and my little Emma. They are both so sweet. It will be hard for me to be away again, this summer.

The Journal

Even over the loud sounds of the wind and rain, I heard the howls of wolves. They must be close. Soon I'd have to check on Blaze. Laying Lars's journal aside, I got up and placed a log on the fire, where it crackled and spit out hot coals.

It had taken me a couple of days to decipher and transcribe just a few pages from Lars's journal. His entries were painting a clearer picture of himself and what he had been doing up at the mine. For the hundredth time, I looked at the faded pictures and studied the little girl more carefully. This must be his daughter Emma.

Standing by the firelight, I opened and read all three of Nelly's letters. Each was written with a delicate hand and was easy to read. The letters were full of her love for Lars and of what she and Emma had been doing. She talked about their home in Seattle and which friends and neighbors had dropped by since Lars had left. The words were warm and chatty, the product of a family that missed its husband and father. I felt a little uncomfortable reading them, as if in some way I was prying into a stranger's personal life. But the letters did tell me about a family whose members had a deep love and respect for each other, something I had not known since Grandmother died. It was then that I decided that, when I got out of this valley next spring, I'd look up Nelly and Emma and return the contents of the tin box to them. I was certain that, after all these years, they'd given up hope of Lars being alive, but they still would want to know his story.

Adjusting the candle by my chair, I sat down and was once

again consumed in the words of his journal.

May 15, 1929

We arrived here at Mills Camp late yesterday. Some of the local workers helped us unload the equipment and our raft from the flatbed rail car. Today we worked on reassembling the raft and loading the equipment and supplies. As planned, the raft pretty much 'snapped' together with its steel spikes and cables, alongside the river. In the late morning, we launched it into the water and started to load. Planning the load took some doing, as the space was limited, and we didn't want our heavy equipment shifting around as we moved down the rapids. Both the steam engine and the rock crusher were shipped to us in wooden crates, broken down to their smallest parts. The heaviest, the boiler unit, weighed over 200 pounds, so we fastened it with large cables in the center of the raft. All the other equipment crates were fastened around the boiler. On top of these crates, we loaded our other supplies, securing them all with netting and additional steel cables. The load takes up almost the entire space on the deck. We only have a narrow walkway on both sides. In the rear, where we'll steer with the oars, we still have a good view forward, as the load is no more than 5 feet tall.

The river seems to be running lower than last year. We are still hopeful that the narrow gorges downriver will be filled with water, making for an easy passage. I am anxious about the trip, for things have gone too smoothly to this point. Tomorrow, we shove off; may God bless Nelly and Emma and our little voyage.

May 26, 1929

This has been the longest ten days of my life. What a journey down that river! I don't believe I've ever been so scared. The chilling, churning water seemed to boil up from every rock, with the current jerking us up then down, left then right. And the noise from all that rushing water was near deafening. We had to beach the raft three times to make repairs and rescue our load. I don't remember the rapids being so wild or dangerous when we came down the river last year in the canoes. We believe that this year there is not as much water in the river, which made it more severe. In some gorges we were faced with rushing white water for as far as we could see. At one point, the raft dropped over a rapid of turbulent white water more than 20 feet and then straight down another rapid, almost capsizing. It took all the strength that Hank and I could muster just to pilot the raft around the boulders protruding above the white water. On two occasions we broke our oars on the boulders and had to stop to make new ones. Whenever possible, we'd beach the raft and walk downriver to see what was around the next bend. And we were almost always disappointed with what we saw—more white water and more rapids. The weather didn't help, either, as it rained during almost the entire trip. At night, just getting dry and warm became our most important duty. On some days, we didn't shove off until near noon, just so our clothes could completely dry by our fires. Yesterday, we crashed against some rocks with such a hard force that two large logs of the raft split open, breaking their steel pins. Now they are only being held in place by the cables, which are also coming loose. I told Hank that if there was one more mile of this "river from hell," I'd give up. But there wasn't and we didn't. When we finally arrived at the mouth of the lake, the weather and our spirits both improved. The last few miles on the lake were like a boat ride in a city park, smooth and peaceful. Tomorrow we begin unloading our heavy equipment. We've rigged a block and tackle to lift off our load, one crate at a time, to the top of the ravine. We hope to be working in the mine in a couple of days. We also found the canoe that we left behind last fall, in good shape after the winter. It will be used for fishing and hunting, and, more importantly, it will be our ticket out to Nascall Bay this fall.

June 5, 1929

With our cabin completed and the steam engine and crusher reassembled, we've started working in the mine again. It's such a pleasure to have the power of the engine and crusher at our hands. We used the engine hooked up to a band saw to cut the timbers needed to shore up the shaft in the mine. We also built a long wooden sluice and diverted some of the water coming off the mountain. Next to the sluice, we crushed the rocks carried out from the mine, placing the shavings into the water to wash away all but the gold residue. This new method is so much faster and easier than panning the gold, the way we did last year. We've already removed over a pound of dust and nuggets. Hank and I take turns with all the tasks. One day, he digs in the shaft while I carry out the rocks to crush and sluice the ore; the next day, we switch. We do the same with cooking and hunting; he does one, I do the other, and then we trade off again. The area is plentiful with game, so we won't go hungry this summer. The only animals we avoid are the wolves, which seem to roam in many, large packs up here in the woods. With the long daylight hours, we work until we are both totally exhausted, then drop, dead tired, into our beds. In one good day, we both can do the work of any four other miners, and we are proud of it. My only concern now is the 4 long months until I can see my family again.

White Goose

Opening my eyes, I sensed something was wrong.

Rolling over on my little bed, I looked towards the fireplace. In the dim light from the embers of last night's fire, I could see Gus lying on the bearskin. His head was up and cocked to one side, as if he was straining to hear something.

That was it: the silence was deafening. There was nothing to hear. No sound of the wind or rain, not even the rippling from the creek alongside the cabin. The room was totally devoid of all the outdoor noises I'd grown accustomed to. Unzipping my sleeping bag, I dropped my stocking feet to the stone floor. It was cold—not just the floor, but the entire cabin. Most mornings were cold like this, but something still seemed strange about it.

Shuffling to the fireplace, I tossed two logs in and stoked up the embers. It was November 23. Tomorrow was Thanksgiving, so today we'd hunt for a special meal to cook.

As I waited for the fire to jump to life, I noticed that I could see my breath in the cold air. This was new. Gus, now on his feet, had gone to the front door to go out. Pulling on my pants and boots, I went to the door and unlatched it. To my surprise, when I swung the door open, I was greeted with an unusually beautiful site. It was snowing. Large flakes dropped straight from the sky onto a white blanket already a few inches deep. It was coming down so hard that I could see only over to the stable, which was already covered.

Gus also was stunned. He stood there for a few seconds, and then started barking at the falling snowflakes. A desert dog, he had only seen snow once before, at the summit of Thunder Mountain. So he wasn't quite sure what to think now: where had the green-brown valley gone? What was this white stuff blanketing the ground?

Walking off the porch, I reached down and made a snowball and threw it back at Gus as he stood on the porch. When it hit him on the side of his face, he jumped back, licking the snow off with his tongue. Instantly, he got the idea and leapt from the porch into the snow, his nose digging under the thick blanket. Laughing at him, I tossed more snowballs as he explored the snow. He now ran full-speed in a circle with a crazy grin on his face. The snow would be a new experience for Blaze too and I wondered how he'd react.

After dressing for the weather, I gathered my hunting gear and walked across the compound to the barn. Along the way it stopped snowing, and I could see out over the lake to the low-hanging clouds shrouding the treetops. Everything looked fresh and clean; the trees were beautiful, their limbs heavily laden with snow. With my boots crunching through the deep snow, I spotted Gus still playing. He'd found a little brown field mouse trapped on top of the snow, which he chased and barked at. The little brown spot would dart from here to there as fast as it could, but Gus seemed to always get in front of it, snow flying as he pounced. I was sure Gus was just toying with the little fellow, as I'd never seen him kill a mouse.

These events with Gus and the snow lifted my spirits and put a smile on my face. Opening the stable door, I found Blaze standing tall in his stall, ready to go. Quickly, I saddled him and walked him outside, watching the expression on his face. At first, the cold snow around his hoofs seemed to surprise him. He lifted one front leg and shook it. Then he dropped his head down and rubbed his nose across the cold blanket. After that, he lifted his head, gave it a shake, and whinnied loudly. He, too, seemed to be enjoying his first experience with snow.

There were no wild turkeys, this far north, so I hoped to find a stray duck or goose for my Thanksgiving pot. My plan was to ride up to Duck Lake to see if any birds might have stayed on this late in the season.

It started snowing again just as we arrived at the creek that led up the ravine to the lake. With the snow already on the ground, it would be slippery going up the rocks, so I dismounted Blaze. Leading him by the reins, we made our way up the gorge. Gus followed, still biting at the snowflakes. By the time we reached the top of the bluff, the snow was coming down so heavily that I could only see a few feet ahead of me. Soon we made our way around the shore of the small lake to the other side, where we moved under a tall fir tree for protection from the snow. When Gus joined us, he was covered with a layer of snow that flew all over us as he shook it off. Moments later, the snow eased up, and my visibility improved all the way out to the lake. While it was beautiful, with a white collar surrounding its almost black waters, it was also empty of any game.

Soon I remembered two small ponds further up the trail that we'd passed when taking the mules to the meadow. Mounting Blaze again, we moved on. The wind had freshened from the south, and I could feel the temperature falling with the wind chill. If I recalled correctly, it was only a couple of miles up to the ponds. Slowly, we went up the hill on the snow-covered game trail.

The first pond was in a clearing, just below the trail. As we rode by, I could see that it, too, was empty of any game. A half-mile farther up the trail, the second pond was the same, and I turned to go back to Duck Lake.

That's when the snow really started coming down. The wind was blowing it sideways into deep drifts, and the temperature seemed to have dropped another 10 degrees. In a few minutes, the snow was so heavy that I couldn't even see Blaze's bobbing head in front of me. Finally stopping, I dismounted Blaze and started feeling my way along the trail, one treacherous foot step at a time.

The wind was now howling, and I called out for Gus to join me. I heard nothing back but the wind. It was such a whiteout that I became disoriented and didn't know which direction I was moving. Wanting to find a tree for protection, I stumbled around in a general downhill direction for what seemed like a half hour or more. By now, the blowing snow was piling high, with drifts up to my knees. Finally, I bumped into a tree limb that I couldn't even see, causing its snow to pour down on my head. Moving under this branch, I headed towards the tree trunk for shelter.

Immediately, I could see more clearly. The tree was tall and offered good protection. Pulling Blaze closer, I brushed his snow off while we waited for the storm let up. Moving to the outside limbs, I called for Gus, but again the wind was my only answer. I worried about him, knowing that what he had played in, just a few hours ago, could now kill him.

A loud cracking jolted me. As I jumped back, a large branch, heavy with snow, crashed to my feet. As I moved back closer to the trunk of the tree, I heard a kind of huffing and snorting noise. The hair rose on the back of my neck, and I thought, Please God, no wolves.

Peering under the overhanging branches, I found Gus bounding through a snowdrift to join me under the tree. He was covered in white, looking a bit like a ghost dog. Crouching on my haunches, I dusted his fur off and gave him a hug. My worst fear had been avoided.

Just as I stood up again, the whole area under the tree got brighter. It was as if a light bulb had been turned on. All of a sudden, the snow stopped, and the sun shone through intensely. At the edge of the tree, I shook a few branches free of snow so I could see better. Sure enough, there were patches of blue sky, and the sun was now bouncing brightly off the snow.

Returning for Blaze, I led him from under the tree, with Gus following close behind.

We'd moved no more than a few steps when I realized that I was standing not fifty yards from the first pond. And there, sitting in the middle of the water, was a large white bird. My first thought was that it was a swan or a snow-covered goose. Then, looking more carefully, I could see that the head bore the markings of a

Canadian gray goose, while the rest of the body was pure white. An albino goose! I'd read about this type of rare bird in one of my books. The author had stated that the Indians thought the "white goose" was a sign of good fortune. And it was good fortune for me, as it became my Thanksgiving dinner.

Later that evening, I cleaned and dressed the goose, then placed it in my cellar. Finding her feathers light and soft, I replaced the duck feathers I'd been using in my flour-sack pillow. They proved to be a delightful substitute, and I slept like a log.

It was Thanksgiving morning; the weather had warmed somewhat, with about half the snow melted away. My plan was to walk Gus down to the bay to bathe and wash some clothes before starting to cook my Thanksgiving meal. I'd leave Blaze behind because of the previous day's long, hard ride in the deep snow back to camp. He deserved a day of rest.

My menu was set for the afternoon meal: roasted goose, fresh-baked biscuits, baked potato, stewed tomatoes, and blackberry wine. While at the bay, I'd see if I could find any clams for an appetizer. This would be the most complicated meal I'd ever tried to cook in the limited space of my stone fireplace. At best, it would take two hours to roast the goose, an hour and a half for the potato, and three quarters of an hour for the biscuits. All would be cooked in my small rock oven, only two feet wide and deep, and one foot tall. Looking forward to this culinary challenge, I wanted to be back from the bay no later than early afternoon.

It was a slushy walk to the bay. There were many signs in the melting snow that other small wildlife had made the trek earlier. Gus was still enjoying playing in the slippery slush and was far ahead of me, following the scent of the other animals. Looking up the valley, I could see that higher elevations were still frozen, the trees still heavy with snow. It had been the soft breeze off the channel that had warmed up the lake.

Arriving at the bay, I took a stick and began poking under rocks, searching for clams. The channel waters were rough, with waves and whitecaps rolling from shore to shore. The low tide I'd expected had been stalled because of a storm out in the Queen Charlotte Sound; the sky in that direction was dark, almost black. It reminded me of looking out at a faraway black curtain. Behind that curtain, there was more than likely another storm heading my way, so I gave up my search for clams.

Moving to the hot springs, I removed my clothing and slid into the hot, sulfur waters. With the storm coming, I'd only have time for a quick bath; the dirty clothes would have to wait. With a coarse bar of soap, I washed my body, beard, and hair. It had been almost ten days since my last bath, and I watched the water turn brown with my dirt before flowing towards the bay. When I finished my scrub-down, I lay back against a large rock, just to enjoy the hot water. Rain had started, a light drizzle, and the cold drops were a pleasant contrast to the hot water of the pool. My mind relaxed, and I began to wonder, where was I last Thanksgiving? Oh yes, with Norma and Red in New Mexico. She cooked the biggest and best Thanksgiving meal I've ever eaten.

Lying there in the water, almost smelling that meal and hearing those friendly voices around their large, festive table, I wished I were there now.

The year before that, where was I? Grandfather's. That was the day I told him that I was dropping out of college and returning to Alaska. Not a happy day.

My whole body began to tense up with that passing thought. Sitting there for a few more minutes, I let my mind ponder about Uncle Roy and what he might be doing on this day. Then there was Captain Skip and his family; I was sure they would be enjoying this day of celebration. For the most part, my thoughts were of warm and enjoyable times, with family and friends that I deeply missed.

Back at the cabin, I began to cook my solitary Thanksgiving meal. The preparations took about an hour, and then I settled in to wait for the meal to cook. This waiting time reminded me of how lonely I was. To keep busy while the meal cooked, I began making a wind chime out of seashells and fishing line.

Soon, the little room filled with the aromas of cooking goose and onions and baking biscuits. These smells and the distraction of working with my hands seemed, again, to lift my spirits. Then, just before sitting down to eat, I remembered a passage from Lars's Bible that simply said, "In all things give thanks. For this is the will of God in Christ Jesus concerning you." (1 Thessalonians 5:18)

There were many things I had to be thankful for. Not just the food or that I was alive and healthy; there was Gus and Blaze and all the lessons I'd learned in just a few short months. What I had seen from nature: the beauty of the sunrises, the fury of her storms, all the magnificent animals that inhabited this little valley. Yes, this was a Thanksgiving of real thanksgiving.

Tragic End

Gus and I gorged ourselves with a meal made totally from my own efforts. It was not as fancy as some, nor as tasty as others, but it was of my makings, and I was proud of that. After dinner, I hung my wind chime outside on the front pouch. Then, taking a candle, I walked to the stable and gave Blaze raw carrots and potatoes. While brushing him down, I told him my thoughts about being thankful for having faith in my God and faith in myself and of the love I had for him and Gus. He nodded his head a few times as if he understood. He and Gus had become important to my life, and such good listeners to my rambling, forlorn thoughts.

Back at the cabin, I could hear my wind chime dancing to its own soft music in the breeze. Placing a couple of logs on the fire, I sat down and sipped some blackberry wine while reflecting on my day's activities. Gus joined me, curling up in a tight ball on the bearskin, where he fell fast asleep. Soon, I had Lars' journal out and continued working on his story.

July 16, 1929

The work is progressing well. The small gold vein we were following started to peter out, last week, so we started a 2nd shaft. After a few days of working, we again found a vein. Hank knows how to use the explosives; he drills the holes in the rocks, primes the dynamite with blasting caps, and lights the fuse. The whole process scares the hell out of me! I'm lucky he has the knowledge and uses it well. Blowing away the rocks has saved us hundreds of hours of work. We estimate that there is about 20 pounds of gold in our pokes already.

Yesterday we had a violent summer storm blow up from the east. The wind must have been near gale force, as the waves on the lake looked to be over 10 feet high. Our raft was pounded against the shoreline so hard that it broke into pieces. Next year, when we return, we will have to build another, smaller raft for our supplies. Both Hank and I believe that a smaller craft can make it downriver better. Another idea we talked about was to fly in on a floatplane. In any case, somehow, we will return, as this mine looks very promising.

Luckily, we had our canoe stored high up on shore and well secured from the storm. Thank God it suffered no damage, as we plan to row out to the bay in it, come September. We use the canoe all the time to fish and hunt, as it's the best way to get around this isolated wildness.

I have read Nelly's letters a hundred times. I wish there was a way to get a message out to her. I'd tell her how much I miss and love her.

August 22, 1929

Only three more weeks and we will be leaving to meet the boat at the bay. I'm so excited to think that in less than a month I'll be home with Nelly and Emma. She is on my mind almost all day long.

Hank and I now believe that next year we should fly in on a floatplane. We think the plane could hold all the necessary supplies and land us right in front of our mine. The plan is a very attractive idea to me, as I wouldn't like forging that river again on another raft. However, I still have my reservations, as I have never flown before. Which is worse, days of cold white water or hours of panic in a seaplane? Time will tell.

Our pokes grow heavier with dust and nuggets. We should have well over $25,000 by the middle of next month. We are now over 200 yards into our 2nd shaft, although we've been plagued with lots of underground water, which makes the shaft unstable. To overcome this, we've had to cut a lot more timbers to shore up the shaft every five feet or so. It gets a little spooky working that far under the mountain in a dark, wet hole. I'm always relieved to walk outside and bathe my body with the warm rays of sunshine. Hank seems not to mind it at all, but then he's part gopher and a better miner than me. We've become very good friends, as we understand each other's strengths and weakness. This wilderness would be unbearable if you were here alone.

September 14, 1929

The worst has happened! I have been laid up in bed for almost a week. We had a cave-in while positioning some timbers deep in shaft two. Part of the ceiling and a large heavy timber came crashing down on me, breaking my left collarbone and hip. I passed out right after it happened, and Hank had to drag me out of the mine. Thank God he was not hurt in the accident. It's serious, very serious, and painful, so painful that I can hardly write this entry. Hank has done as much as he can for me, but we both know that the left side of my body is mostly broken bones. He put me in bed and made some wooden splints to help relieve the pressure on the broken bones. It's the moving that I can't stand. I have never felt so much pain just sitting up in bed. Hank had to leave today to meet the boat at the bay. We both knew I couldn't make it down to the lake or in the canoe, let alone on a bouncing boat ride up to Prince Rupert. Hank assured me that when he arrives there on the 16th, he will hire a doctor and fly back here in a floatplane to rescue me. If the weather holds, he should be back no later than the 17th or 18th. I trust him; I only hope I can take the pain until he gets back. I told him to take two of my three pokes and, if for any reason something happens, to give it to Nelly. He laughed and told me nothing was going to happen but said that, to ease my mind, he'd take the pokes. When he departed, he looked at me and said, "Look, partner, I can't work this mine without ya. Who else would put up with my cookin'? You're gonna be all right. In a few days, you'll be with your sweet Nelly in some fancy hospital in Prince Rupert."

After he left, I prayed to God that he is right.

September 21, 1929

Something is wrong, desperately wrong. Hank should have been here 2 or 3 days ago. I have been delirious the past day or so, and I passed out from the pain a couple times. Each time, I dreamed that Nelly was coming towards me with her arms open to embrace me, a smile on her face, the wind blowing in her silky hair. Then, just before we touch, I awaken with sweat rolling off my body. I fear I will not hold her again.

This morning when I awoke, I was feeling a little better and strained my ears to hear the sounds of a seaplane. Where could he be? A few hours after he left in the canoe, a storm moved up from the south. I hope he made it safely to the bay, but then, even if he didn't, the boat crew would have come looking for us, as that was our arrangement. He had to have made it to the bay and the boat. So why is he not here?

With the help of a thick stick, I've forced myself to start moving about the shack. Just before Hank left, he shot and dressed out a small deer for me. I have to eat, so there is no alternative but to begin hobbling about the room despite the pain. I have gotten myself to the front door a few times to look out and up at the sky. There are high clouds as far as I can see, but I am sure a seaplane could fly below them and land. Where could he be? I'm not sure I can survive here much longer!

October 15, 1929

It has been a month since Hank departed. I now know for sure that he is dead, as he would have never left me here to die. I cannot imagine what happened to him. My hip and collarbone seem to be better. Either I have less pain now or I've gotten used to it. I can walk a little better but still need the help of a crutch. Since the accident, I'd lost any feeling in my left foot, but that, too, is now mending, as I can feel my toes again.

My only plan now is to wait out the winter and try to walk out next spring. That means surviving here for 6 or 7 months. The weather has been miserable with rain, wind, and some snow. Because of my pain, I haven't had much of an appetite and have lost a lot of weight. But I've begun forcing myself to eat, as I need to regain my strength. I must soon start hunting, as what little food was here is now all but gone. But, my ammunition is dwindling, with only a few shells for the rifle and few more cartridges for my pistol. I must make this ammunition last, or I'll be lost for sure.

Each night, I read from my Bible and recall the wonderful days with Nelly and Emma... The words and these memories are the only comfort I have. The Bible tells me to have faith; the memories of them tell me why I need that faith. Without this reassurance, I would have given up long ago.

December 25, 1929

This nightmare continues. I am beginning to lose any hope of living through this terrifying dream. What a way to spend Christmas, the wind and rain blowing so hard against my shack that it feels as if it will fall down or fly away. It hasn't stopped raining for over 10 days now. The creeks are overflowing, and the lake is flooding its shoreline.

I had to build a set of storm shutters for the inside of the windows. A few nights ago, a pack of hungry wolves attacked me in my cabin. They had followed me into camp after I had killed a raccoon. Yes, I am now eating almost anything I can kill. I have even thought about killing a wolf and eating it, but have not yet brought myself to it. There must have been a dozen or more wolves in the pack, all howling and scratching at the door and walls. But one wolf scared me the most, as he was bigger and stronger than the others. He had ghostly blue eyes and was clearly the leader. They are so bold that, a few times, members of the pack threw themselves against the windows, breaking some of the window glass. Had it not been for the inside shutters, they would've gotten in. The sounds of their howling and their bodies hitting the sides of the cabin are frightening. I would shoot at them, but I don't want to waste what little ammunition I have left. Maybe I'll make wooden spears, just in case.

Tonight, I will read my Bible and pray that the Lord will lead me free from this valley of death… I have fear of the evil and I do want. He now must show me the way. God bless Nelly and Emma on this holiest of all days. God, please help me!

February 14, 1930

The past few weeks have been a living hell. It's been 4 days without any food. I've lost so much weight that I have little or no strength to even scribe these words. Now I realize that, even if I had the grub and could be strong again, I couldn't walk out this spring, cuz I can hardly walk across the room without my crutch. The wolves come almost every night now, clawing and snapping at the door. They sense me as their wounded prey, and they're right. I've only been able to go outside during the daylight hours, which are now only a few hours long. I've tried to hunt with wooden spears but have had no luck. I cannot find dry wood to burn, so I had no alternative but to burn all the furniture in the cabin for heat. The nights are cold, long, and lonely. 2 days ago, while I was trying to hunt, the wolves were so fearless that they tried attacking me in broad daylight. To hold them off, I wounded one with my spear and shot another with my pistol. But I am lost! I have only one bullet left, and I've decided that this last shell I'll use on myself. When living has more pain then dying, there is no other choice. God have mercy on my soul. My only fear now is that, after I'm gone, the wolves will break into the cabin and eat my poor miserable carcass. That possibility terrifies me. So I nailed the door and shutters shut.

I pray that someone will find my dead body and this journal. If so, please give the Bible, gold, and this journal to Nelly Larson so that she might know my fate.

I write this to you, sweet Nelly, and it will be my last… Yesterday is gone and we can't get it back, so move forward from what has happened to me. I have never faltered in my deep love and devotion for you and Emma. You've been in my thoughts and prayers since we said goodbye at the train station in Seattle so long ago. The image of you and Emma, waving and blowing kisses as the train pulled out, has never left my mind. Oh, to touch your golden hair and kiss your sweet lips again. Love is for the lucky few and we have been very lucky. Please forgive me for what I must do. The wolves have come back now… it's time for me to go. Give Emma a hug and a kiss for me. Never tell her what I have done to myself… just what I tried to do for all of us. I love you both… God bless. Lars.

Staring at the flames of my fire, I remembered again what that old trapper had told me back at the Firvale café.

"Get out of there by September, boy; if the weather don't get you, the wolves will."

A cold chill ran up my spine. What a tragic end for Lars, I thought. And the passage about the blue-eyed wolf disturbed me. Was there a whole breed of such animals up here? How long could one wolf live? Was I missing something, something the old trapper had not known or had not told me?

Putting down the last pages of Lars's journal, I felt it was a story with no end. What had happened to Hank, and why had nobody come in search of Lars? One thing was for sure, nothing is more forgiving then time. Somehow, some way, I would search out Nelly and give her Lars's tin and his sad story. Sometimes good news comes wrapped in the same package as bad.

Gus broke my concentration with a jolt. He jumped from a dead sleep to standing in a split second, the fur on his back up, barking wildly. His sudden actions startled me, and I jumped to my feet, too. He must've heard something, but the only sound I could hear was the wind as it whirled around the cabin.

We both walked to the door. He wanted out, and I opened it a crack but blocked his departure with my leg. Through the sliver, I could hear what he'd heard. Mingled with the sounds of the wind and rustling trees were the distant cries of a pack of wolves.

Quickly I closed the door and secured the latch. Placing my back on the door, I slid to a sitting position on the floor. Putting my arms around Gus's neck, I looked him in the face, and said, "It's OK, boy. Lars beat them off, and we will, too, because we have each other."

Sitting there a minute, holding Gus, I thought again about the blue-eyed wolf and what had happened to Lars, up on that ridge of gold and death.

CHAPTER EIGHT

From the Sky

After Thanksgiving, my mood turned gloomy again as the days and weeks became blurred with boredom. The weather remained miserable, with torrential rains almost twenty-four hours a day. The creek beside my cabin had almost reached the top of its banks and was now more like a roaring river. The lake's level was up well over the normal shoreline, which caused flooding in some of the low-lying areas. The overflow of the lake's water that dropped down to the bay was so heavy that most of the hot springs were now fully diluted with cold water. The falls themselves had grown from a gentle flow to a torrent of white water, carrying logs and other debris from the lake down to the bay.

During this time, I spent most of my days cooped up in the cabin. With Lars's story now written in my journal, I turned my attention to drawing rough, pencil sketches on the empty pages of my book. Using some of my written accounts, I drew what I remembered of the scenery and wildlife I'd seen over the past six months. My skills as an artist were limited, but the sketching helped pass the time, and the drawings became a visual record of the last half-year. I also read passages from Lars's old Bible, which was proving to be a difficult book to understand. While its stories were interesting and eventful, the old-world language of the Bible was challenging to me.

Gus and I walked to the bay a few times, to bathe and wash clothes, but it was less successful than before, with the hot springs now filled with the lake's cold, littered run off. To cope with this problem, I began to bathe and wash my clothes in water warmed by my fire, using my largest cooking pot. Many a day, the inside of our little home looked like a Chinese laundry, with wet clothes hanging on ropes that crisscrossed the small room.

The storms seemed to wane around the beginning of the third week of December. For two days, we had no rain, and the sun even darted out from behind the clouds a few times. With the days now no longer than six or seven hours, I split this time between making repairs to the cabin, hunting and chopping wood. On the first nice day, I was fortunate to kill a fat raccoon, which was the first fresh meat I'd eaten since Thanksgiving. While it was gamier than deer or elk, I still found it satisfying. The hot meal of fresh meat reminded me that Christmas was coming soon and that I should make plans for a more extended hunting trip. Deer or elk meat would be a special treat for my Christmas table. With that in mind, I kept a watchful eye on the weather and hoped to go hunting within the next few days.

On the second nice day, I repaired the roof on the stable and cleaned out the soiled straw. Blaze grazed where my garden had been, and Gus was hunting. After finishing my work inside the stable, I turned to chopping wood. Several months ago, I'd set up an area behind the stable to split wood, and then I carried armloads of split logs to the depleted stack on the cabin's front porch. The walk was only a short distance, and I was enjoying the exercise after weeks of forced inactivity.

It was nearly 2:30 in the afternoon, and I was on one of my trips to the porch, my arms loaded with wood and my chin resting on the top of the heavy stack, when I first heard the noise. It was faint at first, but out of place, a low humming not made by anything from Mother Nature. Stopping, I swiveled my body in every direction, trying to discover where it was coming from. But I still couldn't make out what it was. Then it got louder. Turning towards the lake, I decided the sound was coming from behind the narrows at its far end of the lake. The low, hanging clouds were just above the trees, with only the lower portion of Comet Mountain visible.

The noise got louder. Finally, I recognized the sound. It was a plane, trying to fly through the small gap at the narrows.

Then, just above the water, I saw it—a yellow seaplane. It was trying to gain altitude, with its motor sputtering. And it was flying right at me!

Still holding the wood, I was frozen in my footsteps. The plane would rise a few hundred feet, and then drop back down, like a crazy carnival ride. It was struggling for altitude, the noise from its motor almost deafening as it flew directly over me. As I arched my neck, I could see the pilot's face and make out the plane's black numbers under its yellow wings. It was no more than four or five hundred feet off the ground, flying just above the treetops.

Twisting again, I watched it fly in the direction of July Lake. The ravine between Harriet and Blaze Mountains was covered with clouds, and I doubted the plane had the elevation to make it through to the channel on the other side. To keep the plane in view, I dropped my bundle of wood and ran around to the trees behind the cabin. The engine was still sputtering as I watched the plane disappear into the clouds like a ghost. A few seconds later, there was a loud, sickening crash of wood and metal. Then there was silence. Total, awful, silence.

Running to the stable, I grabbed my tack and saddled Blaze, calling for Gus at the top of my lungs. Within moments, I was atop Blaze, riding towards the ravine. Gus, as always, appeared ahead of me, not two hundred yards up the valley. I gave Blaze his head, and we rode hard to the timberline.

By the time we started up the trail towards the lake, it was starting to rain. A half-mile later, the rain turned to snow, heavy, wet snow. Soon, we made our way to the trail alongside July Lake. As we moved down it, at the far end of the lake, through the snow and low hanging clouds, I spotted the crash site.

The plane had broken through some smaller trees on the shoreline and then crashed into a grove of large, dense, fir trees. Upon impact, the right wing had sheared off, and part of the left wing lay almost a hundred yards behind the mangled yellow fuselage. It was almost 4 p.m. when I reached the crash site with twilight fast approaching.

The cockpit, main body, and tail section had come to rest in tree limbs about ten feet off the ground. There was no fire, no sounds, and no signs of life. At first the plane's perch looked rather dicey, and I was concerned that it might fall through the trees at any time, but I had to try to help. Using Blaze as a ladder, I stood on his saddle to reach the handle of the small rear door of the fuselage.

It was jammed and wouldn't open no matter how hard I tried. Sliding back down into the saddle, I moved Blaze forward to what was remained of the wing on the pilot's side. Here, I hoisted myself onto the stub of the wing. Cautiously, I crawled up the wing which seemed thoroughly wedged into the trees and felt stable. Creeping across the mangled metal, I reached the pilot's door and tried the handle.

It, too, seemed stuck, but I kept trying. Through the side window, I could see the pilot's bloody face lying against the front windshield, his eyes open, staring emptily forward. It was a spooky sight, and I tried to keep my gaze off his mangled body. Finally the door opened a crack and, with another powerful pull, I opened it all the way.

The cockpit had a strong smell of liquor and gas fumes. The pilot, wearing a leather flight jacket, was slumped forward, still in his seat belt, with blood covering his lap and the control panel in front of him. Grasping his neck and chin, I felt for a pulse but found none. Reaching down, I unsnapped his seat belt and pushed his limp body over the center console to the empty co-pilot seat. Then, from the open door, I crawled inside the plane over his bloody seat and made my way down a narrow aisle to what looked like four more empty seats.

Thank God, there was no one else on board. Returning forward, I turned to survey the cockpit again and think for a moment about what to do next.

Just then, I heard something. The sound of a faint moan raised the hair on the back of my neck. Crouching low, I moved quickly down the aisle again.

There, in the last seat, I found her. Had she not moaned, I never would've seen her in the darkness of the small cabin. She was under a blanket, the top part of her body well below the windows of the fuselage, slumped into a fetal position. Gently, I reached down and pulled back the top part of the blanket, exposing her face. In the dim light, I could see she was wearing a dark parka with a light fur collar that had dark stains of blood on it. Her hair had matted against her face, her eyes were closed, her forehead bore a large welt, and there was a small trickle of blood coming from her nose. She moaned again but her body didn't move. I had no idea of how serious her wounds might be or if she had any broken bones.

Would it be wise to move her? My answer was the smell of the gas, which seemed to be getting stronger. I'd have to get her out of the plane no matter what her injuries were.

Sitting her up, I pulled her towards me, but she didn't move. Finally, I realized her seat belt was still around her. Reaching down, I unsnapped the belt. She was big—no, she was fat—and I had to fumble around for a few moments to find the clasp. Once it was off, I pulled her limp body out and over her seat, down the short aisle, over the dead pilot's seat, and out the small door.

It took all my strength to do this. Once outside, I laid with her on the broken wing for a moment, trying to catch my breath. The snow felt cold and refreshing on my face; with my heart beating rapidly and, adrenaline racing through my veins.

The lady moaned again, and I knew I had to move on. Gus was below me, barking and running around in the snow. Blaze had not moved from where I'd left him. Sliding the unconscious woman down the mangled wing, I maneuvered her over and into the saddle, then dropped down behind her. As I held her upright, I knew her weight and mine would be a burden to Blaze, but I was confident that he would carry us back to camp.

Without having to say a word or give him any commands, Blaze turned and started down towards the lake. It was totally dark by now, with snow still coming down. I couldn't see much further than Blaze's bobbing head, but he knew the way.

Holding the lady tightly, I could hear that Gus was at the point, breaking a path in front us. Gus and Blaze were in charge now. They would soon lead us back to the warmth and safety of my cabin.

By now, I was wishing I'd brought the blanket she had been wrapped in, as it could have helped keep her warm. My mind was racing a mile a minute. Who was she? What was she doing out here? How bad were her injuries? Did I know enough first aid to be of any help? What if she needed a doctor?

The cold rain on my face snapped my attention back to our journey. We were almost out of the woods, at the timberline, when the snow changed to a cold, damp rain.

Once on the valley floor, Blaze increased his pace to a fast walk, and my mind flashed back to the plane crash. I would have to return and bury the pilot tomorrow, or for sure the wolves would eat his corpse. Had I closed the plane door when I pulled the lady out? And there were also things I could use from the crash site: her blanket, maybe a flashlight, and another first aid kit, whatever else I could find. And maybe, just maybe, the plane's radio might still work and I could call for help.

She moaned again. Looking up, with rain rolling off our drenched bodies, I found that Blaze had brought us to a stop in front of the cabin.

The cabin was dark, nothing more than a black shadow against a dark backdrop. Slipping off Blaze, I eased the woman's body into my outstretched arms. She was heavy as we stumbled towards the murky front door. Unlatching the door with my knee, I carried her into the room and felt my way towards the bed.

The only light inside was coming from the embers still glowing from the morning fire. Laying her on the bed, I went over to the fireplace and threw a handful of kindling onto the embers. As the flames took hold, I added two larger logs. Then, lighting a candle, I returned to her bedside.

Her parka was soaked, her face and hair dripping wet. No matter what her injuries, I had to get her dry and warm first, before hypothermia set in. Unbuttoning her jacket, I propped her up and removed it. Next, I used one of my towels to dry and clean her face and hair. Moving to her wet, cold hands, I noticed a simple wedding band on her left hand.

This was the first time I had looked at her closely. She was young, with a pretty face, fair complexion and golden hair. With her jacket off, I started to search for obvious wounds and soon found a two-inch gash on her right forearm that was still bleeding. For now, I tied a towel around it to stop the bleeding.

As I stood to get the first aid kit, I looked down at her and, in the faint light, suddenly realized that she wasn't fat. She was pregnant!

Moving the candle closer to her body, I checked to make sure. Yes, I was right. This woman was very pregnant. Taking off her boots, I felt her wet pant legs. I thought about removing her pants, sopping wet from the knee down, but decided not to. Retrieving the first aid kit, I returned to the bedside with two more candles that I'd placed in slit-open tin cans. These candles would reflect more light as I worked on her wounds.

During the entire time that I cleaned and sutured her gash, she did not regain consciousness. She moaned a few times when I put antiseptic on the wound, but other than that she seemed lifeless.

By the time I was done, the cabin had warmed and brightened. Spreading a blanket over her, I instructed Gus to stay with her until I returned from putting Blaze in the stable for the night. It had been almost an hour since we'd arrived at the cabin, and that whole time Blaze had stood there, in the pouring-down rain, waiting for me. He'd proven his worth once again, and now needed me to tend to his needs.

Grabbing his reins, I rushed him over to the stable. Removing his saddle and wet blanket, I gave him an extra-large helping of the cut and dried grass, then rubbed him down.

As I brushed him, my mind began to wonder again about the woman in my cabin. Fate had brought her to me, but why? As I ran back through the pouring rain to the cabin, I tried to assure myself that she surely would be rescued in a matter of days, if not hours.

After stripping off my wet clothes and dressing in my other pair of long underwear, I brewed some coffee. Each time I returned to the bedside to check her pulse, I found it to be strong and constant. The dressing I'd put on her arm was still clear of any new blood, my sutures were holding. Running my hands over her arms and legs, I checked to make sure nothing was broken, and she seemed to be all right. Placing a cup of cold water to her lips, I trickled a little into her mouth. Although she didn't drink, her lips made some sipping motions. I guessed that she was in shock, and about all I could do for that was to elevate her legs and keep her warm and dry, which I did.

Having done all I could for her, I returned to the fireplace to heat up some leftover raccoon stew from the night before.

Gus, too, was curious about this person lying in my bed. While I was warming up dinner, he sat by the bed, watching her motionless body. I wondered what his reaction would be when she was conscious, since I was the only human he had ever trusted. I would have to keep a close eye on him.

Gus soon joined me by the fire for his portion of the evening meal. He had his own tin plate, on the floor, close to the hearth. Each evening, I'd share whatever we had in the larder. I'd come to enjoy watching him push around the tin as he licked every morsel.

After we finished our meal, I placed another couple of logs on the fire and sat down in my chair. The sounds of the rain, the crackling fire, and Gus snoring filled the little room. Sitting back and trying to relax, I watched the flames roll up the stone firebox, lost in thoughts about the lady who slept only a few feet from me. Had her unexpected presence broken my Grandfather's codicil? He had been quite clear in his instructions: You will be totally alone for one full year. Knowing Uncle Roy, he would interpret all those covenants to the letter of the will. But then, he would never know, and I figured this woman would be rescued soon, maybe after only a few hours or days. To my mind, the whole incident would be long forgotten before my return to Firvale.

But other people would come to recover the airplane and the pilot's body.

Yes, but that wouldn't be until the weather was better, and that wouldn't happen until late spring. By then, I would be long gone.

I had never seen a dead body in all my life, now in just two months I'd seen two, Lars and now the pilot. Was that an ominous sign...?

Her loud moan snapped my mind back to reality. Quickly, I moved to her bedside. Kneeling down, I took one of her hands into mine. Her face was turned upward, toward the ceiling, her eyes still closed.

She let out another low moan.

Leaning over I gently whispered into her ear, "You're okay, lady, you're okay."

Her eyes slowly opened, blinked a couple of times. She seemed to be trying to focus on the beams of the ceiling. I whispered again. Slowly, she turned her face towards me, trying to focus. As she did, her eyes grew wider and, with fear racing across her face, she let out a bloodcurdling scream and pulled her hand away from mine.

Her loud cry caused Gus to awake and start barking. Her eyes then snapped shut and she passed out again.

Clearly, something had frightened her. Was it the shadows in the room from the firelight? I knelt there for a few more moments, trying to revive her, but with no luck.

Concerned and confused, I thought about trying some cold water again. Moving to the water bucket, I pondered other ways that I might revive her. Deep in thought, I stroked my beard... and that's when it dawned on me. What had frightened her was the sight of me! Pulling out my small mirror, I looked and scared even myself. My face was smudged with dirt, my hair and scruffy beard matted and unkempt. I hadn't shaved or cut my hair for months. When I added to this view the well-worn red long-johns I was wearing and the shadows from the firelight, it was no wonder she had been frightened. She must've thought that I was a deranged mountain man or even a grizzly bear.

Placing water close to the fire, I decided that, before trying to revive her again, I'd clean my face, trim my hair and beard, and change into pants and a shirt.

Soon, I returned to her bedside with one of my candles in the can, and positioned it at the head of the bed so it would throw light on my now clean and clipped face. I also brought a wet washcloth and a tin cup of water. Placing the cool cloth on her forehead, I gently lifted her head with one hand. Then I placed the tin cup of water to her lips as before.

This time, her parched lips parted and she took a small drink. Slowly, her eyes opened again, gazing straight at my scrubbed and smiling face. She blinked a few times, trying to get me into focus. Raising one of her hands, she took the tin cup and drank some more. Then, removing the cup from her mouth, she looked around the cabin and said in a soft weak voice, "Where am I? What is this place?"

Moving the pillow under her head, I replied, "You're okay. This is a cabin in Nascall Valley, in Western British Columbia."

Gaining more strength in her voice, she asked, "What happened? Who are you?"

Pulling the wooden stool over to her bedside and sitting down, I answered, "My name is Dutch, and this is my cabin. You were in a plane crash. I pulled you out of the wreck about five hours ago... but the pilot didn't make it."

Slowly pushing herself up into a half-sitting position, with her back against the log wall, she drank more water until the tin cup was dry.

"The plane," she said slowly. "Yes, I remember. He was trying to land in a channel but couldn't get over some mountains. God, I have a headache. Am I hurt?" Running her hands down to her stomach, she gasped, "My baby."

I quickly replied, "You're okay, lady. The crash knocked you out, and you have a lump on your forehead. You might have a slight concussion. And there's a small gash on your arm. But I cleaned and stitched it close. You and your baby are just fine."

"How did you find us?"

Taking the empty cup from her hand, I walked across the room to refill it.

"You flew right over me. I watched your plane disappear into the clouds, up towards July Lake. Then I saddled my horse and rode up to have a look-see."

Sitting back down on the crude wooden stool, I handed the cup of water to her. She took it and looked around the dimly lit room.

"Where are we again?"

"A cabin in a remote valley in Western B. C."

"My arm feels like it's on fire. What did you do?"

Opening the first aid kit once again, I took out a small bottle. "Here, take a couple of aspirins. It will help the pain. Your arm had a gash that I sewed up. You'll be okay."

She took the pills and lay back in the bed.

"I have hot coffee and stew. Would you like some?"

"I don't know… maybe… I'm so cold," she said, her voice soft and weak.

Returning to the fireplace, I poured a half-cup of coffee and scooped a small portion of stew into a bowl, but by the time I turned back to her, she had slumped back down and was asleep.

Making sure she was covered with two blankets, I returned to my chair in front of the fireplace, where I sipped her coffee and ate her stew. How nice it had been to talk to another human being again. It had been so long. Tomorrow, I'd ask her what was going on in the outside world. Maybe I'd look forward to her short stay, after all.

By now, Gus was again asleep on the bearskin in front of the cracking fire. Pulling my damp coat over my body, I too, was soon asleep.

Unwanted Visitor

Her strong voice woke me up. "Hey, Mister? Mister, could you get me some more water?"

I jumped to my feet, startled to hear another voice in my cabin. It took me a few seconds to realize and remember my guest.

Rubbing my eyes, I looked at my watch; it was a just after 5:00 a.m. Pouring some water into a cup, I handed it to her.

She took a big drink then asked, "Did you say something about stew?"

"Yep, I'll warm some up for you. It will just take a few minutes"

"What kind of stew is it?"

Her question caught me off guard. *Why is she picky?* I thought.

"We eat simple here. Raccoon."

Raising her voice, she asked, "Who eats raccoon stew?"

Turning from the pot by the fire and looking straight at her, I replied, "Hungry people."

Just then, Gus began to bark and growl, moving from the fireplace to the foot of her bed. He, too, had been startled by the abrupt reminder that another person was sharing our cabin.

Our newcomer pulled back into the corner of the bed against the log walls with a terrified expression, looking directly at Gus, and said angrily, "What the hell is that?"

"It's a dog, lady——a dog that doesn't much like people."

"Mister, get that mutt out of here... I don't much like dogs. Please put him outside."

Her request incensed me.

"My name is Dutch, his name is Gus. I care more about him than almost any other living being, so if you feel uncomfortable, I invite you to move outside!" Across the dimly lit room, I glared at her and she knew I was mad. "Look, lady, I did not ask you here. But you are here, the menu is simple, and the dog stays. Any questions?"

A gust of wind filled the trees, shaking the cabin, as the sound of the rain still pounded on the roof. After a long pause, all the while staring at me, she crawled back down under the blankets.

"No," she replied in a soft voice, and then added, "By the way, my name is Laura." With that, she closed her eyes and rolled over towards the cabin wall.

The anger she'd brought out in me, surprised me. It was the first time in months that I'd talked to another human, and I'd lost my temper. My manners were rusty and I'd have to work on them.

Motioning for Gus to leave her bedside and lay down by the fire, I slid back in the hard wooden chair. Pulling my coat up and over my body, I soon dozed again.

The next thing I knew, Gus wanted out. He was whining and pacing up and down in front of the fireplace. As I got to my feet, I sensed I'd been asleep for hours, as my body was aching from the uncomfortable chair.

When I opened the door, Gus bolted past me, eager to go on his morning hunt. It was just daybreak, which made it about 9:00 a.m. It had stopped raining, but a low-hanging overcast blanketed the valley and obscured the view all the way down to the lake. Leaving the door ajar, I opened both the inside and outside shutters on the window. Early morning sunlight now streaked into the little room, showing just how smoky it was.

As I passed by Laura's bed, she began to stir under the blankets. Placing new logs on the fire, I poured water for a fresh pot of coffee. By the time I had the pot tucked in close to the crackling fire, I could hear Laura moving about behind me.

Turning, I found her sitting up, with her legs dangling over the bedside.

There was silence for a few moments and then she said, "Dutch, I'm sorry for what I said about the stew and your dog. Please forgive me. I must have been out of my head."

"Look, I lost my temper. God knows you had one hell of a bad yesterday. I promise my manners will be better today. How's your arm?"

She looked down at the bandage and slowly removed it. To my relief, there were no signs of fresh blood.

"You seem to be a good doctor. Your stitches are straight and tight. Either that or you're a good seamstress."

Looking across at her, I could just make out a small smile on her face.

"Dutch, I…er…have to go to the girls' room. Where would I find that?"

"Girls room? Hmm…I don't have one of those out here, but I do have an old-fashioned outhouse behind the oak grove at the rear of the cabin."

"I'll need my boots."

"Sure," I replied sheepishly.

After putting on her boots, she got up and slowly staggered towards the open door. Rushing over to her, I placed both my hands under her shoulders to steady her.

"Take it easy, Laura. You're still a little shaky. Let me give you a hand."

She looked up at me in the diffused morning light of the open doorway. "Will you show me the way?"

"Sure."

In the soft dawn light, I finally got a really good look at her face. She was young—I guessed in her early twenties with soft features, blond hair and deep blue eyes that seemed full of life even in her traumatized condition.

As we walked around to the rear of cabin and the other side of the oak grove, I noticed other things about her. She was average in height, quick to smile, and carried herself and baby with pride and determination. She was curious about my environment and asked a few questions about both the cabin and the stable as we made our way. By the time we reached the outhouse, she'd regained her balance and was walking on her own. Excusing myself, I told her that breakfast would be ready upon her return to the cabin.

A World Gone Mad

It was a morning meal I will never forget. Over biscuits, salmon jerky, and coffee, Laura told me her story. She sat in the wooden chair in front of the fireplace, her large belly protruding from her small frame. Seated on the hearth, I listened with rapt attention. It was such a pleasure just to hear another person speak and her story was spellbinding.

She'd been born and raised in Ketchikan, Alaska. Then, a few years ago, she'd moved to Seattle to attend nursing school. After graduation, she became an emergency room nurse at a local hospital, St. Mary's. During that time, she met her future husband, Ralph Earl Person. He was a Lieutenant JG in the Navy, newly assigned as a gunny officer aboard a battleship that was being readied for sea duty at a local shipyard. They had a whirlwind two-month courtship that ended in marriage before a Magistrate just forty-eight hours before he shipped out for Hawaii. The honeymoon had been short and romantic, leaving Laura pregnant and her husband thousands of miles away. She lovingly talked about her husband and the many letters, telegrams and occasional Trans Pacific phone calls that had poured in and out from the both of them over the months that followed. Then December 7, 1941, came. The Japanese attacked Pearl Harbor, and she knew from the news accounts that things didn't look good for her loving husband and his beloved battleship, the *USS Arizona.*

By now, Laura was crying, and she continued her story through a sea of tears. Ten days ago, the official telegram had come. Lt. Ralph E. Person had perished in the opening salvos of World War II. She was devastated and lonely and with no family and few friends in Seattle, she decided to return home to have their baby. She knew that she had to choke his death down and get on with life, for her baby's sake. But she couldn't find a way home, as the airlines were full and wouldn't take any passengers without a military priority. The ferryboats had stopped running from Seattle north due to the fear of Japanese submarines. She was beside herself, not knowing what to do.

Then a girlfriend's father, who worked for a Canadian wood products company, made arrangements for her to fly from Vancouver, B.C. to Prince Rupert on a company floatplane. There, she could catch a coastal ferry or fishing boat to Ketchikan. The plane had left yesterday morning, after waiting two days for the weather to clear. The pilot, whose name she could not recall, had spent most of the two-day delay at the airport bar, waiting for weather reports. When they took off, about 9:00 a.m., she expected a six-hour flight to Prince Rupert and then a three-hour ferryboat ride home.

The weather had been clear most of the way but just about an hour out of Prince Rupert, it all changed.

The first misfortune was a blinding bolt of lightning that hit the plane, knocking out the radio and most of the navigational instruments. But the pilot continued towards their destination. Then they ran into a storm coming down from the north. The rain soon turned to sleet and snow, the wings began icing, and the pilot had to turn back south.

They followed the coastline, with the raging storm just behind them, but the engine fuel lines began icing. The pilot flew lower and lower and turned to the east, trying to find warmer weather. His idea was to land on a lake to let the storm pass them by, but the ceiling had been too low and he couldn't find an opening. Finally, he saw a hole in the clouds, with a lake below, so he dropped down at a steep angle, making his way under the ceiling. As they approached the lake, it looked too short for a safe landing, but as he climbed up again, with the motor struggling, he could see a channel just beyond some hills, and he tried to head for the channel waters. The last thing Laura remembered was him saying, "We're gonna make it, lady…. We're gonna make it. Hold on!" Then there was the terrible crash, and everything went black.

By the time she reached the end of her story, Laura was emotionally wrung out. She just sat there in the chair, wiping away tears while gazing into the fire. Watching this troubled woman made my heart almost break, and I bit my lip to keep my emotions in check.

Her sad story had rambled on for almost an hour. My head was swimming from the information she'd told me. We were at war with the Japanese! Pearl Harbor had been bombed, with thousands of men lost. What about the Germans? That's where Grandfather and Uncle Roy had said Mr. Roosevelt's war would be.

My mind kept spinning. The father of this lady's baby was lying dead in one of the largest and most powerful battleships man had ever built. What about her rescue? With the pilot losing radio contact and being so far off-course, who would come looking? Stunned, I began reassessing our predicament.

Laura soon regained some of her composure, and we sat and talked for another hour as I reeled off questions. The time flew, and by the end I knew that after Pearl Harbor, both Germany and Italy had also declared war on America. The whole damn world had gone mad! Also, I learned that it was unlikely that there would be search planes this far south on the first day. From the pilot's last radioed position, rescuers would start their search much further north. With the short daylight hours, it would take a couple of days before—if—they came this far down the coast.

That gave me some time, precious time, to get some items from the plane that could help in her rescue. I told Laura that I had to return to the crash site and bury the pilot, drain some gasoline from the plane for signal fires, and remove anything useful from the plane.

Laura told me that she had only been carrying Christmas gifts for her family, along with one leather suitcase in the luggage compartment. She asked me to bring the suitcase back for her, as it contained warm clothes and personal effects.

At first, she was hesitant about me leaving, asking that I wait a day or two. But I reminded her that time was not on our side and that I needed to return without delay. After making preparations to leave, I had another short conversation with Laura.

"Listen, Laura, before I go, I want you to understand something. This is not Seattle or Ketchikan. We are in the middle of a wilderness. There are wolves and bears and other things that do not appreciate us being here. I have to go, but I want you to be safe." With a small grin, I continued, "Weakness is not an option in my valley. Have you ever used a firearm before?"

She was silent.

"I'm going to leave you my shotgun with two shells in the chamber. You cock it like this, then point it and pull the trigger, pump and pull again. The gun will kick like hell but don't let that scare you. Even if it doesn't kill what you're shooting at, it will get its attention. It's for your protection, and don't hesitate to use it! Do you understand me?"

Sadly she shook her head, "Yes.... How long will you be gone?"

"I only have about three hours of daylight left, so shortly after dark. I'd leave Gus with you, but I'm not sure how he would react. Just stay inside the cabin and keep the door latched. If nature calls, use the bedpan under the bed. Are you going to be okay?"

She slowly nodded her head again, looking resigned if not quite convinced.

The ride back up the valley and through the timberline to July Lake was uneventful. Spurring Blaze, we made good time. The weather was still a gray, low overcast, with a cool breeze blowing up from the south. By the time we reached July Lake, we were in a thick fog of the ghostly overcast.

Making our way around the lake, I found it hard to locate the wreckage due to the poor visibility and dense foliage. Once I did come upon it, the plane looked smaller than I remembered from just the day before. The right pontoon had sheared off and was nowhere in sight. Only the left float held the plane upright in the trees. Standing on Blaze, I tried again to jerk open the rear cargo door, using an iron bar I'd brought for leverage.

Within a few moments, I had the door open. Looking in the luggage compartment, I found two canvas bags full of mail and papers for the wood products company. After going through each bag, I took only a thick catalog for reading and fire-starting. Searching further, I found Laura's suitcase and threw it down to the forest floor. Then there were two large shopping bags that had wrapped Christmas gifts inside. Shaking each package, I tried to determine the contents. I should have asked Laura what they were; they might be food or clothing that we could use. Should I open them here or take them back? Deciding to take both sacks back, I hung them on Blaze's saddle horn and, returned to the plane.

Again, I crawled through the narrow passenger compartment, searching for whatever else of value I could find. In and around the seats, I found three small, woolen blankets and an emergency flight kit. It contained a parachute, a flare gun with three flares, a canvas tarp with metal grommets, and a small first aid kit. I reasoned that I could use the parachute as a visual marker and the flares to start a signal fire. I stuffed all these items into my empty backpack.

The inside of the plane was dark and dank. It was spooky, much like Lars's mineshaft. As I made my way to the cockpit, I saw again the dead pilot's body, flopped over in the co-pilot's seat, just as I'd left him the day before. Looking at him now, I noticed the top of a bottle protruding from a pocket of his leather flight jacket.

It was a pint of brandy, half empty. With two fingers, I slipped it from his pocket into mine. Being pleased and surprised that the wolves hadn't found his dead body, I quickly made preparations to move him out of the wreck.

Extricating him from the wreckage proved to be quite a project. His dead weight had to be well over 200 pounds. Pushing and pulling, I slowly inched his body out of the cockpit and slid him down the wing stub. A couple of times, his stiff body fell on top of mine. His wide-open eyes seemed to be glaring at me, sending chills down my spine. The sooner I got him buried, the better.

I'd brought a pick and shovel, and I began digging a grave not twenty feet from the wreck. The ground was hard, full of rocks and tree roots. It took about an hour's worth of digging to make a small, shallow grave. Just before I put the pilot into the ground, I bent over and closed his eyes; his skin was tight and ice-cold to the touch.

Although I didn't like doing it, I removed his leather flight jacket and his wristwatch—which, to my surprise, I found still working—and placed them in my pack. He would have no further use for these items, and I had to plan for the worst. Next, I went through all his pockets, looking for any information about him. The only clue I found was his wallet, which contained his pilot's license and twenty-two Canadian dollars. The license said his name was Henry Woolridge. I placed his wallet and money in my pocket.

After dragging his body to the hole, I said a few brief words to the Lord about Henry and the way he died. Then, after filling the grave with dirt, I stacked a pile of rocks on top. Henry would now be secure from the wolves and other varmints.

My final task was to drain some gas from the engine to start a signal fire. I'd brought an empty gallon honey tin to collect the fuel. It took almost a half hour to find a fuel line that still had gas in it. Even then, there was only enough to fill the tin two-thirds full.

Just before leaving the site, I went back into the cockpit to have a try at the radio. Sitting there in Henry's seat, which was covered with dried blood, I tried every switch and lever on the dashboard, but to no avail.

Then just as I was about to pull myself up and out of the plane, I noticed it. Showing half under the co-pilot's seat was a long, small, cylindrical object. A flashlight. Pulling it out from under the seat, I switched it on. Sure enough, it worked, putting out such a bright light that it illuminated the entire cabin of the plane. It was an exciting find, since it could be very useful in a variety of ways.

Knowing that Laura would be worried about me, I left the plane, hastily packing all my found treasures into my backpack and empty trail bag, which I tied it to Blaze's saddle, and headed for home in near-total darkness.

Just like the night before, Gus and Blaze managed to find our way back. We had been lucky today, with no rain, and there had been no sounds of search planes. At first light tomorrow, I'd prepare logs for a signal fire and place the parachute out on the valley floor. Then, with any luck, it would be only a matter of time.

My mind kept rushing with thoughts, some connected, others just rambling. "Should I tell Uncle Roy about the plane crash and Laura? It's only going to be for a few days. He'll understand that it wasn't my fault.... But what if it's not just a few days, then what? Who cares? The whole world is burning and I'm stuck out here in this God forsaken wilderness with a pregnant lady! I wonder when the baby is due. How much time do I have? I never even thought to ask. I should've kept the mules—at least we might have been able to ride them out.... No, don't worry, the search planes will come."

It was almost 6 o'clock by the time I reached the cabin. I could see light coming from the window, because the storm shutters were still open. "Damn, I should have closed those before I had left." Hopping off Blaze, I untied the trail bag and hurried towards the cabin. As I walked up, I shouted, "Laura, it's just me. Don't shoot. Are you all right?"

Unlatching the door, I swung it open.

There was a smell in the air, a good smell. And the cabin looked different, with things moved about. It seemed cleaner, better kept. Laura was standing by the fireplace, the shotgun leaning against the firewood. She turned, and in the dim light I could see a faint smile on her face.

"Dutch, you're back. I was getting worried."

"What are you doing? Is that food I smell?"

Grinning, she told me that she'd taken some rice, onions, and dried fish from the food cellar and was trying to cook a Chinese dish she knew. But, with my limited supplies and primitive cook stove, she was giving me no guarantees. As she continued to work by the fire, she asked about my day and told me that dinner would be ready soon.

Placing the bags and backpack on the bed, I told her the short version of what I'd found and done up at the crash site. Then, excusing myself, I explained that I had to tend to Blaze and would return shortly.

This was exciting. A meal cooked by someone other than myself. My mouth was watering at the thought of such an unexpected treat. I tended to Blaze in a fraction of my normal time, called out for Gus, and walked back through the front door in just a half hour.

Laura had set the table and had a candle burning in the center. She had changed her clothes, as well, and was now wearing a dark wool sweater over a loose white dress. Removing a pot of hot water from the fire, she told me to wash up in the corner of the cabin. There she'd laid out a bar of real soap, not the abrasive type that I'd packed in, a towel and pan of hot water.

Using soap that smelled like spring flowers, I was wet, clean, and in heaven. As I rubbed the trail off my hands and face, I watched Gus move towards Laura, as she worked by the fire. At first, he just sniffed her, while she paid him no attention. She then reached over to the stack of firewood where she'd placed his dinner tin full of warm rice and fish. Placing the tin plate on the floor, she did not even look at him.

He approached the food and took a good sniff. Then, he looked up at me and then back to Laura. This was the moment of truth. Would he take food given to him by a person other than me?

He turned away, then turned again and looked at me. Wiping my face, I pretended not to notice his concern. He paused a moment more and sniffed his food again. He then gave in and began eating, slowly at first and then with gusto.

Soon his plate was empty as he banged it around the floor. Gus had a new friend! Joining her at the table, I told her I'd never expected to see such a sight. Either she was a good cook or Gus was getting soft.

Her Chinese dinner was the best. It had flavors and tastes that I'd never experienced. We sat there, enjoying our meal and talking of my plans for a signal fire and other preparations for her rescue. She talked about her day of discovery around the cabin and her plans for a meal for Gus and me. She also commented about the provisions down in the cellar.

"Did you grow or hunt all your supplies down there?"

Looking at her in the light of only fire and candle, I found her voice and facial features soft and attractive. This vision of her seemed so out of place for this wilderness. Was this really happening?

With pride, I replied, "Yes, it was a short but productive summer. I only hope the food lasts until the snows melt."

All through our meal, I kept commenting on her fabulous dinner. Eating all that remained, I could have eaten more. How did she do this? Was I just such a bad cook that I don't know how to make my food taste this good?

Finally, after she had cleared the dishes and poured us both some coffee, she said, "Dutch, I have a confession to make. Remember those Christmas gifts you brought down from the plane?"

"Yes."

"Well, one of them was for my mother, and it's a small rack full of spices. When you first walked in tonight, what I was cooking didn't taste anything like this meal. I doctored it up while you were out in the barn."

A broad smile crossed my face as I replied, "Well, lady, whatever you did, it was worth it. That was the best white rice makings I've ever had."

At that, we both laughed.

As we began talking again, she started asking me questions. She wanted to know what I was doing out in this wilderness, when I had come in and when I would go out. I told her my story—well, most of it. I left out the parts about Grandfather's bequest and the true reason I had consented to this mission. Instead, I painted the picture with broad strokes, giving her the impression that I'd been a willing participant in the family tradition, not mentioning the gold and oil that both Grandfather and Father had found on their journeys. Without appearing mysterious, I talked around the subject as best I could. Also, I didn't tell her about my resentment for my dead grandfather. To her, I talked only of the challenges of survival.

After listening to me ramble for almost a half-hour, she finally remarked, "Dutch, this mission stuff sounds a little silly to me. I'd think a young man such as you, could find a more productive way of spending a year."

"Yes, I would have to agree with you."

She got up from the table and moved to the bed, where she knelt down and pulled the trail bag out from underneath. From it, she removed a Christmas package wrapped with red and green paper. Returning, she handed the package to me and said, "But if you had found a more productive way to spend a year, I wouldn't be alive. This was for my father. I know he would want you to have it. Please open it."

Taking it, I felt embarrassed and said, "Maybe you should keep it. You might be home for Christmas."

But she shook her head no, so I opened the package. Inside I found a bottle of twelve-year-old Scotch. Looking away from Laura, filled with emotion, I moved from the table to the fireplace mantle, where I placed the bottle.

"I'll save this to celebrate when you are rescued," I told her. "Then you can thank your father for me." Pausing a moment, I placed a couple logs on the fire, then continued, "You talked about your father, and being raised in Ketchikan... do you happen to know the family of Skip Patterson?"

When I turned from the fire to look directly at Laura, even in the darken light of the cabin I could see a surprised look on her face. There was silence for a minute or so. Then, just as I was ready to repeat myself, Laura answered, "That's his Scotch I just gave you. How do you know my dad?"

Now it was my turn to be silent. Was this just a crazy coincidence or fate? After a few moments, with Laura still staring at me, I replied, "Well, I worked for him on the *Pacific Lady* for about three years. It was your father who told me about this valley. If it hadn't been for what he told me, I would've spent my year in another location. My God, Laura. You're Captain Skip's daughter? I can't believe it!"

We were both choked with emotion. Laura dropped down in the chair in front of the fire and stared at the flames for a moment, then slowly turned towards me and said, "I'm not sure I ever really believed in divine guidance before this evening, but now I'm a true believer."

We spent the next two hours talking about that wisdom and about Laura's family. She wanted to hear details about the years I'd worked for her father. In the end, Laura remembered the time I came for dinner, that first summer that I worked on the *Pacific Lady*. That was about the time she left for Seattle and nursing school. I remembered the dinner, too... but mostly because of the food. Laura and her sister were no more than a cloudy memory.

Rescue

The next morning, I was up early, well before sunrise. I'd slept in the hard chair now for two nights, and it was taking its toll. My whole body was sore from the wooden slats. This will be the last night for that kind of torture, I told myself.

After fueling the fire and preparing the coffee, I made my way to the front door before Laura even stirred in bed. Taking the backpack, I pulled the canvas tarp from the plane's emergency kit and went to the stable.

The morning was still pitch black, with a fresh, cold breeze out of the south, but no rain. In the stable, I lit a candle and went to work, stringing rope through the metal grommets at each end of the tarp. Inside this web, I slid an oak stick. When finished, I had a hammock that I could fasten to the log walls of the cabin above the small eating table. Tonight, I thought, I'll get a good night's sleep.

By the time I'd finished the hammock and cleaned out Blaze's stall, the first signs of daylight were beckoning. Behind the stable, I got busy chopping green logs and moving small pieces of wood to an area about two hundred feet in front of the cabin. After a few loads, I chopped longer pieces and then even longer pieces.

By the time I finished, I'd laid the wood for a bonfire about five feet high and ten feet wide. Next to this, I positioned the open white parachute, anchoring the silk fabric down with stones from the creek. The chute itself was fifty feet across, so I put large rocks every few feet to keep it out the wind. Then returning to the cabin, I went inside to retrieve the flares and gasoline.

To my surprise, Laura was still in bed. Rolling over toward me as I entered the room, she softly said, "Dutch, please don't think me lazy. I just don't feel too great this morning. Maybe it's all beginning to catch up with me."

"Is your arm all right? Was it the food from last night?"

"I think it's more mental than physical. It's been a very bad few weeks. But I'll be all right, so don't worry about it."

At the fireplace, I poured myself a cup of coffee and turned to her to ask the question I'd been avoiding. "Laura, when is your baby due?"

She pulled herself out of bed and onto her feet before replying, "Second or third week of January. At least that's my best guess."

"Guess? That's not very encouraging. This is no place to have a baby!"

She laughed as she joined me in front of the fireplace for a cup of coffee.

"Look, Dutch, don't worry about it. You said yourself that I'd be out of here in the next few days."

Smiling at her, I hurriedly swallowed my coffee, and then moved towards the door with the flares and gas. "Yes, and I'm ready. Today or tomorrow, there's bound to be a plane up there looking for you, and they'll see my signal fire."

I spent the next two days, December 22 and 23, sitting on a log next to the stack of firewood, waiting for any sounds of a rescue plane. On the afternoon of the 22nd, I thought I heard a plane, but its sound faded before I could get the fire started. On the second day of my vigil, as I sat on a log with my poncho on, it rained so hard that I felt like a beaver in a pond.

About 4:00 p.m., Laura ran out of the cabin with her parka over her head, shouting over the sounds of the wind and rain for me to return with her inside. Once there, she took off my wet poncho and boots. Directing me to sit by the open fire, she poured a cup of the pilot's brandy for me. Then, after warming herself, she turned from the fire and said, "Listen, Dutch, I know how badly you want me to be rescued, but we were so far off course and the weather here is so bad, I just don't see it happening."

I was stunned by her comments. As I had never doubted she would be rescued. Not knowing what to say, I finally stammered, "Laura you might be right... but you can't stay here. Your baby can't be born in this valley. I'm no doctor, and I don't have enough provisions for us to survive the winter."

She sat down on the hearth, her back to the fire. The flickering red firelight formed a halo abound her head. Rubbing her hands on the sides of her shoulders, she replied, "I know that, but what can we do? Can we walk out? How far is it to the closest town?"

I pointed north and said, "About 55 miles from here, up the lake and the river that feeds it, is a lumber camp. At least, there was one, ten or fifteen years ago. To get there, if it's still there, we would have to cross two snow-covered mountain ranges." Next, I pointed south. "And this way, as the crow flies another 50 miles or so, is the little hamlet of Firvale. But since we're not crows, it's a daunting trip, some ninety miles over Comet and Thunder Mountains. That's the way I came in. It was still snowing up there in late May. I hate to imagine what it's like now."

She stared at me for the longest while and eventually said, "Well, Dutch, I put my life in your hands once before, and it turned out all right. Now I'm putting my baby's life in your hands. I know it will turn out okay. God has his own destiny for us."

"Thanks. I wish I could say that makes me feel better, but it doesn't."

We spent the rest of the evening talking about options for rescue and plans for our survival.

Christmas

I rolled out of my hammock on the morning of December 24th to the sound of Laura throwing up in the bedpan. Knowing this meant trouble, I took a cup of water and a towel to her, which she gratefully accepted.

By the time I'd stoked the fire and heated the remains of last night's coffee, she was up and dressed. Taking the flashlight and pistol, she made her way to the outhouse. The weather was still overcast, with a light rain. When she returned, we ate some biscuits and elk jerky. Leafing through the tide book, I told her that there was a minus tide at 11:00 a.m. and that I would try my luck for some seafood down at the bay. Asking her to stay in the cabin, I told her to keep an ear open, in case the weather improved and she happened to hear any sounds of rescue planes.

She agreed, then asked, "Tonight's Christmas Eve. What do you want me to fix for supper?"

Looking carefully at her, I noticed she was tired and didn't look well, but I knew how much she wanted to contribute. I replied in a positive voice, "Bake some fresh biscuits, if you feel up to it. With any luck, I'll provide the main meal. Are you okay? Do you want me to stay here today?"

Trying to give reassurance, she replied, "No, you go on about your business. I'll be all right, I just need some rest. But I'll keep an ear open, so don't worry."

By 10 o'clock, Blaze, Gus, and I arrived at the bay. The rain had stopped, and the overcast had lifted to the tops of the surrounding mountains. I was surprised to find the waterfall from the lakes about half the size it had been just a few days ago. While there was still a lot of debris in and around most of the pools of hot water, there were a couple of ponds almost clear enough to use. Tempted to sit and soak for a while, I thought better of it with Laura alone back at the cabin. Soon, I'd tell her about the hot springs, and maybe we could use them in the next few days.

Removing the crab trap from Blaze's back, I made my way down to the shoreline. Needing bait to fill the trap, I thought, with this tide, maybe I could hook a fish and then use its head for my bait.

But then, kicking rocks on the shoreline, I began finding blue neck clams. These were the same kind I'd found over at Eucott Bay last summer but had never seen here before. Quickly, I dug up two of the large clams, removed them from their shells, and placed them into the crab trap as bait. With a mighty heave, I tossed the trap out into the bay as far as I could. Securing my end of the line up the shore, I would wait for the incoming tide.

During this wait, I dug another blue neck and rigged up my fishing pole. Using some small pieces of the clam neck as bait, I cast my line out into the channel. It was a good day as Neptune was smiling on us. I hadn't had this much luck at the bay since late summer. Within two hours, I'd caught two small halibut, each about six pounds, half a dozen more clams, and three good-sized crabs. Kneeling by the water's edge and cleaning my catch, I began making plans for the holiday menu. Tonight, we would eat the crab with fresh biscuits. Tomorrow, I'd make seafood stew just like the one that Laura's mother had served me so many years ago. Excited, I couldn't wait to return to the cabin and tell Laura of our good fortune.

Rain started again in earnest as I returned to my little compound in the early afternoon. Putting Blaze in the stable, I gave him a thorough rubdown, along with fresh straw, food and water. With our Christmas dinner catch rolled up in my poncho, Gus and I ran from the stable to the cabin in the pouring rain.

As I unlatched the door and entered the room, I heard Laura cry out softly in pain. Looking around, I spotted her lying on top of the bed, holding her belly.

Glancing up at me, her face anguished, she said, "Dutch. I'm so glad you're back. The baby... I think it's time." And then she moaned.

"Time? What do you mean time?" I replied stupidly. Kneeling beside her, I saw that she was in such pain that her hair was matted from the sweat rolling off her forehead.

Between ragged breaths, she finally replied, "The baby has turned, and my contractions are about twenty minutes apart. This baby is going to be born soon. Very soon."

With rainwater still streaming down my face, I stared at her like the village idiot. She turned her head away from me, and I walked over to the table. My hands were shaking as I took my coat off and laid it on the table with the poncho full of seafood. I had to face what was happening, so I went back to her bedside and tried to be calm.

"You told me the baby wasn't due for another month. Why now?"

"I don't know, Dutch. Maybe it was the shock of the plane crash, or maybe I was wrong. All I know, as a nurse and a woman, is that it's about time."

"What do I do? What can I do? How long do we have?" I demanded, hearing fear in my own voice.

"My water hasn't broken yet, but even after it does, it could be hours. I'll give you instructions and tell you what's going to happen. It's okay. I'm a nurse, and women have been having babies since beginning of time."

"Yeah, sure... but I haven't been there for any of it. What does water breaking have to do with it?" I asked with panic in my voice.

Grabbing my hand, another contraction rolled through her body. When she found some relief, she looked up at me with a sheepish smile and replied, "Weakness is not an option in giving birth."

Over the next few hours, she explained in great detail what I should do and what I should expect during the delivery. Most of what she told me I found embarrassing and it all sounded a little hideous to me. By comparison, the memory of gutting my first elk now seemed like a walk in a park.

Laura had taken off her clothes and retreated under a single blanket. She asked me to clean and boil the poncho to make it as sterile as possible. She wanted me to place it under her lower body so that, when her water broke, the fluids wouldn't damage the elk skin and bedding.

I began boiling water. Lots of hot water would be needed, and I'd need as many towels as I had, but they were all dirty. So I got busy and washed them in one of the pots of water, then hung them up to dry by the fire. And light—I would need as much light as possible, so I positioned my candle cans and flashlight at the foot of her bed. But, for the most part, I just sat next to Laura as the pain of the contractions continued to surge through her body.

During all of this time, she was as calm as a summer morning breeze, and I was a wreck! I prayed silently, *Dear God, this woman has been through enough. Please give her continued strength and give me strength to be of some help.*

Gus could sense that something was wrong as he couldn't seem to get comfortable in front of the fire. Even after I'd fed him, he paced up and down the little room. Laura's body cast long shadows on the log walls as she rose up in bed during contractions. Her moans, along with the sounds of the wind and rain and Gus's pacing, about brought me to my knees.

Then, just after eight o'clock, Laura's water broke. Afterward, she asked me to help her clean herself, and I removed and cleaned the poncho again. From then on, her contractions got stronger and closer together. Using a wet washcloth, I kept wiping her face and talking to her in a low, whispering voice. All during this time, I kept praying that God would intervene, and save this young lady from her pain, and make the birth happen. Sitting by her, I was frightened, and didn't know how much more she could take. Both her body and mind seemed worn out.

Checking my father's pocket watch, it was 11:45, when she looked up at me and said, in a weak voice, "The baby is coming, Dutch."

Before I could leave her side to move to the foot of the bed, she grabbed my hand. With tears in her eyes, she said softly, "Dutch, if anything happens to me, will you take care of my baby? Promise me."

I squeezed her hand and, without hesitation, gave her my solemn promise.

With my help, Laura scooted down to the foot of the bed and hung her legs over the end. I placed my poncho and the bedpan on the stone floor for the afterbirth she had told me about. Then, lighting both candles and turning on the flashlight, I knelt at the foot of the bed, facing her birth canal. Other than in French Postcards, I had never seen a woman's private parts before, and I was both horrified and embarrassed. But that suddenly didn't matter when, using the direct beam of the flashlight, I realized that I could see the top of the baby's head trying to come out.

"Push, Laura, push. I can see your baby!" I shouted.

Rising up on her elbows, she gave it all she had. She was so weak that her cries of pain could hardly be heard over the wind and rain. She strained and then collapsed back on the bed, giving up.

Another gust of wind blew up, shaking the cabin to its foundation, its whirling noise filling the room. Grabbing Laura's legs, with my mouth cotton dry and a knot in my gut, I screamed, "No! Come on, Laura. You're no quitter. Help me get your baby out." When she didn't move, didn't reply and, didn't give any sign that she had heard me at all, I felt a sense of terror. "Push, damn you. Push!"

Gus, who had been pacing, came to her bedside and began to bark.

This, at last, seemed to get her attention. With a groan that seemed to roll-up from deep within, she finally rose again in the bed and gave another strong push.

With that, the baby's head was out, resting in my hands. The sounds of the wind were now deafening. Steam was rolling off Laura's body in the cool room, and new life was only seconds away. With a cautious finger, I began clearing the baby's nose and mouth, as I had been instructed.

"Again, Laura, again!" I rasped.

With a cry of anguish, she gave the final push. With the baby's head cradled in my hands, I guided the baby's shoulders through, and then the whole body slid free. It was a boy. "Laura, it's a boy!" I shouted, with relief.

But he was so small that it frightened me. With some fishing line, I tied off the umbilical cord and cut away the remains with my hunting knife. But through all of this, the baby did not move or make a sound.

Quickly, I grabbed one of the towels that was warming by the fire and briskly rubbed and cleaned his little body. Then I turned him upside down and spanked his tiny butt softly with my open hand.

That did it! His cry of life overpowered the sounds of the tempest. He didn't like being upside down, and he wanted his mother, and was letting me know it. His energy and defiance made me grin.

While I'd been caring for the baby, Laura had given one last push to force out the afterbirth. Then she'd fallen back onto the bed, utterly spent.

Settling the baby on her chest, I moved her arms to hold him, but I could see that she was only half-conscious. Slowly, I eased her back up the bed. With another damp towel, I wiped both Laura and the baby.

The cool, wet cloth seemed to help Laura, and her arms closed more tightly around the baby.

I whispered in her ear, "You have a Christmas baby, blown in on the wings of angels. A Christmas baby boy."

Confident that she had a good hold on him and that she was fully conscious now, I moved to the foot of the bed and took the bloody afterbirth on the poncho outside.

A few minutes later when I returned, I found that Laura had regained some of her strength and was sitting up, with her back against the log wall, as she fed her baby. Oh, what a beautiful sight that was. Drying myself off from the weather, I moved over to the bed and knelt next to Laura. In a quiet voice, I confided, "You gave me quite a scare. I thought I'd lost you. You have a beautiful boy, born on Christmas morning. God bless you both."

She looked at me, then at her baby feeding from her breast, and with tears in her eyes as she replied, "Thank you, Dutch, for all you have done this night. I told you God would take care of us... now you get some rest."

Collapsing in the chair by the fireplace, I began thinking about how the process of giving birth had sounded so ugly yet turned out to be so beautiful. What a miracle life was.

Gus joined me, curling at my feet. I thought about getting up and into the hammock but I was just too tired. We were both soon asleep. It was a Christmas Eve I would never forget.

Later that morning, I awoke to the sound of a baby crying, it was a magnificent sound of life.

That day, I made diapers out of two flour sacks, about six in all. I even found some safety pins in my sewing kit. All the while, I made sure that I tended to all of Laura's needs. By early afternoon, she felt strong enough, with my help, to visit the outhouse, her baby wrapped safely in blankets on the bed.

After she returned to the cabin, I excused myself and, with Gus in tow, went into the forest to chop down a small fir tree. When I came back, I stood it in a corner of the room where Laura and the baby could see it and then went about starting our Christmas dinner. Our seafood stew would now contain crab legs, clams, and halibut, all cooked in a tomato and onion broth. To this I added some of the spices that Laura had bought for her mother.

The little cabin was soon full of good smells and sounds. As I prepared the meal, I found myself softly humming, my heart full of joy.

While the stew cooked, I talked to Laura and made crude ornaments for the tree with tin cans and lids, twine, and strands of cloth. At one point, she called me over to her bedside to show me her sleeping baby and then said, "Your Godson will never forget this day, and neither will I. And your tree is the best I've ever seen. Merry Christmas, Dutch."

Taking one of her hands in mine, I gave it a squeeze and said, "I've never had a Godson before. Thank you."

That evening, we ate and talked. I did most of the eating as Laura still didn't have much of an appetite. She said the stew was as good as her mother's. But then, what else could she have said?

Later, we sang a few Christmas carols, and she talked about holidays past. But to that I was mostly quiet.

By nine o'clock both Laura and her baby were fast asleep. Standing by the crackling fireplace, I stared for a long time at the bottle of Scotch resting on the mantle. I had been saving it for Laura's rescue, but I thought that Skip wouldn't mind if I had a drink to welcome his grandson into the world. Cracking it open, I poured a shot into my tin cup. Then, easing myself down into the chair, I opened Lars's Bible and began absent-mindedly thumbing through the pages. Gus joined me, curling up in his spot on the bearskin.

The wind and rain had stopped. The only sounds in the room were those of Laura, the baby and Gus, all sleeping. I, too, was exhausted, but I decided I'd read one random passage before turning in. Looking down at the open Bible, I found myself reading Luke, Chapter 2, Verse 7: "And she brought forth her first-born son..."

CHAPTER NINE

Survival

"Dutch...Dutch, wake up!" With my mind still foggy, I tried to focus. Opening my eyes I found Laura standing over my hammock, holding her baby. Just then, Gus awoke and began barking.

"What is it? What's the matter?" I asked, rolling out of the hammock.

"Make Gus stop barking and listen," she insisted.

Gus padded to the door. I joined him and told him to be quiet.

Through the closed door, over the sound of the wind, I could hear them. It was a pack of wolves, not more than a few hundred feet from the front of the cabin, howling and fighting amongst themselves. It was a blood-curdling clamor of growling, crying, and whimpering.

Turning to Laura, I put my hand on her shoulder. "They're close. Gus and I must've gotten used to their racket to have slept through it."

At the fireplace, I retrieved the rifle, slid cartridges into the breach, and pulled on my boots. Gus paced by the door. He wanted to go out and mix it up with them but, of course, that was a bad idea. Instead, I gave him hand signals and told him to sit. Then, slipping my jacket on, I opened the door slowly and eased my way out onto the porch, with Gus just behind me and in check.

It was predawn, just light enough for me to make out the shadows of a half-dozen wolves scraping down by the creek, some hundred yards away. At first, I thought they must be skirmishing over a dead animal, but then it dawned on me: that was where I'd thrown the afterbirth two nights ago. They were killing each other for the taste of human blood, and that made me more distressed. At the time, I'd thought of burying the afterbirth or taking it further into the forest, but I'd been afraid to leave Laura alone. Now, the wolves had tasted blood.

With the rifle at my shoulder, I quickly fired off three rounds in their general direction. The noise and bullets got their attention, and they started running towards the lake.

Behind me, the baby started crying, startled by the sound of the gunshots. Looking over my shoulder, I saw Laura rocking and shushing him.

Stepping off the porch, I ran in the direction of the creek. There, I found that I'd wounded one wolf and with a fourth bullet, I finished the job. As I walked back to the cabin, I could still hear the baby fussing. This was not a good way to start the second day of his life. I knew what I had to do, what I should have done in the first place, bury what was left of the afterbirth and the now-dead wolf.

At first, I hesitated, but I needed to tell Laura what I'd found and done. Giving her instructions to keep the door closed, I explained that Gus and I would return to the creek to do the burial.

She clutched the baby tightly to her hip and stopped me with one hand just as I was about to leave. "Is it true what they say about wild animals getting a taste of human blood?"

Her face was frightened. She had been badly scared. Smiling, I shrugged it off. "Those mangy wolves don't know the difference, they're just hungry. It was my fault this happened as I knew better."

I only hoped that what I'd told her about the wolves was true.

My pick and shovel made barely a dent in the hard, rocky ground. But the hard work gave me time to think out our predicament. Part of me was still hoping, beyond all reason, that Laura and her baby would be rescued. In fact, I felt a little indignant over finding myself in this position. After all, I'd made carefully calculated plans for this damn mission, and now she and her baby had turned those plans upside down. But another part of me was happy to share my valley with other folks, even if it would require additional sacrifices. Still, I had my doubts, many doubts, about us surviving another six months in this wilderness.

After I had shoveled the last of the dirt back into the hole and piled rocks on top of it, I sat down on the grave and looked at Gus, who had been watching me work. A few moments later I finally said out loud, "Well, Gus, the truth is, I can't change any of this. What's going to be is going to be." And, with that declaration, I decided to butch-up and start planning for a short-term future that was very different from my plans of just few days ago. I had to change my attitude to flexibility and optimism. Life can turn on a dime, and I needed to learn how to turn with it.

Gus looked at me with his head cocked to one side, his eyes bright and his manner typically self-assured. He'd always been a good listener.

That evening, I talked to Laura at great length about surviving the winter in our little valley. I explained that, while I held out hope that she and the baby might still be rescued, if it didn't happen, we'd still live and survive. Not wanting to paint a bleak picture, I talked in general terms about the dangers we'd face and the actions we'd have to take.

She listened to me ramble for almost an hour. In the end her only comment was, "God has allowed all this to happen for a reason. He won't forsake us now."

Soberly, I replied, "God won't feed us or show us the way out. That's up to us. We need to have faith, but we also need to believe in ourselves."

Food was going to be our biggest problem; I'd known that since the night the baby was born. The first thing I had to do was make an inventory of what was still in the root cellar. Just a couple of weeks ago, I was confident that my larder would carry me through the winter. Now, I had a family to feed. With that in mind, I took the flashlight and paper and crawled down the ladder to the dark, damp little crypt. Inside that small room, I wrote down our remaining supplies.

From the garden:

• Two trail bags of carrots (about a bushel each). Half of these would have to be fed to Blaze. Without any grain or oats, he needed the nutrition of carrots.

• One trail bag each of potatoes and onions. This was no more than a three-month supply. Because the root cellar was so damp and cool, we'd have to eat these items first, before they spoiled.

• 8 clay pots of stewed tomatoes. These were doing well in the damp environment, as I'd sealed them with wax.

• 5 clay pots of pickles. They were somewhat soft but showed no signs of mold.

• 6 clay pots of cabbage. From the smell, I concluded they'd started to ferment. I wasn't sure if this was all bad; a little alcohol might add flavor to a raccoon stew.

• 5 small clay pots of wild blackberry jam.

• 2 clay pots of blackberry wine. I hoped it would not turn to vinegar.

In addition, I had about fifty pounds of dried fish and elk jerky. This I used primarily as our morning meal. But my big concern was the supplies I'd packed in. They were dwindling fast. Those remaining were:

• One and a half 10-pound bags of flour. This was an unwelcome surprise. Before Laura arrived, I had been baking biscuits every three or four days. Now, it seemed, we ate a half a pan day. The flour would have to be rationed.

• Half a 10-pound bag of beans.

• One 10-pound bag of rice.

• One 5-pound sack of coffee beans. This would also have to rationed.

• About 2 pounds of pepper. No salt… I'd have to distill seawater for this luxury.

• One half-gallon tin of honey.

• The sugar, baking soda and yeast that remained were just enough to be used in baking the biscuits.

• One 64 oz. can of lemon juice.

That was it. Long gone were the cans of fruit, vegetables, and chili. Oh, what I would give for few pounds of sugar, dried fruit, and another 10 pounds of flour and coffee. Was what we had enough? If it was just for me, I could survive. But if Laura and the baby weren't rescued, it was going to be a long and lean six months. We could only make it if we rationed the supplies and were fortunate in our hunting and fishing. Thank goodness the baby would be fed with Laura's milk, but I knew that Laura's milk would only hold out if she was getting decent nutrition, herself.

Folding the list of staples and placing it in my pocket, I crawled back up the ladder to the warm cabin. Laura was by the fire, reheating the last of our fish stew. The baby was sleeping on the bed.

"What were you doing down there, Dutch?"

Peeling off my coat, I hung it on a hook, trying to think of the best way to talk to Laura about this without making her overly apprehensive.

"Just taking a little inventory of our supplies... nothing for you to worry about."

"From the look on your face, I'd say you're not telling me the whole truth."

Laura was a trouper, and I decided we needed to work on this as a team. Removing the list from my pocket, I unfolded it on the table and read it aloud.

When I was finished, she asked, "Well, what does all that mean? Are you telling me we're going to be seagull bait?"

I smiled. "Nope, I'm telling you we're going to navigate some uncharted waters. With a little rationing and some luck hunting, we should be just fine. Anyhow it shouldn't really matter, as you and little Junior will be rescued and long gone by the time I leave this valley in the spring."

Laura carried the iron stew pot over to the table, dished a large portion into my plate, and slid it across the table. "Did I hear you just call my baby 'Junior'?" she asked smiling, as she sat down across from me.

"Just a figure of speech."

With that same smile on her face, she replied, "Well, I was thinking that he does need a name. We can't go around calling him

'Junior.' It would hurt his feelings. So the name I was thinking about is… yours. 'Dutch.' What do you think?"

Her words caught me off guard, other than Grandfather, Father, and me, I'd never met another person named Dutch. I fumbled for a reply.

"Why?" is all I heard myself ask.

"You're his godfather, and you helped give him life, so why not?"

Feeling proud by her answer, I replied, "What about your husband? Or, this is your dad's first grandchild, and if it hadn't been for him, I would have never been here to help. Why not name him after your father?"

She paused while eating the stew and a grin crossed her face. "OK, and I'll be sure to tell him it was your idea. We'll name the baby Marion."

"Marion!" I hooted. "Where the hell did that name come from?"

"That's Dad's real name, but don't tell him I told you. His mother must have wanted a girl to place a handle like that on him. 'Skip' is just his nickname."

Leaning back against the log wall, I shook with laughter. "Well, one thing is for sure—you won't hear me calling your father or your son Marion."

"You're a smart man. Dad would deck any man who called him that, and I would never put such a handle on your godson. How about Theodore? That's Dad's middle name. His father was a Republican and loved Theodore Roosevelt. We could add your name as his middle name."

"Theodore Dutch… What is your last name again?"

"It's Person. I was married to a sweet Swedish boy."

"Theodore Dutch Person has a good ring to it, a very good ring. I'm sure he'll be called Ted or Teddy, as Theodore is so big for such a little guy." I said with a smile.

Later that night, while both Laura and Theodore were sleeping, I sat and reflected on recent events. Only a few days ago, my extended family was Gus and Blaze. Now I had a godson, who carried my name, and Laura, who looked to me for survival. While in some ways, I felt put-upon, yet I also felt what I imagined a proud father might feel: full of hope and thanksgiving at the gift of a newborn.

Gathering my thoughts and my courage, I pledged then and there that I would stand by and protect Teddy for the rest of his life.

That thought made me feel like I was standing on a hillside in a summer breeze. My whole body tingled with warmth and contentment. Taking Lars's old Bible in hand, I wrote Theodore Dutch Person and the date of his birth on the front page. As I closed it, I bowed my head, thanked God for his life and prayed for his future… especially his immediate future.

Over the next few days, I set a second signal fire on the bluff overlooking the channel. My thinking was that, if rescuers had called off the search or couldn't fly because of bad weather, then maybe I'd find a boat down in the channel. The only problem was that the bluff was a good half-mile from the cabin, so I could only check for boats two or three times a day. Even this was difficult, due to the low-hanging clouds and fog that always seemed to obscure my view.

Scanning the horizon with my binoculars, I spent hours each day, but to no avail. Soon, I retreated from this position and thought about only using the signal fire on our travels to and from the bay and the hot springs.

New Year

A clear, cool, dry day ushered in 1942. The only celebration we had on New Year's Eve was a short toast with the last of the dead pilot's brandy. Laura spoke of 1941 as a year of love, hope, death, and birth and looked forward to 1942 as a year of optimism and growth. Raising my cup, I made a short toast to my godson and the young men in our armed forces. Privately, I prayed for an early spring and our safe return to civilization.

New Year's Day was so clear and dry that we were able to open our door and window to air out the little cabin. In the early afternoon, Laura asked about going to the bay to wash some clothes and bathe. At first I hesitated; it had been just a week since the birth of her baby. But she seemed strong and fully recovered.

Saddling Blaze, I helped her and the baby on and led Blaze by the reins towards the bay. Gus, as always, was ahead of us a few hundred yards.

This was the first time Laura had seen the whole valley and the surrounding landscape. She asked many questions about the mountains, the valley, and our lake. Pointing to the south, I showed her the two mountains where her plane had crashed. Twisting to the north we had a good view of snow-covered Comet Mountain. I explained how that mountain was the way I had come in and how it would be the way out in the spring.

When we reached the bluff overlooking the bay, where my second signal fire was laid, we had an excellent view of the channel with Thunder Mountain and its snowcap in the background. Looking at Laura, I could tell that this majestic view had caught her off guard. She finally said, "Dutch, it's so big, so imposing. It's brutally beautiful!"

Pointing towards Thunder Mountain, I told her that the little town of Firvale, the closest civilization, was on the other side of that mountain. We paused on the bluff for a few minutes, just enjoying the sprawling vistas of the area.

Then we made our way down the narrow trail to the bay and over to the pools of hot water. There, we washed the clothes and laid them out on rocks to dry in the sun. Laura soon slipped out of her clothes and into one of the larger pools with her baby. Sometime later, she called out for me to bring one of the towels to her. As I approached the hot spring I could see, through the clear water that she had nothing on.

Handing her the towel, I watched as she dried the baby and wrapped him in a blanket. Settling him on some rocks close by, Laura looking up at me and asked, "Dutch, I have a favor to ask. Let me give you a haircut and shave. I used to do it for my father, and he loved it. I brought along the scissors and your razor. Will you let me?"

My lame reply was, "Why?"

"Let's just say I'd like to see what you look like under all that fur." Wearing only a grin, she challenged, "Well, Dutch, are you going to join me or just stand there, staring?"

Nodding my head in approval, I quickly turned, undressed down to my skivvies, and slipped into the warm water. I sat with my back to her while she rinsed my hair with hot water and then rubbed in soap with her hands. The head massage felt marvelous. Within seconds, I realized there was something about her touch, something wonderful and stimulating, but also embarrassing.

Soon, the water around me showed just how dirty my hair had been. After rinsing my hair again, she used a comb and the scissors and started clipping away. Looking down, I watched the pool fill with trimmed hair that then floated away to the channel beyond. I can't remember when a simple haircut ever felt so good.

When she was done with the back, she asked me to turn. Then, with my bare legs touching hers underwater, I watched as she trimmed the front of my hair. All this time, she was grinning, with her enlarged breasts moving in and out of the warm pool. Next she lathered up my beard and started shaving me. She knew how to hold the blade at just the right angle to give a smooth, painless shave. As she worked, she made small talk, moving the razor from one side of my face to the other. I can't remember a word she said; all I remember thinking was how nice it was being touched by this beautiful woman.

Finally she broke my concentration. "You don't talk about your father much."

"He died when I was very young. So I didn't know him very well."

Sensing my sober reaction, Laura reached for the towel and wiped the soap off my face. Then she placed one of her hands on my clean-shaven cheek and exclaimed, "Well, lookie here! You have a very nice face... a handsome face, under all the grime. Do you have a girlfriend, Dutch?"

Feeling my cheeks go flush and with a cotton-dry mouth, I stammered, "N-no."

Patting my face while looking me straight in the eye, she replied with a smile, "That's too bad, but I'm sure there will be plenty in the future." Lowering her hand, she continued, "You know, Dutch, I don't have much modesty when it comes to you. After all, you delivered my baby, and you've seen me at my worst."

Trying not to make eye contact, I looked away and said, "I guess that was different. It was just something that happened. I didn't think of you as a girl then."

With a silly grin, she replied, "That's not much of a compliment. You're so bashful. Haven't you ever seen a naked girl before?"

"Well, uh, sure," I mumbled, "lots of times... you know."

"Now, Dutch, you can't tell me that the crew on my Dad's boat didn't take you to a few of those 'sporting houses' in Ketchikan."

Now I was really getting embarrassed and could feel my face reddening again. Trying to change the subject, I said, "I should try to catch a fish for our dinner. It looks like the tide is starting to come in."

With a loud laugh, she playfully slapped water at me. "Dutch, you're a virgin! I'll be damned. I always thought Dad's crew could corrupt anybody. Well, that's okay. I think it's wonderful, and you can change the subject if you want."

And I did. This had been the first time in my life that I'd talked to a naked girl. While the crew had taken me to some of those 'sporting houses,' I had partaken only of the free beers and never had the courage to go any further.

We sat in the warm waters of the hot springs for another hour, talking. She told me more about her life, her family, and what was going on in the outside world. She asked me many questions about my family, as well, but my answers were few and vague. Once again, I avoided telling her the total truth about what I was doing out in the middle of nowhere.

As we traveled back to camp, I reflected on the emotions I'd felt for Laura while at the hot springs. Her smile had brought springtime into the winter and her personality was as open as the countryside. I searched for just the right word that would describe my feelings, and I finally found it, envy; I had not admired many people in my life, so this feeling was new to me. She had been so beautiful, so warm and honest, so down-to-earth. But I reminded myself sternly that she was a widow and a mother; I had no right to see her in any other way. Whatever I might feel for her, I had to put it aside.

Over the next few months, these conversations at the hot springs became a habit, and they were almost the only times we talked of personal matters. Weather permitting we went to the springs as often as we could. It was something we both looked forward to, as our normal, everyday conversations mostly dealt with survival.

As the days turned to weeks, the weather changed from a precious few days of clear and dry to stormy and wet, and there was still no sign of rescue.

We soon fell into a routine. My time was spent hunting, fishing and caring for the needs of the cabin and Blaze. Laura spent her time cooking, cleaning, mending, and, most of all, looking after Theodore. As we moved into late January, the days should have started getting a little longer, but, because of the constant cloud cover, I couldn't see any improvement. On most days, in the late afternoon, I'd spend time in the stable, building things for the cabin as best I could. As a result, there was now a second chair in front of the fireplace, with a second small table next to it. Also, I'd made a small, crude, cradle that Laura could use to rock Theodore to sleep. But the most challenging project was the design and construction of a mother's cradleboard for carrying the baby on her back, as the Indians did.

For this carrier, I made a frame of strong oak twigs, secured with rawhide to a thin oak board. For the inner cocoon, I pieced together some soft raccoon fur, the hide facing outward, with a secure opening for the baby. The cradleboard was designed in such a way that it was almost water-tight in a heavy downpour. For the straps, I used pieces from one of my waxed canvas trail bags.

In the end, I was quite proud of my handiwork and told myself I would've made a good native Indian. The project took almost a week and Laura was surprised when I gave it to her. She hesitated about using it, at first, not convinced that the baby would be safe. But she soon developed confidence in her little backpack and used it almost all the time. As for Theodore, he seemed to like his soft, warm cocoon and fussed very little in it.

Much of my time and energy was spent on hunting and fishing, but, this time of year, that wasn't proving very fruitful. The deer, the elk, even the fish, all seemed to have vanished. Each morning, I'd saddle Blaze. Then, with Gus in tow, we'd set off to hunt. We hunted around Duck Lake and around July Lake and even as far as Eucott Lake but with no luck. We fished the lakes and down by the bay, but there, too, we had little luck. I did shoot a few raccoons to fill our cooking pot for a few days. But I knew that, even with all the new spices, Laura didn't much care for raccoon stew because she ate very little of it.

Early each morning, as usual, we let Gus out for his morning hunt. I'd been doing this ever since we'd moved into the cabin. Gus would always be gone for an hour or two and with the short daylight hours, most of his hunts were done in morning darkness. I never knew what he hunted or whether he was successful. This was what Gus had done all his life, and, while we had bonded, he still had his wild side. When he returned from hunting, he'd scratch at the door and I'd let him in.

Then a funny thing happened. One morning, he scratched, and I opened the door to let him in. To my astonishment there, lying on the porch was a small, dead rabbit. Gus was nowhere to be seen… just this fresh kill at the door. Sitting back on my heels, I inspected his gift. Looking up from the porch I called out for him, but he didn't come. Taking the rabbit inside, I was commenting to Laura about the tasty surprise when Gus scratched on the door once again. This time, I opened it to find Gus sitting on the doorstep with a second, larger rabbit hanging limp in his jaws. He had one proud look on his face, and I'd swear he was smiling.

Kneeling down close to his face, I looked him straight in the eye and admitted, "Guess we know who's the best hunter in this valley. Good boy."

With that, I gave him a big hug, which he wouldn't let me do very often. That day, we feasted on rabbit, with Gus getting his share with our deep appreciation. This never happened again.

The Truth

While all the mountains surrounding the valley were white with snow, for the most part the valley floor stayed snow-free in January. But that all changed in the fourth week. A cold front moved in from the east with storms from the southwest, and it started to snow.

At first, Laura and I marveled at the sheer beauty of the clean, cotton-like landscape. On the second day of the storm, however, the temperature outside dropped so low that I was forced into the relative warmth of the cabin.

By now, it had been over a month since the plane crash, and I'd finally come to grips with the fact that Laura and the baby would not be rescued. It now seemed apparent that she and Theodore would be walking out with me in the coming spring.

Laura was standing by the fire starting a pot of potato soup, with the gusting winds outside blowing the smoke of the fire back down the chimney and into the room. She put a lid on the pot as she waved the smoke away.

"Dutch, you told me once that there was another way out of here, up the lake. How did you find that out?"

Getting up from the table, I went to one of the trail bags and retrieved the rusty metal box that held Lars's legacy.

"It's a heart-breaking story, but I should tell you so that you won't get any ideas about us getting out that way."

Laura joined me at the table and pulled her wooden stool close to mine as I opened the box. Over the sounds of the swirling winds, I related in detail the story of Lars and his gold mine. The story took hours to tell; sometimes I'd read directly from his journal, and other times I'd relate what I'd seen and done. In the end, I could see that Laura was visibly shaken by my tale.

"My heart goes out to his wife, who lost her husband for a little gold. I have never understood why people would jeopardize their lives for gold. It's just so stupid."

"Well, sometimes people risk their lives for a lot less than gold. Anyhow, when I get out of here, I'm going to look up Lars's wife in Seattle and give her this pouch of gold. It's what Lars wanted."

The room filled with the gurgles of Theodore waking up from his nap. Soon, Laura had the baby in her arms, feeding him.

"Dutch, tell me again why you're out here. Can it be any more stupid than why Lars came here?"

Finally convinced that there was to be no rescue, I decided to tell her the truth about my family and my required mission in the wilderness. As I told the story, I left out the two covenants of Grandfather's will: "totally alone" and "staying for one full year."

During my explanation, Laura listened intently. When I finished, she got up from the table and moved to the bed. Still holding the baby, she sat down on the blanket with her back against the log wall. Finally she said, "Dutch, your reasons are more stupid than Lars's gold. You put your life in danger just to prove to your dead grandfather that you are some kind of mountain man. This family tradition stuff is just so much crap... why wouldn't your Uncle Roy just forget about the damn will and let you both get on with your lives? It's just ridiculous."

I sighed. "To understand, you'd have to know Roy. He's a man who lives by a very special code. I have never heard him lie, or bend—let alone break—any rules. He wears no robe other than honor."

Laura put her legs up on the bed, propping the baby against her bent knees as she played with and made funny sounds for him. In a few moments, she stopped, staring directly across the room at me. "So what would his *honor* get you if you were dead?" she asked angrily.

Thinking a moment, I then replied, "It isn't about dying, it's about living. My only hope is that someday I'll have that same sense of honor. But it's hard to achieve and with the whole damn world at war, I'd think that honor would be more important than ever."

"You're changing the subject again. I still say he's stupid, and if I ever meet him, I'll tell him so... But then, without his stupidity, Theodore and I would be dead. So let's just call it 'stupid luck!'"

Just then, a gust of cold wind shook the cabin, reminding both of us just how lucky we were.

The snow stayed with us for over a week, and, while I tried to hunt, the only game I got was another raccoon. There were still very few hours of daylight, and one of my biggest tasks was splitting enough firewood to heat the cabin. There was a large stack of wood next to the fireplace that I replenished each day from the larger stack on the front porch. Estimating that I'd burn over four cords of wood during the winter, I had prepared that amount. With the winter now more than half gone, only a cord and a half remained. With Laura and the baby, we were burning more wood, cooking more, and trying to keep the cabin warmer than I might've done on my own. While I was a little concerned about our supply, it didn't worry me too much, as there was plenty of "green" wood available. My hope was that the weather would soon moderate, so I could begin chopping more.

One evening, as I was bringing fresh wood in from the porch, Laura told me that she was going to the outhouse and asked me to keep an eye on the baby, who was sleeping in his cradle. When I nodded, Laura bundled up and walked out of the cabin into the night.

Gus was sleeping in his place next to the fire, making me step over him as I added to the stack of fresh wood. As I turned to get another load, I heard Laura scream from behind the cabin. With Gus right behind me, I ran to the door and saw that Laura had not taken the pistol from the hanging gun belt, as usual. Grabbing the gun, Gus and I rushed out the door and down the path towards the outhouse.

Within a few seconds, I could see the light of Laura's flashlight pointing into the woods behind the small building. Glaring back from the light were three pairs of eyes, two brown and one blue, in the deep bushes not fifty feet from where she stood. The blue-eyed wolf was snarling, his white fangs gleaming in the focused flashlight. Instantly, I sensed that the other two wolves were doing his bidding. Running towards Laura, I pointed the pistol just above the wolves' heads, and squeezed off three shots.

The gunfire cut through the silence of the dark, making Laura jump. Gus raced by me, barking loudly as I reached her side. She grabbed me with a frightened hug and started sobbing. With the flashlight, I pointed the beam back into the bushes and found Gus standing where the wolves had been. The gunshots had made them bolt deeper into the woods. As I whistled Gus back in, I turned to Laura and said, "It's okay, they're gone. You did the right thing by keeping the light in their eyes, it almost hypnotizes them."

In the dim light, I could see her looking up at me. She whispered sadly, "What a God-forsaken place this is." Then a weak grin crossed her face, and she said more loudly, "Dutch, they scared the hell out of me. Damn! A girl can't even go to the outhouse in your valley."

I gave her a quick hug and as we parted, I replied, "Laura, I told you always to take the pistol with you. Here take it now, and I'll leave Gus with you."

She nodded and moved towards the privy. Telling Gus to stay with her, he was soon sitting sentinel duty by her door. Relieved that she was safe, I walked back towards the cabin.

But when I reached the corner of the cabin, I knew something was wrong. The front door, which I thought had closed behind me, was ajar, light spilling into the darkness. Quickly, I climbed to the front porch and moved to the partly open doorway. Pushing the door open cautiously, I looked into the room.

There, standing on the table, eating food scraps, was a bobcat some forty or fifty pounds in size.

Just then, the baby, lying in his cradle at the foot of the bed, cried out suddenly. The cat was startled. He stuck his nose into the air and sniffed, slinking to the end of the table with his fur up. Then he let out a loud hissing noise while I seemed frozen in place.

Across the room, I could see my rifle leaning against the wall by the fireplace, hopelessly out of reach. And the pistol was with Laura.

The cat arched its back, and I knew it was about to jump across the room onto the cradle. Then my left hand grazed the handle of my hatchet, sticking up from a log on the porch.

Without blinking, without thinking, I took the hatchet in my hand and held it over my head. The whole scene seemed to play out in slow motion. I didn't really know how to take aim with an axe at this moving target, but I let it fly. It rotated end over end toward the cat, which was now in midair. The polished head of the axe reflected back at me as it twirled across the room.

The impact was brutal. It hurled the cat further into the room and bounced him, with a thud, off the fireplace hearth. Rushing into the room, I found the baby safe but still fussing. For the moment, I had to leave him in the cradle. Moving across the room to the rifle, I stepped over to the motionless cat.

There was no question about it—he was dead, his neck sliced open, blood everywhere. Pulling the hatchet from the carcass, I saw that the sheer force of the blow had broken the cat's neck.

With my heart pounding, I picked up the dead bobcat, hoping to remove it before Laura returned. But as I turned around with the limp and bleeding cat in my hands, I found her standing in the doorway, with Gus by her side.

"What the hell happened?" she demanded.

Rushing to her baby, she picked him up and started walking the room to quiet him. As I moved past her with the carcass in my arms, I answered, "We had a little problem because I didn't secure the door when I came chasing after you. But Theodore is fine. I'll be back in a minute to clean up the mess."

Taking the bobcat to the stable, I hung it high from the rafters. I knew I'd have to return later that night to skin and dispose of the remains. If I didn't, the wolves would return for sure and cause yet another problem. On my way back to the cabin, I reflected that this had been a rough evening, with Laura badly frightened by the events. When I entered the cabin, I found an edgy Laura still pacing, but Teddy was now asleep in her arms. She turned to me with a look of deep distress and asked, "How long, Dutch? How long do you think we will have to stay in this God-awful place?"

Not having any idea how to respond to her, I began cleaning up the blood from the chairs and hearth. I needed to keep this positive and upbeat. Finally I answered, "I don't know Laura, maybe the middle of April or the first of May. I just don't know. Think of it this way—that's only eight or nine weeks away and, it's up to Mother Nature. We'll make it... we'll be OK."

She moved to the cradle and lovingly placed the baby in his bed. As she tucked the blanket around him, she said softly, "Yes, we'll make it—not for ourselves, but for him."

The wolves remained a problem that we had to deal with the rest of the winter. It was lucky that Laura hadn't noticed the blue-eyed beast during her encounter by the outhouse. The last thing I wanted to do was terrify her with my wild stories of this creature.

Never again did Laura or I go to the privy without the pistol, the flashlight, and Gus. But these animals were so bold that they even began stalking me when I was hunting, chopping wood, or walking to the barn to care for Blaze. I knew they were there, even when I couldn't see them. It was like the shadow you saw in the bright sun that wasn't there in the overcast. And yet, in some ways, I felt sorry for the mangy vermin, as they were only hungry like we were. This was a hard country, only fit for the fit.

Renewal

During February, the weather went from snow to slush, from hail to rain, and then rain to a 24-hour sticky drizzle. I never knew so much water could fall from the sky, and I can't remember a clear day the whole month. But the temperatures were warming, and the wind had shifted from the northeast to the west. Clearly, the seasons were starting to change, and I hoped for an early escape to civilization, as soon as the mountain passes were free of snow.

In early March, I could finally tell that the days really were getting longer, because the earlier sunrises and later sunsets became much more noticeable. With the longer days, the hunting started to improve too. Instead of just raccoon, our game included a few ducks that ventured up from the south early. Then the fish, both in the lake and in the bay, started to bite again. With the rice and potatoes running low, Laura spent some of her day walking the area around the cabin, digging up dormant plant roots, which she cooked with our fish or bird stew. Some of these roots tasted like onions or rutabagas, while others were so bitter and sour that we discarded them unused. We also tried adding young plant leaves to our porridge, but this proved to be hit-and-miss, as well. Still most of her meals were tasty because of the spices she'd brought into the valley.

A new scent drifted over the channel towards the end of March. This smell was in the wind, and its fresh aroma meant renewed life. As March turned to April, the valley floor bloomed with all the colors of the rainbow. There was the bright yellow of wild daisies, the deep red fireweed, the blue of lupine, and the green of new grass. Nature had come alive again in the Nascall Valley. It was a time of rejoicing and renewal, and it gave us hope that we'd get out safely.

It was against this backdrop that Laura and I began taking almost scheduled baths down at the hot springs. One day in early April, we packed Blaze with a load of our dirty clothes and made our way to the bay. As always, Gus led the way, but for some reason, on this day, he seemed more agitated. When we arrived at the bay, I unsaddled Blaze and placed his saddle and bags on a large, gray log snag. Laura, with Theodore on her back, started washing the clothes, while Gus and I cast out the crab pot at the water's edge.

The day was crisp and clear, with visibility unlimited. Fighting the tide, since we were only two hours from flood, I held out little hope for either crabs or fish, but I figured it was worth a try.

Soon, Laura called out to me that the clothes had been washed and that I should come join Theodore and her for a bath. As I approached the hot springs, I could see all the clothes drying on rocks and logs surrounding the pool in which she and Theodore were bathing. Item by item, I stripped off my clothes as I walked towards the hot pool.

All of a sudden, I realized my total lack of modesty. Only a few months ago, I would never have done such a thing in front of Laura. By the time I slipped below the hot water, I was naked.

Laura smiled across the steaming pool. "Well, Dutch, you've come a long way. I never thought I would see you do such a 'strip' in front of me."

Laughing, she splashed water at me. I returned her splash and was just settling back against a rock to relax when all of a sudden the bay was shocked with a loud noise that shook the entire floor of the channel. The blast rolled across the water and bounced off the mountains on all sides of the bay, echoing as it returned.

Boom!

Another deafening report came seconds later.

Boom!

Gus started running in tight circles, barking.

To the southwest, I saw smoke rising in the sky, not more than five or six miles from our cove. Jumping out of the pool, I grabbed my hat and boots and slipped them on as I ran towards the log with the saddlebags. There I grabbed my binoculars.

"Boom!"

The sound filled the air again as I climbed some high driftwood to look. Focusing the glasses as fast as I could, I found an image that both excited and frightened me. There, some miles down the water, was a small ship, steaming from one side of the channel to another, dropping explosives. First, I saw a water plume rise, some two or three hundred feet high behind the ship. Then within seconds, we heard the deafening roar of the explosive. The explosions happened two or three times before I figured out what was going on. This had to be a Canadian navy ship, dropping depth charges at something under the water—probably a Japanese submarine?

Then it hit me... this could mean rescue! Flipping the binocular strap around my neck, I ran back to the saddlebags and Blaze. In record time, I removed the flare gun and loaded a flare into the chamber. Pointing the gun skyward, I pulled the trigger.

The sound was loud as the phosphorus shell exploded, a few hundred feet above me. The flare lit up the sky with a bolt of red light, which, after a few moments, slowly floated back down to the bay.

With our flare now dimming, I turned my attention to the top of the ridge, where I had laid my second signal fire. Not having time to saddle Blaze, I grabbed Blaze's reins and threw my legs across his bare back, racing up the trail to the top of the hill. Using the tin of gasoline that I'd left up there for just such a moment, I quickly doused the stack of wood, loaded a second flare, and fired the signal gun into the gas-soaked wood.

Within seconds, the stack of wood took hold with a roar, entirely engulfed with fire from the hot exploding shell. The flames were high, sending dark smoke rising from the valley floor. The wood was wet but the gasoline did its job, and the black smoky fire created the effect I'd envisioned.

Standing on the cliff, I took off my hat and waved it in the air, all the while jumping and screaming as if they could hear me.

My dance and the roar of the fire must have lasted for almost five minutes before both died down. By then, the ship had moved further south and was almost out of sight. My heart sank. For a few moments, I thought about using the last flare, but a little voice inside of me said, "Save it." As the last of the smoke from the fire rose into the sky, I wondered why they hadn't seen me. Maybe, I thought, they have other things on their minds... like that submarine.

Dejected, tired, and angry, I returned to Laura, who had not moved from the hot pool of water. Approaching her, I yelled, "Sorry, guess my flare wasn't high enough or my fire big enough or my screaming loud enough to get their attention."

Looking up from the pool with the biggest grin on her face I had ever seen, she replied, "Dutch, what a show... I've never seen a naked man in cowboy boots ride a horse so fast or do such a fire dance in all my life. I'm sure every animal in your valley is smiling this day!" Then she dissolved into laughter.

Only then, as my adrenaline began to fade, did I realize that I stood in front of her with only my boots and hat on.

"Oh, Dutch," she chuckled, "I'm not laughing at you.... Well, yes, I am laughing at you. But if you had seen what I've just seen, you'd be laughing, too."

At first, I could feel my face getting red, but then I thought about her words. Pulling my boots off, I slipped back into the hot water and, with a smile on my face, replied, "And what a show it must have been."

We both howled with laughter, on and off, for well over an hour, replaying each moment of the event over and over. Beneath my laughter, however, I knew that this had probably been the last chance for Laura and Teddy to be rescued. In some ways, I felt responsible for not being able to make it happen. Although, that little voice in me that said, "Save it" would prove to be fortuitous.

Whiteout

April dawned with promise; the skies were clear, offering a good view of the surrounding mountains. With such favorable conditions, I decided to plan a short trip back up Comet Mountain, the way I'd come in, to determine whether there was a safe passage through the high ground this early in the year. I would hunt, as well as scout for a trail for our journey out.

Laura didn't like my idea, but I explained that I would be gone no longer than a couple of days and that this was the first step of our journey back to civilization.

With a warm spring breeze in my face, I packed up Blaze and rode off on the morning of April 10. Leaving the shotgun behind for Laura's protection, I also left detailed instructions on how to keep the camp while I was gone. With these preparations, I felt sure she would be safe for the duration of my short trip.

The journey up the side of the mountain from the lake falls proved to be dangerous and slow-going. While it hadn't rained for a few days, the trail was still full of loose rocks and mud and I had to lead Blaze up. With Gus behind, it took almost an hour to climb the few hundred feet to the first crest. Then, after mounting Blaze again, and with Gus at the point, I rode up the hill towards the lake where I'd spent my next-to-last night coming in.

At first, the trail and weather were with us, and we made good time until early-afternoon. Then the visibility turned sour, with low-hanging clouds. Continuing along the trail, I could only see a few feet in front of us. After about an hour, as we reached the higher elevations, the trail began filling with snow. From our little camp on the valley floor, I hadn't been able to tell how deep or dangerous this snow-capped mountain was. Now, on the mountain, I knew—and it wasn't what I'd hoped.

Soon, the way was impassable; with the snow well over six feet deep in drifts. Guessing that I was still another hour or two from the lake and the timberline, I turned back. As I did, the weather turned as well, with cold winds out of the south. First, there was rain with strong winds, but this soon turned to snow as the temperature dropped. When I reached the bluff overlooking the valley in the early evening, the light was waning and the weather wasn't improving. Because of conditions, I decided to stay the night before attempting to move down the steep ravine.

The wind was now pelting me with hail, which turned to snow and then to hail again. With Blaze secured behind some rocks for protection from the elements, I looked for a place to safeguard myself. There was a large crevice in the granite, a few yards from Blaze, so I spread out my canvas tarp and sleeping bag and placed another canvas tarp on top of the bag.

With the wind and wet, I knew tonight's camp would be cold, without a fire or hot coffee. Deeply chilled, I removed my wet boots and crawled into the bag, where I ate some elk jerky for dinner. Soon Gus joined me, lying next to the bag for protection from the weather. He allowed me to spread the canvas tarp over his body, and I pulled him close to me for his warmth. While I was sure he enjoyed our trail time together, I was willing to bet that he'd rather be in front of the fire at the cabin right now.

The evening had now become very dark, and I, too, longed for the fireplace and company of my little cabin. I was disappointed with the day's activities, as I had not even made it up to the timberline of Comet Mountain, nor had I seen any game. The whole trip had been a waste of time, and I'd left Laura and the baby in possible danger. This had been a stupid idea!

The downpour turned to snow, and the tarp covering Gus and me soon turned to a white blanket. My mind was racing. Maybe I should try moving down the hill tonight. It was no more than a mile to the cabin, Laura, and a warm fire... No, it would be too dangerous, I thought. All I needed was to have Blaze break a leg or me to get hurt, and then we'd all be in even bigger trouble. Stay here tonight and go down tomorrow.

Peering out from under my sleeping bag, I couldn't see a thing except the whiteout of the falling snow. The motion of the white swirls mesmerized me. Staring through the shields of white, I conjured up the image of an all-white wolf with blue eyes and the outline of a man chasing behind. The image was blurry at first, yet it seemed real, as if they were moving in slow motion across swirls in front of me. The man was running after the wolf... but then the wolf was chasing the man. The faster the wolf ran, the faster the man ran; the faster the man ran, the faster the wolf ran. I strained my ears to hear them but, other than the roar of the wind, there was nothing.

The whole scene was reminiscent of a book I'd read, The Four Horseman of the Apocalypse. Trying to shake the images from my mind, I soon saw the message clearly. Was the wolf the problem or was it man? Crawling back under the sleeping bag and feeling Gus's warm body next to me, I slipped into a restless half-sleep full of mystical and terrifying dreams.

It was almost 8:00 a.m. when I stumbled back into the compound. The previous night and the way down the mountain had been appalling. When we'd left the cold camp in the morning, there was almost six inches of snow on the ground. An hour later, after slipping down the snow-covered game trail, we reached the valley floor, where we found mud, mud, and more mud.

Stabling Blaze safely in the barn, I washed and dried him off as best I could. He'd had the worst of it last night. Giving him some fresh hay and dry carrots, I apologized for my poorly planned trip, assuring him we would not take such a journey again.

As I walked slowly and painfully across camp towards the cabin, I noticed how achy my body was. This, I concluded, was from sleeping—or, should I say, half-sleeping —on the cold rocks.

Swinging open the cabin door, I savored the welcome sight of Laura adding logs to the fire. My early arrival back had caught her off-guard and she jumped for the shotgun, before realizing it was me.

"You scared me, Dutch. I'm so glad you're back early. I worried about you all last night, camping in that raging storm."

Dejectedly, I dropped my gear on the table and headed to the coffee pot, "We got snowed in before I could even reach the timberline. That storm was just miserable."

Laura came over and poured me some coffee before I could reach the pot. As she handed it to me she, said, "Are you okay, Dutch? You don't look so good."

Pressing one of her cold hands against my forehead, she shook her head as I replied, "My bones are achy, but that's from sleeping on the rocks last night."

"You have a fever, and your face is flushed. Take off those wet clothes and get into bed... now."

Looking her straight in the face, I could see her concern. "I'll be OK," I assured her. "I'm just a little tired. I'll curl up in the hammock and take a little nap, and in a few hours I'll be just as good as new."

Turning, she walked to the bed and said, "This bed, Dutch, and now! I'll wash and dry your clothes while you sleep."

As soon as I slid between the blankets, I was out like a campfire in pouring rain. After that I don't remember much, only what Laura told me later.

It seems that my fever got worse, much worse. For the most part, over the next seventy-two hours, I was in and out of consciousness. I remember little bits and pieces, like Laura washing me down in cold water and the sensation of water in my parched mouth... There was a fuzzy image of her reading at the table next to my bed... Finally, I could remember the taste of a warm stew, with Laura's soft voice in the background.

The next thing I knew, I opened my eyes to find the cabin empty. No Gus, no Laura, and no baby. Blinking a few times, I tried to recall what had happened.

With great effort, I swung my weakened legs over the bed and let my bare feet touch the cold stone floor. With the help of the stool next to the bed, I pulled myself up and staggered to the water pail and drew out a cup of cold water, which I drank in one gulp. God, I was so thirsty.

Soon, my gaze turned to the empty room. The shutters were open, with just enough light coming through the window for me to see clearly. The fire had burned down to just embers, so Laura, Gus, and the baby must have been gone for some time. Slowly, I moved to the woodpile to add a log to the fire. After that, I felt so weak that I decided to go back to bed.

Shuffling by the table, I noticed my journal lying there open and, next to it, my gold watch. That's strange, I thought. I didn't think Laura even knew about my journal, or if she did, I didn't think she would pry. At that point, though, I shook those thoughts from my head. I was just too tired to think about it. Returning to the bed, I soon fell asleep again.

Their return woke me, and I opened my eyes to see Laura carrying a completely dressed out raccoon. Theodore was on her back, with Gus following her every move.

"I thought you all had left me," I said weakly.

The sound of my words surprised her. She laid down the game and rushed to my bed. Placing her hand against my forehead, she said, "Thank God, you're okay."

Putting my hand on hers I said, "This is where we started, just a little while ago. What's the matter?"

She frowned. "That 'little while ago' has been almost three days. Two nights ago, I thought I'd lost you—your fever must have been over 106 degrees. You were delirious most of the time, and it was only last night that I could finally get some stew into you. Compared to that, you feel and look much better." Slowly, she removed her hand. "What can I get you? Are you hungry? Do you want some coffee?"

Cautiously, I swung my legs over the edge of the bed again and rested there with my eyes closed for a moment. Then I opened them, because I felt a head resting on my thigh. There was Gus, with his big soft eyes gazing up at me, his tail wagging wildly. Reaching down to pat him and scratch his ears, I said, "Hi pal. I'm glad to see that you and Laura are getting along." Turning to Laura, I said, "What happened to me?"

"All I can guess is that you came down with some type of bug that caused your body to shut down. Those aren't very good medical terms, but I'm sure, given these conditions, that your body was just run-down."

"I felt all right until that night on the mountain." I offered an apologetic smile. "Right now, though, what I really want to do is go to the bathroom."

She smiled back. "That's a good sign. Are you strong enough, or do you need my help?"

With a small grin, I replied, "No, I think I can make this trip on my own."

My walk to the outhouse, with Gus by my side, was shaky and slow, but I made it and relieved myself. Upon my return, I noticed that my journal had been replaced on the table by tin plates and cups. Laura was cooking at the fireside.

Plopping down at the table I said, "I have a few questions. Do you mind?"

She turned to me. "I have a few, too, but you go first. Dinner will be ready in just a few minutes. What do you want to know?"

"Well, I saw you come into the cabin with a dressed-out raccoon. Where did that come from?"

Turning the meat in the frying pan, she answered, "Gus and I went hunting, both yesterday and this morning. Or, should I say, Gus went hunting, and I tagged along. He showed me the way and flushed out game, both mornings. You know, Dutch, I'm a really bad shot, but today I got lucky and shot this raccoon we're about to eat."

Seeing the expression of pride that crossed her face, I knew that her first kill of game had been a rewarding experience, especially given our circumstances.

"You're the lady who wouldn't eat raccoon stew just a few months ago. Now you're the main source of it," I said, with a grin.

"Yes, I guess so. I never thought that I could or would kill a raccoon or any other living animal. But then, that was before I came to your valley."

Reality flashed in my mind. She had used the rifle, and that was the problem. How could I ask her the next question? But I had to.

"How many shots did you take when you were hunting?"

With a surprised look, she replied, "Two the first morning, and I missed both times. This morning, I used three shots to get this guy before he could get away. By the way, I looked last night for more bullets but couldn't find where you had stored them. You know that the rifle belt only has a couple of cartridges left?"

After thinking about it for a moment, I decided to tell her the truth. "There is no more ammunition for the rifle. What's in the rifle and on the belt is all we have."

The room was silent for a moment. Then she said, "What about the shotgun and pistol? Are we in any better shape with them?"

Slipping off my boots, I replied, "Two shotgun shells and five rounds for the pistol."

I could tell she was surprised, and she remained quiet for the longest time. Finally, with her head down, she joined me at the table and said, "Dutch, I'm so sorry that I wasted what little ammunition we had. I only wanted to make sure that you had some hot, nutritious food."

Reaching across the table, I grabbed her hands and looked right at her, holding her gaze with mine. "Laura, you're one hell of a nurse, and you just saved my life. If you hadn't been here, I'm sure the outcome would've been different. So a few bullets means nothing. I just wanted you to know where we stand. We can't have any secrets from each other."

Her eyes were wet as she pulled her hands back. With a nod, she stood up and returned to the cooking. Soon, she said, "Dinner is about ready, after which I'd like to talk to you about secrets."

Now, it was her turn to surprise me. After a quiet meal of fried raccoon meat and rice, Laura poured me the last of her father's scotch. Putting the tin cup of whiskey on the table, she said, "Do you feel up to talking a little more, or would you like me to save my questions until tomorrow?"

Between her tasty meal and the smell of the scotch, I felt stronger and more alert. And I was also curious about her "secrets" comment.

"Sure. Ask away."

Laura sat at the table across from me nursing Theodore. "When you were sick, and I thought maybe I might lose you, I realized that I didn't really know very much about you, Dutch. I was scared... and I'm ashamed to say that I found your journal and read most of it. Forgive me for that. But I don't think you've been totally honest with me!"

As I listened to the wind swirl around the cabin, my mind flashed back to the journal that had been on table earlier. Laura looked so serious in the dim light, with the baby suckling at her half-exposed breast, that finally I replied, "I told you most of my story, the part I thought you should know. In any event, I didn't try to lie or mislead you. Whatever you read has little to do with you, the baby, and, most importantly, what's happening now."

I could sense she was picking her words carefully. "What does the codicil in your Grandfather's will mean, when it says, 'You must be totally alone for one full year, in the wilderness of your choice, for the executor to deem that you have met all the terms and conditions?' Tell me, Dutch, what does that mean? Isn't your Uncle Roy the executor?"

Shaking my head, I answered, "Look, it's just a stupid family thing that really has no meaning here and now."

"No meaning? From what I read, it has to do with a great deal of money. And now, because I crashed into your life, you're going to lose it?"

Putting the tin cup to my lips, I let the whiskey fill my mouth with its rich, smoky flavor, rolling it around on my tongue before I swallowed. Finally, firmly, I said, "You don't understand. I couldn't care less about my Grandfather's money. I made this journey for only one reason, and that's because Uncle Roy asked me. He was between a rock and a hard place, and I couldn't say no."

"You mean the part about the Mormon Church taking your share of the estate?"

"Everything got all mixed up when Grandfather died. I had my own life until then, my own dreams. And then Roy made me feel obligated. From grandfather's grave, we were both manipulated, making us do things we didn't want to do. But I don't blame Uncle Roy. To me, this adventure has never been about money. Besides, what I'm doing here now doesn't really matter a hill of beans. The whole world is burning, while I'm sitting in a warm cabin, eating raccoon meat and drinking scotch."

Laura leaned down and kissed the top of her baby's head. It was a beautiful sight, in the golden light of the fire. She looked up at me and sighed. "Dutch, we're talking about your future. Surely Roy would understand that you had no control over things like the plane crash and me. He'll make allowances for things you couldn't control… right?"

Looking her straight in the eye, hoping to end this conversation, I fibbed. "Sure. He's a fair man, and he'll understand."

She looked back at me for a long time. Then, getting up from the table, she said, "I don't believe you. And this conversation is not over."

She moved across the cabin and placed the baby, now sleeping, into his crib before adding, in low voice,

"Is that beautiful gold watch your father's?"

"Yes. Roy found it in Grandfather's things and gave it to me before I left."

"What do the words mean?"

By now, Laura had returned to the table with a cup of coffee. Looking at her sober face, I answered, "The first word is 'search' and the last is 'pray.' Just what we are doing —searching for a way out of here, and praying we will find it."

Reaching across, she gently grabbed one of my hands. In a soft voice that was almost a whisper, she asked, "And the 'blue-eyed devil'—what does it mean? And why was Lars chasing it?"

"How did you know about that?"

"I told you, you were delirious for almost two days, and you kept screaming out those names. You would yell for Lars to run from the blue-eyed devil, and then you would shout out at some wolf to run from Lars."

I felt a little embarrassed and wondered what else I'd said. "It was just a vision I had in the snowstorm. I guess finding Lars's body up at the mine affected me more than I thought."

Squeezing my hand tightly, Laura replied, "I think that's right. In fact, I think this whole adventure will affect us both for the rest of our lives."

Laura insisted that I spend another night in the big bed. Still not feeling quite up to par, I tossed and turned for hours, our conversation about Roy racing through my mind. And I worried about the shortage of ammunition. But mostly, I thought of her words about how this adventure would affect the rest of our lives. For now, if we were to have any future, my goal had to be to get us out of this valley. In life, sometimes a door closes while another opens. I had to find another way out. I had to plan an escape–one that would work.

I love the sound of rain falling on a roof, as long as I'm warm and dry. In the end, it was what soothed me to sleep.

CHAPTER TEN

Black Veil

By the end of April, I'd regained my strength. The days were now much longer, but the weather hadn't improved. We spent the last few days of the month fishing and hunting, but because of the rain I always had my yellow slicker on or close by. The results of my efforts had been dismal, with only a few fish and another raccoon to show for my troubles.

On the morning of April 29th, I finally got a chance to shoot some game that could add real meat to our meager diet. About a quarter mile behind the cabin, close to a tree line, a deer was browsing in the underbrush.

Gus sensed the game first, coming to a sudden halt and freezing just in front of me. Dismounting Blaze, I reached for my rifle, with full knowledge that I had only one round of ammunition left. Creeping low in the tender spring grass, I came to where Gus stood, with his back arched and his hair up. Just on the other side of a small knoll was the deer. His coloring blended into the foliage, making it difficult for me to get a good view and a reliable aim.

What I saw, as I eased closer, was a young "spike." He looked to be about 150 pounds, with a dark brown coat. What little wind there was came from the west, so I'd have to move to my right to stay downwind.

Slowly, ever so slowly, I crept down the ridge and through the grass until I was as close as I dared. The deer was spooky and kept moving in and out of the underbrush and trees, sniffing the air for any trouble. I worried that if I got any closer I just might spook him back deeper into the forest. The truth was we desperately needed this meat, so I decided to risk a shot from this distance. Long gone were my conflicted feelings about shooting such a proud and beautiful animal, as I now fully realized that his death would contribute to the lives of three people.

The angle was good, the wind in the right direction, and my aim was on-target, so I squeezed off the last rifle bullet.

In that split second, the deer jumped over a log snag and bounded back into the forest. I'd wasted my last shot! If he'd stayed in place just one instant more, I would've had him. If Laura hadn't wasted bullets on her hunts, I could've gone after him. And, had I brought in more ammunition, I wouldn't be making excuses now.

That night, I told Laura what had happened with the deer. I added that we were now down to two shotgun shells and six rounds for the pistol. We talked about these problems for a while, and then she crawled down the steep ladder to the root cellar. When she returned, she plopped three small muslin sacks on the table. This was what was left of the supplies that I'd counted on: about two pounds of rice, enough flour for no more than two or three pans of biscuits, and enough coffee for no more than a week.

After talking about our situation, she looked up at me and smiled, pointing her finger at the sacks, "But this doesn't count the fish, clams, crabs, roots and other food we might find, so I'm not worried."

"Yeah, and I'll build a bow and arrow and some spears tomorrow. It will be just like Adam and Eve in the Garden of Eden. But don't tell the wolves, bears or cougars that we're down to just a few rounds. What they know can kill us."

With this, we both laughed, united in purpose, drawing strength from each other.

That evening, we dined on the remains of a fish stew with the last of our meager, half-rotten potatoes mixed in. Just before turning in, I walked to the outhouse, with Gus tagging along as usual. As I sat relieving myself in the little house, Gus started howling outside. I yelled at him to be quiet, but he continued his commotion.

As I emerged from the little wooden house, I saw what Gus was crying at. There, in the twilight of the southwestern sky, was the biggest, blackest, thunderhead I had ever seen. It looked like a black veil about to drape over the land to extinguish the last remnants of sunlight. It was a freakish site that could have deadly consequence.

As I looked around the valley, I found that it had become completely still, with no wind and no sounds of life. Something was about to happen. Gus knew it, and I could feel it now, too. Hurrying back to the cabin, I alerted Laura that a big storm was on its way and that we'd have to close the storm shutters and lock and brace the door. At first, she was doubtful about the urgency of my concerns, so I took her outside to see the thunderhead herself. One look and she was fully convinced. We hurried back inside the cabin to prepare.

The first of the winds came up just a few minutes later. It was at this point that I got worried about Blaze in the barn and ventured out to make sure he was secured. Inside the stable, I hobbled him and then bolted and nailed shut the barn doors. Before leaving, however, I took one last minute to comfort and soothe him.

When I tried to race back across the compound, the winds were so violent that they blew me to my knees twice. Each time, I regained my footing and continued. Once inside, I nailed the door and the inside shutters closed and braced them both with long logs as a brace. The wind was now blowing so hard that it had blown out our fire, forcing red-hot embers out into the room. Laura and I chased down the sparks, pouring water on them to make sure they were totally out.

The cabin was now completely dark. Fumbling for the flashlight, we soon had enough light to see what we were doing. Laura then lit two of our last three candles so I could save the batteries. The cabin was shaking with wind gusts so strong that I feared the roof would soon blow off. Laura and I, dressed in our winter clothing, sat in front of the darkened fireplace, where I had now hung a canvas tarp to hold back the flying ashes.

Laura rocked Theodore and tried to make small talk over the roar of the wind. After one especially loud and heavy gust, she asked me to come and sit in front of her on the bearskin floor so we could be close. For almost half an hour, she stroked my hair and talked about her life and family. She was scared, and so was I.

About midnight, we were hit by a gust of wind that I swear I heard coming from miles away. It blew so hard that the large oak tree behind the cabin, its roots soaked with months of rain, came crashing right into the room.

The oak fell with such force that it sheered off the fireplace chimney and tore a hole in the roof across half the cabin. Hearing it coming Laura and I jumped up and ran for the door, seconds later tree branches filling the area where we had just been sitting. Another gust hit, and a second tree from behind the cabin grazed the side wall, shifting the structure some ten or fifteen degrees before landing on the outside tent that held dry firewood.

I was sure the cabin would collapse at any minute. With Laura holding the flashlight, I tried to remove the nails and unlock the door, but the cabin was leaning at such an angle that the door wouldn't give way, even with all my weight against it.

Next, I tried the inside window shutter. Managing to wrench it open, I used the wooden stool to break through the glass and the outside shutter. Cleaning the glass away, I helped Laura, the baby and Gus through the small opening. Before I followed, I handed out the sleeping bag, two blankets, two tarps, and the elk skin. I'd retrieve the rest of the supplies tomorrow, if there was a tomorrow.

Laura and I held tightly to each other as we made our way by flashlight through the blackest storm I could ever imagine. When we safely reached the barn, I was surprised to find it still in good shape. With my hunting knife, I pried out the nails and opened the door to find Blaze moving restlessly, wide-eyed with fear. While Laura laid out the tarps and blankets, I reassured my horse. With Gus at his feet and me in his face, I gave him a hug and a dried carrot. We had been through so much in the last year; a windstorm, no matter how severe, couldn't change the love and trust we had for each other.

Gus let out a single bark as another gust of wind hit the barn. Blaze stood in his stall, pawing the ground. Finally, he shook his head and whinnied loudly. In spite of my fear, a smile crept across my face, knowing we were all together, in fair weather or foul.

The Way Out

The next morning revealed the damage to our little camp. With the wind still blustering through the trees, and a cold drizzle falling, I walked to the cabin, which was now nothing more than a pile of 'Tinker Toys'. Half the roof was crushed from the blow of the falling tree, and the entire floor was covered with mud and water from the storm. What had taken me months to build had been wiped out in minutes. How brutal and wild Mother Nature could be.

What little there was to salvage, I moved to the barn, which had suffered only minor damage. We were thankful to have a shelter and set up camp with the meager means that remained.

By evening, the dark clouds and storm front had given way to a clear view of the mountains that surrounded the valley. This view, while welcome, was not encouraging: the rain that had fallen on the valley floor had been snow on the higher elevations. The spring of warmth and renewal had changed, in a matter of hours, to the spring of ruin and frozen entrapment.

Sitting on one of the wooden stools outside the barn, rolling a cigarette, I contemplated our future. My mind jumped around like a mouse in tall grass. I had lost to the weather, and the valley had won. Like the old trapper had said, if the weather doesn't get you, the wolves will.

With the evening breeze in my hair, and the last rays of sunlight dancing off the snow-covered mountains, I knew we had to leave and soon. But should it be up the lake or over the mountains? It was choosing between the known and the unknown, both filled with hardship, snow, and danger. I didn't have high expectations for either alternative, so I thought about finding another way out. If I could fly like the crow, it would be only about fifty miles to Firvale... but I couldn't fly like a bird. If I could swim like the salmon, it would only be twenty or thirty miles to the mouth of the Dean River... but we weren't fish, either.

Or were we? How had Lars come to this valley? The answer struck me like a lightning bolt from the storm: build a raft from the log snags down at the bay and sail down the channel to the Dean River.

It sounded simple enough, but we'd still have to fight the winds, the tides, and the weather all the way up the Channel, and then trek over Thunder Mountain. Still, this idea seemed to be our best—and maybe our only alternative.

That night, I broached my plan to Laura, and she approved of the scheme enthusiastically. Later, I reflected on what else she could have said. Still, I felt it was the only practical idea for our survival, and she seemed to know it, too.

What I had learned from the mules, I put to good use with Blaze. Cutting the driftwood on the beach to length, I used his power dragging each snag into place. The base of the raft was made from three large, straight timbers, each about twenty-five feet long and thirty inches thick. I placed smaller logs, about fourteen feet long and ten inches thick, crosswise on top of these, and fastened them tightly. Using spikes that I'd removed from the cabin, along with pieces of rope, I secured the top of the raft to the bottom.

At one end of the float, I constructed a rudder station. For the rudder, I used one of the planks from the cabin's front porch that I shaped with my broad axe. I secured it to the station with ropes and a "U" bracket made out of an oak tree limb. The work was laborious and wet, as the rains had returned and never seemed to stop. While Gus joined Blaze and me each morning, he soon found dry quarters under some snags and would only venture out if the sand birds or seagulls tried to land in our bay.

Working from sunup to sundown, it took me five days to finish the craft. After completing the construction and giving it a final inspection, I tied the raft to some large logs on the beach. Now all we had to do was wait as I'd constructed the raft about fifteen feet below the high-tide markings. According to my tide charts, the next really high tide, plus 9.5 feet, would come in the next two days. By then, we needed to be ready to start the journey back.

That night, I returned to the barn and reminded Lara that, within the next 48 hours, we would leave my valley and begin our trek home.

On May 8th at 6:00 a.m., the tide had fully washed the raft off the beach, and I was ready to load our skimpy provisions. We took very little, as we had little to take: two tarps, two blankets, the elk skin, the sleeping bag, and a knapsack containing nothing more than my journal and the rusting steel box that held Lars's legacy. In one trail bag, we carried a few articles of dry clothing, some towels, three diapers, one bar of soap, fishing line and lures, cooking utensils, a half-pound of rice and, in the spirit of "waste not, want not," some used coffee grounds. For protection and hunting, we had the empty rifle, the shotgun with two shells remaining, the pistol with five bullets, and the flare gun with one flare.

The problem was not getting Laura and the baby safely aboard, or even Gus; the problem was Blaze. He wanted no part of the raft or of the choppy waters of the channel. But eventually, with much effort, many stern words, and lots of coaxing, I had him tied to the front railing of the raft. Sliding the boarding planks up, I jumped into the water, pushed with all my strength and, using a small log as a lever, shoved the craft into deeper waters.

With a lot of work, I soon got the raft moving towards the flowing waters of the channel. Laura, with the baby secure in his cradleboard, helped me by pushing with the rudder. The water was ice-cold, with three-foot white caps rolling across the gray channel as I finally dragged myself onto the platform. My body from the waist down was sopping wet, and the cold wind made my wet legs feel frozen.

Using the rudder as a paddle, I worked to move the raft forward, towards the incoming tide. According to my calculations, we had about another hour of flood tide and then half hour of slack tide. During that time, we'd have to reach a rocky island some two miles down channel or risk being washed back down the channel towards the Pacific Ocean.

Laura soon had a towel and another pair of trousers for me, and I changed clothes as best I could without interrupting my frantic efforts to catch the incoming current.

Within the hour, the flood turned to slack, and we were still a mile from the island. With all the effort I could muster, I pushed the paddle back and forth, back and forth. We slowly, ever so slowly, made progress.

Twenty minutes later, I could see that the water was now beginning to flow seaward again and that we were not going to make the island. Fighting the out-flowing tide was a losing battle. Our raft soon slipped past Nascall bay where we'd started and began making its way towards King Island and the Pacific.

As we bobbed pass our bay, I cursed the tides and looked for a way to stop our drift. That's when I spotted a large log snag sticking out of the water on the east shore, about a half a mile down-channel. Jerking the rudder hard, I maneuvered the raft in that direction. As we got close, I shouted for Laura to take the helm and keep us heading towards the snag. Just as the current sent the raft drifting by the deadhead, some twenty yards away on the port side, I threw my lasso like some cowboy in a rodeo steer-roping contest. My aim was on track and found the top of the log snag.

It took every ounce of strength I could muster, but soon I had us tied to the snag, which ensured that we wouldn't end up in the Pacific Ocean… at least for now.

The tide turns about every 12 hours, so we were stuck surfing on the snag until about seven in the evening. Then, with the lengthening spring daylight, we would have about three hours of sailing time before dark. Until then, there was nothing to do but wait.

The weather was still miserable, with both wind and rain from the west. Laura secured one canvas tarp on the deck of the raft, towards the stern. Then, using the other as dry cover, she lashed them down. Confident that we were secure and safe, we crawled under this cover where I removed my wet slicker and dried myself with a towel. Then, turning to Laura, I shouted over the weather, "Are you and the baby okay?"

She smiled and, as Gus joined us under the tarp, answered, "For a while there, I thought we might be sailing straight to Ketchikan. But then, once again, God had a better idea. But will that log hold us?"

As I mopped off my face, I replied, "It should hold, but I'll have to keep an eye on it. Now if God could only provide us with a warm fire, some hot food and coffee."

Her voice was soft as she assured, "He will, Dutch, He will."

Gus moved between us and lay down, the smell of his wet fur filling our little shelter. Taking my towel, I tried to dry him off. He rolled and turned his belly up to help me. It was the first time I had seen him that submissive.

Feeling bad about Blaze being exposed to the elements, I stuck my head out of the little tent to see him standing in the pouring rain with his head down. The look on his face was sad, but there was nothing I could do. Back under the tarp, I yelled, "Blaze looks like a drowned beaver. I wish there was some way to get him out of the weather."

"I'm more worried about you, Dutch. You haven't gotten a good night's sleep since the cabin fell in. Lay back and get some rest. I'll watch out for Blaze and keep an eye on the snag while you get some sleep."

Her eyes were bright and alert. I knew she had my best interests at heart, and, for the first time in many days, I felt tired. With the rolling and pitching of the raft, and the rain pelting the top tarp, both Gus and I were soon asleep.

I awoke about five in the afternoon. Laura was nursing her baby when I opened my eyes. Her features were soft and delicate in the diffuse light under the tarp. It was a beautiful sight, mother and son.

She looked over to me and quietly said, "You talked in your sleep again, something about a white goose. I almost woke you, but I thought you needed the sleep."

"The goose was a snow bird that I shot for Thanksgiving. It was the only pure white bird I've ever seen,"

She smiled. "There is something about 'pure white' that makes a man take notice."

Her statement caught me off-guard as I climbed out from under the tarp. The weather had improved to nothing more than a low overcast a few hundred feet above us. The channel waters were now steel gray and flat. The green timberline, all around us, blended into the jagged rocks of the shoreline, making the water look like a lake. Blaze was almost dry now and looked a little happier. While the tide was still running out, for some reason I felt more confident about the next leg of our journey.

By 7 o'clock, the tide had turned to slack. After I untied the raft from the log snag, I began using the rudder again as a paddle. By 7:30, the tide was with us, and we started making good headway up the channel. Guessing that we had almost another three hours of sunlight, I figured we could make Nascall Island, some five or six miles up the waterway. Traveling any further at night, with no moon, would be too dangerous, so we'd have to camp there for the night.

With light fading in the western sky, we landed on the rocky, green island shown on the charts as Nascall Island. It had no sandy beach, so the best I could do was maneuver the raft close to some boulders on a rocky beach at the north end to unload Blaze, Gus, Laura and Theodore. Tying a rope to the raft, I let it drift with the tide as we made a small camp on the green plateau above the channel.

We had to have a fire tonight, so I searched in the small rock caves and scrounged up some dry firewood. Laura started the fire as I ventured out to find something to eat as it had been almost a day since our last meal. While I searched, Laura started cooking the last of our rice and reused some coffee grounds to brew a small pot of coffee.

The island was small, high, and rocky, some hundred yards wide and three hundred yards long. Climbing up to the highest point, I could see that there was little or no chance of any game living on this green outcropping. But just as I stumbled back into our camp, I spotted a fat seagull sitting on one of the rocks behind Laura. With twilight upon us, my stomach growling, and no other opportunities in sight, I shot and killed the seagull with the second-to-last shell in my shotgun.

Laura was caught off-guard by the loud report of the shotgun going off just behind her. She jumped from the fire and grabbed the baby. With Theodore crying, she whirled and screamed, "Dutch, you scared the hell out of me. What are you doing?"

Scrambled over some rocks to where the dead bird had fallen I raised it into the air. "Shooting our dinner, lady."

"Nobody eats seagulls," she snarled, still shaken. "I heard they were poisonous."

"It's just like raccoon stew," I countered. "You don't know what you'll eat until you're hungry enough to eat it."

I have to admit that, after plucking the feathers and cutting up the bird for the cooking pot, not much remained, and it tasted even worse than we thought it would. But it did add a little meat to the last of the rice, and when you got over the image of eating a seagull, I'm sure it added some much-needed nutrition, as well. At least that's what I told Laura as we choked it down.

After a long night of sleeping on rocks and even a longer early morning waiting for the tide to turn again, we were off the island by 9:00 a.m. This time, I hoped to reach the mouth of the Dean River before sunset. But the weather changed again, with the wind whirling out of the north and white caps filling the channel from shore to shore. For every few yards we made with the tide, we lost a yard from the wind and choppy waters. Try as I might, I couldn't get us close to the Dean River by nightfall. It hadn't started to rain yet, but I knew it was coming. Desperate for a place to beach the raft, I tied up in a rocky little cove on the leeward side the channel at 9 o'clock.

I was exhausted and discouraged, but I knew I had to try finding some game or fish for us to eat. As Laura made the fire, I began searching the rocky cliffs where we'd landed. With the tide now rushing out, I soon found some mussels on the rocks, in waist-deep water. With my knife, I pried off about two dozen, which Laura cooked in boiled seawater.

By nightfall, it started to rain again. Laura, Theodore, and I climbed under the tarp to protect us from the bad weather. It was now pitch black, and the rain had totally drenched our little fire. Soon I felt the Gus's head and body as he joined us under the canvas for protection. Turning to Laura, I said, "Well, we're all here. If Blaze could fit in here, I'm sure he would put his head under the tarp, too."

Laura laughed. "There's no room here for your entire menagerie. But if we make it out of here, I'll keep Blaze dry and fed for the rest of his life."

"I'll hold you to that." Wrestling a blanket from Gus, I asked, "What was this 'pure white' stuff you talked about yesterday, anyway?"

There was a long silence. Laura and her baby rolled over, away from me, in the sleeping bag. Then she said, "You figure it out. Maybe you and my son are unique, as both of you are still 'pure' and not corrupted by life."

Hearing my own breathing over the sounds of the rain, I finally replied, "Pure I am not. Incorruptible I am not. And while I've not yet had a slice of the cake, I'm just an ordinary guy."

There was a long silence before Laura replied, "The statement about being 'pure white' was not about you, Dutch.... Go to sleep."

Bewildered, I eventually did just that.

Late the next morning, we pushed off again. This time, I was confident that we'd reach the mouth of the Dean River by nightfall. The channel had flattened down, with only a slight wind out of the south. But the weather was still miserable with pouring rain and cold temperatures. Standing at the rudder, I could see that we were all soaked to the bone and chilled. It sickened me to see Laura, Theodore, and the animals so exposed to the elements, so I decided that we'd spend our last night on the channel at the old Kimsquit Cannery, about a half-mile down from the river.

As we passed by the mouth of the Dean River, Laura looked up at me, the canvas draped around her wet head, rain running off her face, and shouted, "Where are we going? I thought you wanted to land there."

Pointing down the channel, I answered, "There's an old cannery down there, and if I remember right, one of the buildings still has a roof. We can dry off tonight, and tomorrow we can use the outgoing tide to make it back to the mouth of the river."

To my surprise, Laura made no further comments. She must have realized how wet we were, too. Slowly, ever so slowly, we made our way to the dilapidated skeleton of the stinking cannery.

Pulling the raft ashore next to the tall wooden pilings of the cannery, I carefully guided my little party onto the old game trail next to the buildings. Hobbling Blaze, I let him graze on a grassy knoll close by. Then, carrying Theodore, I led Laura and Gus up the wooden ramp to the top platform. It was still an eerie and lonely place, but it provided the only shelter I could think of. With twilight approaching, I maneuvered our party around the holes of the rotting wooden decking.

Soon, we reached the old structure that I remembered from my journey in. Kicking the door open, I found a dark but dry cabin for us to take refuge in. In one corner was a rusted potbelly stove, still connected to a chimney that ran up through a mangled tin roof. The room was small and looked safe, with no signs of rotten beams or seagull dung. The little hut was large enough for us to enjoy warmth and dryness for one glorious night. Under these circumstances, I was as happy as if I'd landed us a room at a first-class lodge.

Laura lit our last candle and began making the room as pleasant as possible by putting our belongings in place. We needed a fire, so I made my way from building to building, looking for dry firewood. As I moved from one abandoned structure to another, with my arms full of wood, I noticed a large, gray goose sitting on one of the pilings near the shore. Hurrying back to the shack, I returned with my shotgun and killed the bird with my last shell. That evening, after cleaning and plucking the bird, Laura and I enjoyed an appetizing meal of pan-roasted goose—a little burnt but tasty. I was pleased that my last shotgun shell had not been wasted on another seagull.

With a fire in the old potbelly stove, the little shed soon became warm. Most of our clothing was hanging on rope lines to dry, and we were all finally warm for the first time in days. It was the first night since the cabin came crashing down that I'd felt comfortable and snug.

Summit of Sorrow

Early the next morning, I reloaded the raft and paddled with the outgoing tide to the mouth of the Dean River. It had stopped raining and had even warmed up a bit, although the southern sky remained dark and threatening. After unloading the raft for the last time, I put Laura and Theodore on Blaze. As I'd done so many times before, I led Blaze, with Gus at point, and we began the long walk toward Thunder Mountain. With a good pace and any luck, we would reach its summit and that dry little cave by nightfall.

By noon, a storm out of the south reached us, bringing pouring rain and dropping temperatures. Crossing the many streams and creeks, I made sure that Blaze was following close to my lead to ensure that he always knew our trail and the depth of any water. Walking alongside of Laura and Blaze, I commented to her about how quiet little Theodore had been during the entire journey.

Laura looked down from her perch on Blaze's back and grinned. "Maybe you're not the only mountain man in this wilderness."

"Well, one thing is for sure," I replied. "He's definitely the youngest mountain man in this wilderness."

We both smiled and nodded. I was pleased that our spirits were this good on the fourth day of our trek.

The trip up the mountain was difficult. The rain turned to snow a thousand feet before the trail's summit. The way itself was rocky and muddy, giving way to loose boulders as we moved up the switchback trail. Leading Blaze, I fumbled for my footing on the steep knolls, with snow blowing sideways into my face. A number of times, I looked up to see whether we were in sight of our night's destination but found only a tapestry of white. While Gus was still at the point, he no longer roamed hundreds of feet in front of us because of the weather. He was now content to keep our little party in close sight. With the wind in my ears and snow in eyes, I worried about what we might find at the summit.

By dusk, we'd reached the pinnacle, and I found the cave that had sheltered me on the way over. Helping Laura and Theodore, I moved them into the cave, leaving Blaze standing some fifty yards from its mouth. Gus also joined us. Laura and I quickly gathered some dry twigs and wood and soon had a small fire going inside the rock walls. With the wind beginning to pick up again, I decided to secure Blaze as close to the fissure as possible.

As I headed out of the cave, I heard Blaze make an anguished bellow that turned my blood to ice. I knew immediately that it was big trouble. Straining my eyes in the early darkness and falling snow, I couldn't see what was happening. There was another loud cry, and then I heard a wolf howling in the muffled weather.

As I raced towards Blaze, I drew my pistol. Through the blanket of snowflakes, I saw a mangy wolf with his jaws sunk deep into the hindquarters of my beloved horse. The wolf held onto the flesh while Blaze kicked with all his power. The predator had dug deep into Blaze, and, no matter how hard Blaze kicked, the wolf would not let go. By the time I reached them, the two animals were in a death lock.

With pistol in hand and few bullets left, I shot the wolf through the head with a fury and vengeance I hadn't known I had. Within a split second, the vermin fell to the ground dead. But then Blaze also fell and let out a cry of pain that I will never forget. Kneeling, I put my face to his and could see that there was little life left in his eyes. Quickly, I moved to his hindquarters to survey the damage. The wolf had exposed his entire right backside down to the white of his bone. Blood was spattered on the snow for almost 30 feet behind him. Moving back to the face of my horse, I knew it was hopeless. He was now making uncontrolled kicking motions with his legs as he lay dying on the snow covered ground. Lifting his head, I placed my hands around his nose. Looking down at him, I shouted, "It's my fault, it's my fault... I should have stayed with you. Oh, Blaze, please forgive me."

With tears rolling down my cheeks I raised my pistol and sent one bullet squarely between his eyes.

In spite of the muting effect of the falling snow, the loud sound echoed off the cliffs. Dazed and crying, I looked into those brown pupils as they stared up at me. Then his eyes closed. I was thankful it had been quick. But, my God, what had I done?

The next thing I knew, Laura was standing over me, roughly shaking my shoulder. Snow blinded me as I looked up at her.

"Dutch, what happened? Get a hold of yourself!"

After a few seconds, I got up from the wet ground and went behind my dead horse, where I found the body of the dead wolf.

Through the falling snow, I saw its ghostly blue eyes staring up at me. Was this the same animal that had stalked me since my trip over a year ago? And was this—could this—be the same predator that had attacked Lars, twelve years ago?

Kneeling down, I examined the dead carcass. Under the dirty matted fur was a face with graying hair around the nose and muzzle. In his mouth, I found his teeth yellow and rotting. This was a very old wolf. It had to be the one that had stalked both Lars and me.

Standing, I shouted, "You're nothing, just one old, mangy wolf!"

With a swift kick, like a punter in a football game, I airlifted the dead animal across the trail and down the ravine on the other side. My mind was reeling as I felt guilty about Blaze and was furious at the blue-eyed devil.

Gus joined us, sniffing around Blaze's lifeless body. In the dim light, I could see a puzzled expression on his face as he sniffed my horse's head.

Kneeling down again, I reached for Gus and sobbed, "He's gone, pal, he's gone. It's my fault, and you can blame me."

Laura called to me, over the weather, "Dutch, it's the wolf's fault, not yours. Please come inside the cave and get out of this storm. There is nothing more you can do for Blaze."

Jumping to my feet, I roared back to her, "You go back. What I have done here tonight can't be righted. But Blaze will not become dinner for those other mangy wolves."

She looked at me for a moment; she had never seen me this angry and didn't how to respond. Bursting into tears, she turned and rushed back to the cave.

I worked for over two hours, burying Blaze in a large pile of loose stones. I worked without thinking or caring about the snowstorm raging about me. All I knew was that Blaze would rest here without being disturbed by any other vermin. Meanwhile, Gus stood nearby on a large rock, howling into the wind, as if telling the wolves that this was now holy-ground and that none should return. His howls and the whirling wind became my gospel choir for the burial of my beloved horse.

When I finally finished with the stones, I looked up into the sky, letting the snowflakes mix with my tears, and I cried out, "Thank you, God, for this proud and beautiful animal. Death can come for any of us at any time… and it's never a welcome visitor, so take him now. He was cheerful in all weather and never shirked a task. His spirit was pure and his heart determined. Forgive me, for I have let him down. Take him into your kingdom with my prayer and hopes. Oh, how I'll miss him…"

Then, shaking the snow off my face, I slowly walked towards the cave, calling for Gus to join me. With a blood scent in the air, I paused at the opening and prayed there would be no more trouble.

Laura had spread out the tarps and blankets against the back wall of the cave. In front, near the opening, the little campfire was burning. Inside, I knelt by the flames to warm my hands. My head was still reeling as I stared into the red embers.

Without saying a word, Laura was soon behind me with a cup of hot water and a piece of last evening's goose. As I looked up at her, I knew she'd been crying, but she managed a brave smile and returned to the canvas, her baby, and the makeshift bed.

The cave was silent except for the crackling of the fire. Gus curled up in front of the cavern's opening, as if he was on sentry duty. Adding more wood to the fire, I took off my boots, coat, and gun belt, and then lay down beside Laura.

Pulling a blanket over my body, I stared upward. The firelight danced on the ceiling rocks, making strange shadows that in some ways added to my misery. With my eyes watering, a single tear raced down my cheek. I was exhausted and still in shock, grief rolling through my mind as I faced yet another tragedy.

"Dutch, come here. Sit on my lap."

She was such a grand lady, with a smile that made me feel warm and happy. My little five-year-old feet carried me to her as fast as they could. As I leapt into the air, she caught me and pulled me to her big, warm bosom. Placing her arms around me and hugging me, she said, "Your mom and dad have gone on a journey.

They loved you very much and wanted me to tell you that they will miss you and will always love you."

She'd caught me off guard with her matter-of-fact words. I thought for a minute and then looked up into her sweet, somber face and replied, "Where did they go, Grandmamma? When will they be back?"

A tear rolled down her cheek.

"There was an automobile accident, and they are dead. God now has them in his kingdom. It's a most beautiful place, but they will miss you very much until you can join them there."

As I clutched her dress, I raised my little face to hers. "I don't understand. Why did they go? When will I see them again? What does 'dead' mean?"

Gus was barking, but I didn't know why. It seemed as if I had closed my eyes only a few seconds ago, but when I opened them, it was morning. The early light spilled into the cave, still smoky from last night's fire.

Gus barked again, and I had to shake my head to gain my thoughts. As I rolled stiffly to my feet, I saw Gus standing close to the cave's opening.

Then things began to happen as if I was in a time machine set to fast-forward. A huge brown bear rose up at the opening of the cave, letting out a roar that echoed through the cavern.

Reaching for my pistol, I screamed at Gus to move back. The bear, silhouetted against the incoming light, looked to be over eight feet tall.

Laura and the baby were suddenly awake, with Teddy crying. Gus moved back a few feet into the cave, but the bear followed, swinging his front legs and head as he moved inside. By now, Laura had grabbed her baby and was standing behind me, close to the rear of the grotto.

Events were moving so fast that I had no time to think, only to react. The bear made another move forward. Now he was no more than ten or fifteen feet in front of us. Gus had stopped backing up and now stood firm at my left side. When the creature stood on his hind legs and let out another deafening roar, Gus sprang into the air, trying to reach his throat.

The bear lifted one paw and, with a powerful motion, hurled Gus all the way across the cave, against the far rock wall. He let out a whimper as he landed on the stones and slid to the ground with a sickening thud.

The bear was now angrier than before, as he approached Laura and me. Raising my pistol, I knew two things for certain: I had only three rounds of ammunition… and pistol bullets were not going to stop this monster.

On pure adrenaline, I fired all three bullets in rapid sequence. The cave echoed with the noise and filled with the smell of gunpowder. The bear was stunned, his black nostrils flaring and snorting, but I knew he hadn't been stopped. After hearing the "click" of the fourth, empty chamber, I dropped the pistol. My mind said, Pull your knife; my gut answered, No!

Quickly reaching down to my backpack, I grabbed the only other weapon we had, the flare gun. As I stood up, the bear again lumbered towards us on his hind legs, now within swiping distance. He was angry, roaring, and wounded. With my hand shaking, I pointed the flare gun at his face, removed the safety and cocked the breach. There was no more time... I pulled the trigger.

The crimson flare raced from the barrel, sending a deafening bellow throughout the cavern.

We were lucky, that morning, very lucky. The live flare found its way into the open mouth of the bear. At first, the hot shell just made the animal stop in its tracks as he tried to figure out what had just happened. Then the flare went off inside his mouth, the hot fluorescent signal-tip cooking the bear's brain. The monster's entire head lit up like roman-candle. With smoke rolling out of his mouth and nose, and his eyes turned inward with amazement and he crashed to the ground.

But as he fell forward he took one last swipe at me, slicing deeply into my left shoulder with one set of his claws. Dust came rolling up into the still morning air as he hit the ground. A few more uncontrolled movements and the bear was dead, totally dead.

With blood running from my upper arm, I examined his carcass. His head was still on fire, and the awful smell of fried brains permeated the air. My first three shots had hit him squarely in the chest, but not penetrated all the way through his heavy fur and fat. But the flare had been on target. With his dead, open eyes now looking up at me, I knew I would never be this lucky again.

My hands were trembling, and sweat pouring down my face. By now, Laura was hovering next to me, trying to place a tourniquet on my arm.

"Dutch, you're hurt. Please let me bandage you before you bleed to death."

Grabbing the towel, I yelled, "Where's Gus? What's happened to Gus? "

Pressing the towel against my shoulder I staggered across the cave to where Gus was lying. Slumping to the ground, I found Gus with his eyes closed and blood stains on his upper hip from the bear's claws. There in the faint morning light, I pulled his limp body onto my lap.

His eyes opened for a moment and looked up at me. They were bloodshot, and his pupils were dilated. With his breathing labored, he made very few sounds, only a little whimper.

Looking down at him, I screamed, "I won't let you die!"

Laura knelt next to me, with the first aid kit and another towel. While she examined my arm, I wiped the blood away from Gus's hip and examined him. Other than three deep claw marks on his fleshy thigh, which were still dripping blood, he seemed to be okay, but I knew that the claw marks would have to be sutured.

As I turned back to Laura, I felt the fire in my arm for the first time. Groaning, while holding the towel tighter to my shoulder, I watched as she rummaged inside the kit and retrieved the syringe with a small vial of Novocain. As she transferred the pain killer into the syringe, she calmly said, "This is the last of it... only enough for you, Dutch."

Shaking my head, I answered, "No, half for me and half for Gus."

Nodding in agreement, she stuck the needle in me and, seconds later, did the same for Gus.

"He doesn't look good, Dutch. He's lost a lot of blood and might have some internal bleeding. Keep pressure on his hip with the towel while I stitch you up, and then I'll do the same for Gus."

"He doesn't die."

"It's not up to us," Laura replied, sad and steady, with suture in hand.

In the dim light, she went to work with the needle and thread. Some minutes later, I had twenty-two stitches running up and down the six inch claw marks on my upper arm. Just before bandaging the wound, Laura wiped the four cut marks with antiseptic. This hurt like the hell, and I let out a loud gasp of pain.

Wrapping my shoulder, she said, "Sorry... you don't want to get an infection from dirty claws."

As she completed my bandage, I said, "I'll help you with Gus. He won't like that anodyne any more than I did."

I helped Laura as she cut away the fur around the gashes on Gus's hip. Then, with me holding him down, she sutured his wounds. In all, he got fifteen stitches on three gashes, some five eight inches long. During this time, he was semi-conscious and only whimpered a few times. But when Laura swabbed the area with antiseptic, he let out a furious growl, and I had to hold him back.

The growling woke Teddy again, wrapped in a blanket, and he started crying. As Laura moved to him, I reached down and taped a bandage on Gus's exposed flesh. When that was done, I lean back against the rocky wall with Gus's head still in my lap and let out a sigh of relief. Sitting there for a few moments, I looked around the little cavern. The bear's gigantic, stinking body took up most of the cave, and the floor was splattered with blood everywhere. We had to get moving before it prompted another disaster.

"Pack up," I ordered. "We're leaving this place."

"Shouldn't we wait here until you and Gus both have your strength back?"

"No, I'll carry him," I answered, and gestured around the cave. "All this blood is an open invitation."

Laura's eyes widened. "You can't carry fifty pounds on your back. It's just too much."

"If my mules could make it up here with five hundred pounds, I can make it down with fifty."

Just before leaving, I asked Laura if she wanted me to cut off some of the dead bear for trail meat. She didn't blink before responding, "I'd rather eat another seagull than any meat from the animal that almost killed you and Gus."

She got no argument from me. Moments later, I stumbled out of the cave with Gus draped across my shoulders. He was still semi-conscious and hadn't protested when I slid him onto my back. The weather was clearing, and the cool breeze through the pass felt good on my face. Slowly, I walked over to the pile of rocks that was Blaze's grave, and said a final prayer. Gazing down on the stones, with tears racing down my cheeks, I remembered all the times I had enjoyed this magnificent animal. What a loss.

Finally, Laura shook me.

"Dutch, come on. I'm so sorry, but we have to get out of here. Death is part of life, and we can't get it back. We have to move on."

Slowly turning, I saw her standing next to me, the baby on her back and carrying our only trail bag. Her eyes were swollen and her face puffy, but she still looked beautiful, which made my heart break all the more. Knowing she was right, it took me a few moments to regain my composure.

As we started to move down the trail, I stopped one last time to gaze at the summit of Thunder Mountain. *This I will remember as the Summit of Sorrow*, I thought, *and I will never forget what happed here.*

The Last Trail

Just before descending the mountain, Laura checked my shoulder to make sure the stitches were holding, and did the same for Gus.

"How's he look?" I asked.

"No bleeding and his breathing is better. But he's still not really conscious."

I patted his head, where it rested on my shoulder. Then we turned and slowly started our trek down.

While the day was dry, the way was muddy, and we slipped down the east-side game trail. We carried all of our worldly belongings on our backs and in our hands, which made for slow going on the trail. We slid more than we walked, and used our rope to cling from one rock outcropping to the next. A number of times, we lost our footing and slid down the trail in wet muck before we could stop one another.

A few hours later we finally stopped by a big boulder to rest, and Gus started to move on my back. As Laura reached into her trail bag for the canteen, I slipped Gus off my back and onto a tall rock. Still holding him tightly, I looked into his face, to find his eyes open and bright. Taking the tin cup from Laura, I held it to his mouth.

Slowly, he slurped some water. I had worried about him all the way down, but now he was finally moving and drinking. Thank God! As Laura stroked his head and checked out the stitches, she proclaimed, "Gus, you're one hell of a tough dog. Let's see if you can stand."

Gently, I slid Gus from the rock to the ground. He was shaky at first but soon found his footing. Finally, looking up at both of us, he barked and slowly wagged his tail. Then he walked gingerly over to a scrub bush and lifted his leg. With joy in my heart, I watched him do his business and said, "Gus, what guts. I like that."

With Gus slowing down the pace, it was late afternoon before we reached the timberline, covered with mud and wet to the bone. It was a miracle that we were able to keep Teddy dry, but we had him bundled up in everything we could think of. About five hundred feet down from the timberline, I found a small creek that provided us with enough water to clean up and drink.

It was both good and bad to stop at the water's edge. We could clean our wet clothes and boots. And, if I could find enough dry firewood, we could build a fire. But we were still so high up on the mountain that I knew we'd have little chance of finding game or anything to eat. Still, a fire was first. Soon, I had found enough dry twigs and wood from under large fir trees to fuel a roaring fire. We hung our wet clothes and boots as close to the fire as we dared. On this smoky blaze, Laura began boiling water in the coffee pot, adding roots from some nearby plants. Within a couple of hours, our clothes were dry, and we consumed a hot, tart, liquid meal.

Late that evening, lying under the tarps with Gus between us, she commented, "What I wouldn't give for a little raccoon stew."

We both gave a half-hearted laugh. We knew that there would be no raccoons or other game until we reached lower elevations.

Then it started to rain again in earnest, dousing the last of the fire embers. With Gus's warm body next to mine, I reminded myself that I could not look to him for our protection and that while I still carried my rifle and pistol, both were empty. At best, my guns could only be used as clubs or hammers. Our fate was now with God... but then, it always had been.

Oh, how I wished Blaze was here to lead us back. I missed him so much that my heart actually ached. But I rejoiced to still have Gus. Silent tears ran down my cheeks as the sounds of the rain pounding on the tarp lulled me to sleep.

The morning camp was cold, as we had only two matches left. By 7 a.m., we were walking down the mountainside, the weather cool and cloudy, but dry. The way down was getting better, as the heavy green underbrush was drier and provided better footing.

My attitude, however, was still miserable because of my emotional and physical wounds, and I sensed that Laura knew it. My shoulder would soon heal, leaving only claw marks as a tattoo, but the emotional scars would take longer. Along the way, Laura tried many times to engage me in conversation. She kept asking about the area we were traveling or what we'd do once we reached civilization. She was a real trouper, talking even though her questions went without many answers.

By noon, we reached the river in the general area where I'd spent the first night of my journey in. Walking along the shoreline, I kept a close look for any signs of fish. Just after we crossed the river on a downed log, I spotted a fish swimming not more than a quarter-mile from my original camp.

Instructing Laura to rest with Theodore under a large fir tree, I set about trying to catch that one lone fish. He was hovering under a large rock, close to some rushing white water. Through the half-clear water, I could see him dart out into the current to feed and then dart back under the rock again. For over an hour, I fished, trying all three of my lures, but with no luck. He'd come out from under the rock and look at each offering, but then he'd retreat back under the rock for protection.

Time was moving on, and I knew we had move on, too. As I pulled in my line, I was about to give up when Laura approached and said, "Dad always told me that the way to catch any fish was by using the right bait."

She handed me a fat worm she had dug with her bare hands from under a tree.

"Put this on your hook and try again. What are a few more minutes?"

Her industriousness and determination warmed my heart. Smiling at her, I replied, "What can I say to the daughter of the best fisherman I've ever known?" Fastening the worm on the trailing hook of the lure, I placed the line into the rushing current again. It floated quickly downstream and close to the rock.

BAM! The fish was hooked and began taking off downstream.

His pull was great, but my determination was greater. Nothing would stop me from catching this fish. Within a few minutes, I'd landed a fat two-or-three-pound cutthroat trout.

The result of using Laura's bait and of getting the cook fire going lifted our spirits. Within half an hour, we were eating the fat fish from a cooking stick, with Laura commenting that she'd never had such a fresh and good-tasting fish in her life.

After our meal, we rested and even napped a few minutes, but by 3 p.m. I rousted our little party to our feet, and again we headed east towards Firvale. My goal was to make it as far as the timber clearing, some three or four miles from the hamlet. If we walked until dark, we should make it.

Sure enough, by 9:30 we stumbled into the clearing of the logged forest. Tomorrow, I knew, we would only have another few hours of walking to reach the town.

We walked until dark, about 10 o'clock. Then we spread out the tarps and bedding. But because the trees were young growth, only few feet tall, I had problems finding any dry twigs and brush under the tree canopies. What I did find would be difficult, if not impossible, to burn. With our last match, I had Laura hold two twisted papers from my journal. She held them away from the breeze as we attempted to ignite the twigs and the pages, but to no avail. The match and the two lit papers couldn't start the damp pile of twigs.

Looking up at Laura in the last remains of the evening dusk, I said, "Looks like another cold camp. But tomorrow night we'll be sitting inside with a hot meal and a hot fire."

She smiled and replied, "We'll see about that. For now, let's just get some sleep and face tomorrow, tomorrow."

Her comments raced through my mind as I crawled under the tarp and my blankets. The last sound I remember was the peaceful and contented suckling of baby Ted at her breast.

Since leaving the eastern slopes of Thunder Mountain, the weather had been mostly dry, but the surroundings were still rain-soaked and damp. The morning of our final walk out was no different. We broke camp about 6 a.m. My guess was that we had no farther than two or three miles to walk to reach Firvale. But the early morning was cloudy and foggy, and I couldn't see more than fifteen or twenty feet in front of me. With compass in hand we started out. No doubt we were a shabby-looking group. We were all soiled with trail mud, with filthy rags on our backs, and Gus's fur was matted and patchy. Worse, my mood matched our looks, as I was still feeling anger over Blaze's violent death.

As usual, Laura sensed my mood and tried to make small talk as we stumbled across a wilderness of dead tree stumps and heavy, wet brush. Walking in front of me, carrying Ted, with Gus at her side, she kept looking back to make sure I was not out of sight. For the most part, I didn't even acknowledge her questions and observations about the countryside. She rambled on, but I only replied a few times.

By mid-morning, the clouds and fog cleared, and we had a clear view of our destination, just a mile or so in front of us.

Then it happened. All of a sudden, I smelled all kinds of scents that weren't the natural smells of the forest. With one waft, it was bacon; another, coffee, then onions. I stopped a couple of times to breathe deep and try to taste the smells. Excitedly, I called out to Laura, "Do you smell that?"

She turned, beaming. "I think so. It's coffee. No, it's civilization! My God, Dutch, we're almost there."

At those simple words, I lost control. I couldn't believe what she'd just said: We're almost there. Those were the words I'd dreamt about for over a year. Immediately, I forgot my sorrow, and my heart filled with glorious relief. Grabbing Laura, I gave her a big hug. Then I buried my face against little Ted's head, kissing his downy soft hair. This nightmare was almost over, and I wanted Laura to know how happy I was for us. Racing in front of Laura again, I lifted them off the ground and twirled them in a circle, all the while hooting with joy. But Laura's face was solemn as I set her down on the ground.

"What's the problem?" I asked. "I thought you'd be happy to get out of this God-forsaken wilderness."

She looked up at me. "What's the date, Dutch? What day is this?"

"It's May the thirteenth, as near as I can figure, and we are no more than an hour from a warm meal and a bath!"

Removing the cradleboard from her back, she firmly lowered her body to the ground next to a stump.

"Let's stay here until the morning of the fifteenth. Then we can march into town, and meet your uncle, and complete your grandfather's mission."

Being touched, I knelt close to her. Looking her in the eye, I replied, "You're crazy, lady. We have no food, no fire, no bullets... and you want to camp here? We didn't march this far to stay one second longer than we have to. We have a baby to think about. What we'll do, this fine morning, is walk into the Frenchman's hotel and order the biggest steak-and-egg breakfast he has!"

Laura grabbed my hand, sad and intent. "Dutch, if we stay, maybe your uncle will consider your mission accomplished, and you can go forward with your life."

I snickered at her statement, but I could see she didn't like my laughter. Her concerns were real, and her idea of a solution was heartfelt, but she didn't know Uncle Roy.

There was a small breeze in the air, moving a few loose wisps of her mostly matted hair. Looking into her eyes, I could see her resolve. She felt guilty about my future, just as I felt guilty about the fate of Blaze.

"Look, Laura, someone once told me that life has its own way, and there is nothing we can do about it. God has his own destiny for us. Sound familiar? This is not the end, only the beginning and there is no looking back."

To my astonishment, my simple statement seemed to release me from the guilt I had about Blaze. It was if an anvil had suddenly been lifted from my shoulders, and I could see that Laura sensed my relief.

There, next to the tree stump, I found a single yellow dandelion. Picking it, I slipped it into her hair, saying, "I've been alone all my life, until you and Theodore dropped into my valley." Pulling back and looking her straight in the eye, I continued, "When you wear my flower, you make it look beautiful."

Her eyes filled with emotion as she finally realized that we would not stay another night or another hour in this wilderness. A smile crept across her face. Leaning over, she kissed my cheek and blinked her blue eyes in agreement.

Pulling her to her feet, I helped load the cradleboard onto her back. Soon, we were again walking towards hot baths and food. As we stumbled over downed logs and brush, she asked, "Dutch, what have you missed the most during your year in the wilderness?"

Using the empty rifle as a walking stick, I paused and thought about my answer.

"Eggs. No...a radio. No... maybe...yes, a milkshake. Or maybe just a glass of milk. What I won't miss is raccoon stew... you know, that's a hard question."

We laughed as we made our way ever closer to civilization. Her questions and my answers made for good soul-searching about life and what's important. Then it dawned on me. Walking in front of Laura I stopped again, pointing a finger at her. "My grandfather came out of the wilderness with gold, my father with oil, and I came out with two lives. My mission was by far the richest."

She smiled at me and kept walking. As she passed, she grazed my cheek with another kiss and whispered, "You've got it. You searched and prayed and found yourself."

The look in her eyes told me the truth. It had been there all the time, written on the back of my father's watch.

Decisions

By eleven, we scrambled up the embankment that led to the end of the dirt road at Firvale. Not fifty feet in front of us was the hotel and cafe.

We rested a moment and tried to regain our composure before we slowly walked up the street to the front door of the hotel. We could have entered through the bar door, closer to us, but I didn't want to face any patrons who might be inside. Opening the door to the little hotel lobby, we all walked in and found a dark little room lit only with a single light bulb hanging from the ceiling above the registration desk. There was nobody in sight, but I could hear talking and laughing coming from the bar at the far end of the building.

Noticing a small, chrome bell resting on the desk, I banged the plunger three times, the high-pitched jingle filling the room and beyond.

Frenchie's voice called out, "Be right there."

Soon, the wooden doors leading to the café swung open. Frenchie appeared and stopped, seemingly stunned to see what stood before him. And what a sight we must have been. Both Laura and I had not bathed in more than two weeks, and I had not shaved in over three. Our hair was dirty and matted, our clothes tattered and filthy, and Laura carried Teddy in the cradleboard on her back. I'm sure we looked like starving mountain people—which we were—who had just crossed a wilderness into civilization—which we had.

Frenchie moved behind the desk and said in a stern voice, "Sorry, we don't take Indians."

His comment infuriated me, but I collected myself and replied, "We ain't Indians, Frenchie. It's me, Dutch. Dutch Clarke. Remember me from last spring? I was here with my uncle, Roy Clarke, from the States."

His eyes were bulging as he tried to identify me through the trail dirt.

"Dutch, is that you, boy? Where the hell have you been?"

I replied, "Yes, it's me, and this lady is Laura, and this is her baby Theodore. They both survived a plane crash back in December, and we all wintered up in the Nascall Valley. Do you have that suitcase I left with you? We're tired, cold, hungry and in need of a room. How about it, Frenchie? Any rooms for us?"

Scratching his head while looking down at Gus, he replied, "Okay, Dutch... but not with the wolf."

"He's no wolf. He's my dog, and he ain't no Indian, either."

Pausing and then slowly nodding, Frenchie turned the registration book our way and then shouted towards the kitchen, "Margaret, get the hell out here now!" Turning back to me, he continued, "Sure, Dutch, no problem. In fact, your uncle sent me a wire, a few weeks back, telling me that he would be arriving here tomorrow. What in the devil is going on here? Why would anyone 'winter' in the Nascall Valley?"

Signing the book, I looked up and said, "It's a long story. I'll tell later. Right now, I need that suitcase, two rooms close to the bath, and some hot coffee and food. Lots of food! We haven't eaten for over two days. So can you help us out?"

Just then, Margaret appeared at the kitchen door with a shocked expression.

Frenchie turned to her and said, "It's okay, it's okay. This here is Dutch Clarke. Remember the Yank from last spring? And this missus here and her baby survived a plane wreck a few months back, and they all need rooms, hot coffee, food, and the suitcase he gave us last spring. Get to it, woman. I've given them rooms 201 and 202." Turning back to me he, continued, "They are the front, joining rooms, just like last year. The bathroom and tub are just across the hall. My wife will take you up and see that you get what you need."

Beginning to lead Laura up the dark stairs, with Margaret in front, I stopped halfway and turned to Frenchie, "Is there a doctor in this town? If so, I'd like to have him check out the lady and her baby."

"There is, Dutch, but the sawbones is out to one of the logging camps today. He should return tomorrow. I'll see to it, when he gets back."

Margaret showed us to our rooms and made sure we had towels, sheets and blankets. We must have been the only guests in the hotel, as she stocked our needs from a well-supplied linen closet. I helped Laura get the baby positioned safely on the bed, and then she shed some of her tattered trail clothing. Sitting on the bed, with Teddy between two pillows and Gus curled up on the floor, I told her to take the first bath.

As she turned to leave the room, she asked, "What's this doctor stuff? I don't need to see some small-town quack. There's nothing wrong with me."

As I pulled my boots off, I replied, "Then just have him take a good look at Theodore. In any event, we're going to need a birth certificate. Guess the little guy is half Canuck and half Yank. What a legacy!"

"I've taken more than a few good looks at Theodore, too, and there is nothing wrong with him, either." Turning serious she continued, "And what was all that crap about Indians? For a moment there, I wanted to be back sleeping in our valley."

Shaking my head, I replied, "Don't know and don't care. He's some kind of redneck, and, no matter what we do or say, we can't change that."

A flash of anger crossed her face. Slamming the door, she shouted back, "Oh, yes, I can, if that SOB ever says that again!"

While Laura was in the tub, Margaret reappeared, carrying a tray of food that included fried chicken, ham sandwiches, a soup bone and coffee. Placing the tray on an old dresser in the corner of the room, she asked, "Why were you out there in the Nascall Valley for the winter? Doing some prospecting or trapping?"

Seated alongside Teddy, I looked up and replied, "Nope, neither one. I was just trying to survive."

She reached down inside a pocket of her dirty apron and removed a pint of whisky, placing it on the dresser.

"Frenchie thought you might need this, to warm up your bones." Turning her head towards Gus, she continued, "Is that the nasty dog you had last spring?"

"Yes. He made it through."

"And your two mules and horse, where are they?"

I was beginning to lose my patience at all her questions. "The mules might still be alive," I replied testily, my throat tight, "but I had to shoot my horse after a wolf attacked him on Thunder Mountain. Blaze was his name."

Shaking her head as she left the room, she muttered, "Who in their right mind would spend a winter in the Nascall Valley?"

Ted was sleeping peacefully, so I inspected the food, coffee, and whisky. I didn't know what to try first. Taking the bone, I tossed it to Gus, then popped the cork from the whisky bottle and took a short swig. *Yes, who in their right mind would spend a winter in that valley?* I thought.

Just then, Laura returned to the room with a clean towel wrapped around her body and another one around her wet head. After eagerly surveying the tray, she poured herself some coffee and picked up half a sandwich. "It's your turn, Dutch, and it feels great. Take as long as you like."

Crossing the hall, I took a relaxing hour-long bath. But I had to change the dirty water a few times. All the while, I was sipping whisky and eating chicken in a steaming-hot tub with lots of soapy bubbles. Taking my razor, I even shaved—and generally enjoyed myself to the fullest.

By the time I'd finished and returned to the room, Laura, Teddy and Gus were all fast asleep. Moving through the connecting doors into the other room, I took the tray of remaining food, the whisky, and coffee.

The small front window washed the room with enough light to see that Margaret or Frenchie had found my suitcase. They had also laid out a few items of lady's clothes for Laura, a gray sweater and dingy green dress. Stacked on top of this pile was some baby clothing, just big enough to fit Theodore. *Frenchie might be a redneck*, I thought, *but he's a redneck with a heart when it comes to women and babies.*

As I ate the remaining food and sipped coffee that I'd fortified with whisky, I sprawled on top of the bed, lost in deep thought.

The last thing I remembered was looking at my pocket watch at 4 p.m. When I awoke it was 7 a.m. and shaking the cob webs from my mind, I realized that someone had covered me with a heavy blanket and quilt. Laura must have done that, yesterday evening, I thought. I hadn't slept fifteen hours straight since I was a teenager.

Feeling well-rested, I crawled out of bed, dressed in clean clothes from the suitcase, and went to our connecting door, which was closed. Knocking softly, I opened the door to find Laura's room empty except for her meager belongings. Quickly, I slipped my boots on, figuring she must be down in the café for breakfast.

Although I was eager to join her, I first had to do something about my mouth, which tasted like a dirty sock. Going to the bathroom, I found two toothbrushes, one wet and the other dry. Next to them was some toothpowder. Frenchie had thought of everything.

Rushing downstairs after cleaning up, I found Laura sitting at a table close to the front windows in the café, with Gus at her feet. Theodore was still in his makeshift cradleboard, perched on a chair next to her.

The weather outside was a bright overcast. The morning light streamed across the room, making Laura appear beautiful even in the dingy green dress, which was two sizes too big. She looked up at me from her plate of eggs and potatoes as I approached, an enormous grin on her face, and she rose hugging me warmly.

"Look who's up. I thought you might sleep this day away, too."

She looked so bright and refreshed that it took me a minute to connect with the conversation. Pulling a chair out from the table, I sat down and said, "I was out like a fire in the rain. You must have put the blankets over me. Why didn't you wake me?"

She reached across the table and grabbed my hand. "Wake you for what? You needed all the sleep you could get, and that's just what you got."

Frenchie approached the table. "What can I get you, Dutch? What would you like for breakfast?"

His words rang in my ears like music. They were words that I'd thought about hundred times in the wilderness. Now what would I say?

"A couple of eggs, no, four eggs, over easy, with a big steak, medium. And potatoes, lots of potatoes... and toast... and lots of coffee."

Frenchie smiled as he made notes on his order pad.

"I'm good for it, Frenchie. Uncle Roy will be here, later today. He always pays, and I guess that's the way it will be."

As Frenchie left the table, I realized the last thing he was worried about was my tab. But Laura seemed troubled by my statement. Reaching into her pocket, she slid a twenty dollar bill across the table, saying, "This is to cover my expenses. If it's not enough, I'll get you more when I get home. I want nothing from your uncle, and I'll pay my own way, no matter what it costs."

She returned to her meal, and the table fell silent as I tried to understand her feelings.

Soon, Frenchie returned with coffee. Apparently, he sensed the conflict in the air and departed as quickly as he could. Finally I said, "I don't understand your anger about my Uncle Roy. He's a very good man, and someone who has always been there for me. Please give him a chance."

She glared at me from her plate for the longest time and said nothing.

Finally trying to change the subject, I said, "After breakfast, we have to go to the train station to send a telegram to your folks."

With an expressionless face, she replied, "I've already done that. I was at the station at six, when it opened. I guess by now they've already received the message from their long-lost daughter."

Gazing across at her, I was still confused. Then Frenchie reappeared and slid a platter of food in front of me. The smell filled my nostrils and my mouth watered. Taking knife and fork in hand, I asked, "What did you say in your wire?"

Finished with her meal, she picked Theodore up and slid him inside her oversized dress for his breakfast. Once she had him settled, she looked across at me with a grin and replied, "Simple. Ten words maximum, due to the war. "With Dutch Clarke (stop) Baby and I safe. (stop) Home soon (stop). Laura.' Now, there is a heck of a message!"

Devouring my meal, I hung on every word and proclaimed, "Boy, I wish I could have seen your folks' faces when they receive that telegram."

Smiling back at me, she replied, "Me, too."

By 9 o'clock we were both back in our rooms. I knew that the morning train from Vancouver was due at 10 a.m. Within the hour, Roy would know I was in the hotel and would be knocking on my door. In the meantime, Frenchie had given me a newspaper from Vancouver, to catch up on the war news.

And the news was not good. The British were suffering massive bombings in London from the Germans, and our American forces had suffered many naval setbacks in the Pacific and in the Middle East. All in all, 1942 didn't look promising for the free world.

The paper also talked about the war efforts in both Canada and the States, and how every able-bodied man, from eighteen to forty years old, was being called up for military duty. The world had come unglued in less than a year, and I knew I had to help glue it back together, in some way. After my recent adventure, the prospect of enlisting in the army didn't appeal, but the prospect of not enlisting appealed even less. While some might call this Mr. Roosevelt's war, it had now come down to Laura and Theodore. My war would be dedicated to Laura's dead husband and Theodore's father, and it was a challenge I could not forsake.

At 10:20, there was a knock on my door. I was waiting for it and opened the door within seconds.

There stood Uncle Roy in his fedora and pin-stripe suit, his eyes wide with an expression of disappointment yet his hand outstretched in loving friendship.

Taking his hand, I pulled him into the room with a big hug. He looked great, just a little more gray around the temples and a few more wrinkles from working too hard. Pulling away, he looked at me and said, "Wow, you look as skinny as grass. Boy, what the hell are you doing here? Frenchie told me you came in yesterday. Did you lose count of the days?"

"Roy, you look great, and you're a sight for sore eyes. Come in, come in. There is someone I want you to meet."

Walking to the adjoining door, I tapped on it and called out, "Laura, Uncle Roy is here. Please come and say hello."

Roy stammered for a minute and then said, "Who is Laura? And why did you come back two days early?"

Then the door opened and Laura stood there, holding Teddy on her hip, staring at Roy. The room fell quiet until I broke the silence by saying, "Laura is Skip Patterson's daughter. She was in a plane crash, last December, and I helped deliver her baby, Theodore, at my cabin in the Nascall Valley. Can you believe this? Your friend's daughter falls from the sky in the middle of my mission."

Roy, always the gentleman, removed his hat. "Hello, Laura. Does Skip know you're all right?"

She replied in an irritated voice, "He does, as of this morning." Turning to me, she continued, "Dutch, I have to give the baby a bath and then see about that birth certificate. You and Roy should go downstairs, so you can fill him in on what happened. I'll join you later."

Then she smiled and closed the door.

We sat at the same table in the bar that we'd occupied a year before. Here, I slowly told Roy of my year's adventure.

Two cups of coffee soon turned to two bottles of beer. All through my story, I noted that Frenchie was eavesdropping on every word. Roy was quiet for the most part, only asking a few questions as the story unfolded. He was most distressed to hear about Blaze as he had a soft spot in his heart for my horse.

As I wrapped up the happenings of the last few days and completed my tale, he grew even more quiet and withdrawn. Finally, at the end I said, "Well there you have it. No gold, no oil, just life. I'm very sad about Blaze, but then I'm proud to have been there for Laura and Theodore."

By now, the little bar room was filling with noontime drinkers and eaters. Roy leaned back in his chair. "You know, Dutch, you have not fulfilled all the provisions of your grandfather's will, and I don't know what to say. Your story is fantastic and the outcome truly good. But still, it's not what was expected."

Grinning I replied, "Looks like you have a new partner. I'm sure you and the church will come to some kind of an agreement that will work out well. As for me, it's time to move on. The whole damn world is burning, and I'm sitting here on my butt. You keep the money. What I've learned and done on this adventure will be with me forever. Now it's time for me to do something for my country."

Roy leaned forward in his chair with a serious expression on his face. He twisted a near-empty beer bottle in his hands, then looked up at me. "Dutch, I'm well-placed with the war effort. You come back and work for the company. I'll see to it that you get a full deferment by working in a critical industry. There is absolutely no reason for you to go off and fight Mr. Roosevelt's war."

By his expression, I could tell he meant every word. The last thing I wanted was to crush the only family bridge I had. Looking up, I shouted to Frenchie, over the clamor of a now-crowded room, "Two more beers please."

Just then, Laura walked through the louvered barroom doors like she owned the place. Her hair was pulled back, and she even made the dingy green dress look good. With Theodore planted on her hip and Gus in tow, she reached our table and stood there, looking down at us.

The room became quiet as no one had ever seen a woman, other than Margaret, in the barroom before. Roy started to get up from the table, but Laura motioned for him to stay seated. She cleared her throat and then said angrily, in a voice all could hear, "Dutch tells me you're a man of integrity, a man of honor. I hope he is right. For some reason, you and your family thought it was acceptable to send this young man into the wilderness for a year. And because of that decision, he saved my life and delivered my baby in the worst conditions you can imagine. But now you probably think that doesn't make his year acceptable. Now you'll penalize him for doing the right things, the things you wanted him to do in the first place. Well, Roy, Dutch has done his year-long penance, and now he looks to you for absolution. There is no glory in making a person do what they don't want to do or penalizing them when they act with honor and courage."

She turned to me, her face red, and continued, "I'm going down to the doctor's office. He should be back soon. I'll meet you both later." Turning back to Roy, she concluded, "Sorry, Uncle Roy. I just had to get that off my chest."

With that, she marched out through the barroom's front door.

The room, which had been as silent as a dewdrop, started to come alive again with talk and laughter. I was embarrassed, but not for Laura or me. She had only said eloquently what I had thought for months.

Roy smiled as Frenchie brought us two more beers. "Now, there is a woman in love." he finally said.

"Love! What the hell are you talking about?"

"Dutch, you would have to be blind not to see that she loves you. And from what you've told me, you love her."

With a fresh beer in hand, I tilted my chair back on its two hind legs, thinking about what he'd said.

"All the more reason why you should come back and work for the company. If you don't, how will you survive?"

Pulling my chair level again and facing him, I answered, "The same way we did up in my valley, one day at a time. There will be no marriage, no soft company job. That's not going to happen. I'm not committing to anything until this war is over."

Somehow, that allowed us to move on, and we spent another hour debating love, war, and the news events of the past year. In the end, I asked Roy for some money to buy clothes for Laura and Theodore at the local dry goods store. He passed a couple of fifty-dollar bills across the table and said, "You go ahead. I'll check in and see you and Laura for dinner."

As Uncle Roy left the table, I could see that he was deep in thought. I wondered if it was because of my story of survival or Laura's tirade against him.

When I returned to my room, I had new clothes for Laura, Theodore, and myself. Laura still hadn't returned from the doctor's office, so I stretched out on the bed and was soon napping.

The next thing I knew, it was almost six in the evening. Getting up from the bed, I dressed in a new shirt and jeans and a pair of canvas shoes. Laura was still not in her room, so I guessed that she and Roy were down in the café.

Excited that they might be together, I entered the dining room but found it empty. As I passed through the barroom doors, I found a half-dozen folks drinking and talking. It was still daylight, and rays of sunshine flooded the smoky, smelly, room. Frenchie was behind the bar, talking to a patron as I approached.

"Have you seen my uncle and Laura?" I inquired.

I could feel all the eyes in the barroom turn to me as I spoke. For some reason, we had become some type of celebrity or joke in this town.

Frenchie looked up. "Your uncle is gone. He took the 6 o'clock train back to Vancouver. But he did leave a note for you. I'll go get it."

As he left for the hotel lobby, I turned around to see Laura and the baby enter through the front door of the bar. Her eyes were bright, and there was a smile on her face. The local crowd let out a gasp to see Gus walking behind her.

Laura approached me and placed Ted atop the mahogany bar. Reaching into her pocket, she pulled out a piece of official-looking paper and remarked, "He's legal! Here's his birth certificate. Please note the attending physician."

Unfolding the paper, I found at the bottom, just under Theodore's date of birth, the line: "Attending Physician or Midwife; Dutch Clarke."

A smile creased my face, and I broke out laughing. "I must have been the physician, because I'm sure as hell not a midwife."

Laura and I hugged as the rest of the bar room laughed and clapped for our happiness.

Just then, Frenchie returned with an envelope that had my name on it. Laura looked up and asked, "Where is Roy?"

"He's gone."

"Oh, Dutch, I'm sorry. Did I scare him away?"

When I opened the envelope, five one hundred-dollar bills fell to the bar top. Quickly collecting and stuffing them into my pocket, I read the note. Then I handed the typewritten message to Laura for her to read.

```
Dutch, sorry to have to leave so soon but
duty is calling and I know you are in good
hands. She is a lovely lady and I wish only
the best for you, Laura, and the baby. While
all may not have worked out as planned, I
hereby confirm that you have lived up to
both the spirit and text of your
grandfather's will. All covenants have been
completed satisfactorily. As the executor of
the will, I now deem that you have inherited
the balance of your grandfather's estate. To
that end, I will await your instructions on
the distribution and execution of said
assets.


Roy Clarke, Executor

P.S. Dutch, you never asked, but I
thought you should know, your half of the
```

```
estate is valued around four million
dollars. Let me know what your wishes are
and I'll do my best to see that they happen.
Take care and don't die in this war. I will
need you, after it's over!

   Love, Roy

   P.P.S. Your grandfather was right. You
went into the wilderness a boy and came out
a man, a very lucky man!
```

Standing there, I watched Laura read the note with my eyes watering. Finally, she placed the note on the bar, tears running down her cheeks. Then she looked up at me and said, "You were right. He wears not only a robe of honor but also a robe of reason. He is indeed a man of integrity."

A broad smile ran across her face as she hugged me and then kissed me on the lips. Once again, the little room full of people begin clapping and whistling.

Laura turned to the admiring crowd and shouted to the barroom, "Drinks for the house. We have a man here with a future!"

Epilogue

After settling our account with Frenchie, Laura, Theodore, Gus, and I made the 10:15 train north, the next morning. As we boarded the train, the conductor had the notion that Gus should travel in the baggage car but, after trying to touch him, he accepted my $20.00 tip and changed his mind. We traveled in a crowded day-compartment, and the train seemed to stop at every little village and logging camp along the way to Prince Rupert. A trip of only a few hundred miles took almost eighteen hours. We arrived at the little fishing town at 3 a.m. and walked to the ferry terminal, where we booked passage on the morning boat to Ketchikan.

There would be a wait of another three hours for the inland ferry north, so we walked to the Canadian Mounted Police Station a few blocks away. I was concerned that if we told the authorities about last December's plane accident, they might want us to stay while they gathered more information. Still, I felt that it was our duty to report it to them, if for no other reason than for the closure it would provide for the dead pilot's family.

The station was a little brick building. Inside was a single gray-haired officer, seated behind the night desk, reading a magazine. He looked pleasantly surprised to see someone so early in the morning. Putting down the magazine, he cleared his throat and asked, "What can I do for you folks at this hour?"

Laura and the baby took a seat across the desk from him while Gus curled up next to her. Standing, I described the plane accident. As my story unfolded, the officer became more and more interested in its details. Finally, I reached into my backpack and placed the personal belongings of Henry Woolridge on his desk. Behind the officer was a large map of British Columbia on the wall, so I marked as best I could the spot of the downed plane and the pilot's grave with a red pencil.

By then, he was pulling out official-looking forms for us to fill out. The forms were for an automobile accident report, but when we mentioned that to him, he waved a bony hand as if it made no difference. The poor officer truly had no idea what to do in such a circumstance, but he tried his best to act official, so we filled in most of the answers and signed on the dotted line. After we finished, he thanked us for our efforts and bid us a good morning.

Leaving the office, I said to Laura, "That was too simple. Now let's grab the ferry and get the hell out of here, before his supervisor arrives."

She nodded, and we rushed towards the ferry terminal. "So," she said as we hurried down the street, "what color was that car that hit you, and what was its license number? Were there any witnesses?"

We laughed and moved on.

When we reached the ferry building, we still had another half hour before departure. Laura was lucky enough to get a phone line home and was finally able to talk to her parents for a few minutes, so she was excited and eager to leave when she rushed back to the boat.

We stood on the car deck, the sun now showing in the eastern skies as I turned to Laura and asked, "What did they have to say?"

Holding her baby close, she smiled. "They were pretty much speechless, about me, about the baby, and about you. Mom cried and Dad gave orders, about you, about me, and about the baby."

Leaning against the boat railing, the sea in my face with a fresh wind out of the west, I shook my head and remarked, "Well, he hasn't changed, always the skipper. God love him for that."

The ferry arrived in Ketchikan a few hours later. The weather was foggy and cold yet clear enough for us to see down to the landing. Standing below the misty gangway were Skip and his wife, peering and waving to the passengers aboard. By the time they spotted Laura, she and Teddy were rushing down the gangplank towards them. In one fluid motion, all four came together in a big hug, full of tears and kisses. I followed behind with Gus, letting them have a moment alone. There was great joy in my heart as I watched the love that this family had for one another. Then Skip broke away and extended his hand to me, with a somber expression and bright eyes. Looking back at him with a silly grin and the devil in my eyes, I remarked, "Marion, so nice seeing you again."

He gave me a big bear hug and then whispered in my ear, "Dutch, you saved my daughter's life and helped bring my grandson into this world... but if you ever call me that name again, I will personally throw you into the sea."

Pulling away from his embrace, I grinned, "Laura told me you'd say that. God, it's good to see you again, Skip!"

He just stood there, staring at me, shaking his head, for the longest moment. Then he knelt down to where Gus's was sitting next to my leg. He didn't reach out to touch him, just looked him square in the eye and asked, "And what do we have here?"

"Meet Gus. You'll get use to him. He's your daughter's and grandson's protector."

Standing, Skip replied, "I'll take your word for that. He's a beautiful animal. Just know that you and he will always have a special place in my heart."

We were welcomed into Skip and Louise's home with open arms. There was nothing these two fine people would not have done for us. A special meal, a fine wine or brandy, a particular game or entertainment, all I had to do was ask. This made me feel both comfortable and uncomfortable, yet I knew it was genuine, one of the few ways they could find to show their thanks.

This was the first time in my life that I'd experienced family life full of forgiving love and affection. They tended to our needs, all the while taking care of their grandson. In the evenings, they'd clear the dinner dishes and challenge Laura and me to a game or just conversation. Then, as the evening was getting late, they would excuse themselves, leaving Laura and me alone with some quiet time. It was a holiday the proportions of which I would not experience again for many years to come.

Back in the wilderness, Laura and I had each realized that there was a special bond between us, and now that bond was blossoming into love. Our quiet times together, for the most part, were spent exploring that love. We expressed our affectation by both touch and taste and just being close. I sensed that both of us wanted to go further, but this was just not the right time or place.

Also, there was still a barrier between us, and that barrier was the war. We tried to talk it out, but each time I told her about my feelings, she would close up like a wild rose and turn cold to my plans of joining the fight. Finally, I realized it was the memory of her dead husband that stood between us. She didn't want to lose another man she loved to this war. This I understood, so I did not push any further discussions of my future.

Nevertheless, those plans were an itch that I couldn't scratch. I found myself feeling guilty and restless about the comfort that was all around me. So at the end of the first week, when the family was out of the house, I walked to town and found a lawyer. Here I dictated my last will and testament, leaving half of Grandfather's estate to Laura and the balance to Uncle Roy. Instructing the lawyer to send a signed, certified copy to Roy in New Jersey, I then walked to the nearest recruiting station at the end of the public pier. It just happened to be the US Marine Corp.

A large, starchy sergeant in a neatly pressed uniform, with a cigarette dangling from his lips, greeted me by saying, "Hello, young fellow. Come to enlist and kill some Japs?"

His matter-of-fact statement shocked me a little.

"Yes, sir, I think so."

"How old are you, son, and where are you from?"

With those simple questions, we began an hour-long conversation, during which we were soon joined by a captain, the commanding officer of the station. They wanted to know where I had been and what I had been doing during the past year. Next, they had me take a physical exam with some local doctor who was located just two doors down from the recruiting office. The old saw bones must have made notes on my paperwork about my bear-claw "tattoo" because, upon my return to the station, both the sergeant and the captain wanted to see it.

After a few simple written tests, more forms, and another lengthy conversation, I raised my right hand and was sworn into the United States Marines. Before I left the office, both the sergeant and the captain shook my hand and told me that I was about to have another "interesting adventure" in the Marines. Both felt that my survival skills would be a great asset to the Corps and country.

That evening, I waited until Skip and his wife had retired and Teddy was fast asleep in the next room before I told Laura about my enlistment.

She listened intently to my description of the day's events and finally replied, "I'm not surprised. You told me months ago what you wanted to do. I'm only disappointed that you wouldn't consider your Uncle Roy's offer."

Moving closer to her by the fireplace, I knelt by her chair. "I have considered it... and it's not what I'm going to do."

The firelight washed her face with a soft, warm glow. She thought about my words and then took one of my hands into hers before replying, "I have lost one man I loved to this war, and I don't know if I could stand to lose another. So I can't lose you, and I won't lose you! When this war is over and you come back home, I'll be here. In the meantime, I'll be yours until then."

Lifting myself to her chair, I kissed and hugged her in the warm, flickering firelight. We had made a pact... we had a deal.

The next morning, I told both Skip and Louise of my plans and asked if I could leave Gus with them.

Over a glass of orange juice, Skip answered without hesitation, "As I said when you returned Laura to us, you and he will always be welcome here. When you come back, Gus will be here waiting." He paused a moment, his expression turning to a broad smile as he added, "And by then he should have his sea-legs."

Unfinished Business

I had less than seventy-two hours before I had to report at Camp Pendleton, California, for basic training. Nevertheless, when making my travel arrangements I scheduled an eight-hour layover in Seattle to look up Lars's wife, Nelly.

Skip and Laura saw me off at the island airport across the harbor. It was an unusually clear day for this early in the season, and a surprising number of people showed up to see me off. The local newspaper had run a short story about our survival in the Canadian wilderness; and in some ways, we had become local folk heroes. Because of the story, almost twenty total strangers showed up to say goodbye.

Shaking hands with Skip, I bid him farewell and good fishing. Holding hands with Laura, I walked with her through the boarding door to the outside ramp leading up to a Western Airlines DC4.

As I was about to climb the steps, I reached into my pocket and grasped my father's watch. Handing it to Laura, I shouted over the idling engines, "If anything happens to me, give this to my godson. Telling him what the words mean and that I loved him."

Holding the watch, tears rolling down her cheeks, Laura answered, "I will. You have my promise. But nothing is going to happen to you, Dutch Clarke, because I love you! So don't get killed in this war or I'll never forgive you." She forced a smile. "We have a deal, right?"

I bent down and kissed her. "Yes, we have a deal. I'll be back, walking down a gangplank very soon, so you better be there."

Then I kissed her one last time, and ran up the ramp and onto the plane.

That morning, the plane flew only a few miles off shore over the Queen Charlotte Sound, and I tried hard to find the Dean Channel. With my face pressed against the cabin window, I searched the area for landmarks. Then, just under some clouds, I spotted Comet Mountain and, to the right, across the channel, Thunder Mountain, its summit still packed with snow.

My thoughts started moving fast as I thought about what I was doing last year at this time. I thought about Gus and Blaze… even the mules. Then, as I looked again at Thunder Mountain and its 'Summit of Sorrow,' a single tear rolled down my cheek. I had not forgotten, nor would I ever forget, Blaze and the brave part he had played in my incredible adventure.

The municipal airfield was only a short distance from Seattle. But before leaving for town, I had to know exactly where I was going. Thumbing through a phone book at a booth in the airport, I found a listing for Nelly Larson at 1520 Hillcrest Drive. Reaching for the phone, I dialed the number: Madison 1120.

After a of couple rings a lady softly answered, "Hello, Larson residence."

Fumbling for words, I finally stammered, "Is this Nelly? Are you the wife of Lars Larson who has been missing up in British Columbia for a number of years?"

The phone line fell silent for a long moment.

I said again, "Is this Nelly Larson?"

"Who is this?" the lady demanded.

"If you're Nelly, I just returned from a year-long trip up in British Columbia, and I have some belongings that were your husband's."

After another long silence, she angrily answered, "What do you want? He has been dead for years."

"Then you are Nelly? Look, I'm on my way to Camp Pendleton, and I only have a few hours here in Seattle. May I drive out and give his belongings to you? Do you still live on Hillcrest Drive?"

Slowly, she seemed to understand what I was talking about. Finally, she replied, "Yes, please come over."

Saying goodbye, I hung up and hailed a cab for downtown.

The cabbie knew the address but warned me that it was not the best part of the city. Later, as we drove down the streets of the neighborhood, I saw that the homes were, for the most part, poor and run-down. They were all classic turn-of-the-century homes that had not been maintained or refurbished for years. Union Heights was once a good neighborhood, but it had clearly fallen into disrepair.

The cab stopped in front of 1520, a home designed as a Cape Cod cottage some forty or fifty years back, but it was now little more than a drab dwelling. Getting out of the cab and handing the driver a twenty-dollar bill, I instructed him to wait for me, no matter how long it took.

It was an unusually warm and sunny day for early June in Seattle. As I walked up the stone walkway that led to the front porch, I encountered a young girl, about twelve or thirteen years old, playing softball with a catcher's mitt on. With her baseball cap and dusty overalls, she looked the part of the local tomboy. As I walked by her, she was throwing the ball against an old garage and catching it on the return.

Looking up at me, she said, "Hello, Mister. Do you like playing ball?"

"Oh, yes. Is your mother inside?"

She nodded her head yes and then said, "After you see Mama, maybe we could play some catch. I'm really a good player, and we could have fun."

"If I have time, maybe we could do just that. You look just like a real professional player, with that Dodgers cap and big glove."

At the porch, I knocked on the wooden screen that covered the open front door. Soon, a woman who seemed older than her years appeared and greeted me. "Are you the man who called from the airport?"

"Yes."

She opened the door and showed me into the parlor. Seating me in an old chair next to a small table, she brought out coffee in a tarnished, silver set, along with some home-baked cookies. Her home was neat and tidy but old, musty, and in need of paint.

When she sat across from me, I noticed her graying hair and wrinkled eyes and hands, intensified by many years of hard work. She was dressed in a clean but slightly tattered old smock.

Staring at her features, I could see that it was indeed Nelly from the old black-and-white pictures that Lars had locked up in his Bible. While her youth was gone, her beauty remained. She carried herself proudly, but there was sadness in her face.

Pouring the coffee, she looked up at me and asked, "I don't remember you giving me your name. May I have it now?"

"Yes, ma'am. My name is Dutch Clarke, and I just came out of a place in Western British Columbia called the Nascall Valley."

She filled a cup and passed it to me. "How do you like your coffee? Sugar? Cream?"

"Black is fine."

Her dark hazel eyes watched me closely as I took my first sip.

"You said you had something that belonged to Lars," she remarked when I lowered the cup. "May I see it?"

Reaching down inside my travel bag, I pulled out the small tin and placed it on the coffee table.

She stared wide-eyed at the box.

I cleared my throat. "May I tell you my story before I show you the contents?"

She nodded her approval, and I began. A few minutes later, I opened the tin and placed his journal, his Bible and the pouch of gold on the table. She quietly sobbed through the rest of my story and, at the end, took his Bible into her hands, pressing it against her chest.

In an unsteady voice, she said, "You don't know how important it is that I finally know what happened to Lars. He has been in my dreams and prayers for years. Thank you." She looked down at the pouch of gold and asked, "What do you think it's worth?"

"A few thousand dollars is my guess… but what I don't understand why his partner didn't come back for him."

She paged gently through the Bible and replied, "Hank and the pickup boat never made it back to port. I always believed that Lars had been with Hank when the boat went down. The only thing I learned was that the boat had left Prince Rupert to pick them up but never returned because of bad weather. The Canadian Coast Guard looked for survivors but found no trace of the boat or its crew."

Now that she had filled in some information that I had only been able to speculate about, it made sense to me that Lars's partner had been lost at sea and never able to contact any help.

Across from me, Nelly used a pink cotton hanky to clear her eyes.

"Nelly, I don't have much time. I wish that we could talk longer, but we can't. Is that little girl playing ball out there Lars's daughter?"

"Yes, and now she will have a better idea of what happened to her father, thanks to you."

"Nelly, do you and Hank's wife still hold claim to the gold mine up in the valley?"

"I don't know. I think so. When we were granted the claim from the Canadian government, I think it was for twenty years. Why? What could we do with it?"

Reaching into my bag, I pulled out a pad and wrote out Uncle Roy's name and address. Handing it to her, I answered, "You and Hank's wife should get together and talk about what I've brought you. And if the claim is still good, and you want to hire men to return to the mine and try again, I will underwrite the costs. All you have to do is write to my uncle at this address with your needs and instructions. I'll tell him about our meeting, and I'll ask him to make whatever arrangements you might need."

She looked up from the piece of paper with puzzlement. "Why? What do you want out of this?"

To this question, I smiled and quietly answered, "Lars's story moved and comforted me in my despair in that wilderness. All I care about is that girl out there, playing baseball. If you want another shot at the golden ring, I'll be happy to pay for it, for her sake."

With that, I got up and moved to the front door to go. Nelly followed me. As I opened the screen door, she reached out and hugged me, saying, "You're a stranger to me, Dutch, but what you brought this day and said here will change our lives forever. You may be a stranger, but you're also an angel. God bless you for that."

Smiling down at her warm, gentle face, for the first time I silently thanked my grandfather for the mission he had sent me on.

I reported to Camp Pendleton and basic training on June 9, 1942. That was the beginning of my four-year hitch in the United States Marine Corps. I went in as a recruit and came out a captain, spending all of my combat time in the Pacific, where I... but then, that's another story altogether.

Final Business

From the time he was young, Theodore heard stories about that winter spent in the wilderness the year of his birth. As he matured, his interest in and questions about that time and about our survival grew. Right after his graduation from high school, and just before he was to leave for his first year at the Naval Academy, Laura and I took him back to the Nascall Valley for a journey into our past. We left the harbor of Vancouver, B.C., in late July 1959, sailing my beloved sloop, *Pacific Lady III*, north up the Inland Passage. At the end of the second day, I turned the boat east into the Dean Channel by King Island. By nightfall, we had reached Nascall Bay and dropped anchor.

We spent two days here exploring the valley and lake area. I was surprised to find the old barn still partly standing, with grass growing from its roof and walls. The sight brought back haunting memories of Blaze—and even of the mangy, old mules. Sitting on the grass in front of this edifice, I was amazed at how well I'd built it. If I listened closely, over the sound of the breeze, I could almost hear my axe chopping, Gus barking, and Blaze's proud whinny.

The old cabin had not fared as well. It had been nearly leveled by the winds and harsh weather of almost eighteen years. I asked Laura and Ted if they wanted to join me as I explored it, but they declined. They seemed to sense my deep bond to these two structures that I'd built with my bare hands when I wasn't much more than a boy.

Peeking through the twisted window of what remained of the front facade, I could see sunlight streaking across the little room on its cold stone floor. There, lying on the floor was the broken wooden bed-frame and a chair that I'd crafted, now rotting in the weather. The only elements that held the cabin together were the roof rafters that slanted from the floor to the mound of logs that were once the cabin walls.

Crawling through the small window, I found a room full of memories. I could almost hear the wind, the rain, and Laura's screams of pain that had been my symphony during the birth of Theodore. There were ghosts in this room, ghosts of good times and bad, of love and hate, of hope and despair. But then, all of life is filled with these emotions.

On the second day, with the weather warm and dry, we walked the five or more miles to the site of the plane crash. It had all been removed or grown over, and we could find no signs of the plane or its contents. All that remained was the memory of that fateful December night in 1941. Laura had never seen the site and, of course, neither had Theodore.

On our walk back, I recounted again the events that had brought us together, and how Blaze had carried us blindly down the mountain in the middle of a snowstorm with Gus leading the way. I recalled how we'd finally arrived at the cabin and my amazement when I realized that Laura was with child.

Both Ted and Laura had questions and both seemed to enjoy my rambling story. As we made our way back to the valley, we spotted a small herd of elk, grazing just behind the old barn. Stopping, we watched those magnificent animals for the longest while.

Finally, Ted said, "We should get the rifle from the boat and shoot one for dinner."

My mind raced back to the first elk I'd ever killed. Finally I answered, "No, I hope I never have to kill another living-thing in my life. These animals are just too majestic."

Early the next morning, with the sun glowing over the eastern mountains, I weighed anchor and turned the *Pacific Lady III* into the wind and west up the channel toward the Pacific Ocean. Soon, Laura came up from the cabin, handing Ted and me cups of hot coffee.

Ted was seated next to me at the helm, looking back at the early morning light as it danced off the waters of Nascall Bay. He was silent for a long time, deep in thought. But as I tacked the boat into the wind and we lost view of the bay, he turned slowly to me and asked, "Dad, will I have a mission? Is there something you want me to prove?"

My eyes watered at his honest sentiment. Shaking my head, I put an arm around him and replied, "Son, you don't have to prove anything... to anybody but yourself. There's nothing you can't do or be... the future is yours, so grab it!" With the wind in her hair and a smile on her face, Laura hugged and kissed us both.

Just then, an eagle flew above the mast, letting out a loud cry, as if to say all missions had indeed finally been accomplished.

The End

Acknowledgments

Rewriting, reediting and recreating this book (first published in 2002) for my grandchildren was a joyful adventure. I have been blessed in having a supportive and thoughtful community of friends and colleagues as well as an encouraging family, all to whom I offer my heartfelt thanks.

Special thanks to Judith Meyers for a masterful editing job. And thanks to Melissa Weintraub for professional proofreading and polishing. Also to map artist, Scott MacNeil for helping with the illustrations. And special gratitude to Richard Rodgers for his music, Victory At Sea. This classic symphony was never far from my ears during the years of working this book.

Finally my heartfelt thanks to my wife, Tess, who tolerated my absorption on this project with the same grace and humor that she has brought to all our 'adventures' these past forty-two years of marriage.

Everyone who helped me added strength and benefits to this book: any errors, misinterpretations or mistakes this story may contain are solely my own responsibility.

Trailhead Supplies

Mule Harry: Four waxed canvas trail bags, 4' long x 2.5' deep x 2.5' tall, each weighing about 70 pounds full.

6 10-pound bags, flour
4 10-pound bags, beans
4 10-pound bags, rice
1 2-pound bag, baking soda
1 2-pound bag, yeast
2 1-pound tins, lard
4 5-pound bags, sugar
4 10-pound bags, coffee beans
1 5-pound tin, pepper
1 5-pound tin, sea salt
3 Gallon tins, honey
6 24 oz. cans, lemon juice
24 12 oz. cans, fruit
2 5-pound bags, dried fruit (apricots and oranges)
24 12 oz. cans, beans
6 5-pound sides cured bacon
10 pounds beef jerky
50 12" candles, with 25' of extra candlewick
6 1-pound cubes of wax
12 pouches of tobacco with rolling papers
2 iron skillets (14" & 10")
2 iron cooking pots (one 3 gallon, one one-gallon)
2 metal mixing bowls (large and small)
2 metal biscuit-baking tins
1 metal cooking grill
Coffee grinder
Flour sifter
4 metal plates/4 metal cups/4 sets of utensils

Medical kit in a weather proof container (wound cleaners, assorted bandages, splints, razor blades, hemostats, forceps, scissors, suture kit, burn packets, antibiotics, syringe, small bottle Novocain, ointments, analgesics, antacids, salt tablets, thermometer, iodine tablets, aspirin, bug repellent, etc.)

Mule Harriet: Four waxed canvas trail bags, 4' long x 2.5' deep x 2.5' tall, each weighing about 70 pounds full.

> Three axes (no handles): common axe, broadax, and large steel hatchet
> Two shovels (no handles): squared and rounded
> One sledgehammer (no handle)
> One pickaxe/hoe (no handle)
> One froe, used to split shingles (no handle)
> Two drawknives, large and small
> Two iron wedges
> Two grapple hooks with iron chains
> Block and tackle
> Iron plow with leather reins (no handles)
> Scythe (no handle)
> Files for sharpening
> Stone & oil for sharpening
> Wood tool kit (hammers, saws, brace and bits, squares, planes, chisels, etc.)
> One 6' x 10' waxed-canvas tent (with ropes, no stakes or frame)
> One 10-pound wooden keg of 8-penny nails
> Two 10-pound wooden kegs of 16-penny nails
> One 10-pound wooden keg of log spikes, 16"
> Three 10-pound sacks of cement

Three 20-pound sacks of oats. (For Blaze and the mules, I knew there should've been more, but this was all I could carry. The oats would be rationed out to them over the months)

> One 6' cross-cut logging saw (strapped to the side of the mule)

15 pounds of garden seeds (potato, onion, carrot, corn, tomato, cucumber, pepper, cabbage, garlic, beans, and rutabaga)

One large, watertight jar of wooden matches
Two 100' long ropes (one half-inch & one ¾-inch plus a 50' half-inch on Blaze)
Two fishing poles (one fly, one telescopic, with lures, line, net, and flies)
One leather feed bag

Personal items in Backpack (About 30 pounds)

3 long-sleeved wool shirts
2 long-sleeved cotton shirts
3 pairs of denim pants
2 pairs of wool long-johns
2 wool sweaters (one V-neck, one turtleneck)
4 pair wool socks
4 pair cotton socks
4 pairs cotton undershorts
4 cotton t-shirts
4 cotton towels (large)
2 cotton hand towels
2 leather belts
1 heavy, fur-lined, wool coat
1 light denim coat
2 pair cowboy boots
1 pair canvas shoes
1 pair leather gloves with wool inserts
2 pair canvas work gloves
1 Stetson cowboy hat
1 wool stocking cap
1 New York Yankee baseball cap
1 Pair leather chaps
Map and sighting compass

Toilet kit (4 toothbrushes, 6 cans tooth powder, straight razor and strap, 12 bars of soap, brush, comb, small mirror, scissors, needle and threads, etc.)

> 2 metal canteens (military type)
> 1 pair 8 x 30 power binoculars
> 1 gun cleaning kit (oil, swabs, and ramrods)
> 1 set military-style cookware (for use on the trail)
> 2 books - 6 pencils

Frontier Guide To Hunting: 1896 -- covered identifying, hunting and dressing game of the Western United States & Canada.

Surviving The Montana Wilderness: 1888 -- with instruction on building cabins, log furniture, frontier farming, preserving game and garden foods. Also tips on cooking and other survival and medical remedies.

Writing Journal (100 pages, 8" x 12" hard-bound, gray journal. Two Tide Booklets (1941 and 1942) For Vancouver, B.C., 40 pages each. With calendar, times, and moon tables.

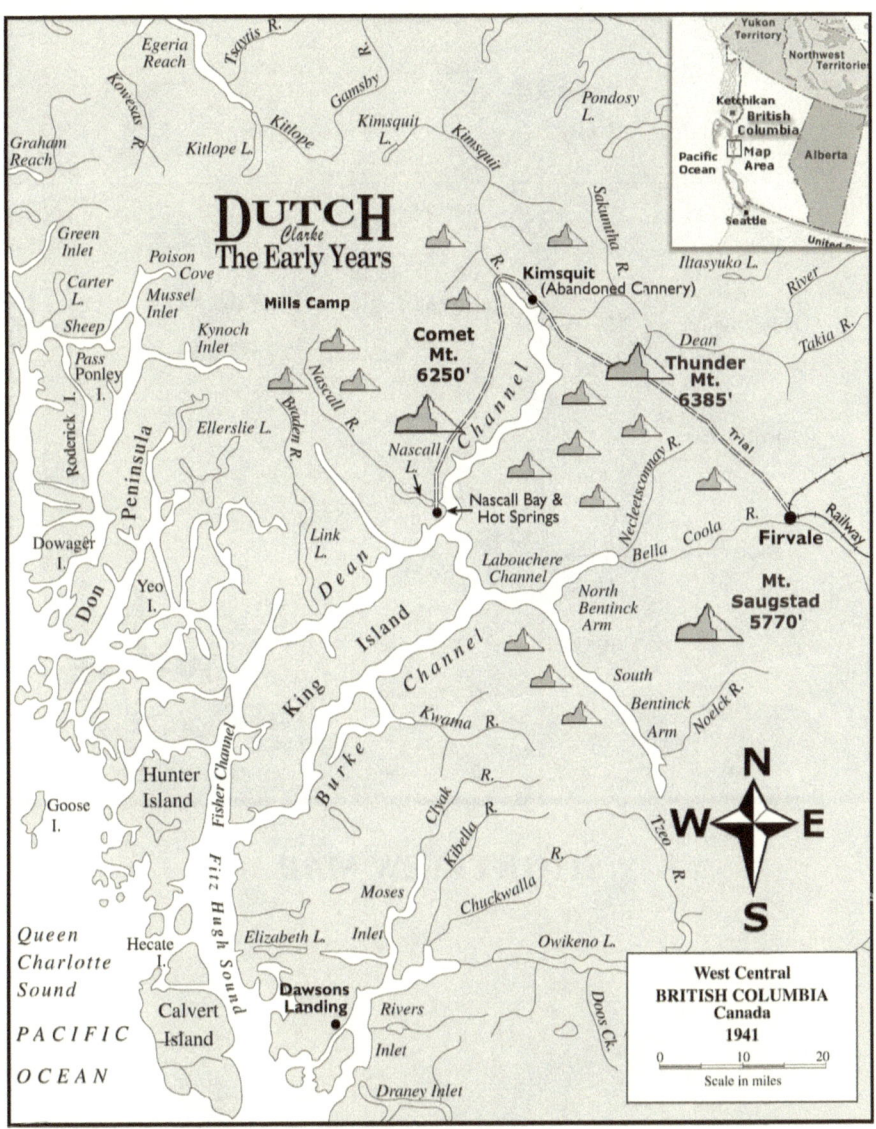

LONGVIEW MAP

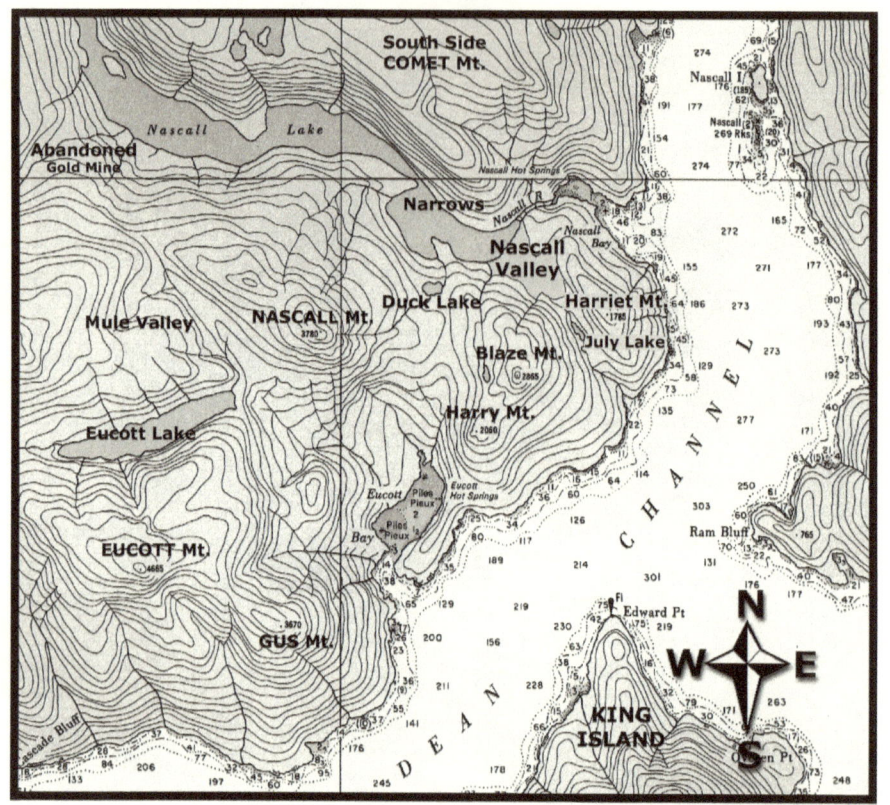

SHORTVIEW MAP

STORY NOTES

Author Bio

Brian D. Ratty, a retired media executive and graduate of Brooks Institute of Photography, also holds an honorary Master of Science degree. He and his wife, Tess, live on the north Oregon Coast, where he writes and photographs that rugged and majestic region. Over the past thirty years, he has traveled the vast wilderness of the Pacific Coast in search of images and stories that reflect the spirit and splendor of those spectacular lands. Brian is an award-winning historical fiction novelist, and has written numerous magazine articles about the Pacific Northwest.

Why I write

I write what I like to read, historical fiction rich with bold characters and powerful storylines. I shy away from gratuitous violence and descriptive sex; instead my stories portray adventure with vivid descriptions and believable plots. My goal is to whisk the reader away to another frame of mind... the results being a suspenseful and brisk read. **Readers Wanted!**

For more information on Brian's books, short stories, articles and recipes:
www. Dutchclarke.com

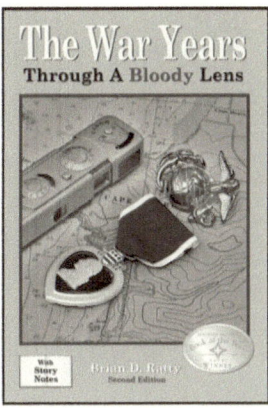

www.ingramcontent.com/pod-product-compliance
Lightning Source LLC
Chambersburg PA
CBHW030345020726
47493CB00003B/687